"My business is complicated and boring." He tilted his head, a smile curling. "No, I withdraw that. My business is complicated and far too exciting for a delicate lady's ears. You will likely faint before I utter the first words of an explanation."

"It is a good thing that my ears are sturdy then, and that I've never fainted before," said Charlotte.

"There is always a first. At least you are on the bed. You would fall so prettily upon your back. Lips and legs parted, in complete surrender."

The reminder of their proximity and position was unnecessary but still brought color to her cheeks.

"See. There. I detect the beginnings of a faint already."

"More likely you detect the stirrings of my temper."

"Really? I'll bet you look quite lovely in a fit. Cheeks all ablaze in passion."

"I thought you were uninterested in beauty."

He smiled slowly. "What I'm interested in is *you*." He leaned forward, and one finger touched her chin. "I'm going to possess you, Charlotte."

Romances by Anne Mallory

ONE NIGHT IS NEVER ENOUGH
SEVEN SECRETS OF SEDUCTION
FOR THE EARL'S PLEASURE
THE BRIDE PRICE
THREE NIGHTS OF SIN
WHAT ISABELLA DESIRES
THE EARL OF HER DREAMS
THE VISCOUNT'S WICKED WAYS
DARING THE DUKE
MASQUERADING THE MARQUESS

ANNE MALLORY

One Night Is Never Enough

AVON

An Imprint of HarperCollinsPublishers

AVON BOOKS
An Imprint of HarperCollins*Publishers*
10 East 53rd Street
New York, New York 10022-5299

First Avon Books paperback printing: March 2011

Avon Trademark Reg. U.S. Pat. Off. and in Other Countries, Marca Registrada, Hecho en U.S.A.
HarperCollins® is a registered trademark of HarperCollins Publishers.

Printed in the U.S.A.

10 9 8 7 6 5 4 3 2 1

To S, because you are awesome

Acknowledgments

One line of thanks is never enough—giant, heaping thanks to May Chen, Matt, and Mom, as always! And to Dad, for your neverending support!

One Night Is
Never Enough

Chapter 1

S he needed to slow down. To saunter and smile gently as a well-bred lady should. To embody the kind and soft woman she wished to be.

Charlotte Chatsworth strode the pavement instead. Long, hard strides. Trying to shake the feel of chains that had always been there, that she had tried to ignore for so long. Chains that were settling more firmly over her shoulders, growing tighter around her wrists and neck.

A distended feeling, full of panic and weariness, pushed outward from her belly, pushing against her ribs, reaching for her throat, to choke her—a balloon grown too large. Emotions too tangled within and around it—creating an almost physical pain.

If only it were a physical pain, a stomachache. Something that could be cured or relieved.

But the swelling desperation—the mixture of bitterness, pride, and fear—had been growing inside her for so long that she didn't know if anything would be left of her true self should the balloon finally pop.

If an unladylike walk down the crowded street could give relief, if only for an hour, she'd seize whatever she could scrape.

She felt a warmth at her elbow and a strange desire to shift—toward or against the heat, she wasn't sure—

ran through her, then slipped from her body, attached to two men who were brushing past, one dark-haired and the other light. Long strides outpaced even her determined ones, paving a path through the large crowd ahead. People seemed to unconsciously give the two men space to navigate before closing the gaps created by their fleeting presence.

Barely in her view for more than a few seconds, and hard-pressed to think of their passing as anything other than an odd imagining, a strange feeling lingered nevertheless.

Shaking her head, Charlotte looked over her shoulder. Her maid, Anna, trailed behind her, dragging her feet and peering into the windows of the nicest milliners on Bond Street. Dreaming about pink hats, most likely. Wishing that her mistress would purchase a stylish one, then toss it to her when she tired of it.

But Charlotte looked dreadful in pink.

Other ladies, more delicate, with readier smiles, wore pink like the innocent and lovely color it was. Full of hope and femininity. Fragile and tender.

Emily, even with her rampant mischievousness, was a picture in pink. Charlotte's mouth relaxed for a moment as she pictured a jaunty cap on her boisterous, but sincere sister. Perhaps she would return this way and purchase a cap for her.

But there would be no pink hats for Charlotte.

Rich, deep navy blue. Indigo. Midnight. Stark white. Occasionally a hint of cream when she couldn't deny herself. Her entire wardrobe was comprised of the combinations therein.

She'd heard more than one of her rivals snidely remark upon the choice and how her father must have stolen a shipment of blue and white muslin and satin years ago, forcing her to survive on the palette.

Three girls walked toward her, heads pressed together, giggling. "—so sweet and kind. He makes me feel safe." Another giggle. "And Father said I could pursue him. So I did."

"You kissed! And you didn't tell us! What was it li—"

Charlotte could hear the giggling happiness behind her as they passed. The girls laughing together.

She touched the pin at her breast. A lift of soft metal wings. A hint of flight.

A gift from the unlikeliest of new friends. With a clasp that was sure and strong. Well crafted and steadfast.

She blinked to clear suddenly moist eyes. She didn't know what she would have done this last year without Miranda, the new Lady Downing. Most likely she'd have become crushed by Bennett Chatsworth's machinations, crumbling to dust.

Emily would always be a dear confidante, but Charlotte was fiercely determined that her sister wouldn't share her burdens. That she would be free of them and of their father, as Charlotte had never been.

So she couldn't share her difficulties with Emily. And the distended balloon grew.

Now into her third year on the marriage mart, waiting for her father to decide on "the largest crown," the looks she received had started to turn from envy to smug satisfaction. She smiled bitterly. People relied so heavily on appearances.

Fleeting. So fleeting.

That the recently gifted pin was created to withstand an ocean gale, pinned even to the most damaged flag, made her throat tight. Charlotte had worn the pin often enough in the past few weeks that it had started to cause comment. People calling her *The Dove*.

But even with the glow of the gift, she'd never felt less free to fly.

She put an extra clip in her step, fingers slipping from the unusually sharp metal tail. Determined not to fuel the bloated tangle inside. And not to succumb to melancholy. She would weather whatever desperate plan her father next invoked and turn it to her advantage. Build an empire. Carve her own happiness. Allow Emily to be free.

She *would* do it. She'd gather whatever emotional scraps she needed in order to succeed. Without mawkish sobs into her pillow over what would never be. Their mother hadn't endured twenty-four years as second-best with nothing to teach Charlotte from it.

Charlotte turned down a less-populated side street, thankful for the fewer acquaintances she might encounter. She had four social visits left in the afternoon, then an outing in the park, supper out, two galas, one ladies-only party, and a musicale that evening. The stretch of the social smile that had lately been frozen about her lips strained.

She touched the pin again. But at least now there were ports in the storm.

A passing couple leaned into one another, smiling, their heads touching, melding together. Happiness in being with the one they loved.

She closed her eyes, then opened them again, quickly. For there must be nothing seen to be amiss with the Chatsworths. Just some bad luck at the tables that would turn *corking* any day now.

She didn't allow morbid laughter to escape the tangle. One of these days, her father was going to embroil them in an entanglement from which they couldn't break free. Or someone was bound to collect on debts they couldn't pay.

The bell on the door of the ribbon shop jangled as the door opened, and two women emerged, shrugging. They turned in a direction away from Charlotte. Charlotte caught the door, somehow prevented the bell from sounding again, and she and Anna slipped inside before it closed.

The shop was dim—none of the lamps were lit in the corners to brighten the merchandise and enhance the meager light that seeped through the front windows facing the alley. She would think they were closed, but Charlotte had scheduled an appointment to pick up the special bows and intricate knots she had ordered. Mrs. Hunsden, a shy woman who made the best ribbons in London, was prompt with orders, and Charlotte planned to wear one of the exquisite creations around her arm tonight.

"Good afternoon?" she called, aiming her voice to the back of the shop.

"Perhaps they went out for a nibble, Miss?"

Before she could respond to her maid, she heard a door bang in the back room. A raised voice. Mr. Hunsden screeching. Charlotte had never liked him—smarmy smiles and slick brows, and when he thought no one was looking, quick kicks behind the counter to the shins of his wife. She took a few steps toward the doorway that separated the customer display area from the back of the shop.

She heard Anna mutter about the man's parentage. Charlotte longed to agree but resolutely walked on, eyes narrowed.

Mr. Hunsden might bully his wife, but he would never dare raise even his voice to Charlotte. The man was a coward. He'd be glib, with an insincere smile, even if she caught him red-handed striking his wife.

Perhaps she could *do* something though. Convince Mrs. Hunsden to come with her. Encourage the Ladies Society to invest more money in her program for disadvantaged women. Or recommend an additional program as part of the Delaneys' new venture. *Yes.* The itch grew. She could see it already. And Mrs. Hunsden would be *free.*

Charlotte would free *someone.*

She peered around the corner, her gloves curving around the splintered frame of the door. Crates littered the space, but sweet Mrs. Hunsden was nowhere to be seen. Instead, she saw a tall, dark-haired man holding stout Mr. Hunsden by his lapels.

She jerked back instinctively. Her body gave a sudden lurch in the opposite direction, and she had to clutch the chipped wood to stay upright.

"I do hate to repeat myself. Where is the money, Hunsden?" The man's voice was silky and sinister, sending a chill through her.

"I don't have it."

"That is unfortunate. Coupled with your poor choice of friends, we've decided you've *come due.*"

Sweat matted Hunsden's hairline, curling in rivulets down his cheek and pooling at his chin. Charlotte felt her own body respond in kind. She pulled back again, to run, to go for help, but once more her body lurched, her pin sticking in the splintered wood—the forked tail of the dove embedded like small daggers in tree bark. She tried not to panic. She pushed her chest forward, fumbling to unhook the broach without causing noise or putting herself in full view.

"I don't have it," Hunsden said, palpable fear lacing the words.

"That's unfortunate for you." There was a smile in the man's voice. As if he was *glad.* "Tell us which rock Noakes has crawled beneath."

"I don't know."

Charlotte felt an insistent tug on the back bow of her dress. She pushed a hand behind at her maid, trying to still her. She was still hooked. And she'd never make it to the street with Anna in tow if the man chose to stop them. She reached shaking fingers to her chest and tugged the muslin. She'd apologize to Miranda for losing the pin, if she could only free herself.

"Your ignorance is quite to your misfortune. Noakes has been *blacklisted*."

"That's—that's none of my concern," Hunsden stuttered. "That's between you and Cornelius."

"Oh, Cornelius will get his too." The words were darkly promising. "But word has it that Noakes is here. Perhaps hidden behind a *wooden* rock in this very space?"

Charlotte shifted her darting gaze between the caught fabric and the tableaux, not wanting to take her eyes fully away from either. Using her teeth, she yanked off her right glove, thankful she had worn a short pair.

Hunsden's face mottled. "I'm surprised you didn't send your lackeys."

She nearly triggered the unyielding silver clasp, her shaking, bare fingers almost disengaging it from its lock. She swallowed. Nearly there.

The dark man twisted his hand, and Mr. Hunsden's skin purpled. "I don't need lackeys. Now tell me where—"

Charlotte's vision blurred as a man charged from behind a stack of crates at the far end of the room, the top crate pivoting on end, starting to fall. Charlotte froze in terror at the new threat, a wave of pressure crashing from her throat to her gut, her fingers rooted uselessly over the clasp. The man's hand descended, silver glittering in a downward arc toward the dark man's back.

Her body, her thoughts, went cold. Inactive. Immobile. Mr. Hunsden being manhandled and threatened was terrible, yes. But she was about to see a man stabbed while she was pinned to the doorway.

Murdered. She tried to close her eyes, to look away. The crate crashed to the floor.

A golden angel appeared as if by ghostly apparition from the side of her view—another man she had neither seen nor heard amidst the wooden crates and her own panic. A well-tailored angel. Gieves and Hawkes, she thought inanely, still frozen.

As the knife descended, the well-dressed man caught the assailant's hand and twisted, the blade arcing to the side of its intended victim, narrowly missing the tall, dark-haired man. The assailant gave an agonized cry as his hand contorted, and the knife slipped from his fingers. The blond man caught the knife deftly as it fell and had the man pinned, twisted, and chewing the bent nails protruding from the wooden floorboards in seconds.

He flipped the knife, wrapping the handle in a golden fist, and punched the man once in the face. Blood sprayed from the man's nose and mouth like the cantaloupe Bobby Drayton had once dropped from the top of a three-story building. The man went limp on the floor. Still as death.

She had just seen someone murdered after all. And the man had been killed *by hand.*

Self-preservation triggered movement once more. She pushed her body forward, then tried to forcefully pull back, hoping to rip the fabric from the pin's unexpectedly traitorous grip.

The man rose, his profile to her, and she caught her breath, fingernails still clawing the pin, at the horrible dichotomy. Angelic-looking, beautiful really, but for the feral grin he shot Hunsden and a long scar curving his cheek. A fallen angel straight from hell.

"I, on the other hand, prefer lackeys." His voice was

gravelly, with an edge to the cadence. The hint of a previous accent unsuccessfully removed. A street accent not quite covered by the polish of his clothing. "Much less mess."

Charlotte's moist fingers slipped over the dove's sharp beak in her white-knuckled terror.

"You killed Noakes." The shopkeeper looked frantic. *More* frantic. She didn't know how she was able to follow the conversation, both what was said and what wasn't, when everything in her was screaming dire warnings, terror, and escape, but it all set out for her like words on a page. Hunsden must have known Noakes was there, biding his time, his ace in the hole.

At his words—*killed,* in particular—hands suddenly gripped Charlotte and started pulling her violently. Anna, in obvious—though fortunately silent—hysterics behind her, madly tugged.

"You'll be arrested," Hunsden said feverishly. "Hanged! And Cornelius, he'll come after you. Send assassins. Unless I help you. Help you dispose of the body. I—I know just the spot."

"Well, that's bloody accommodating of you. Because I'm shaking in my boots at the thought of Cornelius's *assassins.*" The blond man twirled the knife on his palm and addressed the tall, dark man, who had maintained a crushing grip on Hunsden. "Anything interesting left in him, Andreas? Or has the piece of goat shit dried to chips?"

"My—my wife . . ." Hunsden stuttered before the darker man, Andreas, could answer.

"Whom you beat," the blond man said, almost pleasantly.

" . . . she will tell someone. She will . . ."

"Rejoice in her widow's weeds?"

Charlotte gave up on trying to unclasp the pin, Anna's

violent tugging wouldn't let her get her sweaty fingers around it again. She pulled on the fabric once more, trying to rip it from the embedded dagger.

"I—I . . . you can have her."

"Did you hear that, Andreas? Hunsden's wife is all ours. All we have to do is, what was it? Let the goat go? And he'll help us dump the body? But there are so many choices for *where* to do the dumping." The blond man affected a look of studied indecision, tapping the heel of the blade against his palm. It should have made him look less dangerous, but instead his expression seemed to glow with a demonic light, relishing the game. "Should we really leave it to Hunsden here to decide?"

Charlotte sent up a prayer, hoping that Mrs. Hunsden was safe, somewhere else. There was nothing Charlotte could do for her but to escape, to call the watch, to get help.

"I'm not in the mood for theatrics, Roman," Andreas said. His hand twisted the fabric near Hunsden's throat a little further.

Odd and fleeting recognition that these were the two men she had seen briefly on the street struck her.

The blond threw out his blood-smeared knuckles, and one drop flung to the floor as he carelessly motioned. "I never get to enjoy these things anymore."

The pin suddenly came loose, and she caught it in her hand, staring at the little metal body in shock for a moment. Dear God. She was free.

She pushed back to run. Anna pushed forward to more insistently get a grip and the force of the two propelled Charlotte's chest and hand into the edge of the door. The pin lifted into the air, flying free for a few suspended moments, then dropped sharply, the weight of it too much, and clattered across the floor like the opening shots at Waterloo.

It stopped, almost gently, against the fallen angel's foot.

All heads turned, eyes looking between or around the crates. Charlotte met the pair of icy blue ones. The pair that so far had proved the most deadly.

"And what have we here?"

Run. *Run.* But Anna was pressed up behind her, quaking. With seemingly no self-preservation to be had.

Her maid gave a sharp squeak, and Charlotte half turned to see a man had come up behind them, a grisly smile on his face, a patch over one eye. Blocking their only escape.

Charlotte turned back and lifted her chin, eyes meeting iced blue once more, running through her options.

"Hunsden doesn't have a daughter." The man's—Roman's—voice was pleasant, but she wasn't fooled. "And you are showing far too much spine to be his downtrodden wife." He regarded her, looking her up and down somewhat lazily with his fallen-angel eyes. "And far too expensively dressed. With a maid hiding behind your skirts. A beautiful customer experiencing her first taste of darkness?"

"Run! Get help! They killed Noakes!"

A sharp shove pushed Hunsden farther up the wall. The darker man, Andreas, looked as if he might finish the double murder right there. Charlotte tried to still her shaking hands, pinned as she and Anna were between the one-eyed man and the murderer.

Roman smiled at her with a too-charming grin. "Don't mind One-eye." He motioned lazily to the man hovering behind her maid. "He's reformed. He now only harms those who require it."

Roman spoke over his shoulder to the other two men, without looking away from her. "Unfortunately, Hunsden, your dear Noakes is alive. I *should* kill him though. Trying to put a knife—rather fond of knives, isn't he?—in my brother's back?" His expression grew barbaric again as he swung to look at the shopkeeper, who was already purpled and mute. "Perhaps I will dispatch him still."

Her eyes went unwillingly to the dark-haired man, Andreas, who was watching her as well, but in a far colder manner. Brothers? They looked nothing alike. Not their coloring, their features, nor the expressions on their faces. They both wore their expensive clothing well though. Too fitted to be stolen or tailored for anyone but the person whose frames the garments graced.

But even if she had spied them walking into the most expensive tailor on Savile Row, she knew her heart would have jerked. A need suddenly pressing against her to cross the street, some deep survival instinct kicking in, as it had to the people they had passed earlier. There was something about both of them that was unnerving. Their eyes far too quick. A dangerous lethality coating the air around them.

They had *passed* her fleetingly, coming from behind on the street, and even then she had felt it.

"Hmm? No?" Roman turned back to Charlotte, face easing again. "Too many witnesses now, I think." He flashed her another charming smile. "And I'd never harm a lady."

"Is that so?" She somehow managed to say it calmly. Long practice with her father and the dour matrons of the *ton* helping.

"Especially not one as lovely as you are." He grinned. It was almost boyish under his far-too-seasoned, penetrating gaze, and there was something about the curve of his lips that made her frozen heart skip a beat. She wondered if there was something wrong with him. Or with her.

He bent to the floor, crouching, his eyes not losing contact with hers. Two fingers curled around the pin, red knuckles enclosing it. He lifted and examined the dove for a moment before looking back to her.

He held it up between two fingers, his other hand upon his knee, half sitting, balanced on the balls of his feet.

She would need to cross five paces to retrieve the pin. Five paces that would give her a lead should she need to run.

She needed to run *now*. Even with the one-eyed man blocking freedom.

"Come now." Those lips—it was hard to look away from them—curved slowly this time. "I'll be a good boy."

She broke her gaze and concentrated on the cool blue of his eyes. "I have no assurance of such, sir. You haven't been particularly hospitable so far."

He twisted the pin, the tail touching his forefinger, the head kissing his thumb. Back and forth. Back and forth. "I blame Hunsden." Back and forth. "You should too. Inhospitable cuss."

"Mr. Hunsden hardly seems in a state to open his larder," she said, trying to pretend he was just a man at a rout, and she was simply exchanging pleasantries with him in order to pass the time. Not a ruthless killer, unusually charismatic and crouched before her. "Or his liquor cabinet."

He might not have killed the man on the ground. Yet. But none of his words or actions indicated a lack of knowledge of the art.

The smooth, cold metal of the dove kept a steady circuit between his long, capable-looking fingers—roughened digits protruding from the black and white of his tailored cuff. Not the lily-white fingers of a pianist at a musicale but of a man who could fell another with a single blow.

"His liquor cabinet? A grand idea."

"Would you care for a drink? I believe Mr. Hunsden would be willing to fetch you a dram if you release him. Or I will send back some spruce beer if you give me a minute to cross the street."

"Mmmm . . . One of my favorites." His quick eyes seemed to miss nothing, and she couldn't hide the motion of her fingers squeezing the fabric of her skirts. His gaze rose back to her face, lingering on her lips, then meeting her eyes. Even giving away her nerves with the telltale sign of her pinched fingers, she refused to look away.

"Andreas, I think I've fallen in love."

"Roman." There was a wealth of unspoken meaning in that one word, so darkly uttered. But Roman's too-beautiful mouth crooked, head cocked, eyes watching.

Heads and tails. Touching his finger, kissing his thumb. The choice before her.

"I think you are making the lady's maid nervous, Bill," Roman said to the one-eyed man near them though he kept his eyes on Charlotte. "Perhaps you might back up a bit."

Bill moved. Charlotte wondered what game his master played.

"Come." Roman smiled at her, a lovely lift of his lips. "Take your pin."

It was a dare. A test to see if she would cross to him, retrieve the pin from his bloodstained hand.

"It would be a shame to lose something so valuable. Unless you care little about its loss?"

There was something in his eyes that said he knew the piece was precious to her. But that was silly. This man, who held all the power at present, didn't know her at all. And he could do anything to her he wished should she decide to retrieve the pin or not.

And yet, something about the look in his eyes and his instruction to Bill to move gave her pause. If she chose to run, she had the odd notion that he would not stop her.

Which bled into the thought that she wouldn't be harmed if she retrieved the pin. She didn't know why or what made her think that when nothing about the situation should reassure her. Perhaps it was the way he sat, or the absence of any physical menace toward her or action against her. Easily able to rise and overpower her if he chose to or to step into her space and intimidate her mentally and physically.

Her left foot stepped forward. She paused, her weight switching.

But there was also something in his eyes that said her actions might be irreversible if she went to him. That it would change her life.

A ridiculous thought.

She swallowed, lifted her chin, and took another step toward him. The edges of his eyes tapered, satisfaction and anticipation deepening the blue. She took three more measured steps until she stood in front of him. Kneeling before her, he seemed at a disadvantage, but for the way he commanded the space.

He twisted the pin so it rested in the palm of his bare hand.

She slowly reached forward and touched the pin, gripping the small metal body, the bare tips of her fingers brushing the strong, worn skin of his palm.

The blue of his eyes held hers. His fingers curled up as she lifted the pin, his tan knuckles speckled with red, the edges of his own bare fingertips caressing hers as she lifted the dove, and he slowly relinquished his hold.

The beat within her jerked and began drumming more insistently. His eyes dropped to the curve of her bare throat, then lifted, his smile growing, the creases at the edges of his eyes deepening further.

She quickly stepped backward, clutching the pin against her thigh, then stepped again. "Thank you, sir. I believe we should be on our way now."

He tilted his head, smile still in place, eyes dropping again to the thumping beat at her throat, down to the torn fabric at her chest that had been damaged by the jerking pin, back to her lips, then up farther.

A feeling close to panic but without the cold edge—warmer somehow—pulsed through her. She took two harsh steps backward and, feeling Anna's dress, pushed her maid so she stayed behind her, backing them roughly through the frame between the rear and the shop proper. Anna clutched her, pulling Charlotte's dress in her terror-filled grip, forcing Charlotte to make an extra effort to stand tall.

Roman rose and followed them, his eyes never leaving hers, even as he motioned lazily to his left, then over his shoulder with his thumb. The one-eyed man appeared at their side in the shop proper, then promptly disappeared into the back of the shop, into the belly of the crime. Her internal pounding remained.

Charlotte continued walking backward, pin clutched in one set of fingers, the skirt of Anna's dress bunched in the other.

Her tormentor leaned against the splintered doorframe of her imprisonment, arms crossed, head cocked, amusement about his mouth, but something unreadable in his eyes.

"Run to the street, Anna," Charlotte murmured over her shoulder, letting her maid free. Anna's hand jerked and disappeared from her dress, and Charlotte heard her maid's footfalls and the yanking of the door, the jangling of the bell, and the crash as it closed.

Charlotte continued to back away, never taking her eyes from the man. But he didn't come any closer. Simply watched her as she wrapped her bare hand around the cold handle of the door behind her.

"Farewell, little bird," he said, his voice cultured marble on top of jagged rock.

She pushed through, whirled, and ran after her maid, up the street to Bond. To call the watch. To get far, far away from here. From him. From the strange and dangerous thoughts he had engendered.

Chapter 2

Roman Merrick tapped the cards on the table as they were dealt to him, treating them more recklessly than he normally would.

A hundred decisions awaited his judgment that eve, and yet all he could picture were lush lips parting, pulse jumping under a long, smooth column of flesh. On a different night, he'd be out there, finding her at one of the half dozen events she might be attending.

Waiting for her to walk into the garden to cool her heated flesh. Lounging back on a bench in the shadows, scaring the devil out of her with a lazily uttered, "Good evening." Seeing her eyes widen as she recognized him, watching her chin rise, her hand clench.

Women came easily to him. But he had a feeling that this one would require a unique form of persuasion. That she wasn't used to men like him had been quite obvious.

He smiled slowly. Thoughts of what he could do with her pride and innocence tumbling in quick succession.

His smile grew as he examined the intoxicated man seated across from him. If the man only knew what he was thinking, he'd likely drop dead of apoplexy right there, face forever embedded in the wood of the tabletop.

"Charlotte is a good girl," the man said. "Sometimes

thinks too much. Not her best trait, but she can be broken of it. Her beauty would pardon heavier sins."

It was the twentieth such thing Bennett Chatsworth had uttered. Roman felt he could adequately reel off Chatsworth's daughter's likes and hobbies, sterling characteristics and faults, like a dossier on a war criminal. John Trant and Chatsworth had been circling each other for hours, playing a game both on the table and through words.

"You plan to have her betrothed at the end of this season then?" Trant asked.

"Yes. Can't keep holding my girl in. Too many interested parties for her hand. Been holding off for too long as it is." Eyes widening, Chatsworth could barely contain his drunken glee as he looked at his first three cards.

Roman would rather be out there right now, watching those lush lips—or even better, *feeling* them against his. But when he had seen the players at this table form, he had felt the draw. The tug of his gut that said he needed to be a part. And so he'd smiled charmingly and invited the four men to join him at one of the back tables used for special games and the wealthier clientele.

People always accepted the invitations. For to retire later to a club and casually mention that one had been playing in a Merrick anteroom was a much-sought-after thing.

But that meant that he had been detained here for the past two hours when he'd much rather be *elsewhere*. And as with anything, when he was doing something that wasn't *the* something on his mind, it chafed and rubbed, the pull to do what he wanted tugging relentlessly.

Andreas had tried to rid him of the trait long ago, but even Andreas had to admit that sometimes it was bloody useful. Roman's intuitions were always important, even if they didn't seem so at the time. His muddied Rom blood never failed to come in handy, especially hidden behind his decidedly antithetical blond hair and blue eyes.

"You have been holding out for a long time, Chatsworth. Heard that Binchley was thinking of coming up to snuff soon," Lord Pomeroy said at his right. "You willing to part with your daughter for the marquess?"

And now there were two tugs. The one assaulting him with what he wanted to do—find the gold-crowned girl he had chased away that afternoon—and the one that his gut said was the more important at the moment—stay in the game.

He impatiently tapped the edges of his cards against the table in front of him, uncaring for once if the sharp man on his left noted the actions. It was going to be a bad hand anyway—an easy choice to throw in once he was dealt his final card. He'd spotted the card he needed toward the bottom of the deck, out of play. Pomeroy had never been a stealthy shuffler. And Roman was simply going through the motions of playing, his mind on other games.

"Might be, might be. Think she could go even higher"—like a parcel being bid on—"but the marquess has much to offer. Have a few other offers already coming in this season—*good* offers"—Chatsworth shot a biting look to Viscount Downing, who only lifted a brow in return—"so the marquess will need to express himself well."

Chatsworth was a fool. Still holding out for a bigger title—and a bigger pot of gold—when he was in such dire financial straits. Dangling his beautiful fish on his barbed hook. Not realizing that the bait had stopped swimming. That she might even be torn from the hook completely if he wasn't careful.

Swallowed by a shark, if *she* wasn't careful. Forever separated from the rest of the silver school.

"Your daughter is a lovely woman," Viscount Downing

said coolly, at Roman's left. "I expect you will make her a fine match. Perhaps even utilize her tragic use of *thought* and allow her some choice in the matter."

Downing's wife was a close friend of Chatsworth's daughter. And Downing had nearly been betrothed to the lady in question two years ago. It would be hard not to know such information, as Chatsworth had been sending Downing darker glances and uttering more sarcastic jabs as he'd gotten increasingly drunk. He was obviously piqued that Downing had escaped being his son-in-law.

"Fine eyes, she has. Heard one of the puppies wrote a sonnet to them last week," Pomeroy added.

The edges of Downing's eyes pinched, as if in pain. "And read it to the assembly at the Peckhursts'. My wife delighted in repeating the lines at every opportunity for three days. Gave me nightmares of which I am not yet rid."

Roman felt a tug at the edges of his mouth. He'd always rather liked Downing. Before the viscount's marriage, he'd been a marvelous customer. Even if he won more than he lost, he had an innate ability to pull others to and with him, and that was worth any loss to the coffers Roman and Andreas might suffer. Because rarely were Downing's acquaintances so lucky.

The only reason Downing was at the hell tonight was because of a ladies' party to which he wasn't invited. Roman thought that sounded as good an excuse as any. He shuddered to think what might happen at a party for ladies only.

Though he might find *her* there. Or else at one of the other events, dancing with some stringy cad just out of Oxford, unable to tell which of his two left feet should be leading.

He wondered what she looked like as she danced. He bet her skin warmed, pink blooming just beneath the creamy surface. She had reacted so beautifully earlier. The pulse at her throat. The lift of her chest. With her proud posture and determined eyes, those very feminine reactions, the stirrings of desire, made the whole encounter incredibly potent.

That he hadn't been able to purge the earlier encounter from his mind wasn't surprising.

"Going to need to offer a great amount for her hand to beat out Binchley's title," Chatsworth slurred. "And any shortcomings will need to be compensated."

Compensated monetarily, of course. Bennett Chatsworth had high standards—he had outright said that he wanted no less than an earl for his daughter—but he would need money, lots and lots of money, to cover his debts.

Downing was the heir to a marquessate, and exceedingly wealthy, so he had been a good match. Trant had no title to claim—at least not yet, though there had been interesting rumors lately—but the man, too, had money to spare.

"I wonder that you aren't looking at the larger scene, Chatsworth," Trant said casually.

Unlike his positive feelings toward Downing, Roman had mixed regards concerning Trant. The man's deep pockets and outrageous wagers made him a good client. He lost about as much as he won, so he wasn't a liability to their businesses. In fact, he seemed to frequent the tables more out of a desire to gain a social edge than to add to his own wealth. He played with those who could provide value. Whether that was to gather information or plant seeds. The man hadn't become a brilliant politician by chance.

"I'm looking at the prospects perfectly well, *Mr.* Trant. Binchley is at the top of the list at present though that could change provided circumstances change."

Maintaining a smooth expression, Trant tipped his

head. A tick of irritation pulsed under his jaw, the only tell that betrayed otherwise calm equanimity.

Roman frequently encountered men like Trant in his line of work. Ruthless. Cutthroat. Determined. But coupled with Trant's deep need to climb ever upward, crushing anyone in his path, the qualities, while making Trant an interesting associate at times, at others made him decidedly predictable and boring. After all, a ladder contained a single directional path. Someone like Trant rarely tried the twisting vines, tree branches, and handholds to the side.

Trant had insinuated to Roman that he'd be interested in purchasing Chatsworth's debts if the price were right. Had danced around the issue on two separate occasions in so many weeks. But Trant hadn't been willing to commit to the high sum that came along with commissioning the collateral exchange and, frankly, although Trant was wealthy, he didn't have enough money to acquire all of Chatsworth's debts. Trant would have to gamble and purchase *just enough* of Chatsworth's debts if he decided to go that route.

Roman had never agreed to *take on* the project though.

Roman watched the man tuck his final card in with the others before Trant pulled the hand toward his chest.

It was little wonder what Trant would do if Roman chose to purchase Chatsworth's London debts, combine them together, then relinquish the lot to Trant's possession. What Trant could force Chatsworth to cede. Charlotte Chatsworth was a diamond of the first water. Even with her father's pockets to perpetual let, she sparkled like a gem amidst paste.

A wedding gem. Which Bennett Chatsworth counted upon—*bet* upon. That she would restore the family fortunes *and* increase their status.

Roman thought about her confident chin, about what the flesh of her jaw would feel like when he put his fingers beneath to watch the emotions tumble through her dark blue eyes.

He would put his money on Charlotte Chatsworth succeeding.

There was something about her. A proud tilt to her head, some survival spark that he seldom found in the wealthy.

At least not the *ton* wealthy.

Those like him, self-made men, tended to have it in spades.

That she was beautiful and obviously intelligent didn't hurt. He wasn't above a pretty face or a witty repartee. But there was always a pretty face to be had. And there were plenty of well-read and sharp courtesans who intermingled with his establishment's clientele.

No, there was something else about her that stuck with him. Like the points of her little pin.

He had seen her fleetingly in the market a month past. Just a glimpse of her face and the expression upon it as she'd looked at the cages filled with fowl, the penned creatures shoved together with barely room to breathe. But it had been enough of a glimpse to ignite something inside him. He had seen her before that, as beauty such as hers stood out, but it was that particular glimpse of her that had attached some sort of invisible cord to her within him.

He rarely emerged during the day, except for the rare occasions like that afternoon. His world was that of dark, soaked nights and the blurred eyes of early morning. Quite the opposite of the girl who was the toast of the social scene.

The dove of London.

The feel of the metal bird echoed between his finger pads.

He'd heard all about her, of course. She was in the papers frequently, for her charity work and her beauty, and the patrons or her father spoke of her at the tables—as happened with many of the people of society. Roman could run his own gossip column with the amount of information he casually collected.

And he knew exactly how much financial trouble Chatsworth was in. Deeper than he let show. He was liable to do something stupid soon.

That Roman felt a spark at the thought was troubling. He closed his eyes, his thumb and forefinger going to the bridge of his nose, then pushing over his eyelids, rubbing in opposing directions. He really needed to get the girl out of his thoughts.

Else *he* was liable to do something stupid.

"Turning it in already, Pomeroy?" Trant said, the edge of a sneer mixed with something approaching excitement in his voice.

Roman didn't look up to see what was going on with the two men at his right. Instead, with his open fingers resting in a bridge over his brows, the weight of his head pressing down to his elbow on the table, he looked across the table to observe Bennett Chatsworth more closely. The slope of the man's nose. The set of his eyes, which at the moment were gazing at his cards in undisguised, drunken glee— more so the fool to continuously drink true spirits when desperation clung fiercely and pots grew large. A once-distinguished man, though more hunched and furtive now, there was a hint there, a promise, if one looked closely enough, of the beauty held by the girl this afternoon.

A chair was abruptly pushed back. Roman let his hand fall and looked over to see Pomeroy stuffing a pocket watch into place. "Gads. Just remembered I'm supposed to be at the Winphors'. The missus is going to have my privates. 'Pologies about leaving midhand. Have an extra five crown on me?" He didn't wait for a response, just tossed the coin into the pot. "Evening, all." He rushed from the table like the devil was at his heels.

Downing, at Roman's left, threw his cards to the center as well. It was obvious that Chatsworth finally had a winning hand. Roman was about to throw his in too when he caught sight of Trant's eyes, narrowed on Chatsworth, determination in their depths.

Roman placed his cards facedown on the table instead, curling his fingers around the edges of the hard paper.

"Pomeroy was nearly drained anyway. And Chatsworth, I see you are at the end of your night's credit," Trant said, after a moment of letting Chatsworth examine the hand he held. "But I'm feeling indulgent, and a bit reckless. What say we up the stakes?"

"Oh?" Chatsworth's eyes went from his cards to the pot in the center.

Roman felt the rim of the cards denting his skin. The feeling that had been curling in his midsection, the tug, sent out sharp tentacles, waiting, on edge.

A sliver of respect wound through him as, like the others at the table, he watched Trant. The man had finally taken a look at what opportunities surrounded the ladder, broken as it was with Chatsworth's continued denials and the amounts of money it would require to force him to capitulate. All of the little tells on Trant's face spoke to his excitement, to his determination and fierce motivation.

Roman could have clapped.

He might have, if his fingers weren't clutching his cards.

"Say my ten thousand . . ."

Chatsworth's eyes flashed and lit on his cards once more.

"To your . . . oh, what can you put up . . . say, a night in your daughter's company?"

Movement at the table stilled. Downing carefully set his drink on the table. Too carefully. Chatsworth's eyes narrowed on Trant but then turned shrewd and greedy as he reviewed his cards.

Roman kicked back in his chair. "What an utterly tasteless suggestion, Mr. Trant," he said, as lazily and indifferently as he could manage over the tug of fate, the pull, which was growing stronger, wrenching at him. "I'm shocked."

Trant didn't look his way, his gaze concentrated fully on Chatsworth, the only person who mattered to him at the moment. Trying to determine how the man might respond so Trant could react accordingly. "I hardly think you could be shocked by something so banal, Merrick."

"Banal? This is the most exciting thing that has happened all evening. I applaud your tastelessness in earnest."

Downing shot both of them black, furious looks, to which Roman issued a lazy grin.

"Chatsworth, don't be a fool," Downing said bitingly, turning his body, a cutting move against Trant. "More fool than you already are, that is."

Yes, Roman had always liked the man.

Chatsworth's jaw clenched, but there was a glimmer of pause in his drunken, watery eyes.

"Downing, you are out of this hand," Trant said quickly, and as dismissively as he dared. "You have no say in the wager. You turned down the gentle lady's presence two seasons ago."

Roman stroked his finger along the edge of his cards,

his dead hand that Trant, even though he had jumped the starting gun in his excitement, in all correct likelihood, expected him to throw in. Roman had given no sign that he had anything other than rat shit.

"That doesn't preclude me from telling you that you are a bastard to even pose such a bet." Downing was beyond furious. "And Chatsworth is more ass than fool for not telling you immediately to go to Hell."

"What do you care, Downing?" Red spots of pride and embarrassment dotted Chatsworth's cheeks. Embarrassment giving way easily to anger. "Turned my girl down, didn't you?" He looked back at his cards abruptly. "I'll take the bet."

Roman could see the rusty, gin-soaked cogs in Chatsworth's brain turning. If he lost, he wouldn't lose everything. Granted, Trant was nowhere near the top of Chatsworth's high list, but then again, Chatsworth had great cards.

And he *needed* to win a large hand.

Ten thousand pounds more, on top of the already generous pot on the table. Roman could almost hear the devil whispering in Chatsworth's ear.

"And you seek to ruin her instead?" Downing asked in his deep, clipped tones.

But Chatsworth was ahead of himself in dreaming up new ways to gamble away his prospective winnings—unable to mask the emotions flitting across his face.

Roman should have cut the man off three hands and two whiskeys ago and sent him packing, but he'd been thinking about other things, distracted.

Thinking about the man's daughter, ironic as that was now.

The lady who was about to find herself gracing the bed

of the man to his right. For Trant held the best hand. It didn't take Roman's well-honed instincts to sense it. Trant had waited for just the right hand to make the bet. Had waited for Chatsworth to get into his cups and to have some decent cards.

Had waited to place the bet when only two men would witness the wager. One, a man who was utterly devoted to his wife, and whose wife was a close friend of the lady of the bet. Who would hold the scandal secret. The other, a man who held the debts and markers of over half of London's citizens. Who would make sure the wager took place. Who wouldn't interfere—for it was his business not to interfere.

It was his business to be impartial and ruthlessly fair. Their gaming halls and the collateral exchange thrived on their lack of meddling. It was part of what made their reputations so fierce and successful. As long as you kept within a Merrick law, you were fine, but step one foot outside . . .

Trant was going to win this hand, no matter what Chatsworth could scrounge from the deck. He would take Chatsworth's daughter. Ruin her. Use it to gain her in marriage, as he no doubt sought. And for quite a cheap price.

Roman should be pleased with this turn of events. He knew how Trant worked, knew how to manipulate him, if he chose. And given a year or two, Charlotte Chatsworth would undoubtedly need a lover. He could lie in wait, possibly strike up a rummy friendship with her. Be there just when she needed a shoulder to cry on. One-eyed Bill swore by the tactic.

Roman had never been patient, however. That was Andreas's cold trait. Roman would much rather seduce her into descending the latticework next to her window. To throw her over his shoulder and carry her into the night.

And the vision of the girl he had met earlier that day lying beneath another man, his for the night, to do with whatever he wished, made Roman's hand twist around his cards, nearly crushing them. His dead cards.

"Ten thousand, Chatsworth." Trant shrugged idly. "To my dismay, it does look as if your luck is turning."

His *nearly* dead cards.

Luck and fate that Roman needed one particular card. The card near the bottom of the deck, a deck that couldn't be moved from its position without causing comment. A very particular card indeed.

Roman felt the hard smile slip over his lips as Chatsworth nodded tightly, accepting and confirming the wager again. A coiled, springy sensation tightened in Roman's gut. A sensation he hadn't felt since he'd been on the streets, throwing dice for bread, needing that extra bit of luck so they wouldn't starve.

Andreas was going to kill him.

"Stanley." Roman called over one of the young boys who ran errands between the tables and rooms. "A round of drinks for the table." He motioned a circle with his finger. "And tell Andreas to come round. To bring the luck of the streets for Chatsworth."

Stanley's head bobbed, and he disappeared from view.

Chatsworth was avidly examining his cards, a tight smile about his lips. *Liable to do something stupid?* Roman had thought no more than a minute previous. Sometimes his revelations had the rottenest timing.

Trant was silently gloating. Downing looked as if he were contemplating murder. Two of them. Possibly even throwing in Roman for good measure if he thought he could get away with it.

It didn't take the whisper of twenty ticks of the standing clock before Andreas appeared in the doorway, eyes moving around the room in short order. Trying to determine if there was a physical threat he hadn't been alerted to.

"Merrick," Downing greeted, eyes returning back to the table's participants and hardening again. He tapped his fingers against the table. "Come to witness the debacle?"

Andreas met Roman's eyes. Fiercely questioning what the bloody hell was going on.

Roman gave a tilt of his head. "A bit of an extra bet to oversee. Tonight, Trant chooses to amuse and annoy."

Trant shot him a look but said nothing.

It was a lovely trick of theirs. For even with Roman's tendency to be chatty with the aristocracy—so much easier to extract information when people thought you a friendly face—when the two of them were together, even weathered old dukes grew silent. Intimidated. Unsure of the disparities they displayed and the absolute hardness that snapped together when they chose. Of course, too, Andreas could sometimes just be a fiendish beast.

Andreas strode forward, passing behind Roman, behind Trant, continuing to the right side of the room and standing in front of a messy pile, where he withdrew a ledger. He turned to face them, leaning back against the counter and lifting a pen. "What should I record?" he asked in the perennially bored, irritated tone he used in public and with anyone not close to him.

"Oh, I doubt Chatsworth will want it on the books, isn't that so?"

Chatsworth looked up, and something about the whole bet seemed to be sinking in to his gin-soaked mind, because a fine line of sweat had gathered on his brow. "No, no, leave it off."

Andreas snapped the book closed and turned his back to toss it to the counter, obviously annoyed. "Well then?"

"Chatsworth has just put up a night with his illustrious daughter against Trant's ten thousand."

Andreas stilled, his fingers tightening on the pen as he replaced it in the well. Just for a hair of a moment. Too short for anyone else to catch it. Anyone who hadn't been tossed to the streets and then spent twenty years with another person, scrapping together, watching each other's backs, forming an uncompromising bond.

Andreas didn't turn around, didn't look at Roman. He didn't have to. Every line of his body said what he was thinking.

Neither of them needed to win a hand for a paltry ten thousand pounds.

A boy entered with drinks, pulling the table's attention briefly as he set them down. Roman turned his attention to the boy as well, keeping the movements of the other men in his peripheral sight. Andreas's boots harshly struck the boards behind, his long strides eating up the floor, as he brushed Roman's chair. Roman leaned forward, catching the falling paper surreptitiously as it slid down his back, then scooting his chair forward to cover the actions.

"Consider it witnessed," Andreas said without turning, as he strode from the room, anger in motion.

"Your brother is barely polite these days, Merrick," Downing observed, a little too casually. As if his own fury had suddenly been partially contained. Vibrating under the lid of its box.

"He's never polite." No, Andreas was angry. Furious. *Livid*. Enraged in the way that Roman knew he was going to be called every obscenity in his brother's vast vocabulary—every gutter jab known to the lower east side, every intellectual snub the hoi polloi used as verbal swords. "But he comes through."

Roman folded the fan of his cards and slid Charlotte

Chatsworth's fate in between, discarding the dud into his sleeve in one easy motion. He tapped his cards on the table. "Now then, I don't have a daughter to bet, so I believe I'm in for ten thousand as well."

He pushed a marker to the center of the table, and the wild, coiled sensation exploded.

Chapter 3

Charlotte descended from the carriage, lifting her skirts to avoid the puddles that littered the road. Not giving in to the volatile impulse to drag the edges through. To dirty the far-too-expensive gown.

"Your father is sure to be displeased." A grim, sardonic little smile curved Viola Chatsworth's lips. "Marquess Binchley watched you behind his glasses of port all night, and you didn't speak with him more than two minutes at a time. Tut, Charlotte, you will be old and unmarried, and we will be poor and ruined if you don't fall in line with your father's *grand* plans."

Fall in line. As if Charlotte had been anything other than a foot soldier her entire life. She had coolly made her way through each party tonight—and had done everything short of violently flirting with all of the men and women alike. Of course, she *hadn't* flirted, she'd likely give the whole of London the vapors should she be seen frolicking.

And speaking with Binchley required fortitude. Two minutes was an eternity.

Charlotte met her mother's gaze steadily, nodding in agreement with the words of her failure. Charlotte had learned long ago simply to agree with her mother. For her unpredictable moods, especially around anything concerning her husband, could prove devastating otherwise.

The creases around Viola's eyes pinched, and she crisply handed their items to the butler. "I believe I feel an oncoming megrim," she told the butler. "Send Anna up with my herbs. I doubt I will be available come the morning. Tell anyone who comes by tomorrow that I am with Aunt Edith."

Viola strode into the bowels of their house without further comment.

Charlotte's stomach tightened. She had failed at that communication as well, as her mother was obviously displeased with her response. What Viola wanted with her these past few weeks, with her sharp glances and steady looks, confounded her. She had come to depend on the steady melancholy punctuated by raging fits her mother had displayed for years. This sudden change had upended Charlotte's life further.

Charlotte gazed blankly at the floor, pressing the heel of her hand to her forehead. Trying to deal with her mother's vagaries these days was almost as hard as dealing with her father's demands. Too many crystal expectations. And far too many encased in shadow.

Father would yell that explanations were for the weak. That she should always know what to do. That she needed to be perfect.

But Father wouldn't be back until the morning, so she had a respite before she received her castigation about her lack of ducal offers. Or her failure to entice the marquess that eve.

Every time she had thought of anything marriage-related, though, the balloon had simply extended. Knuckles bathed in blood and light eyes dark with promise pushing into her thoughts instead.

Why she would be thinking such things was the question foremost on her mind. For she was used to her father's threats and her mother's apathy and cutting remarks. No reason to feel the need to rebel now. Perhaps just knowing the end was near . . . but, no, she needed to keep to the plan. Nothing could go wrong as long as the Chatsworths followed the plan. As long as her father didn't do something stupid.

As long as *she* didn't.

Her fingers brushed a bright swath of pink fabric that had been placed over the banister rail, forgotten by its owner two weeks past, finally sorted from the rack to be returned to an armoire above stairs. Charlotte pulled her fingers along the pink. Perhaps she could ask . . . yes. The thought brought a smile to her lips. One that didn't pull or hurt. Her schedule could be rearranged surely for a few days next week?

An abrupt banging interrupted her forming plans.

She turned to see her father stumble inside, brushing off the butler's helping hands.

"Let go of me," he roared, eyes bloodshot. The butler's face remained stoic as he closed the door and stood to the side, waiting.

Charlotte swallowed, fingering the pink fabric. She couldn't remember the last time her father had returned home for the night.

He looked up, his eyes meeting hers, rage in their depths. She froze—surely news of her lack of success that night had not circulated so quickly? She bowed her head, pretending deference, watching his physical movements for any sign of his emotional state, which might indicate how she should respond. The shaking of his hands seemed to indicate some sort of personal devastation.

"Girl, follow me. Now," he barked.

She stiffly followed, still fully dressed in the elaborate navy-and-white gown she had worn all evening. It was hard not to feel as if the bare walls and surfaces she passed had been bled, leeched, into the cloth encasing her. Stripped paint and sacrificed heirlooms clinging to her, demanding she make everything right once more.

"A good evening to you, Father," she stated as she entered his study and closed the door behind her so that any remaining servants would have to press an ear to the door to hear. "It is a pleasure to see you this night."

He ignored her, violently shuffling through the piles on his desk.

She stood for a minute watching. "And I was thinking perhaps Emily—"

"Emily?" He didn't look up as he searched unsuccessfully through the scattered papers. "Bloody peasant fodder. And as useless to me tonight as always."

Charlotte tried to control her own anger. *Caution.* "I was thinking—"

He sliced a hand through the air. "Don't *think,* for god's sake. Just get rid of her in the morning. Send her back to the country. God knows she can't keep her gob shut." Though his ruddiness pointed to obvious alcohol consumption, there was something overly controlled about his movements and words.

Charlotte's unease grew. "She is already in the country, Father. She has been for two weeks. In fact, I thought perhaps I too could—"

"What?" he asked coldly, running a hand through his hair, causing it to stick out in strange angles. The strands were thin now, where they had once been thick and strong. "Go to the country? Hide with your useless sister?"

Charlotte held herself still, stiff. "Emily is not useless. And yes, I—"

"You can't, you have an appointment tomorrow night in the *heathen's* den," he spat.

Ladies didn't sweat. *It was a rule.*

Nevertheless, Charlotte could feel the brimming moisture in her hairline—cold, not hot—frosty like the icicles gathering in the very marrow of her bones. "I believe I heard you incorrectly, Father."

She wasn't sure how her voice remained so even because she was certain she had heard quite correctly, indeed, no matter her words.

Bennett Chatsworth looked away for a moment, fingers playing at the flap of his disheveled jacket, stroking the pocket watch there, an ill look to his features. The rage momentarily gave in to the devastation that simmered beneath.

"You will be staying the night elsewhere tomorrow. I will have your mother make your excuses to the Drumhursts."

She felt the cold certainty spread to her stomach. She unconsciously clutched the silk of her skirt. Of her *investment*. One of many that cluttered her wardrobe, robbing the rest of the house of its once-glorious grandeur.

Unreal. Like a dream. She'd wake and find herself in the country, three years younger and eagerly awaiting her debut, everything in the past two years a fading nightmare. "I am also expected at the Mandells' and the—"

"Yes, yes," he said sharply, interrupting her wooden recital. "I'll have your mother cancel everything. Only thing she is useful for these days."

This existence she now found herself in was real, of course. She had painfully pinched herself far too many times in the past only to have the throb remain. She schooled her expression, closing the cold pane over her features, not allowing anything to show on her face. "Very well, Father. And where might this heathen's den reside?"

"It doesn't matter. No one will know of it, not even your mother, and the less you know the better."

Bitter laughter bubbled, and she fought to keep it down. What was he planning to tell Viola? That Charlotte was spending some choice time with his mistress in order to learn the trade? "Afraid I'll do something to ruin our marriage chances?"

"Don't get smart with me." He shook a finger in her direction, darkness in his expression. "Trant will fix things should they go awry."

So he had lost to Mr. Trant. And somehow a bet had been undertaken before that loss. Given his attention in the past few weeks, Trant was hardly a surprise aspirant for her hand. But she hadn't anticipated that other aspects might be negotiated first.

She should only be surprised that it had taken her father this long to venture down this avenue. Selling her to the highest bidder in marriage was little more than stringing together a lifetime of sold nights.

"I see. You chose to skip the direct route to marriage. I thought you were aiming for an earldom. Trant won't even make your grandson a peer."

"If only that were it."

She narrowed her eyes on his face, watching the expressions that he had once kept close to his chest—it seemed so long ago now—expressions that every day grew more obvious, furtive, and desperate. "Who exactly did you lose to, Father?"

"It is of no consequence. He did it on a lark, as he seems to do everything." Bennett Chatsworth fisted his watch. "Makes money hand over fist, despite it. *How?* Blasted nobodies. His reputation though . . ." Her father shuddered. "He will *destroy* us if the bet is not satisfied."

The ice turned to dead stone as the circumstance grew

tangible. "What did you do? Who did you sell me to, Father?"

Overheard conversations overlapped her lifeless thoughts. *Charlotte Chatsworth doesn't know how lucky she is. Did you see her standing there, nose in the air? She thinks she is better than all of us.*

Those girls in the retiring room had no concept of the definition of "lucky."

Her father turned without answering. "I will tell your mother you have taken sick."

Nothing felt closer to the truth.

"I—you can't mean for me to spend the night alone with some gentleman?" Or with someone who couldn't . . . even be deemed such.

His silence was answer enough.

"What-what if it gets out?"

These things always did.

Years of scraping and posing, holding together her pride under constant barrage, showing calm in the face of gathering anxiety and increasingly pressing desperation. All lost to her father's gambling and greed. And Emily . . .

"It won't."

"But—"

"Then you'll do what needs to be done to fix it," he said harshly. "That is all, Charlotte." He moved toward the door, conversation finished.

She reached out and gripped his sleeve. "Father." *Please,* echoed, unsaid. *Don't do this to me.*

Everything she had endured. For *him.* For the family. For her own small, desperate longings.

He ripped his sleeve from her grip and strode from the room, taking her remaining courage with him, along with what was left of the packed snow dripping from her chipped ice. *So lucky. So arrogant.* Having to stand there night after night and hold herself together with pick, with axe, with painfully gathered snow.

She sank onto a hard wooden chair in her beautiful ball gown and tried not to let the tears fall.

Tried not to think of what would happen to Emily.

Tried not to think of what would happen to *her*.

Tried to pull together cold pride to save her once more. For one day soon, she was simply going to melt and drain away instead, just like her tears.

Roman watched his brother throw back a shot of coarse whiskey. Andreas was angry. Furious. Livid, as expected. But had said nothing until they were alone. Also, as expected.

"Tell me again why I should not throttle you, Roman?"

"Because you love me more than your flesh-and-blood kin?"

Andreas shot him a look of distaste. Roman was used to it. Used to Andreas darkly stomping the sensibilities of all in his path. But Roman didn't allow much to faze him, and long ago he'd waited out Andreas's savagery and found the man beneath.

And beneath was a man who would die defending those he loved. Of course, Roman only knew two people who fit that bill, so to most people Andreas was a bit of an ogre.

"That measure is in place for *emergencies*. The virginal fate of some fool's daughter is not an emergency, Roman." Andreas's arms were clenched so tightly that Roman was afraid they might splinter right off his tall frame. "I could murder you where you stand."

"But then I'll never get to enjoy my ill-gotten spoils." Roman smiled charmingly. Charm that rarely failed him. Even with someone as immune to it as his brother.

"They'll lock you up in Newgate," Andreas said harshly.

"Then you'll have to bust me free. Two picklocks. Maybe a little bribery." Roman waved his forefinger around in a circle.

"This is not amusing, Roman. Trant suspects you cheated. Rumors need little to evolve—you know that—*you use that*. And Cornelius is just looking for an opportunity . . ."

Andreas's lips were white.

"I know." Roman couldn't help it—his voice tightened, smile dropping. Their entire operation ran on their hands being clean when it came to the tables.

"I know," he said more softly. He'd deal with Trant later. And put Cornelius, the latest man vying to usurp their position in the underground, out of business for good. "I'll make it up to you."

He shouldn't need to make anything up. He shouldn't have *played* the hand. He *knew* that. And yet . . . everything in him said he would *still* do it if he had to play it all over again. As if bewitched.

"If you take this night with her, and the *ton* finds out, *we* will be the ones blacklisted. And I see your eyes, Roman. You *will* take the night with her. You will risk everything." His brother's harsh lips twisted, his dark patrician features mirroring his frustration. "Why? Beautiful, yes, but you know better than anyone not to be swayed by a pretty face."

Roman said nothing for a long moment, the memory of blue eyes haunting him. "There's something about her, Andreas."

"For God's sake, you just met her, Roman. Hell, you didn't even *meet* her. You picked up some bauble of hers from the floor. After nearly killing a man in front of her eyes."

"Yes. Yet . . ." He rolled a pair of dice in his hand absently. "Yet I have found her fascinating for a long time. I must know her somehow. This morning made me sure of it. I can *feel* it."

"Then drag some jackass in front of her house. Beat the snot out of him. See if she drops something from her window for you to retrieve."

Roman looked at the dice in his hand. Sixes. "You know we can't ignore my gut." Ignorance of it had always resulted in death.

"I can ignore it if the feeling is emanating from your *genitals*. My God, you normally don't look at the same woman twice, and now this?"

"I couldn't let it happen."

"Let what happen? One night in bed with the man who won her? And what are you going to do? Play chess with her?"

"Do you think she's any good?"

"Roman." Andreas's mouth thinned into a dangerous line.

Roman rolled the dice more roughly in his palm, gaze drawn to a navy handkerchief on the table, carelessly discarded during the game. "Did you see her eyes this afternoon? The girl deserves a better fate."

"Than marrying a wealthy man of the *ton*?" Andreas gave a dark laugh, old bitterness rising. "That is quite the worst fate I can think of for a girl fishing the mart."

Roman didn't immediately respond. Instead, he turned over the facts he knew about Charlotte Chatsworth against his own perception and awareness after meeting her. "She reminded me of Little Penny."

"Don't try to blame this on your damn savior complex."

"No." He rolled the dice again between his fingers,

giving them an extra twist before looking. Sixes again. "She intrigues me. She has since the Delaneys first mentioned her six months past."

"Enough to risk everything?" Andreas asked harshly.

The easy, charmed answer was, "Of course not." But Roman said nothing. It would cheapen the entire incident. And worse yet, there was something that tickled the edges of his emotion when he thought of the girl. The tickling of fate. He'd had it when he met Andreas that day long ago.

He looked up at his brother.

As furious as the tick in his jaw stated, Andreas had given him the card tonight. Had relinquished a piece of his honor and given it to Roman, even to use in perceived folly. Because Roman had asked.

He would support Roman even in this, because Roman had asked.

Furious, Andreas might be. But on Roman's side and at his back? Always.

The deep tie was part of what made them unstoppable, something even beyond what a flesh-and-blood sibling, if Roman had ever possessed one, could claim.

"I will make it up to you," Roman said in a low tone. A promise. "Even if everything goes rocks up and hampers your revenge. I *will* fix it."

There was a knock at the door, and, for a tense moment, Andreas did nothing. Finally, he turned and barked for the person to enter. Stanley peeked around the corner and met Roman's eyes, then pattered across the floor. "A note for you, sir." He extended his hand.

"From whom?"

"Don't know, sir. Didn't say. Liveried chap."

Roman took the envelope and flipped it. An ornate seal fastened the flap. Andreas said something to Stanley, then the boy's footsteps faded. Roman broke the seal and emptied the contents into his hand. A well-known object fell into his palm.

Roman stared at the single black shovel printed on the paper in his palm. The twin to the card slipped down his back earlier that eve. Obviously retrieved from the deck by the sender. He could hear Andreas swear as he caught sight of it. Roman flicked the card onto the table in front of him.

He wondered what the sender would one day ask of him. Or of *them*. But Roman would go to his death and take the whole of London with him before allowing Andreas to pay the price as well.

Of course, Roman didn't have to initiate this particular game. He could leave events as they were, the cheat, the threat, fading to obscurity. Find the girl later and spark a different game. Not use the opportunity within his grasp.

He threw the dice on the table. Sixes. Andreas's swearing echoed in his mind.

What the hell was it about Charlotte Chatsworth that called to him? He narrowed his eyes, thinking about what he was going to do to her to determine the answer.

Chapter 4

Charlotte perched stiffly on the carriage seat as it rocked them to their destination—somewhere east of Mayfair. She could almost feel the polish slip from the buildings and roads as they ventured into a seedier section of town.

Her father sat across from her, his back as straight as hers—like a board propped against the cushions behind. He hadn't had a drink all day, and the strain of it was starting to pull at his eyes, deepening the creases there at the edges. She knew his abstinence was likely to end as soon as he delivered and washed his hands of her.

"Lord Downing and Mr. Trant demanded to attend the exchange."

The exchange. Her father's marker for hers.

She didn't respond or change her expression.

"Stop staring at me in that way," he said harshly. "If anyone can talk Merrick around, it's Downing."

"I thought you said the man would destroy us if the bet weren't satisfied?"

Bennett sneered, but there was fear there, deep in his expression. "Downing wields enough power to negotiate with Merrick. And you were smart enough to become friends with that wife of his. He might get Merrick to take something else."

There was that pinched look to his features again, and she wondered what her father had tried, and failed, to negotiate. What else did the Chatsworths have to "take?"

"And what might Downing then ask?"

"That will be dealt with when it occurs." He licked his lips—he *needed* such a thing to occur, for his fear was far too palpable. She tried not to let the feeling bind her too, but nausea rose from the pit anyway. "I am sure you will be able to flap your lashes and get us out of it entirely. That wife of Downing's is soft in the head."

Charlotte wondered if Miranda knew what was to happen tonight and what her reaction had been or would be. Soft in the head she was not. Charlotte could almost see her stowing away in her husband's carriage, coming to rescue her.

Charlotte allowed the image to warm her a little. But she was too used to rescuing herself.

She was a rational girl. She had to be to survive. And she was of the *ton,* where sex was often a tool of the trade. Something that was bartered. For marriage, mistresses, pride, money. And obviously for debts to be paid.

She had been silly last night to let her desperation show through. This would be a cold business transaction. Part and parcel of something that she would do in order to survive in this world and keep it clean for Emily.

The fact that Charlotte was in her third season with virginity and heart intact made her think perhaps she was truly the ice queen she was called. Doomed like her mother for a frosted marriage bed and a brittle future of turning the other cheek.

But she'd use the cold. Use her mind and social standing to ascend the peak. She'd host elaborate parties. Rule the *ton*. Sit high on top, untouchable and likely acidic. Eyes jaded and brittle, like some of the matrons and dowagers who decided the fates of all.

If she had been married her first season, she would already be in the running for a cicisbeo or two. Perhaps a man to warm her, to make her laugh, to stop the constant push of the balloon.

The start of her first season had been magical. Her second, increasingly chaotic. Now in her third, she felt the stretch of skin about her mouth like a sunburn that never eased.

"And if this Merrick does not accept alternatives?"

She had heard of the Merricks. Nothing very specific—they were whispered about in back rooms, the topic of conversation deemed unsuitable for ladies' ears. They owned a number of very fashionable—and a number of very seedy—clubs in London. The young men-about-town frequented the more fashionable establishments, though occasionally those fresh from school, without a care in the world, ventured into the latter. Usually with nothing left in their pouches—or of their pride—when they emerged. Lucky to emerge *physically* unscathed.

She had never cared much about listening to such talk except to curse gambling in general. She wished now that she had paid closer attention. Hadn't Margaret Applewood said something about one of the men in a hushed conversation in a retiring room last week?

There had been a lot of tittering going on, but Charlotte had shoved that conversation along with a dozen others out of her mind, thinking them inconsequential to her present course.

"Then Downing will keep silent about the whole matter," her father said. "And we will deal with Trant. You will do what you must to keep him at arm's length until we can get Binchley or Knowles to come round. We must move forward quickly now regardless," he said, wiping his hand along his thigh.

She chose the better part of valor and didn't respond.

She should have sent a note to Miranda. Surely she would know about the Merricks as she knew far more about what happened outside the *ton*. Or Downing would have filled her in, if not. But Charlotte had been unable to set her humiliation to paper. To make it real.

She had hoped with each passing hour that her father would appear and say the matter had been resolved. A vain hope that she had clung to until the end. Until she had stepped foot inside the conveyance.

The carriage stopped, and she took a series of deep breaths as she felt the vehicle shift to indicate the unknown coachman had dismounted and was about to open the door.

She pulled her mourning net farther down and descended onto the uneven pavement of a back alley. Dark shapes slithered along the walls, and scuttling noises conjured images of things better left to nightmares. Raucous laughter boomed from somewhere in the distance, indicating a lively part of town on the other side of the buildings. But the voices were far enough away that she and her father would most likely be unaided when they were mugged here and left for dead.

Her father walked briskly toward the back door of a large building and rapped on the wood with his cane. He whispered something briefly to a head that poked around the edge.

The door opened, and her father gestured sharply for her to move.

Upon entering, she could see a short corridor and a heavy door. From the voices and light emerging from the crack beneath the oak, it was likely the floor of a gaming hell. Lovely.

Her father snapped his fingers, and she followed numbly up a set of stairs, away from the voices. Stepping from the landing, she noticed that Downing and Trant were standing halfway down the hall to her right.

Charlotte allowed a grim little smile to form behind her veil when her father made a cutting motion toward her. She stopped, while her father walked toward the men to discuss her fate, as if she were a goat in a stall.

She stared straight ahead at the corridor in front of her instead.

She didn't know what she'd expected. Peeling paint or dents and holes from cracked elbows and skulls. But it was a plain hallway, nothing extraordinary. Lamps hung every few paces—more light than she'd expected.

She wondered if this was a gaming *establishment* or a gaming *hell*.

Morbid humor, unfortunately, didn't seem to help her nerves. She swallowed and tried to focus elsewhere. From her vantage point, she could see in both directions.

A door opened down the empty hallway near an extinguished lamp that dulled the light in that one small area.

A woman emerged, tears streaking her cheeks as she stepped into the light. A well-made man followed her, his shadowed back to Charlotte as he closed the door with one hand. Something about him put Charlotte on edge. Tall, though not overly so, he looked strong enough to handle himself in a fight yet not tire easily the way a heavier man might.

He reminded her of the man from the ribbon shop. Standing as if he owned the place. Well dressed. Hair that seemed to reflect the golden light of the hall for a brief moment when he parted from the shadow.

He made a violent motion with his hand, and the woman flinched. Charlotte did as well. She could see livid marks crisscrossing the woman's face as her cheek touched the lamplight—as if someone had taken a shallow blade to her skin a few nights before.

Prostitutes could often be found near Covent Garden, and she had seen quite a few, even when her father tried to hurry her through the gates. The woman's face looked cleaner than most, as if she had recently taken a bath, but her hair was wild, as if she had forgotten how to use a comb.

The man held out something, and the woman paused, then snatched it from his hand. She looked at her closed fist, nodded at something he said, then turned and ran down the hall and through a door at the end.

The man was likely the woman's handler. She had heard of them. He had probably beaten her too, cut her up. The stories that people liked to tell at parties often grew quite lurid in the details of what happened on the London streets.

And here she was in the midst of the carnage, sold to a man who played in the game.

The man turned fully into the light, and her thoughts stopped churning. Her entire body stopped. And she could still feel the ripped fabric of the dress where her pin and her jerking had irreparably torn it, a dress currently buried in the dark recesses of her armoire.

"You."

There was a distant expression on his beautiful face for a moment before he caught sight of her. The shadow immediately cleared, and the edges of his mouth curved, lifting the edge of the thin scar along his cheek, as if he knew exactly who she was behind her dark veil. As if the sound of her voice had been imprinted upon him.

"Me."

He looked even more angelic than he had before, only the scar showing him of the earthly plane. Blond hair curled at the edges of his face, iced eyes were warmed by the lamps, and the lights caused a halo of gold to appear about his crown. He was garbed once more in impeccably tailored clothes.

But this time, there were no visible speckles of blood on his sleeves. Only the metaphorical kind.

Her mouth moved without thought. "Shouldn't you be in prison?"

"Should I?" He lifted a brow, walking toward her. A lazy gait that she shouldn't have seen as prowling, *stalking* her, but the jump of her heart wasn't listening.

"I told the patrolman. He ran off to arrest you." What was she doing? Telling him that she had sent the watch after him? Even with her father only two dozen paces away, she still had the distinct impression that this man could take them all down before she so much as made a peep. Murder her father, Trant, and Downing with one hand as he pressed her against the wall with the other.

"Patrolman? Ah, you mean Robert?"

She opened her mouth, but nothing emerged. She took a step back toward the others, not taking her eyes from him.

"An old *family* friend, Robert. It pays to have friends in many places." The edge of his mouth curled, and he continued toward her in that same lazy, stalking gait.

"So you just, what, beat Mr. Hunsden? Nearly kill a man? And get naught but a friendly visit from the watch?"

"Don't feel sorry for Noakes." There was something dark in his eyes. "Don't waste a thought for him." The darkness lingered for a long moment before it cleared. "As for Hunsden, he is as well as he was when last you saw him. Perhaps requiring a new pair of trousers, but otherwise, physically untouched."

She took another step back as he advanced, hating the need to retreat but not feeling stupid enough to indulge in holding her ground.

"What . . ." She swallowed. "What are you doing here?"

He watched her for a moment, his eyes roving her veil as if they had successfully pierced the dark fabric and were tracing her features. Or as if he already had them committed to memory and was playing the image through. He raised a brow, something darkly amused in his eyes. "Shouldn't I be the one asking you that question?"

She opened her mouth, but nothing emerged for a moment. She squared her chin, pushing dark thoughts aside. "I am here on business."

"What a surprise." He ran a hand along the wall, cresting over the bend in the hall, as he closed the gap between them. "I am as well."

"Not for a pleasure visit?"

He lazily surveyed her. "I do so hope that too."

She tried to say something rational through the fluster he caused, gazing instead over his shoulder in the direction of the woman who had fled. "You are looking for another victim?"

His brows furrowed for a second, then eased. "Ah, you mean Marie. No, I assure you that I have been saving myself for the night to come." He seemed to find something terribly amusing about that.

"I see." She tried to think of something else to say as he pressed closer.

"Do you? Will you oblige me then?" His voice was low and smooth, nearly whispered. He lifted her hand, the back of his lips only touching lightly but searing her skin beneath the silk.

Everything froze for a moment. Even the flickering lamps seemed to pause, flames surging upward and waiting. She tore her hand away, hardly able to breathe.

"No."

She had never been so near to a man who set her on edge. She had never *had* a man set her on edge. And she didn't find the feeling particularly pleasant. Her breath was harsh and odd in her chest. Frozen without the cold. Her hands were trembling, and she was just thankful that she wasn't holding a glass or some other piece that might give her away.

"No?" One long finger slowly lifted the middle of her veil to form a triangle of cloth. He was even more golden when unobstructed from view. His eyes sought the pulse at her throat—just as they had done in the ribbon shop—and his lips slowly curved. "Folly indeed, but worth it in the end, I think."

"Merrick."

Her father's voice was crisp. But the heat in the eyes of the man in front of her, the increase in the curve of his lips, kept her attention.

Then the single, uttered word registered.

Panic initiated and spread in all directions. No, it wasn't possible. But she could hear the footfalls behind her. The men drawing alongside her again.

Her heart stopped for a second time.

"Merrick, I didn't see you come up."

Having his identity confirmed just made the halt lengthen. One absent beat, then two. She didn't know if the organ would restart.

She watched the beautiful face of the man, who continued to lazily assess her, to drink in her reaction, all dark amusement that she was suddenly putting the pieces together, before he glanced away, dropping his finger and her veil, to answer her father.

He, standing with the flush hand, and she, carrying the discards.

"Chatsworth."

"If I could have a moment to speak with you."

Roman Merrick—good God, she had never heard or kept the knowledge of the Merrick brothers' first names, or else she would have put it together sooner—smiled charmingly. "Surely."

Her father motioned to the man in a deferential manner—and in a direction *away* from her.

Roman's eyebrows lifted. "Don't you think the lady should be able to have a say in something that concerns her?" The words were delivered in a charming and innocent manner, but there was something entirely false about the simplicity of the statement.

Downing strode into her periphery and flipped open his pocket watch, obviously irritated. "Something that was stated last night, I believe." His eyes softened slightly when they focused upon her, her face hidden from view once more, but turned hard when he looked back to the men.

"Lovely Miss Chatsworth seems hardly knowledgeable about what occurred." Roman hummed. "But strangely resigned to what will happen." His eyes were hot on her, and she felt her body traitorously respond. What was wrong with her? Had her own eyes not told her enough about this man that she should respond only with coldness? Was this some sort of internal rebellion against the pressure she had been under? She gripped her skirt in both hands, trying to keep from trembling.

Something snapped shut, the sound like a shot in the suddenly silent hallway. "Merrick, a moment." Downing strode down the hall, obviously expecting the blond man to follow the strict command.

Roman shot her a slow grin before turning and following.

Charlotte swallowed, trying not to follow their progress with her eyes, trying to sort herself out and reinforce her battlements. To think about what might happen if Roman Merrick did claim her tonight. Would her face be scarred in the morning? Would other parts of her? A comforting lick of terror rushed through her. Fear she could deal with, for pride answered to fear.

She didn't know what answered to desire.

Something inside her kept trying to reason that Roman Merrick could have hurt her before but hadn't. Irrational feelings and rational thoughts collided, bleeding into one another. She tamped down all thoughts on the matter.

Her father took a few steps toward the two men, then stopped, seeming to waver on the choice. It was hard to say what Downing and Merrick were discussing. The walls seemed to constrict toward them, tightness in every line, sucking in the surroundings.

Trant looked at her, then at Roman Merrick, something steely in his eyes. "Have you met before?"

"No." It wasn't hard to inject a clip to her voice. She hadn't truly met him, after all. And she didn't wish to speak of the situation with Trant, whom she didn't trust.

"I will ruin him." He looked back at the man, his eyes dark. "For you."

"I hardly think that will fix the situation I currently find myself in, Mr. Trant." And she thought the part about the ruination being for her was more of an afterthought to the statement.

"It is an outrage. Let me fix it for you." He took her gloved hand in his, steering her a little ways away. His hands were warm, but not scorching like Roman Merrick's. And though the touch also made her uncomfortable, the feelings surrounding the discomfort were not the same. "No matter what happens tonight. I will still find you a desirable match."

She smiled, a hard, brittle smile he couldn't see, before smoothly removing her hand in a way to which he could not take offense. For even though she didn't know the details of the bet—yet—she had a feeling that Trant was not inculpable. "That is kind of you."

"Say that you will—"

She cut him off. "Mr. Trant, I hardly think this is the time to discuss such matters."

"There will be no time more opportune."

"Father says this *exchange* might not even take place."

"But if it does, you should have a plan in place. I would hate to have to harm Merrick."

Something alerted her that someone stood behind them. Outside in the alley, the knife would already be sticking from her ribs. This was not her world, and she couldn't pretend that she was in any way equal to fooling it.

The tingling of her skin told her who stood there. She could feel the heat of *him* before he spoke. "I wouldn't have such trouble in return."

The words were silky and dark. Promising. The hair on the back of her neck stood on end. She turned to see Roman Merrick standing there, eyes disturbingly lazy upon Trant. Downing was saying something to her father a few paces behind, arguing with him in low tones that she couldn't pay attention to, too caught by the man in front of her.

Trant shifted. "It was a foolish wager, Merrick."

"It was. And yet here we are." His eyes didn't warm one bit. Fathomless pools of blue ice. Though there was that idleness to them, as if he didn't find Trant much of a threat. And looking between them, at the lethality that surrounded the blond man, she'd have to agree. Trant was fit, and he liked to boast of his boxing prowess, but Merrick looked like he didn't follow the rules of any sort of gentlemanly match.

More likely he would incapacitate the person while they were bowing to start, then *lazily* stride away before the person hit the floor.

"You should concede it." Trant's words were fainter than usual. "Force Chatsworth to pay the amount equal to my wager."

"Should I?" Merrick asked, *idly,* a thin layer of smooth liquid flowing over jagged rocks. He moved smoothly around them, putting the empty corridor at his back, and everyone in his view, forcing Trant to twist awkwardly. "What say *you,* Miss Chatsworth?"

She swallowed, turning as if her chest were connected to his and, like a marionette on strings, she had to shift when he did. She looked up to see him extending a hand to her. The same strong hand that had beaten a man a few days before.

For some indefinable reason, her hand automatically twitched toward his.

"Outrageous." Trant was a good-looking man though she could imagine the mottled red assuredly spilling over his flesh would not aid his coloring. But she couldn't look away from the hand extended to her in order to see. She curled her own fingers together to keep them at her side. "Offensive." She could almost imagine Trant's words contained a sudden hint of panic underlying the anger, but with her own hands trembling and her eyes locked, she wasn't sure she was a good judge of emotion at the moment.

"Is that so, Mr. Trant?" There was just the slightest

twist on *Mr.* Belied by a charming laugh. The menace was suddenly gone again, mercurially replaced with the rogue instead. "You don't believe the lady should be able to voice her own complaint?"

"Of course she should. Miss Chatsworth, tell him you will not follow through with this outrage."

Roman Merrick laughed. "Is that what you would have said should you have won the hand and *your own bet,* Mr. Trant? I had the distinct impression that you would have claimed the winnings yourself should you have won. Held Chatsworth to his *honor,* and thus his family's in turn."

Trant didn't respond. Charlotte thought that wise, as nothing he could say would do him much good. She felt the curl of embittered anger but tried to tamp it down under her swirling emotions. What good did it do to be angered over another man's lying to her? Or perhaps not lying to her in the pure sense but simply leaving out details while trying to dictate her fate.

And it wasn't *surprising.* Trant wanted to further his own plans. What difference did her opinion matter? Not a whit. She was the commodity. If he had won, any rumors of a night between them would be squelched by their certain marriage.

She squeezed her fingers together to stop the digits from shaking as they tried to lift toward, and twitch away from, the extended hand—the hand that came from a totally different sort of danger.

His motive, *his* participation, was not quite as easy to discern. She broke her gaze from the offered hand and looked up.

"I *know* you would have," Roman Merrick said silkily to Trant, still smiling, still dripping charm. His eyes caressed her veil as they slid to look at her father. But as they slipped over her, something in his posture changed.

Something almost infinitesimal. "I applaud your initiative though, Trant, in forcing Chatsworth's hand when he was—and is—so weak."

"Now see here—" her father said, pride overcoming fear.

"You dare?" Trant's voice was deadly.

"I do dare," Merrick answered Trant, smiling, charismatic amongst enemy combatants. "Getting twisted around in your recollections, aren't you? And Chatsworth too? Selling his daughter for a few pounds?"

"I can do as I please," her father said, bristling. "I take no judgment from *you*."

Merrick's eyes traveled over her again, *stroking*. "You should look to whom you take judgment from. You do not show enough care of your possessions. Perhaps they should be removed."

His hand was still extended to her, the gesture somehow not awkward. "I promise to take good care of you, Miss Chatsworth," he said to her, silk and gravel in the words.

His eyes met hers somehow, piercing her veil, glittering in anticipation over the carnage the words would provoke. But there was a depth, a certainty underlying his words, that tightened something in her belly.

"I will *destroy* you. Take *everything* you have," Trant hissed at him, fury and some strange panic overriding his initial caution toward the man.

Cacophony. Voices rose, collided, melded, and battled.

She looked away from the man in front of her, whose motives she couldn't begin to discern, and at the men surrounding her. Trant and her father were yelling at the man in front of her and each other, Downing was speaking coldly about deals and choices, and Roman Merrick was fending every parry as if it were all a game he had orchestrated.

All speaking over her, dogs circling a bone they didn't

really care about—other than that it was a bone the others might want. The tickling ivories of a glossy fillet. She had been little else in her adult life.

Scrape the luster . . . destroy the patina . . . remove the bone . . .

Her mouth pulled into a shape that she would have said was grim but probably looked much more horrifying and ugly beneath the dark cloth. It felt ugly on her face, in her heart. Brittle.

"And your wager? Your *honor*?"

Her father's honor. Perpetually left to her to satisfy. And he, speaking over her head as if she had no choice in the matter. No choice, though she would be the one to gratify, fulfill, and meet his obligations and the results of his greed. She always would.

Scrape the luster . . . destroy the patina . . . own your actions . . .

"My honor?" Her father's voice shook. "You dare? You inferior rif—" His voice stopped, choked, as terror caught up, though the statement still hung.

"I prefer *modest. Modest* riffraff. As long as you don't lump me in with Trant as *upstart* riffraff." Roman shuddered theatrically. Mocking, mocking, mocking. Taunting. Fingers reaching toward the glossy fillet. His words to her still hanging in the air with his fingers.

"I will turn every seat in Parliament against you." Trant could barely get the words out. "I will *destroy* you."

"Gads." The word was all kinds of mocking awkwardness. "I do believe my boot is shaking a little there at the heel." He looked down to examine it, twisting his ankle around, hand still pressed toward her.

Those blue eyes rose lazily from his examination of the firm leather, passing over her again, caressing, provoking that strange discomfort, adding to the tightness in her belly, her soul. "I must find a way to recollect myself."

"They will have your head," her father said, though in a far-less-confident tone than the one he used to berate her—the one he used when telling one of his hunting dogs to heel.

"For what? Collecting on your wager? Should I put the matter to White's?"

Scrape . . . destroy . . . be free . . .

But she'd never be free. Not while her father had control over her sister's fate.

"Merrick." There was a decided threat in Downing's words.

"Downing." Roman's voice lost its amusement. "Perhaps I recall what we discussed better than you do."

Something passed between the two men along with the coded words. Downing's chin squared, and his eyes narrowed.

Roman Merrick smiled. A simple smile really. "We are getting far afield, are we not? What do *you* choose to do, Miss Chatsworth?"

"Why do you ask her anything?" her father demanded. "She does as she's told. Take what you want of your amusement, Merrick. It is obvious you seek only to play and mortify."

"Do I?" He tilted his head toward Charlotte, a slow smile curving. "But that would be foolish of me indeed, to release such a prize. You wouldn't release such a prize, unless it was in return for a very large pot, would you Chatsworth? It would be foolish of me to trade your honor for mere amusement."

Something about that particular smile and those particular words, along with her father's reaction to them, shattered the swelling tide inside of her, popping the balloon. She pictured her father's fear when speaking about the man in front of her. The fear on his face now, even with his pride badly damaged. And still, he had bet his honor, and her, in a game with a man who terrified him.

"Let this thing be done." Charlotte's voice was hard. The taunting words curled, like a demon whispering in her ear. *Remove the bone. Be free.* "This childish bickering ended."

Charlotte straightened and folded her arms stiffly over her chest, unwilling to grab the extended hand, even in grim capitulation to it. Let *none* of them win here in this hall. "The matter *settled*. The marker *completed*."

"Charlotte—"

"Charlotte—"

"No," she said coldly, interrupting, finished with it all. "The bet will be fulfilled and completed. And then I expect none of you will speak of it again. *Ever.* Good evening." She brushed by Roman Merrick, no destination in mind other than to get far away from the farce.

She could hear the men arguing behind her, but she blindly turned the curve of the hall, then traced the steps that the scarred woman had followed. Hoping that her pride would save her. As one thing after another fell from her, it was her cold comfort to claim.

Her father had almost sealed her fate. Trant had tried to seal her fate. Roman Merrick might attempt to do so.

Just this once, Charlotte would damn well seal her own.

Chapter 5

She felt him pull even with her, but he wisely said nothing. One hand touched the small of her back to lead her, bringing forward every unnameable emotion and fear she had. They bypassed the room she had seen the previous woman emerge from—she couldn't contain a hitched breath at the thought of the woman's face—and instead climbed another set of stairs. The hall stretched and there only appeared to be two doors on the top floor.

Using a strange key, he unlocked the one on the left and pushed the door open, gesturing for her to enter. She walked stiffly inside.

The large space, one entire half of the building floor it seemed, was decorated in shades of deep blue, gold, and mahogany. A deep, inviting room with rich trim and a warm, thoroughly masculine, interior. Not exactly the cheap and tawdry place she had been expecting in this part of town.

The room echoed the man, in a way. Solid, strong, and dark, shimmering with bursts of gold.

"You continually surprise me, Miss Chatsworth. Or not so much surprise as *please*."

She didn't answer as the door closed behind her, the lock engaging, sealing her inside. The heavy edged shadows at the periphery of the gold were full of secrets.

"You fit right in." He moved around her, a whisper of wind catching and fluttering her veil.

"Pardon me?"

He motioned lazily to her dark navy coat as he sprawled in a plush chair that looked lumpy and worn, unlike the rest of the fine furniture. With the wall firmly behind it, it was obviously a well-used chair, placed in a circle with three others of various shapes and comfort levels, surrounding a table inlaid with oak and walnut squares.

She could see another room, farther back, a hint of a navy-and-scarlet-patterned coverlet in view.

She swallowed and walked to the high-backed chair across from him, a chair that looked much more ornamental and much less comfortable. She removed her cloak and carefully draped it over the back. She paused, swallowing again, and removed her veil.

Not to do so would convey fear.

"That is far better," he said, eyeing her as he rolled a bauble under his fingers, across the hard surface. "It is a shame to cover such beauty."

"Mr. Merrick—"

"Roman."

"—I realize you have far more experience in this sort of thing than I do—"

"You think I win women every day?" He looked amused. The bauble spun.

"—and," she forged on, the fury from the hall giving way to nerves once more, as she realized exactly what she had done in her sudden unladylike rage. Now locked in a room with this man, alone. "Perhaps we might be able to come to our own terms in the matter."

"Our own terms?" he asked lazily. The expression around his eyes was still intense, but . . . hooded, less open, than it had been when they'd been alone in the hall.

"You want to renegotiate the bet? You think that a man would resist the bet as it is already stated, explicitly and implicitly?"

She squared her chin. Folly to have even broached the subject. And something inside of her seemed to have disconnected from her usual comforting coolness. "Very well." She reached down and lifted her right foot to remove her slipper, balancing with her left hand upon the stiff, ornate chair.

"I have to admit that I think it also a shame to hide what are undoubtedly equally lovely ankles," he said, his voice smoothed bark. "But must confess myself perplexed by the action."

"I am simply making matters easier for you," she said as calmly as she could muster within this odd new emotional state, as if she had been stripped and bared of a second cloak she had never fully understood was there. She slipped her foot from her shoe.

He raised a brow, rocked his chair back, and wrapped his hand around a decanter on a side table along the wall. "Easier for me?"

"I am not so naïve as you think me, sir." She dropped her other slipper to the floor.

"I don't recall expressing my thoughts on your naïveté."

"Nevertheless, you undoubtedly think you have a shy virgin"—she tried not to react like one—"on your hands—"

"Indeed," he murmured, the edges of his mouth curving.

"—and I'm not one to hedge."

"I'm more of an all-in player myself." The front legs of his chair reconnected with the floor, and the smile reached his eyes, but they were alert all the same. She had the curious notion that she had taken him by surprise.

"It was a foolish thought to try to negotiate, and I don't

plan to physically fight. Or to play stupid or coy. My father lost. I am paying his debt."

He eyed her for a long moment, then poured a brown liquid into two glasses, motioning for her to sit. "Have you had to do so before?"

She smiled tightly and continued to stand, now shoeless and trying to hide her fear. Even here, about to lose the last semblance of her innocence and edge toward the meaning in truth, she didn't like being called a doxy. "No."

"I wouldn't hold it against you if you had. Though I'd lose even more respect for your father." She thought she caught an edge of distaste in his eyes as he capped the crystal.

"My father is not a bad man. He is—" The rest of the possible endings to that sentence—he is desperate, he has fallen on hard times, he is loving despite it all—lodged in her chest, unable to form. She cleared her throat. "He is too fond of gambling. I'm sure that he and his kindred spirits help you greatly."

She motioned to the unexpected accents in the room—the expensive and the exotic. "Their losses fill your pockets. Their stupidity overflows your coffers."

"It's the truth." His smile was lazy once more, and he pushed a quarter-filled glass across the table. "We find their generosity an onerous burden, but we deal with the weight."

She narrowed her eyes, not appreciating the jest.

He motioned toward the seat of the chair again. "Sit. Please."

The "please" wasn't exactly an order, nor was it a simple courtesy. She had a feeling that he rarely needed to ask for things.

"Would you rather not satisfy the wager and be done?" Then she could return home and forget everything—or try to.

She couldn't meet his eyes as she finished. As her thoughts caught up.

Negotiating? Forgetting that the man across from her was mercurial at best. Teasing Trant and her father into rabid anger—no sane person would do such a thing—while retaining that piercing quality to his eyes, the one that said he could easily eliminate all of them, if he chose.

Mercurial . . . maybe even unstable.

If she offended or angered him, it was possible she'd never see the light of day.

She looked up, unprepared for her fate no matter how much she wanted to pretend otherwise, but he appeared simply amused.

"The wager was for an entire night of your company. And I'd be a terrible host if I didn't offer you some spirits to lift yours. Sit. Please."

There it was again. The silky order, belying that she had a choice.

She stiffly sat.

"I find it quite complimentary for you to offer to pay the implied terms of your father's debt so promptly and with such zeal."

She couldn't decipher whether the sarcasm on the last word was for her lack of—or presence of—zealotry. She had just offered herself up coldly and abruptly after all.

"Perhaps you would care to make a bet yourself?" he said, idly twirling the liquid in his glass.

She wanted to *negotiate*. She knew far too well what happened to people who continued to bet, thinking they could turn a win on a losing streak. "Under the circumstances, betting would hardly seem wise."

"But you might win."

"The odds of that are highly unlikely. This is your business after all, is it not?"

"One of them." His lips spread easily. "But everyone has a lucky day." He made a careless motion with his glass, the liquid sloshing inside. "It's what sparks the obsession."

Anger surged within her. Anger at her father, her predicament, at everything around her. "And what would I bet, Mr. Merrick?" she asked curtly.

"Roman. And you have plenty to offer, Charlotte. May I call you Charlotte?"

She could hardly credit that he was asking her permission. Then again, on the face of it he *seemed* to be one for charming something out of a person before using force. She'd bet that nineteen times out of twenty it worked too.

That he would secure what he wanted, regardless of the eventual method, hung in the very air around him.

"Mr. Merrick—"

"Roman."

"What might I possibly possess that would be of interest to you? You are hardly in need of more money—"

He smiled. "Every man is in need of more money."

"Then I must confess now that we have none. Which means my father was betting everything on a very large pot. You must have surely won a good sum the other night."

"I'll have you know, I donated all of Trant's monetary losses in that hand—nearly twelve thousand—to the Orphans of Liberty."

She stared at him, unable to comprehend the amounts of money her father played and squandered. "Indeed."

An angelic expression graced his face. "They needed the funds."

"I find your attempt at humor vulgar."

He clutched a hand over his heart, the other continuing to swirl the liquid nonchalantly. "Maligned without cause."

Donated more than twelve thousand pounds to a fund for orphans—did he think her stupid? "I hardly think without cause. Besides, I've done work with that charity, and I've never heard your name mentioned as a donor."

He smiled lazily. "And called on my crockery. Starting at such a deep deficit just makes the game far more interesting."

"You find this a game?"

"I find you a diversion too entertaining to pass up."

"I am hardly that interesting."

"Men do not compose ballads to you night and day?"

Her lips thinned into a strained smile. "I don't know why *you'd* be interested."

"No?"

"I doubt you lack female companionship." There was no way the women in the retiring room had been giggling over the other Merrick. He had been far from unattractive, but he was *not* the sort of man over whom one giggled. A charming rogue—that was the type of man who caused unknown hearts to flutter.

And the man in front of her seemed to switch easily from charming rogue to lethal killer at will.

"You say that as if I would grab the nearest woman who winked in my direction."

"I'm merely pointing out that you have little reason to find me a game or challenge."

"You don't think yourself beautiful—beauty so uncommon as to cause comment?"

She felt the cold pit open. "I have been told such by men before, yes."

He tilted his head. "But you do not think that of yourself?"

She lowered her eyes. She could claim modesty with

the look instead of simply trying to hide her expression. "I see the lines of my face. Symmetrical, with eyes shaped the way men seem to enjoy. I know my hair is the desired color. I've been told I have pleasing lips and chin. And our seamstress gives us a discount just so she can continue to clothe me." With gowns well above their means even then.

"So you know you are beautiful."

Each day she looked into the mirror and saw a beautiful portrait. Perfectly motionless. Frozen in time.

She met his eyes. "Yes."

"So why wouldn't I be interested in you?"

She smiled, the social smile she had long perfected. "Of course. My apologies, Mr. Merrick."

"If you call me Mr. Merrick again, you won't be able to sit for a week." There was a teasing quality to his words, but she froze all the same.

"Of course. My apologies, Roman." His name formed strangely about her lips and tongue, curling into the top of her palate. "I will not forget myself again."

The edges of his eyes creased. Irritation. She had provoked him. Did she desire to be harmed? His eyes were unreadable as he lifted the glass of amber liquid to his mouth.

The words slipped from her without her consent. "I will do as you say. As offered upon entering the room. I'd rather not end up like the woman in the hall."

Everything about him stilled. The half-empty glass hung in the air, freed from his beautiful lips. He didn't respond for a long moment. "You fear I will cut you?"

Damage her beauty. There was an uncomfortable thread deep within her that hungered for the freedom from it no matter the cost.

She met his eyes, lifted her chin. "I can beg you not to, of course. Quite prettily, I assure you."

His eyes shuttered. "You think I did that to her? Slashed her?"

She looked at the thin, faded scar that curved down his cheek and around the back of his neck. She hadn't noticed before that it continued around his throat. She wondered how he had survived the wound.

"I don't know, Mr. Merrick. And if you didn't, then I have probably insulted you greatly." Her throat felt raw, it was hard to swallow. "But I know little about you." She wished she had listened more closely to the gossip. Wished she had contacted Miranda and damned her pride. "And though the eyes can be deceived, they are all I have to go on."

His fingers gripped the glass—knuckles turning white before loosening. He tipped his head, any amusement completely gone. "I will never harm you, Miss Chatsworth. Of that you have my word."

She said nothing for a long moment, their eyes linked. Then she nodded. But she didn't have any reason to believe him, and the further tilt of his head seemed to acknowledge that.

"And I did not do that to Marie. Noakes did."

She felt a rush of emotion over that statement. Relief, anger, curiosity—caution that he wasn't telling the truth—that it was a convenient tale.

"Did you kill him?"

One eyebrow lifted. "Do you really wish to know?"

A part of her did, in truth, but she said nothing. He pushed the other glass closer to her. "Here. Drink this. I promise it isn't poisoned; nor will it incapacitate you in sotted glory. You will feel better."

She grabbed the glass in shaking hands and tossed the liquid back as if she'd done so a thousand times previous. The spicy drink burned as it coursed down her throat, and she gave a slight cough. A trail of warmth spread down her neck and pooled in her stomach, spreading tendrils through her midsection.

"One-eye's specialty. Perfect for the appearance of drinking true spirits. Especially for when a man—or woman—needs to keep his wits while feigning the opposite, since men tend to get suspicious of other men with empty hands."

The thought that he had just told her something she could use against him gave her pause. She wondered if it would make a difference if people knew that he might not be consuming alcohol when he played against them.

He watched her, as if he knew what she was thinking. "Best not to ask what it *is* made of though." He swirled what was remaining in his glass. "Feel better?"

An automatic response in the affirmative formed to placate him, but she realized that she *did* feel calmer.

He smiled knowingly. "Back to the question of why I'd be interested . . . it is a good one. For I know many things about you, and yet nothing about *you* at all, do I?"

He seemed to imply with the statement that he did somehow know her beyond what he might have heard from others. Her stomach tightened at the thought that he was separating her real self from the one she presented to the world. Her eyes narrowed automatically, too used to calling upon pride to react with lingering fear instead. She allowed him to pour more of the liquid into her glass.

"And though I find you beautiful, I understand what it is like to rely on beauty and know the shallowness of it." His eyes were lazy, but there was a sharp point there in the center, acknowledging her. "Yet, it is impossible to say if you would have caught my attention the first time had you been plain and wrapped in brown. Thus remains the endless dilemma of beauty's impressionable curse."

"The first time?"

"Oh, I'd seen you before, Charlotte." His lips pulled into that slow grin that did funny things to her.

"You knew who I was at the Hunsdens' shop? Then, you knew when you were gambling with my father who I was?"

She hadn't had enough time to process the events. She had only discovered less than half an hour past that the man in front of her, the man who had won her, was the man from the shop. But he had shown no surprise to see *her*.

He tilted his head. "Had you been hard to forget the first time, beauty or not, you were impossible to forget the second and third. And this last time, alas, sealed your fate."

She had no idea what he meant by that.

"I'd never seen you before the shop," she said. A man like Roman Merrick would be hard to forget as well.

"Like vampires, we are." His lips slashed charmingly. "Waiting to suck the wealthy and damned dry, only dealing in twilight."

That brought to mind a feral image of pale skin, yet the man in front of her looked as if he spent time outdoors. "Your brother looks as if he's never seen the light of day, but you have more color than he."

"The curse of some long-dead Romany ancestors. Blessed with their fabled luck though, so can't complain about my lack of pedigree in the mixture of odd lines." He shrugged and swirled his glass, his decidedly non-Rom blond hair and blue eyes exhibiting the truth of the odd mixture he claimed. It was as if each bloodline had given him its best trait, mixing together for a stunning whole. "But my brother and I venture out only for auspicious occasions. Of course, the sun would never dare pierce Andreas's skin."

He seemed amused at some private joke.

"Now, as to what you *have* . . ." He tilted his head. "You have exactly this at your disposal, do you not?"

Something strange tightened within her. "More nights of the same? Surely you are not a man who requires a woman to scathingly or insipidly talk him dumb?"

He twisted the glass, coating the sides in amber. His gaze saying far more than words as to what those nights would entail.

She took a moment to answer, trying to keep herself together, for she'd never felt farther from control. "I doubt even marriage to Mr. Trant could cover such goings-on should I lose."

"But think of what might happen should you *win*?" Lips curved charmingly, pulling and promising. The pleasures of a game, of a simple bet. Dangerous.

"And what would happen should I win?"

"That is where we come to terms." He drew a finger along a furrow in the table. "What do you desire, Charlotte Chatsworth?"

The husky, almost scratchy syllables shivered along her skin.

Freedom. That is what she desired. In all guises.

She smiled, strained. "Nothing that can be given, Mr. . . . Roman."

"But there are many things that can be given, Charlotte. You are thinking far too hard." His eyes were amused, but piercing all the same. "For example, it could be something as simple as returning home posthaste, virtue intact. Or something more pedestrian, such as money to cover your father's debts. Or something as complicated as . . . relief."

"Relief?"

He looked entirely too satisfied that she had asked. He reached across the table and lifted her gloved hand from her glass. Pulling it between his, he slipped each fabric channel over each knuckle, medium-grade silk brushing her skin in a roughened caress. She removed her gloves multiple times a day. She knew the feeling as they popped free. But never had she felt like *this*. Warmth penetrated the material, bare fingers brushed each half-freed digit. Promises in each removal.

He smiled, predatory and dangerous, his eyes linked to hers before dropping to the freed silk in his hand. He examined it for a moment, then idly tossed the glove to the empty chair between them. He leaned back in his chair, lifting his glass again.

She stared at him for a long moment, unnerved and unaccountably warm, but gathered her wits back together. "I can remove my other glove, should I win?"

"You can remove whatever you like. Or ask me to do it for you, a slave to your whims." For a moment, she wondered how she had ever thought his eyes like ice. More like molten silver. She blinked, and his light eyes were idle and amused once again.

"It sounds far more like you would win."

"Oh, in that instance I *would*. Perhaps you could play with that in mind. I'll take the choice off your hands. Free you. Give you that relief." Glittering eyes, full, decadent lips. Her eyelids felt heavy as her gaze moved between the targets. "For each game you lose, I could remove a piece of your clothing."

He leaned over and lifted her bare hand, his bare fingers, rougher than what she was used to, inspecting her forefinger. He looked up, his lips pulling dangerously. "Or suck a piece of you dry."

Her finger disappeared into his, and she felt them pull from root to tip. Dear God, there was something in her that reached up, coiling around the feeling in her finger, almost *feeling* his mouth there, tongue curling around the tip, and she almost said yes.

She pulled her finger back, cradling it against her chest, breathing hard. "I . . . I think not."

He seemed amused as he leaned back, lifting his drink again. "No, that would bring an abrupt end to the game, would it not? And now that we are playing, I hardly want it to end so soon."

"I—I haven't yet agreed."

"No?" His lips curved, as if denying the claim.

"I couldn't possibly win a portion of the money my father is in debt for. And even if I could, he would simply gamble it away instead of settling the debts."

"I could settle those debts." There was something very silky about the way he said it. She wondered if this was how Lucifer bargained. "Easily. And without your father."

She didn't bother to ask how. It wasn't the most pressing question. "Why would you?"

He merely smiled. "Will you play?"

"For a relief of my father's debts?" she asked in disbelief.

"For more nights together?"

"Those are your terms? One of my father's markers for each game you lose. A . . . a night for each game I lose?" She could be indebted to him for eternity by the morning. "I could not fulfill those terms."

"No? But you would simply need to pick the game wisely. Unless you *want* to be deeply indebted to me?" He smiled temptingly, and she clutched the finger he had abused in her lap. "You might be able to keep the game going until dawn, and forestall all losses . . . or wins. Even the implicit one in the original bet for this night. For at daylight, I cease to exist." His fingers pushed quickly outward like an evaporating shot. Those lips slashed, pulling further in pleasure.

She heard her voice ask, as if from afar, "What kind of games do you play?"

"I will let you choose." As if it had already been de-cided and agreed upon.

It was enough presumption to raise her hackles. She narrowed her gaze. From the glittering of his eyes, he ap-peared a little too pleased at that stubborn response. She also wasn't so naïve as to see that should she *refuse* to play a game, he would be free to do . . . whatever . . . he wanted with the rest of the night anyway.

"Like chess?" Not a game she would associate with the man in front of her. And one that she might stand a chance at winning—or at least playing through to the night's end.

His lips curved. "I'll start to think Andreas has Rom blood after all," he murmured.

An odd comment. For hadn't he said that he carried the strain, which would indicate his brother would as well?

But understanding took her, as she remembered the other man from the shop. They weren't brothers. At least not by blood. She wondered how they had come to share a last name. Adoption?

Roman lifted an ornate box from the shelves behind him. He slid the top off to reveal striking figures and of-fered it to her to choose. A box that was far too close at hand.

She let a breath escape, a tinge of hysteria escaping with it. She needed to quell such a response before it cascaded with other feelings and opened up the metaphorical box to the rest.

Instead, she concentrated on the very real box before her and the figures therein.

It was a beautiful set. Charlotte touched the head of the white queen. They had sold their heirloom pieces a year ago. She still mourned their loss. But ivory and gold provided spare comfort when worse fates loomed.

"I can't tell you how pleased I am with your choice." His lips stretched, and the flutters in her stomach beat harder. Of course, a man with a chess set so near at hand was likely to be skilled.

In her beloved sister's foul words, bloody great.

Chapter 6

Roman watched her lips pinch and turn down before quickly smoothing out. He tried to maintain a bland façade but found his own lips quirking.

"I haven't played in years," he said as idly as he could. "I keep the set handy only if someone deigns to indulge a poor beginner."

"I'm hardly stupid, Mr.—Roman."

He hummed, not looking up to see her reaction as he put pieces in place. "No, I've not yet taken you for lacking intelligence." He brushed his fingers across hers as he retrieved the black king.

Her fingers clutched into the velvet lining as the king lightly slipped across her knuckles.

She wet her lips, pulling them together and inside. It made his muscles clench from his stomach to his knees. "And it is just my luck that you are probably a master of the game."

There it was again, that hitch in her voice after he touched her.

The sound made him want to do things to her. Dirty, animalistic things. To bruise her lips with his, muss her perfectly coiffed hair while scraping her on the sheets, blotch her skin with feral color as she lost track of her own name—head tilted back, eyes glazed, unintelligible sounds emerging.

Something in his thoughts must have come through his eyes, because the pulse in her throat leapt again, and her breathing increased. Whether from unknown desire or from fear, it was hard to tell.

He hummed and resumed his naturally charming façade. The one meant to put others at ease. But it seemed to elicit the opposite reaction in her, smart woman, and her eyes grew wary—warier—and watched everything about him, studying him in the same way he studied her.

Well, not *quite* the same way. After all, they held very different perspectives and had very different reasons for sitting across the table from one another.

He felt a small twinge of conscience. Very small and easily repressed.

He *almost* felt guilty for playing with her in this way. *Almost* felt guilty for putting her in this situation where she had a distinct chance at being ruined. Almost felt guilty for holding all of the power—sitting across from her where he could drink in her reactions and discover the secrets she hid beneath her cool exterior.

But the more ruthless part of him demanded that he chain her there until he figured out what it was about her that pushed at fate. What it was that had prompted him to jeopardize their empire.

It was what had kept him from releasing her in the hallway. Releasing her back to her father and Trant.

He had felt malicious glee over thwarting the other men, true. But each glance at Charlotte, picturing her eyes, had purged any thoughts of the others, consuming him with the need to protect, to *possess*. And not even Downing's threats had been enough to sway him.

He had told Downing that they would let the lady

decide. That perhaps it was in Charlotte's best interest to accept and show her father what his actions had wrought.

Downing had been coldly furious but had agreed, undoubtedly thinking she wouldn't accept.

But Roman had been relatively certain that she *would* accept, which is why he had made the slick offer to Downing. She exuded too much pride to refuse. Of course, with or without Downing's threats, if she had said that she was not going to hold to her father's part of the bet, Roman would have let her go. Would have found her again, in a garden or at some ball, and possessed her then.

But she had cut the conversation short, said *adieu*, turned from all of them. Strode directly to her fate without another word.

Not just from pride or anger though.

He looked at her, at the delicate skin of her flawless neck, and smiled. No, her pulse didn't jump like that as a result of pride or anger or fear. Her voice didn't hitch from chagrin at an unfortunate turn of events. That jump, that hitch . . . what the telltale signs meant . . . that was why she was doomed.

"It is far more enjoyable to play games with an opponent of near-equal skill," he said, idly, leaving it to her to pick up on any hints to other things. "It is my hope that in the end, we are evenly matched."

He didn't have to look at her to gauge the effect of his words. She wouldn't be willing to believe them yet.

Being the one in power was desirable in order to put one's pieces in place. To test an opponent. But uneven power grew unendingly boring. And it was why most of his liaisons were short-lived. He wanted someone who waited and plotted, then struck back and made him move and *think*.

"In that case, I will endeavor to knock your king to the

floor," she said. "And then wipe his crown into the boards."

Someone who was far more than she showed.

She moved her first piece forward. A white pawn for the slaughter.

He obliged, and they traded a few turns and pieces. "I do love the idea of a woman who could make me grovel." He said it in a way that implied that he didn't think it would happen. Ever.

Her eyes narrowed, then she smiled sweetly, with a tilt of her head, a drop of her chin. In that way that women were somehow taught from birth to do. "I *ache* to fulfill your desires."

He watched the way her lips met and parted just the smallest bit at the finale of the last word. Curling her fingers around the tip of her bishop, contemplating some sort of crazed move. She looked up at him through her lashes and plowed it into one of his pawns. Not the safe move one would expect from a woman of her station. But he didn't *want* her to make safe moves.

She set the captured pawn at the side of the board, squaring it up carefully, before looking at him with an expression that made him hard. Inviting him to reciprocate the reckless play.

Fulfilling his desires. He suppressed the manic smile that threatened to break across his face. And nonchalantly moved one of his pawns—rote and secure.

She massacred his king-side bishop with hers.

It took everything in him not to pull her across the table right then. This woman who was absolutely cool and collected on the outside and a bubbling mess on the inside. Need pushing out from behind eyes forced to maintain a steady calm. Not trying to lose the game, no, only a less-attentive man would think that. But that she would push back against whatever fate pushed on her . . . yes.

She could delude herself into thinking otherwise. But he simply needed to nudge her the way he wanted.

While giving them *both* what they wanted.

God, he could already feel her legs wrapped around him, see the sweat on her face, and picture the fierce expression riding her features. He gripped his piece and moved it forward.

The wrong piece.

He lifted his hand, keeping his brow cocked, as if that were the move he had meant to make. Damn.

His wishes for the future were getting ahead of him. It wouldn't do to lose sight of what was in front of him. He replotted the next twelve moves, clearing his mind.

He hadn't slept a full night—or day—in a week, catching only a few winks here and there. Which probably accounted for part of his overall recklessness in the last fifty hours. Though sometimes he tended to grip logic more clearly the more tired he became. Having to keep his head in dangerous and extreme circumstances had been a way of life for far too many years.

Her brows furrowed at his shifted piece, and she furiously looked at the board for a few intense seconds, trying to figure out his game.

He spoke to keep her off-balance. "I'm so pleased you decided to play."

She studied the board. "For the relief of one of my father's debts? And in a way that might mitigate the one he entangled me in for tonight? The irony of it was too much to resist."

That wasn't the only reason she was playing. He knew it even if she was as yet unwilling to admit it.

"If your father's debts were suddenly to disappear, what do you think would happen to you?" he asked in a deliberately idle manner.

She gave a short, bitter laugh. "My father's aims wouldn't change. Only his timetable. Still, room to breathe—"

She shot him a sharp look, cutting off the admission.

Come, come, he internally coaxed. *Bare all your secrets.*

But she clamped her lips together and moved another piece. A safer move.

"You have the power, Charlotte, you should use it."

She narrowed her eyes on him. "Spoken like a man."

He shrugged. "Your father can't force you to marry. You can run off to Gretna Green with some puppy barely able to lace himself, stars in his eyes."

She gave a rough laugh. "And do what? Live disgraced in the country?"

"I'm told that love overcomes all obstacles."

"Yes, until disillusionment sets in."

He tried not to let the satisfaction show on his face. *A little more, give me just a little more to discover exactly who you are.* "Quite bitter of you."

"Love is wonderful for those who can afford the pleasure of it." She tried valiantly, vainly, to cover the wistfulness in her voice with sarcasm. But the admission of it wrapped around him. "However, my father would turn such treachery against—"

She roughly pushed a piece forward, cutting herself off again.

He raised a brow in question to her unfinished sentence, but he didn't need to hear the answer. Based on what Bennett Chatsworth had offered him for this night instead, he could guess. He moved his next piece automatically, still watching her.

She suddenly looked at the board, then at him, eyes narrowed. She tapped the edges of her fingernails against the table. Obviously trying to figure out how to slow the pace of the game, for they were barreling through.

He'd let her slow it down, and the game in front of them would play until dawn, all while he was coaxing secret after secret from her.

The games she should really be worried about were just beginning.

He smiled, *patiently* waiting.

Everything in Charlotte responded to that smile—excitement and alarm.

He seemed far from a patient, strategic type, so why then was he acting like one? She had thought at first that he would be reckless, making moves with little regard. And indeed his moves *seemed* that way. Quick and without thought. But the way the play was progressing spoke to something else entirely. It wasn't *patience*. He was playing a game that was far deeper than simple chess.

And he was talented enough to know his moves—and hers—far in advance. That he could guess at her strategy—strategy she rarely employed, for she was usually a safe, rote player—terrified something deep inside of her.

Excited something far deeper. The volatile mixture seizing her.

Knowing eyes pinned her, lips curved. Knowing that she was out of sorts. "You do not seek the intimacy that love might gain you?" he asked, silk and gravel in his voice. "Above and beyond the consequences of your actions? Is it the thought of true intimacy that frightens you?" He asked it nonchalantly, moving a pawn.

She moved her remaining bishop in retaliation. "Frightened of intimacy? Something which can be so easily bartered and exchanged?"

"Can it?" He looked amused, but there was a hardness to his eyes. "If I were to take you to bed now—throw you upon the covers and steal your virginity, do you think that would connote intimacy?"

She stared at him.

He leaned forward, stroking his queen, drawing her along the boxed edges of the square she currently owned. "Or do you think that sitting here, across from me, sharing your thoughts freely and giving away your dreams . . . could be a true type of intimacy instead?"

"I suppose the act of—of copulation—" She swallowed, trying to push away the feelings—that strange mix of fear, anxiety, and want—his latter words provoked. "Isn't a reflection of intimacy. Perhaps I should have stated it an intimate pursuit. But, we are not being intimate." No matter what her suddenly sweaty palms stated.

"No? I have a feeling though that there are very few people you truly speak to outside of talk of the weather and the latest *on dits* or even your charity work. That few people truly know you."

His smile grew lazier. "And yet, here I sit, quite sure in the fact that the Charlotte I see before me is the one who bleeds away in the deep of the night. Painted expectations dripping from her, naked and free."

"You are unbalanced."

"Perhaps. Or perhaps I've simply tricked you into thinking you are safe for the night, here in this game. Still safe inside your stiff boudoir made of white. All the while I subtly remove the starch, bathing the white in shadow, turning it to cream."

She stared at him, unable to move. Unable to look away from his eyes, the shadows of the queen he drew along the boxed square the only thing in her peripheral vision.

"Like those whites and dark blues you wear—the darkness never bleeding into the crisp, clean, untouchable color. Purely surrounding it or using it as accent."

She had to clear her throat to remove the block but refused to look away. "And you think this is intimacy we are exchanging? That you are pulling my secrets from me?"

"Perhaps. Or perhaps you are pulling mine from me."

"You've given me nothing but taunting words and seductive phrases. I hardly think right now that you are the Roman who 'bleeds away in the deep of the night.'"

He leaned forward. "That you even admit as much . . . But I have given you such details should you seek to unwrap and use them." He smiled. "I hope you do."

She didn't know how to deal with the emotions he was provoking, so she motioned to the board. "It is your turn."

"So it is." He hummed a bit. "Do you enjoy working with the Orphans of Liberty?"

She looked up at him through her lashes, relieved to be on a safer subject, wary of what he might twist the conversation toward. "Yes. They are not one of my primary focuses, but I enjoy the group immensely."

"Not one of your primary focuses? You don't think orphans should be a prime focus?"

She narrowed her eyes but thought she read his expression right. "You are being deliberately difficult. They are already supported by a generous set of benefactors. They don't require my efforts like other groups do."

"Mmmm . . . like the London Women's Group? Giving underprivileged women a second chance."

She moved her queen-side bishop in a jerking motion, snatching one of his pawns, without meeting his eyes. "Should I be flattered that you know of my interests, Mist— Roman?"

"Merely something I heard in passing." He waved a hand above his king-side rook and pushed it along its crooked path. "And I am always looking for new interests myself. Perhaps I should donate to some of the causes you find worthwhile?"

"So that you can brag of them to your conquests? Not be called on your duplicity?"

"Duplicity, deceit, deception—such useful skills, no?"

"I hardly think so." She viciously plucked his rook.

"No?" The corner of his mouth lifted. "But you employ them so well."

"Pardon me?"

"And on yourself most of the time, mmmm?"

She clamped her lips on an automatic chilly refusal. Something within her not letting the *duplicitous* denial through. Panic spread sharply.

He reached over and touched her chin, thumb skimming her lower lip, releasing it from its tight grip. "But not now, no? Is there something here in this night that makes you feel the release, Charlotte? Something *intimate*?"

She watched his eyes as they traced her lips, felt the pad of his thumb in their echo. Drugging something in her.

"Is there something about me that allows you to brook the thought of relief? Or have I simply provided you the means at the perfect time?"

She spoke, his thumb brushing her lip with each whispered syllable. "You think much of yourself."

"Only in the way that I read your reactions. I would not play these games with someone I found uninteresting, or with someone uninterested in me."

"I don't believe you."

"No? Is that because you don't see your own worth? Or rather *know* it? For I have a feeling you *see* it quite frequently."

In the mirror, every day.

She tore herself away from his grasp. "And you, Roman? What is your worth? In the games you win?"

"Perhaps. Or in the people that are mine."

Something slithered through her, an insidious thread. "And you? Do you belong to them as well?"

He leaned in again, smiling, a dark, delicious smile. "Of course. For that is the risk and the quest, is it not?"

"I don't believe you. Few men wish to belong to someone else. And you do not strike me as a man who would belong to *anyone*."

"Where is your sense of adventure, Charlotte? Your desire for competition? For winning?"

"I am playing am I not?" She shoved her piece onto an empty square. "But most of those feelings are long past. Matured."

Safely buried.

"Then we will simply need to dig them back up. Rejuvenate them. Return Charlotte Chatsworth to her vibrant glory."

She didn't look up from the board, but his words wound through her, hooking in, provoking want. Panic and desire. For he somehow knew exactly what to say to her. Pulling her like the marionette on strings she had been in the hall hours ago. The sands of time slipping through her fingers as they played, just like the metaphorical paint dripping from her skin, baring her with each uttered word.

"Come."

He reached beneath the table, and she could hear a series of snaps. He lifted the top of the table and stood. She stared at him. At the stump of the table left. Neck and legs without a crown.

"Come with me, Charlotte." The words sang of sly promises and seductive creatures of old, almost making her squirm on her chair.

But she looked to his eyes, to the circles that had gathered beneath. Strangely, they made him look more like a fierce, sleek predator.

Was he done with the game then? Exhaustion pushing to other things? Falling back to the threat of leaving her virginity on his sheets?

He balanced the tabletop on one hand, like a servant carrying a platter. He bent, and his fingers curled around hers, sneaking beneath her palm, slowly lifting it and her to standing.

"Come."

She didn't know if she would have had the remaining presence required to extricate her own hand, so when his just as slowly descended, still wrapped around hers, softly leaving it at her side, his fingertips pulling along hers, the hoarse words popped forth.

"Where to?"

"It draws toward morning, and like all creatures of the night, I find myself wanting a darker, softer place to hide."

He carried the board gently, balancing the pieces on top, and walked toward the room at back. The navy-and-red coverlet sang of illicit purposes.

"I promise I only have a continuance of this game in mind," he called over his shoulder. "For now." The last was lower in both volume and register. Almost as if she weren't even required to hear it. It being more of a stated promise.

He turned the corner with the board, disappearing from view.

She approached the room at a much slower pace. Curious and apprehensive. Wondering where this night would lead. A faint flicker built within her as she stepped through the portal.

The bed was large, and it was hard to notice anything else in the room at first. She and Emily could share it with an extra person to either side. She didn't think her own room was large enough to accommodate such a massive piece of furniture. Dark pillows scattered the top as if hastily thrown on. She thought she saw a tucked trouser leg sticking out from under the bed where the coverlet brushed the boards.

That small peek of disarray allowed her to draw a shaky breath and continue forward.

The counterpane itself was magnificent. The scarlet-and-navy pattern wove together into a tight sculpted print, like an oriental rug shot through with gold. She had never seen such exquisite cloth. She touched it with her finger pads, running them along the surface. The fabric was silky, smooth, the gold threads making just the slightest hitch. She curled her fingers into the fabric, feeling the layers beneath. He sat upon the bed, sinking heavily into the layers before arranging the chessboard on top, situating it in its own divot of goose down.

He scooted up and reclined on his side, a charming smile about his lips. "Much more comfortable."

Decadent. Lush. Not comfortable.

She perched on the edge, determined not to be enveloped. A part of her, here in the illusory night, wanting the opposite. Just a little part.

"Come now, Charlotte. You can hardly see from that position, much less reach your pieces. It will be detrimental to your play."

"I find myself thinking this change of venue can hardly be anything but detrimental to my play. Or to me."

He raised a brow. "Not up to the challenge? Even with my most gentlemanly promise?"

She frowned and scooted up, dragging herself across the luxurious fabric half in protest, and sat with legs tucked to the side on the decadent bed, her voluminous, prim black skirts spread about her, her back ramrod straight, as her undergarments dictated. He reclined on his side, propped on one arm, shirt open at the collar and hitching beneath him. Creasing the covers under and around him in a depraved way.

She pulled her lips between her teeth, wetting the undersides, a feeling she could only identify as nervousness running through her.

"Suddenly afraid for your virginity?" He seemed to find some amusement in this as he arrayed the pieces that had scooted from the centers of the squares during their movements.

"Should I be?"

"It depends on what you keep doing with those delectable lips of yours. They keep promising different things."

She raised her chin, the thought that she could be seen as deliberately trying to tempt him making her uncomfortable even as her lips strained to pull into her mouth again. "I am not a loose woman."

"Oh," he said in decided amusement as he met her eyes. "Of the state of your virginity, I have no doubt."

"You didn't seem particularly prone to the thought at the beginning of the night."

"With you offering yourself up? There was a moment there that I thought I had been mistaken about your maidenhead, or lack thereof. That would have made things easier if it had been true. And more difficult."

She blinked at the opposing statements.

He smiled at her look. "I'll leave you to interpret that, shall I?"

"I don't think it difficult to do so." She narrowed her eyes. "Men don't like others traveling the path they want to tread alone, even if their own paths are strewn with couplings," she said coldly, thinking of one of their neighbors in the country. Of the woman's fall from grace, of her mistake in trusting the wrong man. Of the men who had sought her out afterward—none of whom would ever have marriage in mind. Not for someone soiled by another.

A mistress could be soiled. Not a wife.

Even Trant's eyes had been edged in distaste tonight. He wanted her badly enough that he was willing to overlook this, but she had no doubt that she would pay for this night forever should she marry the man.

But the man across from her continued to look amused, as if she were trying to explain a too-complicated riddle and failing.

"*Some* men desire the claiming of a woman's virginity, true. A staked claim to say something is *theirs* alone." He laughed—the sound warm and smooth, with just the edge of the roughness that seemed to travel beneath. The irregularity causing her to shiver but not in aversion.

"But what good is it to be first?" His lids fell a fraction, making him look far less affable and decidedly more dangerous. "The first hand in a game means nothing for the win. Some men say it sets the tone. I've often found that only a green gambler stakes anything of true value on the first hand. More likely it is a complete fluke. Merely practice. Warm-up."

His partially hooded eyes surveyed her lazily. "Lasting until everyone else is a mere shadow at the table, until you've milked everything from them . . ." Dangerous eyes caressed her throat. "*That* is where winning lies."

She didn't know how to respond to that, nor to the reactions he caused as his eyes touched her lips, her wrists, her neck. Here on a bed, no less. And a decadent one at that. "Contrary to appearances, that makes you sound like a patient man," she said, trying to focus on safe things.

Even though he had played as if he had all the time in the

world, *this* wasn't patience. *This* was—as she had thought earlier—playing a game far deeper than simple chess.

He smiled. "Andreas despairs of me, of course. If I want something enough, I will risk everything on a single toss of the dice." He looked at her throat again, at the damn pulse she knew had to be jumping, and smiled slowly. "But it's not so I will be first. It is so I will be the absolute winner."

Her heart sped up. "What do you want from me?" she whispered.

"That is an excellent question." He tilted his head. Then he carelessly motioned to the board. "But it is your move."

She nervously touched the shoulders of the knight closest to her. The conversation, the night, had soothed and put her on edge in increasingly violent turnabouts. "Do you plan to play with me all night?"

There was that *affable* smile again, incongruous and edged in danger. "Are you not enjoying the game?"

She had never played *this* game—the one that truly mattered here—at all. She looked down at her piece, moved it, then looked back to him. She couldn't help meeting his eyes. Directness had cost her at least one suitor in the past, and she had tried to rein in the tendency, but the man across from her seemed to thrive on her natural inclination.

"Strangely, yes, but I'm not sure I am equal to the overall challenge."

Equal to any of the challenges in her life. For at any moment, she felt the hairline fissure would crack, split down the middle, splinter the remaining pieces like a cup of china dropped carelessly to the floor. Shattered.

"You seem more than equal to it. It makes me literally coil inside, wanting to spring."

There was something about the words that snapped something within her.

"But why? I—I'm broken." The words came out in a whisper.

Everything stopped within her. She had not just uttered that to a man completely unknown to her. A stranger and threat. Uttered something she could hardly admit to herself.

Her eyes were frozen on his. But his eyes didn't widen, nor narrow, nor show any reaction at all. He simply tilted his head in that relaxed, deadly manner he seemed to own, his fingers caressing a piece. "I've found that life equips those who are determined. And everything about you fairly screams determination, Miss Chatsworth."

She sat there, stiff.

"Determination, shackled irons longing to be picked, and survival. That is why you caught my attention. And that is why I took you from Trant."

And as if he had said nothing of note, he moved his castle forward in a languid motion.

"Took me from Trant?" She had the strange but distinct impression that he had left *something* out of his listed reasons, and unbelievably, she hungered to know it, though the thought of what it could be terrified something in her as well. The same illogical feeling that had halted her movement toward him in the Hunsdens' shop halted her here—that something irrevocable might occur should she follow through.

"You must know that he desires you."

If it were someone in society, one of her acquaintances, she would freeze them with a glare for their daring. But there was some need deep within her to speak to someone. And the man in front of her, dangerously charming and friendly at the moment, called the words from her. "He has danced around a proposal of marriage. But so have others. Father has turned down more offers than I can count, holding out for a larger title."

Her mouth opened and closed twice before the words spilled forth. "And it doesn't matter, in the end. I have no say."

Like a stopped-up waterfall suddenly undammed. She scrambled for sticks and logs to stem the flow.

Roman surveyed her. "It will only grow worse. Your father has stupidly held out these past two years, declining offers, and Trant will finally be able to take advantage of it."

"How do you know?" It came out as more of a demand than she'd intended.

He waved a hand. "It is my business to know these things."

"What exactly is your business, *Roman*?"

"My business is complicated and boring." He tilted his head, a smile curling. "No, I withdraw that. My business is complicated and far too exciting for a delicate lady's ears. You will likely faint before I utter the first words of an explanation."

She felt much better trading barbs. Easier than to look within. To fear an empty pit. "It is a good thing that my ears are sturdy, then, and that I've never fainted before."

"There is always a first." His fingers went to his temple and chin, his head resting upon them. "At least you are on the bed. You would fall so prettily upon your back. Lips and legs parted, in complete surrender."

The reminder of their proximity and position was unnecessary but still brought color to her cheeks.

"See. There. I detect the beginnings of a faint already."

"More likely you detect the stirrings of my temper."

"Really? I'll bet you look quite lovely in a fit. I missed the vision earlier owing to your veil. Cheeks all ablaze in passion, I'm sure."

"I thought you uninterested in beauty."

He smiled slowly. "What I'm interested in is *you*."

She didn't move for a second, then she lowered her lids to keep her emotions from him. *Wanting* to know that reason he had left out. "Why?"

"Is it not enough that I simply am?"

"Everyone has a motive." And for some reason, she desperately wanted, *needed*, to hear his, here in this strange, drugging night.

"And so I do." He leaned forward, and one finger touched her chin. His elbow pushed the bed farther down, causing one of the pieces to fall and roll off as he leaned across. "I'm going to possess you, Charlotte."

His free hand caressed the flesh of her throat, then threaded into the hair at her nape, pulling the strands there, tipping her head back. Not harshly, but not gently either. "I'm going to take you and claim you and make you beg."

Her lips parted, and heat spread through her. The part of her that housed her immense pride screamed through the heat, overwhelmed.

His lips were breaths from hers. Breaths she couldn't count or take.

"The question is, will you passively accept such, or will you possess me right back?" he whispered, nearly against her lips. "Take me, claim me? Make me beg? Push from my mind any thought that isn't you?"

He was too near her for her to see his lips, but his eyes darkened, melting, and the curves of his cheeks, the crinkles at the corners of his eyes, indicated their whispered lift. "What will you choose to do, Charlotte? Hmmm? The answer to that, the desire to know that answer—that is my motive." The lightest touch of skin, of the very tips of their lips, brushed. His hand withdrew, then his body. He picked up the fallen piece, putting it back in its place as if nothing had happened.

Charlotte stared at him, at the top of his head as he moved the piece, then at his face, cleared of some of the emotions that had been there a few seconds before but still full of challenge. At the dichotomy displayed. That he thought she *might* be able to do it coupled with the doubt that anyone could.

She looked down at the board, thinking of more than her next chess move. Knowing that there was a motive that he had not yet admitted. Wanting to know everything and yet terrified of the emotions he made her feel so strongly. Of the way he pushed any thought from her mind that wasn't *him*. That wasn't *her*.

"You look exhausted," she said instead.

"I've been up far too long. Winning and debauching maidens takes a lot out of a man."

Her lips lifted of their own accord. "I can see that." She moved her piece, and they settled into a rhythm of play that while not entirely comfortable with the ribbons of tension threading through, was soothing all the same.

He laid his head back on the pillows, eyes closed while she contemplated her next move. It would make all the difference in the game, this choice.

She finally edged her last pawn forward. Something that she couldn't put her finger on fluttered on the edges of her mind. Some pitfall she couldn't see. She waited for his warm chuckle to tell her he would now lay claim to everything.

Nothing.

She peered at him. At the long golden lashes resting against his cheeks. The even lift of his chest. An angel resting upon cloudy pillows.

He was *asleep*.

Disconcertment ran through her. He had said he had been up for days, and the slight circles beneath his eyes proclaimed such.

But . . . but where was the wild seduction? The claiming? The making her beg?

She shifted on the covers, uncomfortable with the nature of the thoughts—the feel of them echoed in her belly as if they were natural and normal. The edge of the intoxicating danger that he made her feel when he gripped her chin in his dangerous hands.

Instead, he was lying on the pillows, at ease. A strange thought that he didn't seem the type of man to let down his guard floated through her. That she could do anything to him in this moment.

Though if she shifted forward, would he catch her arm in his grip? Punish her for her thoughts—harmful or seductive?

She could flee. Though to where she would flee, and why, she didn't know. There were only a few hours until her father would arrive to retrieve her. Far safer to spend them here, where she had already released some of her fear.

And she had. Released *certain* reasons to fear, that is. For he could have done anything to her without much recourse from her father.

Yet he had replaced initial fears with the keener concerns over her own body's responses. Dark paths calling to her to turn the corners. To see what lurked around the hedges.

She did something she wouldn't have believed possible the moment she had heard her father's outrageous mistake—or the moment the man across from her promised he *would* possess her—she curled up at the foot of the bed and, a few minutes later, felt her own lids fall.

* * *

She woke abruptly. Her head was nestled on a pillow, covers pulled over her chest. She distinctly remembered falling asleep outside of the coverings though, and she pushed herself up against the headboard in a flash.

But she was alone.

Faint light had gathered at the edges of the windows, dull gray morning shadows allowing her to see that the clock said it was a quarter to six. Her father would arrive at any moment.

She slipped her legs to the floor, the covers pulling at her dress as if unwilling to relinquish their hold. She drew upright and smoothed down the crinkles. She had worn a dress more suited to mourning than to lascivious activities, and it hadn't taken well to being creased under the covers for so long. She would remember such things for liaisons in the future, she thought humorlessly.

She stepped to the door between the bedroom and living quarters, wondering where her erstwhile host had taken himself off to. It didn't take long to discover.

He stood at the window, the drape pulled back by one hand. There was a stillness to him standing there, gazing out the window to something beyond.

There was a minute tightening in his posture— enough to indicate that he knew she was standing there, watching—but he didn't move.

The clock struck the first of its six peals.

She cleared her suddenly dry throat. "I suppose this is farewell then, Roman." Her voice sounded unusually scratchy.

He said nothing for two peals, then let the drape fall and turned to her. As he bridged the distance between them, the slow smile that heated something within her spread across his face. "Is it?"

He was far too close. Looking down at her face in that manner. Making strange feelings curl within.

"I—yes."

Another peal.

His capable hand wrapped around the back of her neck, pulling her the short distance to him. Her mouth opened in exclamation, her quickened breath needing escape. "Then I suppose there is only one thing to do," he said.

And his lips were upon hers.

Not the light press of a gentleman's lips. Not the perfunctory kisses she had seen from established pairs. Not what she heard about in the back rooms with marriage-hungry misses saying they had exchanged quick butterfly touches with their loves.

This was something far more consuming. Scorching. Claiming.

A thump beat within and around her.

And then they were skimming, barely touching hers. There was something even more serious in the brush. A promise.

But a promise of what? For there was only one more peal for the night to be complete, and assuredly footsteps would be drawing closer, stopping on the other side of the door. Her father coming to escort her home. Roman's hand slipped from her nape, his fingers drawing along the edge of her chin, rubbing over her lower lip. His other hand took hers and pressed something into her palm.

"Knight to D6."

His voice sifted over her skin, silk over gravel, and she processed the words as the door opened, the last peal sounding.

"Checkmate, Charlotte."

Chapter 7

Charlotte watched the polish build layer by layer on the houses, the façades lengthening and widening as they drew closer to Mayfair. Her knuckles traced her lips, the white king clutched in her fist. Roman Merrick was . . . complicated. She thought that was the best way to sum up the man at the moment.

And dangerous, very dangerous, to the path she needed to travel.

"Charlotte."

She waited a moment, unwilling to break her vigil, then turned to observe her father.

His shirt was slightly unkempt. Undoubtedly, he was fetching her after spending the night with his mistress. Consoling himself in the woman's arms, as usual. His marriage bed cold and fallow, as it had been for as long as Charlotte could remember.

"You are well?" he asked gruffly.

Charlotte often saw her father's mistress on the edges, in the market, at the theater, in the crowd at Vauxhall, waiting for the family to leave, eager, almost desperate, to service her longtime lover in the dark walks as soon as he broke free.

Her knuckles fell from her lips, fingers curling more tightly over the chess piece. "He didn't beat me, if that is what you are asking," she said in a voice as dismissive as she had ever dared with her father.

His hands fisted. "That wasn't what I was asking."

"Ah. Then in any other instances of wellness, I assure you that I am as fine as I can be, given the circumstances. He didn't touch me."

She resisted the urge to brush her lips again. He hadn't touched her in the way her father was thinking, at least.

Her father's worn features relaxed a measure. "Good." Though she wasn't sure if he believed her words or if he just *wanted* to believe them. "I tried to bargain him out of it. To offer . . . other things. But he refused. I will remember better in the future."

She again wondered what else her father could have offered. The danger of her words of assurance hit her a second too late. She could see his thinking twisting to assume there had been nothing wrong with what he had done.

Something about the night, about the strange and twining conversations she had had with Roman Merrick, wedged within her, in part confusing her and in part giving her added strength.

"R—Mr. Merrick seemed to think of the situation as a lark." She kept her voice as even as she could, for nothing about Roman Merrick's eyes had indicated anything of the sort. "But, if you do such a thing again, I will not save you." She said it calmly, making him meet her eyes. "I will let you burn."

"You—" His voice was clipped.

"No." She smiled without humor. Her father's actions had led to her spending one night with the man, a night on the edge of scandal and ruin. Her own actions had promised her to him for another. "You have nothing to say to me on this matter, Father, unless it is to tender an apology.

I will marry well. For the family. For Emily and Mother. But you will have to save yourself next time, Father."

The carriage pulled to a stop, and she exited without turning to see the expression on his face.

She opened the front door. Her father had wisely dismissed their four servants the night before—giving them a rare night off. All had been eager to take it. For every servant her father dismissed added additional burdens to the others.

He closed the front door behind them. "Charlotte."

There was an appeal there, wrapped in the hard dignity that continued to break and crumble around him with each passing day. An appeal for which she had so desperately yearned a year past. One that promised more pain should she open herself to the plea. She hardened her thoughts instead. Survival.

She would be the proper daughter. The proper society miss. The proper hostess. All she had to do was wrap her mantle of cold dignity tight across her shoulders. And that included shutting out anything that caused pain.

If there was one thing the night and events surrounding it had taught her, it was that she needed to secure Emily's fate herself before anyone else did it for her.

She clutched the chess piece in her grip as she headed for the stairs without turning. "Good day, Father."

Charlotte held herself firmly upon the edge of the embroidered seat, chin set, as she accepted a saucer and cup from the hostess. She offered the illusion of a smile and crisp words of thanks, as the hostess preferred. Charlotte balanced the delicate china upon her knee, calmly surveying the dozen other women, young and old.

Looking for any sly glances or uncontrolled body positioning that would suggest that one of the women had something to reveal. News that would indicate last night was anything other than a strange dream of hers alone. That the knowledge of her night in Roman Merrick's lair had escaped into the rumor mill.

It had taken every ounce of courage to come here, her first and most important stop. The place where ladies were broken every day.

Miranda, Lady Downing, took her offered cup more enthusiastically and immediately lifted it to her lips, as two of the other ladies had done. Before she could take a sip, she caught Charlotte's eye over the rim, caught the slight signal Charlotte was sending, and set the cup down without a taste, making the china give a tinkle. Miranda didn't quite cover her chagrin, and Charlotte sought to direct attention elsewhere.

"What a lovely new stitch, Lady Hodge." She nodded toward the delicate webbing on the table. "I regret that I haven't quite mastered the turn of a needle so well. Your work is to be admired and studied, as always."

"Nonsense, Miss Chatsworth." The woman smiled. It wasn't a warm smile, but neither was it the cold one she had leveled on most of the others in the room. "I have seen your pieces, and they are the work of a budding lady of great import. If only all of the young ladies held such an eye or grace."

The older woman cast a dissatisfied look upon a few of the young ladies, who sent discreet glares in Charlotte's direction when the hostesses holding this "social" weren't looking. But Charlotte was well used to the glares. And was simply grateful they weren't accompanied by the smugness of knowledge awaiting revelation.

She didn't let her shoulders droop in relief, nor any other expression of release cross her features. Indeed, she strangely felt *more* tight. The balloon distending further.

She shook the peculiar reaction aside. What mattered was that Miranda's blunder had been forgotten. Downing would sneer that his wife didn't have to please or impress *anyone*. But Miranda had confided a week ago, at the beginning of the season—Miranda's first, since she hadn't been a part of society before marrying Downing, and they had taken a year after their marriage to tour the continent—that she was determined to breach the inner sanctum of one of the strictest matrons in society in order to make things easier for some of her husband's scandal-ridden family members, a notion Charlotte was quite familiar with. And here, impeccable manners spoke for themselves.

A plate of wonderfully fragrant scones was spread on the table—smelling of cinnamon and sugar and fresh-from-the-oven sin—and Miranda's shoulders hunched forward ever so slightly, nose edging toward them. Charlotte tipped her head a fraction to the left, and Miranda straightened with a wistful look. She copied Charlotte's posture, squaring her shoulders, ramming steel down her spine.

Charlotte withheld a grim smile, partly from amusement at her friend's response but mostly from an edge of irrational anger at the game she was forcing her friend to play. She pressed the thoughts down, into the void, and tipped her head to the right and "Mmmm'ed" in feigned curiosity to another lady's comment on a painting. A neutral gesture that withheld judgment but didn't show support. The other woman would do well to stop speaking.

"It is a piece with great composition and detail. Why look at how the tree sits just so," the woman said, words tripping over each other as she gathered momentum and took the gathering silence as support. "It must have been in your family for generations."

"Lord Hodge picked it up last weekend." Cold scorn

underlined each word. "Wretched new painter with none of the classic strokes. As soon as a requisite amount of time has passed for Lord Hodge to forget about it, I shall have it removed posthaste."

The matrons exchanged coldly amused glances about the nature of "handling" husbands. But Lady Hodge sent a frigid glance to the woman who had made the comments. The woman blanched. Miranda looked at her sympathetically.

Charlotte felt the emotion too, but knew that to display such would only cause anger. Miranda could express sympathy. From Charlotte, people interpreted it as scorn.

They saw what they wanted to see. And she didn't possess the emotional skill to pull people into a warm embrace. She hadn't even known how to properly hug another person until Emily had come into her life. She was . . . broken. Uttered in the dark of night, but true nonetheless, no matter what Roman Merrick said. Destined for a pedestal and a glass case. To be taken and displayed, coldly admired, then returned.

Miranda opened her mouth to say something but quickly shut it again when Charlotte tipped her head left. Her friend looked as if she wanted to sigh, but gave an infinitesimal nod and held still.

Miranda wanted the constraints. But she could play within them as soon as she wanted. Could cast them aside completely, should she choose. She was a viscountess, and she'd be a marchioness someday, married to a man powerful in his own right. For her, this was a case of dressing up, learning what society dictated, and shedding her domino should she decide she wasn't having fun anymore.

Miranda enjoyed that freedom because of her position. And that was directly due to whom she'd married.

Charlotte gripped the edge of the delicate china. Emily

would be able to do the same, would be able to revel freely in her emotions, when Charlotte established them so deeply into the *ton* that a typhoon wouldn't shake a leaf from their tree. It was the promise she had made to herself. There was more than one woman in present company who got by on her sister's reputation or that of her family. It was the way of the world. Leeway was given to those attached to the favored and to those in power.

But such a path wouldn't work for Emily or for Charlotte if Charlotte didn't marry well and secure that legacy. Her present existence in the *ton* was based on *future* goodwill. People *expected* her to marry well and were trading on her future status.

"And you, Miss Chatsworth. Are you recovered from whatever ailed you last eve?"

Charlotte looked at her questioner. Bethany Case hated her with a depth of feeling that Charlotte didn't think the woman even possessed for her own child, born a few months past.

"I am. Thank you, Mrs. Case. It is kind of you to ask after my well-being. Merely a headache of the variety we've all experienced." She dipped her chin but didn't fiddle. Didn't allow the thought that her whereabouts last night would destroy everything.

In direct contrast to Emily's fate given her success, should the tide turn, her sister would be drowned in the same. Emily's fate was tied to hers. Should anyone find out about her father's bet or about Roman Merrick . . .

No. Her stomach gave a vicious squeeze. She wouldn't allow that to happen.

The conversation continued. Waits and feints, thrusts and parries. Some were brutally slashed, withering in their chairs, while others gained courage in given praise or known standing.

"The lovely purples of the season are sinfully delicious," said the daughter of a duke, who could get away with a bit of fast language.

"Yes, though it's unfortunate that *some* are so set in their ways that they will turn up their nose at the rest of us," Bethany Case said. A number of the women smirked and nodded without looking anywhere in particular. It was the fifth such snide comment directed toward Charlotte.

The barbs were meant to sting. Charlotte let them wash over her, having long practice in doing so. Let them flow off to join the gathered ice at her feet. The matrons watched, weighing and waiting.

No matter her favored status, they wouldn't "save" her; nor did she wish them to. How she handled conflict and jealousy was part of what would gain her their ranks. Besides, she didn't allow Bethany Case's utterances to hurt anymore. At one time she had wished to be Bethany's friend, but she had come to the realization deep in the night that there were some women who were not meant to be her friends. That she would never overcome certain perceptions or insecurities. And that she had plenty of her own issues to deal with without shouldering someone else's.

Only the thought that Emily could be hurt by Bethany's younger sister, and the other women in the room, if there wasn't a shield hovering in the shadows, made her wish to prostrate and sacrifice herself. But she could be patient and wait. And they would deal with her in the same way they tiptoed around Lady Hodge.

Charlotte smiled. "Lilac is a lovely color that will look well against your features, Mrs. Case. I have always thought your eyes a lovely shade. Soft purple will only enhance their color."

This is what she'd been bred for. What she knew. Where she excelled. A respected husband would cement her place.

Allow her to build a fortress. A cold, wintry stronghold surrounded by a Stygian trench.

Her teacup gave a tiny jerk on her knee, unnoticeable to the assembly, and she steadied it quickly, smiling. This was her stage. And every actress suffered from nerves, or so she had heard.

She'd rule with kind words, underlined, if needed, with steel. But it was far too late for kind words to matter between Bethany and her. At least on Bethany's side. Charlotte could find it well within herself to forgive Bethany if for no other sake than her sister's. Still, kind words uttered did far more good than savage responses in a game like this.

Lady Hodge's teeth gleamed their dull gold. Bethany looked as if she had bitten straight through the rind of a lemon.

"Kind of you, Miss Chatsworth." Having to utter those words just about brought Bethany to her knees in distaste. And everyone in the room knew it.

Game to Charlotte.

Talk revolved around fashion for a few minutes before Bethany skillfully, with the determination of Sisyphus, got another chance.

"I heard a rumor that the Shooves are bound for the Continent." *Permanently* went unsaid. The couple had been in deep debt for years and had finally reached the end of their very long, knotted rope.

Talking about it specifically was vulgar. But Bethany uttered it in such a way that she could have been simply saying that the couple was going to France or Italy for a monthlong visit. For she'd never say anything so *rude*.

Bethany smiled at Charlotte. "Miss Chatsworth, I heard mention that your family was also interested in a trip to Paris."

Point to Bethany.

Bethany continued. "It would be lovely for your mother to have an extended *vacation*. Such a *dear* woman, taking care of your paternal great-aunt so devotedly."

Two points to Bethany. The wretched woman had always dug as deeply as she could into why Viola Chatsworth was absent so frequently in society.

Charlotte inclined her head. "Mother would love to see the Louvre again, of course."

"We were just discussing a trip," Miranda said brightly. "Paris is fabulous. And in the summer, the Seine simply sparkles."

Charlotte felt a tendril of warmth curl, easing her stomach a smidge. She had been on her own for so long in this arena, it was hard to remember that she had an ally.

"That is right, you were there, were you not, Lady Downing? Before your marriage?" Bethany's voice sweetened though her words were pointed all the same. After all, Miranda had traveled to Paris after publicly showing herself as Downing's mistress, then leaving him.

"I was." Miranda smiled brightly, then deliberately took a sip of her tea, something wicked shining in her eyes. "And Lord Downing wooed me back after our nuptials. Paris is a beautiful place to be in love."

More than one of the older women showed their distaste, yet Charlotte knew her own expression was just as wistful as those gracing the faces of the younger women.

Bethany's eyes narrowed before she smiled again. "How sweet. You are such a lovely new addition to our social gatherings." A subtle reminder that Miranda was an interloper—another point to Bethany. "I'm so happy that those awful rumors of bets at White's turned out to be false."

"Did they?" Miranda sipped again, eyebrow raised.

"Perhaps they didn't. What bets might you be referring to?"

Bethany set her teeth behind her smile, obviously having expected her comment to simply pass by. "Oh, I wouldn't give credence to such things by speaking of them."

And Charlotte knew better than to say a word, but the words emerged anyway. "But you're speaking of them right now, Mrs. Case."

If there was one thing someone like Bethany hated, it was to be directly confronted. "I am decidedly not, Miss Chatsworth. It is obvious that Lord and Lady Downing have a happy marriage, not in the least influenced by vulgar rumors of their prior relationship."

Charlotte said nothing more, for Bethany would simply snake through more passive, sickly sweet language designed to cut and entrap. Designed so that she could claim victimization—that her words had been taken out of context.

Charlotte fleetingly imagined beating Bethany to a social pulp by taking the reins and getting Marquess Binchley to offer. Or finding the Duke of Knowles and dragging him to the altar.

Or better yet, perhaps Roman Merrick might be enticed to "take care" of the woman. He was unlikely to require marriage to do so.

The thought of marriage to him froze her stiff, so much so that she barely participated in the conversation for the rest of the visit.

Miranda bumped her shoulder companionably as they walked down the path to the street. "You are going to the Delaneys'?"

"Yes."

"I am as well. I can't wait to see what they have in mind for the new charity center. Share a carriage?"

Charlotte smiled, relief and uncertainty flowing through her equally. "That would be lovely."

It wasn't an unusual request, or unwelcome. And far better to discuss anything . . . disgraceful . . . in the closed confines of a conveyance. It was that she would be asked questions at all . . . questions she wasn't sure she could answer . . . that provoked the uncertainty.

"The long way around, Giles, Benjamin," Miranda called. Both men nodded, and Benjamin helped them ascend, then jauntily shut the door. The carriage moved slightly as Benjamin hopped into place next to the driver up top. Miranda turned back to Charlotte as they settled into place on the comfortable cushions. "I requested the closed carriage today on purpose."

"Oh?"

Charlotte wanted to look anywhere other than at her friend as the carriage began to move, but found her eyes glued, unable to focus anywhere else.

Miranda reached over and touched her hand. "Are you well?"

"I am." She tried to relax now that she was with a friend. Not needing to be strict and cold. But her body wasn't responding—straight, frozen, unyielding. "What did Downing tell you?"

Best to face things head-on.

"He said Roman Merrick won you in a card game two nights past and that you were handed off last night. He also mumbled something that sounded like a death threat, but waved it off when I asked." Miranda's lip caught between her teeth. "So . . . did . . . did you wish to speak of it?"

Charlotte called up some semblance of feigned amusement. "It all sounds like a grand adventure, but nothing happened. You can assure Downing of that."

"I will." She touched her skirt. "So, what was Mr. Merrick like?"

Charlotte shrugged, the thought of heated lips brushing hers making her shift. "Pleasant." It was true. Somewhat.

"And your father—"

"I don't wish to speak of him."

"Of course," Miranda murmured. "But I want you to know that you have our complete support. Maxim and I will do everything to help you should something occur." Miranda maintained direct contact with her for a moment before looking out the window. "Or if something already did," she said too casually.

Charlotte gave a false laugh. "It might be a grand tale to tell, but we simply talked. And played chess." She didn't want to think about the fact that she had *lost* the game. That losing came with distinct . . . consequences.

Consequences that were somehow steaming part of the ice inside. Turning it into a swirling maelstrom that demanded outlet.

"Chess?" Miranda's brows drew together. "Chess? But I thought Maxim said . . . well, no bother. Roman Merrick does have a mercurial sort of reputation. I didn't notice anything strange at Lady Hodge's, and goodness knows Bethany Case is a dreadful woman and would be the first to spread any such rumor. Though Mr. Trant might . . . be a bother. Maxim and I will help with anything. There is nothing that we can't all fix, should we do it together."

Maxim, not Downing, of course. Miranda never referred to her husband by his courtesy title outside of the drawing rooms.

"You have a love match, Miranda," she whispered. "Of course it would seem that way."

Miranda's brows rose before she looked at Charlotte searchingly. "Charlotte?"

They were a love match in every sense of the words. Even when the betrothal papers between Charlotte and Downing had nearly been pressed with ink, Charlotte had known with cold certainty what her fate in life would be.

Had accepted that she would always be second fiddle to her husband's mistress. Had calmly prepared herself for such—after all, she had lived with her parents' mirror of the same her entire life.

Now it simply would be a different man pressing his signature into the paper. She hadn't known Downing well or loved him even a little, so the matter of a different band upon her finger meant nothing. In truth, nothing had changed. Though the extra crack, straining the already distended balloon, said everything had.

"Anything seems possible to you now that you are together." Charlotte wanted that feeling. *Yearned* for the hope of it. Buried the admission of it deep inside. "But here on the other side . . . I can't believe that yet."

Miranda blinked, then opened her mouth, but the overwhelming burst flooded from Charlotte.

"And I am unbelievably happy for you, I always will be, but I am *jealous* and can't quite accept the same rosy outlook." Her pride was yelling at her to stop speaking. "And I will have to do as Father says. Or I'll put Emily in jeopardy. And even if I figure out a way to remove Emily from peril—familial and social—I am still . . ."

She waved a hand. Empty. Unlike all of those vibrant women who had learned to love themselves instead of living up to some ideal.

"Oh, Charlotte," Miranda said, grabbing her hand. "You are in a precarious situation. And there is nothing wrong with desiring a love match." *Nothing wrong with you.* Miranda's fingers gripped hers almost uncomfortably. "There *is* nothing like the feeling of being in love," Miranda whispered. "And Charlotte, you *will* find love. I believe that."

Charlotte forced a smile, trying to keep her voice light. "Yes, of course." Who was to say that Trant, should he finally convince Father to accept his suit, or one of the others, wouldn't love her, and she love him in return?

Just being near Miranda and Downing, befriending them in truth, feeling their love, seeing their shared glances, had spread fissures like a hand pressed against an already splintered pane.

Miranda's gloved hand pressed into hers again, against that cold and broken pane. "There are many men who would be delighted for you to show them interest."

Charlotte looked to the window. "But Father will simply turn them away. He is going to ruin us completely with his insatiable urge for the match of the century. We are little more than upstarts, yet he conveniently forgets."

"You're not alone in this anymore. We would support you should you even run to Gretna."

"One more scandal to add to Downing's clan?" she said lightly, removing her hands.

Miranda grinned, relief showing. "There is no family who does scandal better."

Charlotte pinched her thigh, trying to keep the emotions down. Emotions that threatened the pit.

"Charlotte?"

Charlotte waved, tears threatening.

"Charlotte?" Miranda sounded frantic.

They could help, it was true. But even their unconditional support wouldn't stem the tide against her. The filth of the rumors staining Emily. No money or family title to cover any loss of standing.

In society, she was nothing but her reputation. And her beauty. It was the empty shell of which she consisted.

The carriage rocked to the side as they pulled onto the Delaneys' street.

"If anything of your night should be discovered, or re-appear . . ." Miranda was obviously frantically trying to figure out what to say.

An empty shell on a beach crowded with them. She thought of the night before, of the heated feelings that had thrummed through her, filling the void. Of the relief she had felt. Yes. Someday . . . someday she *would* be more.

"Thank you, Miranda." She dragged comforting, false, coolness to her. "But I doubt I shall ever even see Roman Merrick again."

Irony, even sarcastic irony, could only be trumped by punctuality.

Chapter 8

Charlotte halted at the open doors to the Delaneys' sprawling backyard. A vision of the white king—sitting mockingly atop her dressing table—flitted through her head.

People milled about the expansive patio, speaking and laughing, waiting for Mr. and Mrs. Delaney to call the gathering to order. There were people everywhere, but Charlotte couldn't look away from one.

Miranda bumped into her back.

"Oh, my apologies, Char—Miss Chatsworth," Miranda said.

"No, it's my fault," she murmured, unable to shift her attention to any of the other guests or to move out of the way of others who might be queuing up behind her. "My apologies, Lady Downing."

But still she didn't move.

Golden hair brushed handsome features as he stood, relaxed in conversation with Mr. Delaney. Thoughts of kings and pawns, feathers and blades, fear and temptation, fanned across her skin like the breeze that drifted through the spring trees, blowing petals to the ground.

There must have been fifty people in the yard, and still she couldn't look away from one.

"Miss Chatsworth?" Miranda's voice rose slightly higher, more urgent.

Charlotte snapped to and walked through the opening, turning to a group of ladies, who coolly welcomed her and Miranda.

Miranda, bless her, looked as if nothing out of the ordinary had occurred and quickly joined in the conversation.

Charlotte exchanged cool greetings with the women. On any other day, she would don her social, charitable skin, the one that had a bit of a bite in order to get things accomplished—to woo donors to part with their money the way her father parted with all of theirs after a few drinks and few rolls of the dice, but instead, as she strained to hear a conversation farther away, she felt only the skin of the nervous debutante she had been so long ago.

A white petal fell to her sleeve, a gift from a flowering blackthorn, and she lifted it between two fingers, his voice drifting over her skin in a similar manner, smooth on top, grainy beneath. "We would be delighted to extend our assistance, Mr. Delaney."

She shivered, everything in her tightening at the sound. He was claiming attendance for charity works. But *why,* was the question. And the timing of his presence, even though his presence itself was nominally acceptable considering the agenda, led to a more pertinent question for her. Had he come for a *collection* instead of a donation? And would he do so during the gathering?

"Excellent, excellent," their host said enthusiastically. "The missus had a good idea with this, what, what?"

"I have been looking forward to it all morning." Roman's voice purred, and she could picture the smile forming about his lips, the casual direction of his gaze as it brushed her, causing her to shiver again.

Miranda's elbow clipped hers, and Charlotte snapped

back to the conversation in front of her. It was the second time she had forgotten herself in so few minutes. She stiffened, making sure her face was composed.

"I wonder what they have planned," Miranda said, in her soft, friendly voice. "Miss Chatsworth is keeping her lips sealed." Miranda gave her a mock frown, and the rest of the group looked at Charlotte without surprise. "But I find it unbearably intriguing that the Delaneys decided to call benefactors from all over London to join together. I think it a splendid idea."

Charlotte had thought so too until ten minutes past.

One of the ladies sniffed. "There is nothing wrong with preserving the current societies."

The *separate* societies. Merchant class, upper class, outer class . . .

"Of course, there is nothing wrong with them," Charlotte agreed, choosing her most aloof manner of answering, as the elder matrons liked that best. "And they will be preserved. The Ladies' Society itself is without equal. But by pooling our ideas and resources, think of the good that can be accomplished for all of London? For what makes life safer and better in the East End also affects the safety of the West. Think of the knowledge that can be shared? Generating information from different perspectives. A tapestry of views. There are some things that only the lower classes can understand, and others that only those born to privilege innately know."

The lady seemed only willing to concede the latter. But her nose dropped a hair. "You have expressed interesting thoughts, Miss Chatsworth, but some just innately know better for everyone."

Charlotte had the urge to say something that would get her into a lot of trouble. She swallowed the retort and tried not to examine from where the itch had sprung. As if Roman had given her some sort of coiled spring to thrust her to her social doom, and just being near him activated it.

That she wanted to activate it was what worried her most. Just like the insidious distention of the balloon at Lady Hodge's parlor when she realized no one had discovered the truth of the previous night. That Roman had somehow allowed her to acknowledge some dark need within herself. Something deep and deadly that had waited far too long to burst forth.

The woman sniffed again. "But did we need to meet together? I heard that the couple over there, near the rosebushes, owns a *dress* shop. What next? Our butcher at the King's ball? We could have met separately, voted, and formed a coalition to meet."

Which would save the woman from being dirtied by the touch of anyone not of the highest caliber.

Miranda's foot was tapping. Not a good sign. But Charlotte was feeling incredibly responsive to the idea of *not* restraining her friend.

"Mrs. Kerringly, you didn't have to attend today," Miranda flatly said.

The woman gave a look of great affront. "Of course I did. Silly child." She didn't dare cut Miranda, for she was no longer simply the niece of a common bookseller. Charlotte found herself less concerned for her friend than she would have a few days past. Miranda had more grace and good fortune in her little finger than Mrs. Kerringly could ever hope to possess.

She and Downing could simply flip their noses, should they choose. Like Roman Merrick, languid, with an expression beyond amused, as he took in the surrounding faces. People were both appalled and enthralled as they surveyed him.

Mrs. Kerringly nodded coldly at the group. "Boundaries, like rivers, are in nature for a reason. Good for you younger ladies to be reminded of that." She excused herself and stiffly walked away with two of her equally starchy friends.

Boundaries were already clearly defined in the spaces, pockets, and groups gathering together, even now. There were very few places in the *ton* that were accessible to outsiders, and even where they were found, like at Lady Banning's literary salon, the divide was still visually apparent.

"Grumpy bats. We don't need a coalition to sort things." Mrs. Johnson slid a string of her bonnet, pulling it back and forth, a gleaming, speculative look in her pretty eyes as she looked out to the groups on the grass. "Not when there are a number of people here who I've never seen before. Such a good thing, to expand one's acquaintances, don't you think?"

Charlotte didn't have to follow her eyes to see where she looked. She *knew* where she was looking.

Another woman did follow her gaze though and laughed. "Better rein in those impulses to meet new acquaintances, Mrs. Johnson. Those *grumpy bats* will have you banished to the country."

"Whatever for?" She pulled the string, head tilted, gleaming eyes still observing him. "This is a unique initiative, to learn from others, a gathering to stretch boundaries. I merely seek to *stretch* myself."

"Indeed. We will mourn your passing, my dear," Mrs. Tapping said. Though Charlotte knew the lady was far more likely to hold a celebratory ball instead.

"Mrs. Tapping, you are being absurd," Mrs. Johnson responded. "The man in question is speaking to our esteemed host right now. And there are at least three other men vying to enter the conversation."

"And assuredly the other men will gravitate that way sooner or later, but they sure as rain in February aren't going to introduce any of us. Not the introduction you seek. They will introduce us to some of the people here, but they will *definitely* not introduce you to *him*," she said pointedly.

"He's obviously a wealthy man." Mrs. Johnson extended an eye down his frame. "*Very* wealthy. And it's evident to anyone with a pair of eyes, that man knows the right way to get things *accomplished*. Ways most people don't observe." She smiled in a catlike manner. "And I have never let silly rules of etiquette get in my way."

Charlotte could already see the woman plotting the best way to bump into him. Charlotte didn't understand why her own muscles tightened at the thought.

"Your mother and father will have a fit." There was an actual warning there, underlining the singsong words, as if Mrs. Tapping wanted her rival to dive off the pier, yet at the same time felt compelled to warn a fellow swimmer. There was also an undeniable hook to her words, and Charlotte finally understood the woman's game.

"My parents don't control my actions anymore." There was a smugness to the words that Charlotte envied. "And Mr. Johnson knows better." Her smug smile grew, that of a woman who knew she held some key strings.

"Mr. Johnson is not part of this equation. Easily wiped aside. Do you see the man you are ogling? Look at how he holds himself. He is more than you can *handle*, Mrs. Johnson."

The woman scoffed. "No one is more than I can handle. And how he holds himself? He looks like a gentleman."

One of the younger women looked dubious. "I don't know. There is something quite alarming about him. He is almost too handsome, don't you think? And he looks more like he is *pretending* to be a gentleman. Something about him makes me want to find Father."

Charlotte thought he might as well have "would be in Newgate, if I weren't rich" imprinted on his forehead. Or maybe "would be in Hell, if I weren't so beautiful."

Mrs. Johnson waved a hand. "That is because you are a silly little twit of a girl." She looked at Mrs. Tapping's smug face. "Fine, Mrs. Tapping, my interest is heightened more than it was already piqued. Who is he?"

The other woman looked pleased that she had won the battle to reveal her knowledge, securing all eyes in her direction.

"Roman Merrick."

Charlotte listened to the inhaled breaths and fervently drank in the expressions on all the faces around her, feeling her own brand of internal smugness at what they contained—shock, fear, heightened interest, dismay.

Mrs. Johnson looked as if she'd been smacked. "I don't believe you."

Miranda, bless her, didn't look Charlotte's way, though Charlotte *knew* she wanted to. Her friend suddenly found her lace cuff very interesting, eyes wide. Charlotte didn't even want to guess at her thoughts.

"Who is Roman Merrick?" one of the bolder, younger girls asked, not exactly softly, mystified.

Charlotte hoped Roman hadn't overheard the girl's question. Knowing he assuredly had, with her luck. That now he might be thinking that she was speaking of him. The consequences, if he formed his own opinion of their conversation, were too dreadful to contemplate.

He could do anything from smirking at her to coming over and pinching her rear.

She sealed her lips together and managed a bored, somewhat aloof expression, trying to look uninterested.

She wanted to leave the group and distance herself from the conversation yet was unable to do so because she might miss what was said. She *had* to hear what was said.

She was beginning to understand what emotions might go through her father's head when spirits were placed in front of him after a long day without.

"Such a sweet girl," Mrs. Tapping smiled, a sneer beneath her curved lips, at the girl's question. "He is only one of the richest and blackest people in the city."

Mrs. Johnson looked excited, intrigued, and perturbed, in equal measures, as her eyes narrowed in his direction. "Are you sure it is he?"

Mrs. Tapping nodded, more than pleased by the group's response and delighted at being the center of the attention. "I'm quite sure. He met with Mr. Tapping a few weeks ago, and I observed his entrance."

Mrs. Tapping preened under the admission. As if having one's menfolk on the edge of danger was a good thing, desirable and nervy, even as speaking to that danger, as a woman, would be disastrous.

"And?" The younger girl gritted her teeth at the response she had received.

"And Mrs. Johnson will be cut something fierce if she *engages* with him, you silly twit. No matter how handsome and angelic he looks."

"Why?" The girl gazed in his direction, her features showing her displeasure with the conversation, taking it out on the subject. "He looks completely at ease and in control speaking to Mr. Delaney. And Mr. Delaney looks *eager*."

"Money, you twit. He has *money*. Of course Mr. Delaney is speaking to him eagerly. Where that money comes from is the issue."

Mrs. Tapping was in her element. None of the older

matrons who would squash the conversation were in their vicinity. She was setting herself up as *the* lady who *knew* things.

The young woman stared mutinously for a moment before giving in, asking the question her more timid friends obviously wanted to know as well. "Where?"

"Hells, debts, prostitutes, crime, *underground and back-alley slaves*. They say if you don't watch yourself around the Merrick brothers, you can disappear from the streets—just like that." She snapped her fingers. "And wake up in a brothel, chained to the hold of a ship, or worse."

Charlotte caught her tongue between her teeth, hard. She wanted to ask what exactly would be worse to wake up to. To see if Mrs. Tapping even had anything in mind, or if she was just making things up as she went.

She shook her head. Fiction mixed with fact was often the most engaging. Where the two separated in the accusations surrounding the blond man was the question.

"You have something to add, Miss Chatsworth?" Mrs. Tapping's eyes narrowed upon her at the shake of her head.

Charlotte continued her cool look. "I don't believe even a king's ransom would buy entry into an event like this if one dealt in slave traffic—especially of the kind you are implying. Otherwise, the Delaneys, and all of the rest of us by our compliance, potentially would be providing bodies for their use, would we not?"

She felt amusement sift over her. Amusement that was not her own—nor that of any of the women in the circle. She tried to push it away and flicked the petal caught between her fingers to the ground as well.

"I doubt the Delaneys would begin this venture with such a taint." She was defending the Delaneys, not *him*.

"Why don't you put your considerable reputation on the

line, Miss Chatsworth, and introduce yourself and ask him in order to make sure?" Mrs. Tapping said sweetly. "Go to his lair and see if you make it out unscathed."

The amusement curled again, seeping within her this time. She would cause the entire circle an apoplectic fit should she reveal that she had already visited his lair and survived, thank you very much.

"I do not remember expressing interest in meeting him, Mrs. Tapping." She smiled calmly. She hoped that Miranda too was feeling absurd amusement that there was no need for Charlotte to *meet* him. "I was merely expressing doubt about the aspersions on a man attending an event such as this. You insinuate we are in moral and physical peril, yet the man is here on a mission to assist the very people you claim he violates."

She tried to rein the feeling in, but the amusement remained, coiling and entreating her to open herself to more. Aloof, cool Charlotte Chatsworth—laughing? People would run screaming.

"Bah, Miss Chatsworth. Money. And the ability to whitewash it."

"Just need to wash the chaff away, is that it?" she asked lightly.

"Exactly."

"Well, I still think—" Mrs. Johnson started.

"I think you should, Mrs. Johnson." Mrs. Tapping smiled unpleasantly at her once and still-current rival, irritation that she had lost partial control of the conversation apparent. "Introduce yourself to him, please, and engage his interest."

Mrs. Johnson pinched her lips together. "Watch your tone, Mrs. Tapping. I am off to speak with Mrs. Delaney."

And likely to see if she could figure out a way to meet and seduce Roman Merrick without scandal. Mrs. Johnson didn't have the social cachet to pull it off though, or the sense to remain quiet about it.

Someone who stood above the social fray could do most anything she wanted, but the members of the presently formed circle were all unfortunately *in* the social fray. Except Miranda, but Charlotte didn't think Downing would be too chuffed to sanction his wife having an affair, and Downing was the reason she was above the fray.

Charlotte shook her head at the ridiculous thoughts.

The circle shifted to close Mrs. Johnson's vacated space. Mrs. Tapping looked marginally more pleased at the interested looks on the remaining faces.

"You said brothers? There are more?" One of the younger women was looking a little nervous, suddenly seeing pitfalls she hadn't expected. "Are the others here?"

Mrs. Tapping tossed her head and leaned forward. "There is just one other. He doesn't enter society, though. You'd have to venture into one of the hells or—have something *happen* to you—to see him."

Which meant the woman had no idea what Andreas Merrick looked like. Charlotte nearly smiled, thinking about the reaction if she were to suddenly describe him.

Why the devil am I even thinking such thoughts?

What she should really be examining is how much more dire the news that she had spent the night with Roman Merrick would be if discovered. Her amusement vanished. And even if it looked as if she was going to get away with last night's adventure . . . a vision of a white crown flashed. Her reputation was far from safe.

The conversation continued and moved to parallel topics, but Charlotte was having trouble paying attention. She wondered which was worse—the old, distended, empty balloon inside her or the new, uncontrollable, uncomfortable maelstrom of excitement and fear?

Miranda skillfully shifted and excused them so that they were walking toward a refreshment table a few minutes later.

"Well, that explains your rather stilted entry," Miranda said in a low voice, trying to keep her eyes forward. Obviously trying to fight the urge to stare at a particular person on the periphery of the yard path. She was rather a circumspect woman usually, not taken to watching others. And Charlotte knew that the urge to stare would be springing from Miranda's curiosity and protectiveness, not from the revolting, sweet, or excited (in the *dangerous man in our midst* kind of way) glances the other women had cast.

"And that explains Georgette's physical description of him," Miranda muttered.

Charlotte looked at her. "I thought you knew who he was," she murmured.

"No." She shook her head. "Heard of him, yes. But putting faces to names is Georgette's hobby, not mine," she said, speaking of her friend.

"Where is Georgette, by the way? I thought she'd be here," Charlotte asked, trying to change the subject as they neared the area where Roman stood, the hair on the back of her neck lifting on end as they passed within a breadth of him. She kept her eyes focused straight ahead.

Charlotte swallowed and forced other thoughts. Miranda's friend, Georgette, was a wealthy merchant's daughter. Charlotte hadn't thought on her absence yet, as they weren't friends outside of knowing Miranda, but they got on well enough.

"No. She is in Dover helping her father. Nearly had apoplexy when she realized her schedule would prevent her from returning for this." Miranda let silence fall until they were safely past him. "So . . . so that is he?"

"Yes," Charlotte answered almost unwillingly.

A paused beat. "I must say that if you *did* give in to—"

"Miranda!" she hissed.

"Well, he is incredible-looking." She tapped her chin, feet moving steadily forward. "Not as handsome as Maxim, of course, but an unattached girl would be left to wonder—"

"Miranda!"

A sound emerged from Miranda, a sound which quickly turned into a small giggle before she coughed into her hand. Her friend grabbed two cups and led them into a less-populated area. She was unsuccessfully trying to hide her grin.

Charlotte felt the urge—inexplicable, horrific, and uncharacteristic—to cross her arms in public. "Just because he is pretty doesn't mean anything for his character."

The humor immediately wiped from Miranda's face. "Oh, Charlotte. You are too right. Forgive me?"

Charlotte took one of the cups from her and looked to the men again. "There is nothing to forgive. I'm just having a little trouble with everything at the moment."

Great. Roman Merrick seemed to have permanently loosened her floodgates. Admissions kept slipping through.

A small hand slipped over her arm, giving it a reassuring squeeze. "Of course you are. And I was only jesting with you because you seem far from scared of the man. You defended him, in fact, and seemed amused." She looked as if she was going to say something else but was thankfully cut off by their host.

"Good afternoon, ladies, gentlemen." Mr. Delaney clapped his hands. "We want to welcome you to our small gathering, and we hope to welcome your time and pocketbooks as well."

A genial round of laughter followed.

"If you could gather round, Mrs. Delaney would like to outline our plans."

The various groups gathered more closely together, though separations remained. Charlotte could feel Roman standing no more than a dozen paces away, the bodies in between them no more than shifting mist.

It was fortunate that she knew of the plans already as she couldn't concentrate a whit on what was being said.

"And I can't help but notice," Miranda whispered, a smile about her lips again as she pretended to be paying attention to their hostess, "that he shifts his body every time you move. Always keeping you in view."

"Stop watching him," she hissed back.

Mrs. Delaney spoke for a good fifteen minutes about their plans to allocate resources. Though her father would reluctantly fork over the minimum amount to keep up appearances, gambling or borrowing it from somewhere, Charlotte always volunteered her time instead to these endeavors.

Charity work made her feel *useful* and alive. Not so empty and on display.

Other people would be far more generous with their pocketbooks, some because they truly cared and others in order to make public their act of generosity.

People like Roman Merrick . . . he'd probably donate a substantial amount, then use the fact later either to gain favors or leniency, when needed.

She narrowed her eyes. Like buying off patrolmen.

Another fifteen minutes of questions and answers, and the gathering drew to a close, people having other appointments and gatherings to attend.

Throughout it all, Roman had been surrounded by people, yet somehow still occupied his own place. Attracting and repelling.

She walked with Miranda to the open doors, prepared to leave.

A hand brushed her waist.

"Pardon me, ladies." His voice slipped over her, just as his hand brushed her sleeve, over the handle of her bag, almost connecting to the fabric covering the inside of her elbow.

She could see in her periphery that Miranda had tilted her head to him, watching him with a slight pull of the right side of her lips. But Charlotte couldn't look. No good would come from it. She could feel the pull of his eyes, just as she had in the Hunsdens' shop, or sitting across from him, *lying* across from him, his eyes pulling her to him, brushing his lips across hers as his fingers wrapped hers around an ivory claim.

Absolutely no good would come of meeting his eyes.

She looked directly into eyes that seemed to reflect the sky today. The edges creased in pleasure, then he was gone, disappearing into the belly of the house.

If only he were a man of the *ton*. This man who could so easily stir emotion in her. Emotions that had been steadily deadening, pocketed only for Emily, then opening to include Miranda as well.

But he wasn't a man of the *ton*. And she wasn't a silly young girl.

Miranda looked at her speculatively as they walked down the drive.

"Yes, Lady Downing?"

"Oh, I was just thinking that you looked much as I probably did two years past," she uttered nonchalantly.

Charlotte's brows drew into a frown. "What do you mean?"

Miranda shrugged, the smile still about her lips. "Charlotte, it's hard to tell with you much of the time, but that didn't look like *fear* on your face when he brushed past you. In fact, I distinctly remember Georgette commenting on my expressions when Maxim and I were first getting to know each other, and I would bet ten pounds that many of them looked just like that one."

Charlotte's feet stuck to the ground for a full ten beats, and laughter spilled from her friend, who continued to walk jauntily down the drive, a smug smile about her lips.

Her friend who believed in eternally happy endings, when Charlotte knew that life rarely provided them. That one wasn't likely in store for her.

But she couldn't stop her heart from racing minutes later when she reached into her reticule for her handkerchief and withdrew a note. There was only one word upon the page.

Soon.

Chapter 9

The Lancaster soiree was in full swing. Music spilled through the open doors and onto the patio beyond. People laughed gaily or talked in low, charged tones—forming ties—social and political.

Bethany Case pretended not to notice Charlotte as she and her group of followers cut directly in front of Charlotte's path. Charlotte simply waited for them to pass before continuing on.

"Look at her. Far prettier than any of the other girls. Carries herself like a duchess too."

Charlotte kept the stiff smile firmly in place as she passed her father holding "court." She nodded to the group and fought the bile that twisted up her throat. The swirling feelings had been colliding against each other all day.

"Can you imagine the heirs?" A broodmare. "Stock like that . . . you can see it." A porcelain vase. "Brought her up right too. Knows her position." A mannered hostess who would turn the other cheek to indiscretions without comment or messy emotion. Her father had had an *indiscretion* for nearly all her lifetime.

She felt the chill invade, a chill that never seemed to dissipate anymore at these events. Her father's behavior had mortified her once, but she was well used to it now. He used her future stock, her promise in the eyes of the *ton,* to get away with increasingly bad behavior.

She thought on Roman Merrick's words to her instead. His words about beauty—that there was something far more interesting about her than her form and face.

Her smile tightened. Plagued by thoughts of him, even now, even here, in a place he couldn't touch.

She kept her feet moving toward the refreshment table, wishing she could find a beverage spiked with whatever concoction he had poured. The drink had curled down her throat and coated her insides, allowing her nerves to settle without making her drunk.

"Miss Chatsworth." Mr. Trant stepped before her, lifting her hand. "A pleasure to see you this eve looking so well."

She tilted her head, keeping her breathing even. "Mr. Trant."

He surveyed her, as if he could determine from the perusal whether she had been ruined the night before. Ruined, sullied, despoiled. A favorite crystal vase blemished by muddied hands.

He held up an arm and set her hand on it. "If you would do me the honor?"

She hesitated, but Trant's arm tightened under her loose fingers. She nodded, and he swiftly moved them into the natural lanes around the floor where people had been treading paths all night. She felt odd holding on to his arm. Which was strange, since it was a natural gesture and position. Indeed, there were at least ten other couples engaged in a similar stroll. But she felt heated eyes watching her from somewhere, and her instinct was to push Trant away.

Ridiculous. She tried to shake off the thought. There were always eyes on one during an event. Even the least-watched wallflower was observed some of the time. It was the gossipmonger's way to pick out even the most insignificant tidbit. And walking a path with a gentleman wasn't insignificant. Nothing extreme, no, but worthy of comment all the same.

"You look beautiful tonight, Miss Chatsworth." Unspoiled.

She thought of the conversation in the night regarding the state of a woman's virginity. Roman Merrick had said . . . Her free fingers caught the skirt of her dress, clutching the fabric.

Stop thinking of him.

"Thank you, Mr. Trant. You look handsome as well." And he did. Though his eyes were sharp and glittering. Always trying to find the flaw he had yet to discover.

She couldn't imagine relaxing around a chessboard with this man. Oh, she had a feeling chess was a game he relished. Not for the pleasure of the game but to destroy his opponent.

Roman played to win as well, and was by far the more dangerous man overall. Still, there was an ease she had found with him, despite, or maybe *between*, the cracks of danger. Bewildering.

And she was still thinking of him.

Her fingers tightened on Trant's arm.

"You are well?" he asked.

"It is as I told my father this morning. My untimely illness has passed, leaving me none the worse. In fact, said illness seemed merely to find amusement in creating its mayhem in the first place. I feel quite as I did two mornings past."

Which said everything Trant wanted to hear. And was mostly the truth besides. She could feel the tension in Trant recede. The muscles of his arm relaxing.

"I am pleased to hear it. Though should your illness return, please notify me immediately, so I can extend my assistance."

"I'm sure that will be unnecessary."

Why did she feel the throb of hot eyes resting upon her?

"Nevertheless, some illnesses have a tendency to linger. Left untreated, they can fester and destroy."

She laughed lightly, falsely. "Yes. Thank you for the caution and warning."

"I worry about you, of course. And have a care for your future." He steered them deftly about the floor. "Our future."

She tried to replicate the laugh, but without the empty echo. She failed. "Though I am flattered, you step ahead of yourself, Mr. Trant."

"It would be . . . unfortunate should anyone learn of the events. I only look after your interests, my dear." He smiled, then relinquished his hold on her. "Perhaps a dance later?"

She murmured automatically, mechanically, as he bowed and stepped back. Leaving her to linger over his words, his carefully veiled threat.

Her gaze brushed her mother, who was observing Charlotte from her seat near a group of matrons. Sitting on the edge of the group, as always, never quite an integral part of the inner circle, where she could help her daughters.

Coasting through life without much notice or care. Malaise clinging to her like a second skin. Though this was one of her "good" days, and Charlotte was glad. Viola had henpecked Charlotte all day, leaving no time for Bennett to interrogate her. Since Bennett treated Viola as if she were a highly allergic substance, he had stayed far away.

Charlotte wasn't going to question her good fate. She'd take her mother's sourness over her father's greed any day.

Though, as she met her mother's eyes, she wondered if she *knew*. If she had initiated the constant barrage of scolding over a guise of concern. But Viola had never shown a desire to save her daughter from any threat or fate.

And Trant had initiated a threat. There would be no cause for Trant to share her whereabouts last eve—if she were pledged to him. Otherwise . . . well, Trant would remain silent only for as long as it was in his self-interest to do so.

Her father would simply tell her to clean up the mess. Then obtain him what *they* desired. For the good of their family.

She watched a friendly young man ask a friendly young woman to dance. A pretty blush bloomed on the woman's face—as did similar high color on the man's. They exchanged besotted gazes as they walked to the floor.

She wished she were at home, tucked beneath her covers.

She watched other young women laugh and play, dance and make merry with the gentlemen of their choice. Gentlemen who were enamored of *them*. Individually charmed. Not with some false notion of beauty and winning. Gaining a trophy, then shelving it, when she proved not as exciting as first thought, the glow of the win falling to dissatisfaction.

She watched a group of unattached young women whispering behind their hands. Waiting for a lick of gossip to spread—or starting it themselves. Thus far, Charlotte had proven unavoidably boring to the gossip mill, and had thus skirted much of the negative flow. There was nothing exciting about ice except when it started to melt into a messy puddle, spreading in all directions, falling down uneven ground. Destroyed.

Her mother had been beautiful once, so she'd been told.

On a good day she could see a hint of it in the curves of her mother's cheeks. But it was her father's mistress who received his attention. A mussed woman half as pretty but twice as vibrant.

Such was the life she had thought, a year past, that she would split with Miranda. But Miranda, warm, vibrant Miranda, had it all.

Unfortunately, Charlotte would likely take after her mother in more than just icy blond looks and cold-mannered regard.

Though she couldn't imagine her mother lounging about the bedcovers across from a man with his shirt open, gaze untamed. Lighting sparks within her, causing silly dreams that held no basis in reality.

Stop thinking of him!

Who was to say that Trant wouldn't love her for herself? That he wouldn't dig deeper and help her uncover all that she wished to be. Thawed and vivacious. Or that Marquess Binchley wouldn't?

A bitter laugh escaped at the image, and she quickly coughed into her hand.

She looked to the shadows beyond the open doors. The garden blooms and night whispered of release. Away from the games and conversation. Strategy and laughter. Laughter that wasn't hers.

She tried to shrug off the heavy feeling that seemed to pierce through the ballroom doors, straight from the dark shadows outside. Dark shadows that whispered of danger.

Her feet moved toward the open doors and the shadows that lay beyond. The lure of escape.

Of breathing free air.

She crossed the stones, exchanging pleasantries with people lingering outside, then headed for the greenery, the garden calling to her more forcefully.

She passed a hand along the trailing clematis vines falling from the wall bordering the property. She had danced earlier with the Earl of Tewksbury, a man whose rheumatoid did not promote a second turn, which meant their one dance would be cause for comment. She had danced twice with an increasingly bleary-eyed, red-rimmed Marquess Binchley. And Trant would claim at least one dance later.

Fine old titles with the first two, high ambition in the third. She'd secure a solid social place with any of them. More than one of the women inside would happily dismember her for her melancholy. Those same women would never realize that when she let the emotion free, Charlotte felt jealousy toward *them*.

But now . . . now instead of an empty pit, there were strange new emotions and sensations swirling within her, dark and uncomfortable, restless and unnerving. But they were *there*. Filling the distention.

Making her feel as if she were ascending *in* the balloon, the ground far below, the restless excitement overwhelming, springing and growing over the past few days. A mirror of Miranda's expression. Of Charlotte's disgraced country neighbor. Of the young ladies free to choose their beaus.

It was frightening and exhilarating at once, for what was she to do with the knowledge? The feelings?

The edge of a silken purple flower slipped from her fingers, and she walked farther into the low garden without breaching protocol. It was a lovely spot, easily seen from the terrace. She needed a few moments to herself. A chance to dream other dreams.

However, seeking freedom came with consequence. If any young buck had noticed and decided to follow her, she would be forced to speak to him in the garden shadows.

But the more rakish men who flourished in the shadows usually left her alone. She was too cold for their tastes, too distant.

What Roman Merrick had seen in her, she didn't know. A simple challenge most likely. A challenge that would come to a disappointing end.

For it seemed easy for men to see that she was a crystal vase, not a warm bulge of clay.

She shook her head, biting her lip hard, and looked ahead. From other escapes, she knew there were two benches in the back of the open garden and yard, near the more wild and twining vines and higher bushes along the wall, and she could see the vague outline of one bench as she moved closer. If the stone wasn't too damp, she could sit back, lift her feet, breathe in the scents of sweet jasmine and gardenias. Take a few stolen moments to watch the guests on the veranda, and keep to herself.

She ran her fingers along the surface of the bench. Still dry. She pivoted and sat, a relieved breath escaping her as she lifted her legs slightly off the ground, the nearest guests far enough away so as not to bother her unless they were expressly seeking her out.

Was it wrong to feel the echo of his fingers in her nape, of his mouth on hers? Better than a well-executed twirl on the dance floor. Something alive and wild. Something that was intimately *hers*.

She put her hands on the stone and leaned her head back, lifting her face to the moonlight and closing her eyes.

"Much lovelier with all of that gorgeous freedom upon your face."

She jerked her head forward and to the side. The voice, straight from her imaginings, caused the hair at her nape to tingle, her skin to heat, her lips to part.

Unrelieved black met her view. Only the gold of his

hair—flashing silver in the slight moonlight—and the flesh of his carved skin stood out from the shadows of the high bushes in the corner. A scandalous alabaster statue garbed in twilight. Legs on the bench and head tilted back to the darkness.

A thousand emotions curled inside her, ramming together, trying to escape through her throat, her skin, the heart of her chest.

His lips curved, and white teeth flashed. "I thought I might find you here."

Her mouth opened and closed, heat blazing a rapid trail upward through her body. She suddenly felt as if she were floating above the ground in that rapidly ascending balloon.

"*What?*"

He slowed his speech into deliberate syllabic chunks. "I thought I might find you here."

"I heard you the first time," she hissed, looking about in sudden panic, hands frozen, clawed around the stone. Panicked by her reaction. Panicked by the threat of discovery. Panicked that the man she couldn't stop thinking of was here in front of her, able to see any flaws or defects—that she was truly as unexciting as she'd been bred to be.

The guests continued milling about. No one had looked in her direction yet. No one had noticed that there was a man clothed in darkness, violating the space. That he was sitting awfully close to an unmarried lady in a darkened spot.

Suddenly, the shadowed bench, though still public and safe, seemed wildly dangerous and wrought with reputation hazards. Wrought with the most dangerous hazard she had ever encountered.

"It took longer than I'd expected, but I was right."

She refused to gape more, so she pressed her lips together until she could control *some* of her thoughts.

"*What?* You—you've just been lying here in wait? Thinking I might—might come out here on my own? Are you *mad*?"

"I knew it was a matter of time. You suffocating indoors, needing to come out and be free."

She stared at him, words stuck in her throat. "You know me not." Her voice came out in a cracked whisper, the balloon ascending that much higher.

"Then I guessed correctly, did I not?"

She glanced back to the veranda, swallowing. She should rise and return to the other guests immediately. Remove herself from his suggestion. Remove herself from the very real danger he represented in all forms.

She turned to him instead. "Why are you here?" she hissed.

He smiled, fierce triumph in his shadowed, silver eyes. "To see *you*."

The tingle of awareness became a rush, a heedless tumult of sensation.

When the young swains, brushing up on their wooing, sang her songs or read her lines, she would politely applaud or smile. Perhaps feel a bit of embarrassment for herself or the person wooing. But never had she felt the rush of feeling that some women expressed. Their hands going to their chests, their breath coming in gasps, their lids fluttering in invitation.

She had scoffed at such reactions before . . . all the while, secretly wishing she could experience such foolishness, such emotion. One lift of perfect lips and three uttered words by this man was all it took.

Thrilling foolishness. "And now that you have?" she

asked, her voice little more than a whisper as she watched his lips.

"Ah. The real question." He didn't break the shadows, but something about him seemed to lean toward her. "Now that I have, I can't seem to resist wanting more."

Want. That was the ache in her belly that had turned from cold marble to heated brick. "Do you know what would happen if you were found here?" she asked, all cold decorum lost.

"I'd be forced to move my feet nimbly like one of the oafs inside? Bowing and fumbling and positioning my cravat ever higher?"

"You'd be arrested."

"Taken away in chains, I hope."

She narrowed her eyes. "It isn't something to be taken lightly. A man sneaked into a gathering just last week and is up for sentencing on charges of fraud and trespassing."

"Mmmm . . . but I have . . . coerced many of the men inside, and have information on most of the others. I think I might get away with a . . . lesser punishment."

She couldn't respond for a second. "If that is true, then I think you in more dire straits should you be found. I imagine many men would be well pleased to be rid of you."

He just smiled. "Concerned for my safety?"

"Your sanity, perhaps."

"But I risk it all to be in your presence, dear, magnificent Charlotte."

Again, a tingle of awareness restarted its sweep.

He smiled. "Quite the array of clodpots vying for your favors, aren't there? I was surprised you managed to extricate yourself from their grasp."

There was a hint of something in his words. Some emotion quickly covered.

"I am hardly as sought after as you suggest." Most men were put off by her coldness—and unavailability— here in her third season. "And you could hardly see from here."

"No?" His smile curled farther, darkening. "Mmm . . . that decrepit man asking if you liked the expensive lilies he sent, when everyone knows you are partial to flowers with Sainfoin-like spikes."

She stared at him. "What—what on earth . . . how do you know what Lord Tewksbury said? And what I like?"

She would have known if he had been in the room. Behind her. Breathing against her neck. He had to be bluffing. No one was that stealthy. Especially not someone as remarkable as the man in front of her.

The man in front of her who was currently wrapped in shadows, unnoticed until he chose to reveal himself. A man who could creep up and stick a knife in one's gut and be on his way before the victim hit the floor.

Hot eyes watching . . .

The edges of his eyes crinkled in darkly amused knowledge.

Her heart picked up speed.

"You are guessing."

"Am I? Or I could be using knowledge gained from listening to your father's prattle."

She pressed her lips together. "Hardly something to admit to me."

"You don't admire my honesty?" His eyes were lazy.

"I question your purpose."

"I'm simply on a mission of collection." He hummed. "Is there anything I should be collecting from you, dear Charlotte?"

She felt her skin heat at the mention, at the look in his eyes. Inexplicable giddiness that there was collection to be had . . . uncertainty that this was a simple transaction for him.

What was wrong with her?

"I'm not sure there is. We didn't properly finish the game. You fell *asleep*." There. She had firmly impugned his manhood. And in the cold light of a new day, it seemed slightly depressing that a man hadn't even been able to stay awake to ravish her. Maybe she really *was* just that boring.

He chuckled, a deep rumbling sound. Water over rocks. "With another woman, I would have taken the pleasure offered, then turned her away for a full measure of sleep. We are *not* finished, Charlotte, you are correct."

God, she couldn't stop the lift, the euphoria. *Wrong, so wrong.* "And what is it that you propose? Did you bring your chessboard? Shall we play in the garden? Use one of the rooms inside?"

He smiled lazily. "You know well that we finished that particular game. I am quite sure that your quick mind played out the game to its conclusion. Five moves more. You are perfectly aware of who the winner was and what *he* won. But would you rather I take you into one of the closed rooms within to . . . discuss . . . it?"

"What? No!" Her heart was nearly beating through her chest. Anticipation. Anxiety.

"At your next stop then? Or one thereafter?" He moved closer with each word. "Perhaps I should lie in wait. Make you anticipate my presence around each shadowed corner, ready to twirl you into the darkness.

"And I will, Charlotte. You can think of our night together as a prelude. You escaped with your virtue intact. And you could remain that way." Eyes languid with promise pinned hers, and she could hear the thumping beat of her own heart. "But you don't want to remain that way, do you, Charlotte?"

His lips brushed her cheek, then the lobe of her ear, as he whispered the last. She leaned into him, terribly aware of the leap of her pulse beneath his fingers. Of the way his mere presence seemed to tilt her toward him, her head automatically giving him better access to her neck. Waiting for a vampiric kiss.

Her eyes closed, the steady beat becoming louder. Like footsteps in the grass, the beat of her heart.

"I should be done with the game and depart with you now." Her heart raced at the words, at the tickling of lips against her skin. "Alas. I'm not sure you'd forgive me. And I plan to make the taste of your skin a serial pleasure. One that neither one night or two can satisfy." His lips brushed her neck, the side of her throat. "Soon."

A whisper of fingers ghosted the flesh of her wrist before lifting.

"Come to cower in the shadows," a strident voice challenged. "Or to meet with a lover?"

Charlotte's eyes popped open. And she frantically looked at the *empty* space before her, her body leaning across the bench and almost touching the foliage. She nearly gave in to a hysterical little laugh before composing herself and turning to the voice.

"Simply smelling the jasmine," she said. "Is that what you came to do as well?"

Bethany Case's eyes darted about the space, actively seeking another body. But Charlotte had chosen the spot for the *lack* of real privacy it afforded. Which had made Roman's successful concealment all the more baffling.

And her subsequent actions all the more alarming.

She half expected him to be spotted at any moment. A cry erupting about an intruder. About her indiscretion. And yet the garden seemed void of anything but invited guests.

She smartly chose not to look too closely, for inspection would prompt her nemesis to do likewise.

"I smell something foul."

"Yes, now that you are here, I do as well." Charlotte rose, brushing her skirt.

Bethany's fingers wrapped around her arm, clawing satin. "Soon, Chatsworth. Soon you will be naught but a distant, *fond* memory."

"Oh?" She peeled the claws from her arm. "Are you leaving dear England?"

An ugly laugh issued. "You have been very fortunate so far, but no one is that perfect. You will slip. And I will be there to watch you fall."

"I'm sure that you will," Charlotte said simply, and stepped to the side. "You've always been a cockroach."

She heard the murderous growl, but continued walking calmly along the path.

"Soon, Chatsworth," the ugly voice called. "And the damage will be irreversible."

Charlotte tried to shake off the portent. The echo of Roman's promise, dangerous in a different way. Bethany's tune had changed little. Why should she listen to her now?

Because you are skating the edge of ruin. Half-willing to shove yourself into the mill.

The dance floor was full, and she was happy to walk around it, not meeting anyone's eyes. Not wanting to be trapped into a dance.

For there was no wild, drugging happiness to be found for her here on the floor. Merely political moves like the shifting of the chess pieces over a cold board. It seemed a lifetime ago that she had thought otherwise in this venue, but she remembered it in a secret part of her soul, a part that was yearning to bloom once more. That chaotic passion of youth.

The tendril of it peeking up and threatening to overtake her with its insanity.

She located the Downings. Leaning into each other. Blowing toward each other like trees in favorable winds. Charlotte's smile stayed firm, and she kept her eyes on them instead of glancing back to the garden.

"Did anything of note take place before we arrived?" Miranda asked brightly.

Charlotte's gaze strayed unwillingly, unwisely, watching the lights from the room bounce off the glass of the open doors. "No, nothing of importance."

Bethany Case entered from the garden patio, her sickly sweet smile turned Charlotte's way. Challenging. Promising that no good would come to her enemy.

And for the love of everything proper, a man who ruled part of the underworld had just been there, lounging in the fronds, touching her, drawing her steadily toward him, wanting. *Collecting.* Which meant he could show up anywhere, at any time. *Soon.* Could come to the next event and throw her over his shoulder and make off with her into the night.

"Well, perhaps we will have more luck at our next destination. You are going to the Slatterlys'?"

"Yes." There was a low wall at the Slatterlys'. She bet Roman knew exactly how to hold her properly in order to scale it together.

"I must tell you all about—"

But Charlotte couldn't concentrate on her friend's words.

He could sate the edges of the bet in whatever form he found her. On a bench, on the grass, on the dance floor—dress skirts whirling above them as she arched beneath him. Her face wild and passionate, and nothing like what she saw in the cold reflection of her mirror.

"And then—"

A wild half-formed emotion rose within Charlotte, pushing at tight binds, trying to shred consequences. And she had to employ every tactic she possessed to cage and bind the feeling. To speak to and answer Miranda and Downing with calm precision. To dance with Trant. To behave as she ought to for the rest of the night.

But when she entered their rented carriage, two events later, at the end of the night's festivities, it was to find a single Sainfoin conicle—red-veined and unusual—for it was far too early for said flowers to bloom—resting on the seat, a white pawn and note attached to the stem by a golden string. One word was scrawled upon the paper.

Soon.

Chapter 10

Roman tapped the note in his hand. Where could he leave this one? Heaven forbid he grow stale and repeat himself. Which eliminated a garden bench, her reticule, her carriage, a runner at the park, and down her décolletage—she'd squawked charmingly when he had pulled her into a back room at a charity event last eve and deposited that one.

By far it had been his favorite drop.

He wondered if he slid the folded paper into her stocking . . . would it count as duplication? It was technically *up* her dress, after all.

He twirled the paper fold around his fingers, playing with it. The game was heating up nicely.

On her pillow.

It was past time for that really. He'd get One-eye to identify her room. He couldn't trust himself to do it, too liable to do something prematurely.

Removing himself from temptation's grasp was the best way to control his impulsive nature.

Removing himself . . .

Like not playing cards with Bennett Chatsworth and Trant.

Like not recklessly cheating and putting their lives and livelihood at risk.

Like not thumbing his nose and taking the night with her anyway. A night that hadn't been full of physical pleasure but had been awash in its own pleasure all the same. The pleasure of anticipation. The spark that maybe . . . *maybe* . . .

The spark that had already fanned into a flame.

Removing himself . . . A tight smile pulled his lips.

He had learned to listen to his gut. Yet even so, even to him, his list of temptation's grasp and how he'd flung himself into it lately was long. And frequent.

And centered solely around one person. One woman.

He tapped the heavy stock against the desk he was reluctantly sitting behind. He hated desks, but they served a purpose. Proper and stiff. Expected.

He'd wait on the pillow.

A knock sounded on the door, and he called out for the person to enter.

Two boys entered the room. The first was scrawny and looked as if one stiff breeze would fell him. But his eyes were quick—as if he'd catch the signs of such a breeze before the current reached him. The other boy was larger, stockier in frame, but without the meat to be a true threat— yet. There was a hunched-in quality to his big shoulders and movements. A future glimpse of a hulking presence.

A quick glance at the two would have most people immediately claiming the first one as a small, fast messenger, and the other as brute force in the making. Only a deeper look would say otherwise.

The smaller one stared at him, lips pressed tightly together, a jagged scar crossing the length of his forehead. Roman would bet the age of the scar and the boy's initiation to the streets coincided. Which one preceded the other would be the question.

The boy gripped his cap in his hands, twisting the

cheap felt. A clear show of emotion in someone who didn't have enough money to purchase a new one.

"There is no need to be nervous," Roman said, keeping his voice even.

"Am not nervous," came the mutinous reply. But small hands twisted again.

A little Andreas. A little One-eye. All ruffled pride.

"No?" Roman let his eyes pointedly stray to the cap.

Behind hollowed eyes, the boy looked irate. He squared up his shoulders, jutted out his chin, forced the cap to his side.

The other boy hunched, lips pressing, eyes wary. Waiting in reaction. Anticipating the kick. Knowing that one always came even if he didn't deserve it.

A smaller Milton. A smaller Lefty. All extinguished hope.

Roman focused on the hunched, hulking boy for a moment, keeping his voice even and somewhat disinterested as he watched the exact way he twitched. "We have many posts open. On the floors, in the streets, as messengers, in the classroom, in the kitchens, in the gardens—"

He smoothly followed the direction of the telltale sign of interest at the second to last. "We have posts for helping with the groceries, prepping supplies, learning how to cook—"

A twitch of life. Perfect.

He motioned to the larger boy. "Head down to the kitchen and speak with Henry the Henfisted. He'll feed you and talk to you about opportunities. Peter will show you the way."

The boy nodded quickly, not waiting for the offer to be withdrawn, and ducked through the door like a large wraith, seeking the boy in the hall who had brought them there.

The remaining boy fastened beady eyes on his. "You have posts open in the kitchens?"

But Roman could see the way the boy's small body moved, the way the muscles of his face showed what he was thinking. Not that it was hard to deduce when one saw as many gaunt children as he did.

"Yes, but you can get something there to eat as soon as we are done—without pretending you want to work there."

The boy's eyes narrowed, yet he said nothing, watching, watching, watching, as Roman did to him, but without the added years, full stomach, and full sleep—well, full *enough* sleep—that Roman possessed. Still . . . smart, little, prideful beast. He'd have to keep him away from Andreas for a few weeks. His brother would kill the tiny bugger. Too much alike in disposition for his brother's peace of mind.

Roman allowed the boy to take his measure for a few moments. To *try* to, at least.

He likely wouldn't suss out *exactly* what this boy wanted yet. However, he could address an essential need. "Peter says you have a knack for thievery."

The flat, sure look in the boy's eyes said everything. "So's what if I do? You gonna hire me out?"

"We don't *hire out*, as such. Though Peter can tell you about what we *do* accomplish with men of your talent should you wish to pursue such paths. There are many. Thieves are especially good at catching other thieves." Roman shrugged. "Or for pursuing their pure skill, if they wish. Did Peter tell you the rules?"

There weren't many, but those they had were encased in iron.

The boy made a noise. "Yeah. We'll see."

And they would. Trust was hard wrought. Not every child—or man—wanted to play by someone else's rules.

But most of them did want somewhere to belong. A natural feeling of having a place. It's what kept some so long in other situations—that they would lose their place in the world, even if that place was frightening or dangerous.

Roman gave the boy in front of him a fifty percent chance. There was brilliance there, but it would be the boy's choice. And sometimes the past was too difficult for some to overcome.

"When Peter returns, tell him to take you to Milton. He'll shore you up. He was a thief too before he became one of our managers." He kept his eyes locked with the boy's. Saw the glimpse of hope before it was ruthlessly squashed. He upped the boy's chances to sixty.

"Yeah? How many people you send *his* way?" he challenged.

Fifty-five, if the boy couldn't gain some control of his tongue. To know when to use it as a frontal assault and when to wait and lash from behind was an essential skill.

"Few."

The boy's eyes narrowed.

"It doesn't matter if you believe me." Roman shrugged, putting his elbow on the desk. God, he hated desks. So unnatural. "I'm neither stupid nor green to think you would. And you look neither of those things either. Meet the others. Talk to them. Live with them. See where you want to be."

The boy's eyes slipped, internal want showing through for a few precious milliseconds.

His score soared to seventy-five.

Belonging was also what kept the ranks together in their dysfunctional little empire. For internally it was a safe zone. The streets were still the streets, and sometimes things happened outside the walls, but the unit was fiercely loyal to itself and to them. It was a safer place to be and provided a haven where they could try new options.

The boy nodded, eyes returning to their distrustful state, as self-preservation dictated. Roman dismissed him.

Sometimes seeds needed careful nurturing, and sometimes they just needed a sprinkling of water and a good plot of land.

Unless he personally oversaw a case on the streets, he let the boys stock their own ranks by bringing in others who would work well within their units. That Peter, prideful, prickly Peter, had suggested these two said volumes, both about how Peter was fitting in to the group and how he viewed these two potentials.

But, again, sometimes the past was simply too much for some to overcome.

Sometimes he saw it in Andreas's eyes. The pulling weight. The revenge coldly plotted for so long, *too* long. Warmth dwindling behind an iced wall.

Roman could only do what was within his power to keep that wall from turning into stone, pushing him out as well. But in someone else . . . cool blue eyes and wintry flaxen hair . . . he could melt it now. Or try. The urgent pull just made it more personal.

He tapped the note again. Yes. He had the perfect spot in mind.

He pushed away from the desk and left the room. Plans and decisions in his head.

He tapped a boy on the shoulder as he walked down the hall, not pausing, turning to walk backward as he rattled off instructions. "Round up One-eye, Travers, Johnson, Burns, Crowny, and Deuce."

The boy nodded eagerly and ran to the stairwell. Roman turned and continued on—he hated to pause when he had a plan. He swiped up the papers he needed downstairs.

Some marks required more *convincing* than others.

The men gathered quickly and received their instructions. It was a routine job—coerce and buy. And it had been one that had been hanging for weeks. Needing only a signal to begin.

Waiting for that certain something to slot into place.

The dice—chance and recklessness—in his pocket burned heavily. He reached in and tossed them to a boy in passing. "Table twelve."

With a quick nod from the boy, Roman knew they would be returned to their proper place.

There were many who wished they could do the same with Roman. *Upstart.* All it would take was a few mistakes . . . a few opportunities for their enemies to exploit. And each opportunity had *her* name written all over it.

Roman walked to his destination in the heart of London, unable to send any of the others to this particular man. Some visits required a more . . . sensitive touch.

He waited in the shadows, watching as a well-dressed group passed by. The men were oblivious to anything around them. Simply following their expectations. Unsuspecting. Unaware that someone lurked in the shadows. He could gut the first one and finish with the last of them before the first even realized he was bleeding. Stupid, not to pay attention, even out here during the day, where one might feel safe.

Charlotte no longer bypassed dark corridors, not for the last week now, without sending each one a searching look. He tapped the note in his pocket. Always looking for him, aware now of who or what could lurk in the shadows. It was a lost innocence, but far better than to be surprised by the monsters in the night.

The thought that she'd need to be prepared for far worse if she fully engaged with him tickled the edges of his conscience, but he flicked the thought away before it could sink in claws.

A man exited the building, and Roman slipped through before the door closed.

Darkness watched and waited. Always. But giving people options—watching their eyes widen at the knowledge that dreams were possible—was an addictive game. Especially since many dreams were well within his ability to grant. Going to school to become an esquire. Running a business. Becoming a cook.

One thing that their empire had wrought was the ability to allow those things to occur. Helping one was in the natural order of the other.

But undertaking tasks and desires outside of that . . . desires that threatened their very existence . . . desires that he couldn't justify rationally because they were solely gut-wrenching feelings . . .

He slipped into the inner sanctum easily. Evading the heavily guarded areas, choosing the lesser paths and shadows.

No guard stood inside the room.

Foolishly arrogant, those with power sometimes were. Roman himself was far too guilty of the failing. He clicked the door shut, letting the noise announce his presence.

"What do you want?" the man on the other side of the heavy desk asked, hand clutched around a pen, shrewd eyes unreadable, wealth and breeding in every line of his body, every accent in the room. He didn't bother to ask how Roman had gotten to him. They had been beyond such questions for a long time.

"Now is that any way to speak to an old friend?" Roman smiled and flipped the lock. Ah. The sweet knowledge of fear bled into the man's gaze before he capably stifled all visible emotion.

Roman smiled more broadly and sauntered forward, dropping into the opposing chair and kicking his feet up onto the desk.

"One of these days, Merrick, you are going to die with that cocky expression upon your face." Dark promises. "What do you *want*?"

Roman lifted a negligent shoulder. "Oh, nothing grand. Just a small matter I'm sure you can help me with."

The powerful man across from him went rigid under the tension of the lie—so unused to people demanding things from him. Other people, peons, didn't *demand,* they jumped to *his* commands, and nearly every citizen in England was a peon to the man across from Roman.

But, alas, Roman had *always* been terrible at knowing his proper place. "What do you know of the Chatsworth family?"

The man eyed him. "Upstarts. But the oldest daughter is considered unnaturally beautiful." His eyes narrowed. "What could you possibly want with them, Merrick?"

Roman smiled and flicked a paper containing Charlotte Chatsworth's *possible* future onto the desk.

Chapter 11

*S*oon. Four simple letters in a word that caused her to tremble in anticipation and dread.

Charlotte curled her fingers around the note in her fist, staring at the door before her. A riot of conflicting emotions flowed through her. Knocking would make everything real. Would take her imaginings and flights of fancy from the past two weeks and thrust her fully into motion.

Would take the enticement of words spoken from silken lips and make temptation tangible. Instead of finding her in the shadows, this visit would anchor something between them in rising daylight.

He had asked, amidst inked notes and freshly plucked, dewy flowers. And she had responded. Jumped to the call.

If she were the Charlotte she had been born to be, it would have grated against her pride and her judgment, that she was falling so easily. Falling into whatever her role was in his *patiently* crafted plan.

But today, she was someone she hardly knew, alive, and on edge. Expecting him to emerge from the shadows—for he always knew where she'd be, as if she were a blooming flower in a bare field instead of the bare flower in the blooming field.

A bud really, *desperate* to bloom, desperate to open herself to the hot sun. Sucking in water, air, and soil in order to do so. Planting herself in places best designed for the sun to appear. Allowing the sun to stalk her slowly, to push away the dark shadows. Waiting.

Every evening she gambled on that bloom, putting herself dangerously in reach of Bethany's clutches, cursing the way her heart jumped each time she caught a flash of golden hair—feeling disappointment curl alongside the relief when the head belonged to someone else.

Yet every once in a while, the Charlotte of old peeked through, demanding an explanation. Demanding decorum. Demanding accountability.

It was that Charlotte whose hand paused atop brass and painted wood.

That Charlotte who was responsible for far more than her own reputation.

That Charlotte who rebuked the new Charlotte when she drew too near the shadows or the blazing sun. Not yet allowing the *patiently* waiting hand to pull her through to either sunlight or unending darkness.

That Charlotte who demanded an answer—*why was she here?*

She curved her fingers around the note.

Seven in the morning. Your park. Wear a cloak. Bring this note.

There had been a hack. A driver. An already paid fare. A trip to the north of town. A brick house surrounded by a profusion of pink flowers, delicate and feminine.

It was the old Charlotte who didn't know if she would actually rap the knocker her fingers rested upon.

And suddenly the decision was made for her. The door opened, her fingers gripping air, and there he was, leaning against the frame, arm stretched, holding the edge of the swinging wood.

Darkness underlined his eyes but didn't diminish his

attractiveness. It simply provided a more accurate representation of a deeper part of his nature, bringing it to the surface. She wondered how much sleep he had caught and why he wasn't currently abed.

"Good morning." His lips quirked. "I nearly expired from old age, waiting to see if you would actually knock on the damn thing. My heart couldn't take it any longer."

She lifted her chin and stepped inside, brushing past him as she did so. "So you are saying that if only I had had a few beats more, I would finally have been rid of you?"

She caught his lazy grin as she passed. "I plan to haunt you even in the afterlife," he whispered, the air of his words brushing her ear, the door engaging behind her.

She swallowed, then lifted her chin. "You haunt me now. I doubt you will have trouble then."

His lazy grin grew. "I had wondered if you would come," he said, leaning back against the door.

She had wondered that quite keenly herself. For she could no longer use the excuse of him seeking her out. She had made the choice to come.

"Rather cocksure of you to think I would find your note. That I will find each of them."

Pressed up against the wall of a cupboard. Stroked in the fronds of a back garden. Lips and hands on hers.

She tipped her head in order to keep the blood firmly from her cheeks.

She could feel the echo of those hands and lips each night as she closed her eyes, and each morning as the shadows slipped away. Could feel the whisper of them on her now even though his body wasn't touching hers.

He pressed back against the door, shifting, smiling. "I am rather fond of that feeling."

A pair of children scrambled down the stairs, one screaming after the other, hair on both in extreme disarray.

"Give it back t' me, ya bloody bugger!" the little girl yelled.

"You'll have t' catch me, wench!" the little boy yelled back, leaping down the last four steps in one go, then racing around the corner. The girl tore off after him, pushing a swinging door wide as she raced through. The door hit its apex, revealing a woman inside the room. The door swung the other way, showing the woman still standing there, dressed in pink with her hair pulled back. Their eyes met, and the woman's widened, then narrowed. The door hung for a moment, then swung closed, its next jag not opening far enough to show her again. Only bits of blank air and nondescript cupboards.

Charlotte stared at the swinging door as it gave its final death knell, something in her freezing. Stupid, girl. To make assumptions based on whispers in the dark.

"Yours?" Her voice was calm, even. Polite inquiry her refuge, as always.

"Good God, no." He shuddered, pushing away from the door. He couldn't have seen the woman to know that Charlotte was asking about more than just the children. But the thought of her presumption was still accurate. What difference did it make if they *were* his, all of them? None. *Silly, stupid girl.*

"Come. The fleabags will be back soon." He held a hand toward the stairs. "After you. First door on the right."

She stiltedly climbed the stairs, thoughts and lingering questions choking her. Why she had come, what she was doing here, where she was going . . . was she so resigned, or heaven forbid *eager,* to be ruined that all rational thoughts ceased around this man?

She stepped into the first room on the right and was surprised to find herself in a study that was less appointed than his rooms at the hell though still comfortable.

He motioned for her to be seated. She was surprised when he sprawled in a cozy-looking chair to the side and slightly behind her, which required her to turn in her seat in a less-than-ladylike manner in order to see him. He smiled.

All of which unnerved her. "I must be back by noon," she said coolly.

He waved a hand. "This should only take an hour. Today."

She simply stared at him, her arm pressed against the back of the chair, waiting for him to elaborate. Wondering . . . but no . . . he couldn't mean . . .

"Working off the night in one-hour increments seems far removed from the spirit of the bet we undertook."

He laughed with a tenor approaching delight and picked up a lash from a side table. A *lash*? Did he mean to bind or whip her?

"You didn't assume I was calling in your night's debt when I asked you here, did you, Charlotte?"

He examined the leather, amusement curving his lips— whether at the implement he held or at her assumption, she didn't know. He obviously knew what she was thinking though—he *winked* at her—the bastard.

"I *assumed* nothing. But with your blatant *summons* cast in parchment, and your whispered words in the night, I wonder what you think I might be willing to do."

"I am *hoping* that you will be willing to do quite a lot." He continued to smile, pulling the leather strips through his fingers. Like a recalcitrant schoolboy lounging in his chair, turning the tables on his strict teacher. "But I am *thinking* that we might negotiate your father's debts. Give you time to breathe." He said it as if he savored the taste of the word.

Breathe. Just as she'd stated—a confession—in the

middle of the night. Breathe. She could barely accomplish the task at the moment. As if he had taken all her secrets, yanked, then exposed them to the world.

"Pardon me?"

He looked at her below hooded eyes. "It is what you desire. You said as much. Time to breathe. I can give that to you." Artful, silky promises.

She wanted to ask *how,* but it wasn't the most pertinent question. "Why?"

"Oh, it will benefit me too. Mutual benefit, that is the key, is it not? Using each other to get what we desire?" He smiled, something unreadable in his eyes. "Like the Delaneys' plan."

"I . . . yes." She had thought of the Delaneys' plan as *working together,* but someone else might easily see it as mutually using each other to gain a desired result.

"Then we are settled."

She stared at him. "Nothing is settled. I have no idea of what you are specifically speaking."

"Is there something you'd be unwilling to do for obscene amounts of money?" he asked nonchalantly, his voice a smooth layer covering jagged edges.

"Yes," she said forcefully. "Of course there would be."

There were many, many things she'd be unwilling to do.

The uncomfortable tendril of thought wrapped through her though the list dwindled significantly when she substituted "to forge a good marriage" instead. But her world was of social survival. Insignificant things, such as having enough money to purchase food, weren't pertinent. Her father had repeated that sentiment for years now. Gospel.

And if she was as good as she was supposed to be, then she would secure a title *and* a plethora of money. Gospel—the chapters that Bethany, and those like her, would love to gleefully revise, striking her family's name from their registers.

She gave Roman a tight smile. The right side of his mouth curved, but the expression in his eyes was dark. As if he knew of what she was thinking.

"What if I can assure you that you will have space to breathe?" he asked, voice less casual, more enticing. "For what would you be willing to bargain?"

Her heart picked up speed. "I already owe you one night. I can claim no grasp of intelligence if I were to wager with you again."

The edge of the waterfall of leather, the apex as the strands drew, then fell, touched her chin. "I don't doubt your intelligence." He lifted her chin with it gently, examining her throat. "What I want is you, unrestrained, and out of control."

Want. Desire. Longing.

"You already have that," she said, knowing the heavy beat more than gave her away already. "I find no semblance of control when you are near."

He smiled, real pleasure in his eyes now. "I crave your admissions, and you give them away so freely." He whispered the last, pulling the leather underneath her chin. "It is enough to drive a man from drink totally, addicted to your lure instead."

Baited folly. "And you know exactly what to do and say to make me think beguiled thoughts," she whispered in return.

Pathetic, enchanted thoughts. That had no business in her mind or on the path she had to tread.

He leaned forward, his lips so close to hers. The odd arrangement of him sitting in the chair, with her half-turned, canted toward him, just made it more like they were bridging some invisible divide.

"Do I?" The bound-leather strips disappeared from her flesh, and two bare palms touched the edges of her cheeks. "Will you tell me what those thoughts say?"

"No," she whispered. A thousand times this scenario seemed to have played in the last two weeks. And each time she just became more entangled in the net. It had started to get so that she couldn't see the escape. Knotted. Drowned. "It would give you far too much power. And you already have it all."

"Do I?" He smiled and drew her lips to his. A soft touch. Then a more consuming one.

She shivered, her own hands clenched around the edge of the chair as she strained toward him. The Charlotte of old clung in that clench. In that lingering refusal to give in completely to her own insanity. The craziness he called up within her. Everything else about her—her own mouth upon his, her body heating, edging toward him—was the new Charlotte who was one heartbeat away from grasping the dark fingers of the devil's temptation.

If he pulled her from her seat, if he bent her over the desk, or laid her upon the small settee by the fireplace . . . right now, the new Charlotte would win. Would defeat the old Charlotte with one easy flick of her wrist. One easy lift of her skirts. One beautifully engaged press of bodies. Hot, not cold; wanting, not simply satisfied.

He pulled away from her slowly. Letting the invisible net stretch along her skin, twisting about her. His eyes connected with hers, hot and dark, unreadable.

"What you do to me."

She wasn't sure which of them said it. But new Charlotte owned every word.

"Why are you sitting there, and why am I over here?" Her voice was breathless, half-turned and inclined as she was in her position—which was *not* thrown over the settee.

His eyes examined her, some cool amusement sinking back in, covering the darkness, the naked want. "I could have chosen to sit on the other side of the desk, but I hate desks."

She took a moment to process his statement—his lack of an answer to her real question—as he reclined in his chair, lash back in hand. Sprawled and casual.

"Desks are pieces of furniture. You can't hate them."

He lifted his brows. "It's quite possible to dislike furniture." He smiled, a bit slyly. "You probably like desks, though, as they are very proper and stiff."

She narrowed her eyes, unnerved by his continual press, advance, then withdrawal. "And you prefer lumpy, disreputable chairs, where the stuffing is poking through?"

He patted the arm. "Disreputable old chairs you can count on."

"Chairs you should probably replace," she said tartly.

He gave her a chastising look. "Now, Charlotte, it's bad form to replace a solid, comfortable chair just because you see a pretty, sleek, new one. A thoroughly loved chair never disappoints."

Her lips twisted at an odd angle, frozen on her face. "How do you know the desk won't turn into a well-loved companion piece then? Once the patina wears and the nicks appear? Perhaps it might unbend in time." She clamped her lips together to stop from uttering something even more ignorant, such as, "desks need love too."

His eyes pinned hers. "Ah, but instead I choose the *right* chair in the beginning instead of trying to change the desk."

She smiled, her social smile. "Of course."

He examined her for a moment, but she couldn't read the expression. "And sometimes a chair has been used as a desk for so long, it stops believing it is anything else."

He waved a hand suddenly, flicking out the lash so that the cords snapped. "Now, footstools. I think we can both agree that there is something inherently wrong with them."

She stared at him. "Perhaps you really do require a woman to talk you dumb."

His mouth pulled, and he stroked the lash threads from root to tip. "Oh, you aren't giving yourself enough credit, Charlotte. I want you to *suck* me dumb."

Her mouth opened, but nothing emerged. She should be used to it by now since even when he lured her into thinking of him as cultured, he reverted to uttering something base. Making all manner of things sputter inside of her.

His lips curved into a smirk that she longed to wipe free of his face. "Ah, it's the smallest of pleasures really that make my day."

As if the reference to time triggered something, he glanced at a clock in the corner of the room and briskly pulled himself up. "But there isn't much time left."

"You mean we aren't going to sit here for the morning, angled oddly, exchanging repartee while you fondle that . . . that whip?"

Wanting to kiss you?

He smiled, as if he had heard the silent addition. "Unfortunately, no; Samuel will be here any moment."

She stiffened. "You have invited someone else here?"

He waved a hand. "It's his house. And you needn't worry about him keeping your presence a secret. Samuel is a tar pit when it comes to information."

The relief that came from knowing that the house—and likely everything and everyone in it—belonged to someone else was irritating. Along with the realization that she had *forgotten* any initial thoughts of a harem of other women sometime between climbing the stairs and being devoured.

"That is easy for you to promise. It isn't your reputation that is at risk," she said stiffly.

"Isn't it?" He regarded her for a moment. "But anyway, to the task at hand. Samuel wants to participate in the Delaneys' project, but he, hmmm, how can I put it, isn't exactly on the guest list."

She looked around the study. It wasn't grand, but whoever owned the house wasn't poor.

Roman rubbed a hand along the back of his neck. The gesture alarmed her. He was always a self-assured man. "Not everyone's money is . . . clean."

Someone involved in crime then? "You were invited," she pointed out.

"Our main businesses are aboveboard. It is our tactics that are questioned."

She wondered what "other" businesses they might have that *weren't* aboveboard.

"Well, prostitution is really just a matter of making sure the prostitutes are happy, right?" she said.

She meant it to be a joke, but Roman's eyes lit up. "Exactly. Perfect."

"Wh—?"

He waved a hand. "I should have known you wouldn't hold it against them. Here is how things will work then. You help with this each morning for a week, and I will pay one of your father's debts each day."

Her mind was whirling, still clamping around the prostitution response. What the devil did he—

"The most important debts, of course," he said. "Easy enough to see which ones weigh the heaviest."

Something suddenly sparked through the swirling confusion. She lowered her eyes briefly, before meeting his. "Oh?"

His lips curled, his fingers pulling along the lash again.

"Only your father's debts. You didn't think I'd relinquish such a claim on *you,* did you? Tsk, tsk, Charlotte."

She tilted her head, trying not to come to terms with how she felt relief at *that* too. "What is this task you need help with?"

"Simply a matter of some advice. Linking resources together. Helping where you can."

She frowned. She hardly needed to be paid to give advice, but before she could ask anything else, the door opened.

A large man ambled in with an odd sort of gait. His hair was carefully combed and his shirt freshly pressed, but he appeared uncomfortable as he nodded to both of them quickly, then sat behind the desk. He appeared out of sorts, brushing by social consideration and going straight to business.

He put his hands on the top of the desk. "Merrick ain't be telling your name, and that's how we gonna keep it. Name's Sam. I'll be calling you Lady."

It took a moment before she was able to form a reply. She very slowly leaned forward in her chair. "Very well, Sam."

"Look, I don't know how they be doing it in yur parts, but I like straightness."

Luckily inborn replies were automatic. "Straight works well."

"Good. Here's the matter. Our money's no good some places. And we don't care to spread it much, but the missus wants to do a lil bluh"—he coughed, sending Roman a nervous look before looking back her way—"sweepin'."

She stared at Sam, unknowing how to respond, or of what he was even speaking.

"'Bout time for a lil swa—cleanin', sweep the bluh—dratted, bug—blighters."

An odd feeling settled. Was this to be an etiquette lesson then? To clean up his language? She somewhat hoped so, or she was going to be hard-pressed to figure out exactly what he was saying.

"Not every woman wants to remain a tro—prostitute, as ye know."

No, no she didn't know. The odd feeling changed into something that was suspiciously more alarming.

"Some women just do it to fur—make a lil money, get a cu—leg up. Others have nuthin' better. Lil work and bad bluh—money in the as—factories."

If she weren't stunned into stupidity at the moment, she might have nodded for him to continue. As it was, thankfully, he didn't need the encouragement.

"We want to change the bluh—conditions. Prison, alley, abb—er, brothel. Get some 'greements. Lor 'knows that when I was whor—hirin' Sally out, I started to feel a bluh—pinch about the emotions."

"I . . . see."

Roman Merrick had asked her here in order to give a whoremaster advice. A whoremaster. And the man's . . . wife? About how to spread money to help women working the streets?

Sam looked relieved. "Ah, good. Cuz there's nothin' to be doing for us bluh—street types. Even when's we fall into money. Need backin' from Tur—*named* money. Who have the ear of Perlament."

Charlotte decided to divide the rather odd conversation into compartments. She concentrated on the task rather than the participants. "Do you have specific ideas, or did you want to allocate money to groups that support your aims?"

"Both." He settled into his chair, looking more relaxed. "Right good of you to de—figure it, Lady."

She could almost feel the amusement at her back, but there was something more serious in the air behind her as well. She pushed the question of it aside, concentrating on the man seated in front of her as he spoke about specifics.

Half an hour later, Sam exited the room, more excited and relaxed than when he'd walked in. His shirt had been pulled loose from his trousers, in comfortable disarray. He had obviously been uncomfortable putting on whatever show he had thought he needed to perform when he'd first entered.

She stayed facing forward in her seat for a long moment before turning. Roman was still lounging in his chair, pulling the leather through his fingertips.

She waited until he met her eyes. "I believe you have something to say?"

He raised a brow in question.

"Something that might start with, 'My apologies, Charlotte, I didn't realize what I was asking you to do' or maybe 'Wake up, Charlotte, you've been abed too long.'"

A lazy smile curved. "If only it could be the latter." His face grew serious a moment later. "Will you help?"

She examined him, the lazy posture with just a hint of tightness to it.

"Yes."

He smiled again, everything about him relaxing.

"His—their?—aims are good, and he has some interesting ideas," she said. "There are a few well-placed women who champion such causes. I know with whom to speak." She shook her head. "Not quite sure how I will introduce the subject, but I do know the right ears for this."

"Thank you."

She examined him again. "You could have asked the Delaneys."

"Why, when I could ask you?" He smiled slowly.

"The Delaneys have more power than I do."

For now. Someday . . .

"But then I'd be beholden to them when I'd much rather be beholden to you." His smile stretched lazily.

"You don't need to be beholden at all." Bad idea to release the winning cards already in her possession, but pride was pride. "This is something I will do without payment. Surely you know that." Active participation in her charities was something that cleansed her soul. To accept money would go against her every principle.

And if he knew anything about her . . .

"Yes." His eyes dropped, lips still curved. "Though I will settle a few of your father's debts anyway. A selfish desire, I assure you. As I want you *free*."

"Why are you helping Sam?"

He looked up at her through lazy eyes. "Need to *clean* money sometimes. Need to care for different types of employees. I'm not doing it because I'm kind."

She narrowed her eyes. His name wasn't mentioned in charitable circles—beyond his singular appearance at the Delaneys'—so his selfish words made sense. Still, he seemed terribly interested in her charity work whenever the subject was raised. And when speaking on the subject, the lines of his body belied the amusement invariably present in his face.

She left her high-backed chair and walked over to sit across from him in one more comfortable.

He watched her, that insufferably light smile about his lips.

And she thought of her options. Of what she had been feeling every night before she fell asleep, every morning as she woke. Every time his lips or fingers touched her.

She could . . . choose her fate. Or at the very least, she could choose the way she fell. Cold and brittle, shattering upon the stones. Or hot and writhing and . . . alive.

"I wish to pay my debt. To give you the night I owe. I can clear my schedule tomorrow and say I've taken ill."

He continued to lounge in his chair, but his eyes were alert, quick. "Why?"

She met his eyes boldly. Thinking of all she knew—and had yet to learn—about the man in front of her. She posed her own question in answer. "Don't you wish to meet on even ground?"

His eyes sparked, he scooted forward in his chair, elbows on his knees, the lash forgotten. "Oh, Charlotte. You play with fire."

"Do I?"

Roman looked at the woman in front of him, calm and collected, but there was heat there, such precious heat that was straining. Offering.

It only took one second for the words to form and emerge. "Consider the debt of the night wiped free."

He saw her blink. Stunned.

Watched the disappointment form. He felt nearly *giddy* as her disappointment formed.

"What, but—"

"But what?" He smiled, loving the look on her face, even the desire that was slowly shuttering—for he would obliterate those shutters with his next words. "You think I am freeing you?"

Uncertainty. Delicious uncertainty. She pulled her bottom lip in. "Aren't you?"

"No." He leaned forward, pressing on his elbows, until his lips were so close to hers that he could feel the heat of her, soft and delicious. "I am a selfish man."

"A selfish man takes what is offered to him." Was that doubt in her voice, doubt of her charms?

"No, a selfish man destroys what is offered to him and demands more. He demands *everything*."

He touched her chin, pulling his finger beneath it, bringing her lower lip to brush against his. "I am a selfish man, and *all* of you, Charlotte . . . that is my demand."

Chapter 12

If she thought it had been a hell of a week, it had proven to be a crazed monster of a morning. Confusing, overwhelming, unnerving. Giddy with desire, knots of tension overtaking rational sense.

"Charlotte, come into my study."

She stiffened when her father imperiously waved her forward. What was he doing home so early in the morning again?

As a child she had entered the room to a myriad of warm accents and plush fabrics, beautiful, leather-bound books, and lovely paintings. But like everything in her world, it had been stripped and bared. They should have sold the house last year and rented a smaller home in a less prestigious section of town, but appearance was everything to her father, and they would cling to these crumbling walls until the bitter end, when there was nothing left.

"Where have you been?" he snapped.

That Charlotte had been out wasn't the issue. That she had been taking an early-morning walk in the park down the street wasn't either. That she had left Anna behind, and that someone had obviously gone looking for Charlotte and had not found her *was*.

She assumed the proper demure stance behind one of the uncomfortable, upright chairs in front of his overly grand desk—the last piece he would ever part with. "I was out for a walk in the park and took the long way around. I needed to clear my mind."

He was prowling behind the desk, lifting papers and discarding them as was his recent habit when agitated. "Don't do it again. Do you want us ruined?"

"Of course not. But a walk in the early hours is not a social crime. The *ton* isn't even awake yet."

"Any breach of protocol is detrimental for us right now."

"I will remember that." The best time to remember would be when her lips were about to be pressed to Roman Merrick's, and yet that was when those thoughts were farthest from her mind.

"Foul rumors are making the rounds."

She kept her breathing even. "Oh?"

"And you do *nothing*."

Had someone seen them? Finally? In the shadows, the devil seducing the virgin? Hades seducing Persephone?

"Your mother is working against us." He clenched his fists. "Someone remarked about her fading looks. Her lack of status. That *you* only have another good year or two in you. That you are aging quickly. And they are right." He slapped a hand against the desk.

She stood perfectly straight and unmoving. The relief when she didn't hear Roman's name quickly falling to cold emptiness at her father's words.

"Scandal looms upon us, girl. The walls are closing in. And we must play the hand we have *now*."

She loosened her jaw enough to say, "I have heard nothing concerning your bet. And there are those who would not remain silent if they knew."

His mouth twisted. "Don't be a fool." His eyes went to the scattered papers on his desk.

She pushed the feelings down into the pit, concentrating on her father's bills and credit notes instead. "What do you have there, Father?" she asked. *Breathing room.* What had Roman done? "It looks like a bill that has been paid."

Paper crumpled in his fist. "*It is none of your concern.*"

Frightened that it had been paid? Or was there something more . . . something worse?

"If it isn't that night, then—"

He slammed a hand on the desk, scattering the papers. "Your concern should be *working your wiles and securing a title.* No more drifting through ballrooms and pasting on smiles. You show no *urgency.*"

She pasted on her *calmest* smile. "My apologies, Father. But it seems beyond vulgar to show our *desperation.*"

His eyes narrowed dangerously. "Don't get impertinent with me."

Her eyes locked with his, volatility shifting the cold. "How many offers have you turned down in the past two and a half years?"

"They weren't up to par!"

"I *will* marry well."

"I have seen no evidence of this!"

"Just last night I danced with—"

"Dancing! What difference does that make?"

"Dancing isn't purely a physical and joyous pastime, Father. And it doesn't simply entail moving across a floor." She took a breath, controlling herself. "But you know this."

"I don't see any *progress.* Any urgency on your part. Even now." He swiped a hand toward her. "You stand there as if you have no life within you."

"I assure you I have a heartbeat." And that it far outstripped his.

"Then show it," he said viciously. "Get them panting at your skirts instead of admiring you from afar."

She stood rigidly. "I think you unsure whether you want me to be the trophy or the vixen."

"Be both!"

A smile twisted her face. "Perhaps you should encourage more card games to teach me the other side."

He advanced rapidly around the desk and grabbed her chin in his hand. Anger underlined the embittered anxiety she could see in his eyes. "You will hold your tongue."

His hand shook. Nothing to drink yet then. She held herself stiffly.

His fingers gentled. "You are superior to every woman in society. My prize. I knew it when you were thirteen. Nurtured it. You have the makings of perfection. Flawless."

She didn't reply, just stared at him.

"Do this. God knows your sister is useless."

She wrenched her chin away. "Emily is far better than you—"

He grabbed her arm, though he was careful not to mark her. Her father knew better than to mark his art. "I'll marry her to Lord Kinley."

"You wouldn't." The distention hardened into something dark and deadly.

He narrowed his eyes. "He offered for you once. I could talk him around. He likes them young."

The darkness reached up. "I'd make sure she was widowed the night of the wedding."

Her father laughed without humor. "Then maybe it should be done posthaste."

Charlotte mourned as the last warm feelings for her father slipped away. For the softer father he had been before debt and drink had turned him to the edge of anger and despair.

"Trant will make an offer soon," she said evenly, bitter

cold and heated fury mixing, leaving numbness behind. "And I'm sure it will be a generous one. I wouldn't even need to *work my wiles* on him."

His lips tightened.

She shook her head, a cheerless laugh upon her tongue. "Trant's not enough for you, even now, pressed and desperate. Even now you look toward a bigger pot."

"You could be a duchess, given time and opportunity." He reached out to touch her cheek, but she slowly, deliberately pulled back. "My grandson, a duke. But Trant has made subtle threats. I made a mistake not wrestling Downing to the ground immediately your first season. Our timetable must be advanced. We do what we must with the hands we have been dealt."

No. Her father had dealt himself—and her—their hands.

He released his grip and retreated behind his desk. "I talked Trant around to wait to offer for you until the end of the season. But . . ." He quickly pushed a paper beneath others littering the desk. "Events have occurred that give us time and yet choke us with the same. You have six weeks to find a better prospect. *Work your wiles,* girl. We have been hoping for the Duke of Knowles, but the blasted man hasn't shown his face. We might have to push and invite ourselves to his home, get you compromised."

Bitterness drifted through her that he was even thinking of engineering such a plan.

"Until then, the Earl of Tewksbury. Marquess Binchley. Net one, and we will hush up any gossip that emerges from Trant's mouth."

The Duke of Knowles, an extremely wealthy and reputedly handsome, man, had disappeared into the country four years before—the phantom crown of the marriage mart. The Earl of Tewksbury, not a day under sixty. And the Marquess, an inveterate drunk.

The cavity had never been deeper or more empty. Desperately needing something to fill it.

Something that could give her . . . relief. She swallowed, feeling the tiny ivory crown of the chess piece as if she were stroking it in her fingers.

"Six weeks." She grasped the time as if it would somehow knit her family into an affectionate whole. As if the answer to everything lay at the end. As if she could find freedom in the ticked calendar squares. "Not a day less."

His fist thumped against the desk. "Do it."

She usually loved Vauxhall. The spectacle, the lights, the merriment, the people from all walks of life. The ease with which one could enjoy the festivities.

But with her father's words ringing in her ears and stuck in a dining box, the cloth walls felt like they were closing in on her. The supports bending, ready to break. Marquess Binchley belched next to her.

She could feel the eyes of the crowd watching her movements as if the king himself had entered her theater box. She was an actress playing a role in a cloth tomb, fragments of remembered lines upon her tongue.

She touched her napkin, creasing the fabric, and maintained a cool smile about her lips. The papers would praise her for it.

Sudden pleasure slipped over her like a shift warmed in front of the fire, sliding heatedly down her bare arms, her breasts, her hips, brushing her ankles.

She tensed. Only one man elicited those feelings. She looked into the densely mixed crowd, scanning each group, until her gaze fell upon golden hair. Even surrounded by masses of people, he dominated his own space. She recognized the two men who were earnestly speaking to him. At him, really, for he didn't seem to be paying them much attention. When her gaze locked with his, he slowly smiled and turned his attention back to the men, speaking as if he had never glanced her way.

Charlotte, however, was incapable of looking elsewhere. The urge to vault from the box, to embrace the night shadows, nearly drowned her in its intensity.

"Like a frog. Without those . . . those flippers!" the man next to her said.

She could feel the slip of paper she had found that afternoon after her chat with her father. A bit of parchment tied around another spiked, red-veined flower. She could feel it as if it were still in her fingers—bare digits crinkling the page—instead of tucked inside her gown, next to her breast. The feel of something exotic and forbidden in the scrawl.

She swallowed and turned to Marquess Binchley, whose eyes were already reddened in drink. A familiar sight. "My apologies, my lord," she said softly. "What were you saying?"

She could feel those other eyes on her though. Amused. Possessive. Forbidden and desired. Stripping her bare. Pausing on the line of her neck and the underside of her chin.

"Wash it," the marquess said, startling her, waving his arms—a whirligig motion that caused her to pull back lest she be whacked. "Then when it finds the worm it drowns in the puddle. Like a toad."

"How true, my lord."

For the crowd, she had made sure to react for the last thirty minutes as if every utterance concerning toads and frogs had the makings of a glorious sonnet.

The moment Roman Merrick disappeared from the crowd, though, her smile started cracking. She knew he had disappeared because she couldn't *feel* him anymore. The thought made her slightly hysterical.

But the shadows of the gardens reached toward her all the same. Whispering of escape. Of finding him.

There was no easy way to extricate herself from Binchley, though. Even if, drunk as he was, he would take no notice of her leaving, others would. And there were definitely people watching. Avidly. She had carefully cultivated it to appear as if the two of them were having an involved conversation. She'd seen her father's pleased nod and Trant's narrowed eyes.

Binchley took another drink. "Can't find toads in the sky."

"It is not known to be their natural habitat," she answered, trying to keep her attention on Binchley instead of searching the crowd—or thinking on the repercussions of the always full glass in the marquess's hand.

And it only made the whisper of words uttered in the dark of night that much more potent. That Roman read her desires so correctly and said all of the right things.

But were his words true?

She could stay here, on this path, or she could embrace the opportunity to find out. So when Miranda peeked into the box, she grasped onto her like a dying woman given a last request. "Lady Downing!"

Miranda's brows shot straight up. Which meant that Charlotte had successfully convinced her friend that they were having a grand time as well.

"Lord Binchley. Miss Chatsworth." Miranda ducked inside. "I hope you don't mind the interruption."

"No, not at all." Charlotte hoped her tangled emotions weren't as obvious as the sucking whirlpool pushing them out from within.

"Leeady Downing. Pleasant." Then Binchley frowned. "Frogs."

Miranda opened her mouth for a second before the words emerged. "A pleasure, yes, Lord Binchley. I say, let me grab Downing. I believe he wished to speak with you."

Miranda disappeared, and Charlotte smiled more genuinely at the man next to her, wild anticipation squeezing her belly, mixed with the heady relief of escape and the fear of the uncertain.

He muttered something unintelligible, and when Downing ducked inside, looking first to Charlotte, then her companion, Binchley gave a sloppy salutation.

Downing shifted from the shadows and into the light, dark clothing and hair making him look like a demon sweeping up an appalling minion. "Binchley. Your mother is searching for you. Said something about an appointment."

"Dragon," he muttered, but shakily stood. "Worse than frog puddles."

Downing's face gave away nothing as he stepped into Binchley. But suddenly Binchley was closer to Charlotte, his arm in front of her. Binchley stared at his limb as if unsure how it came to be there.

Charlotte wrapped her hand around it and conveyed wordless gratitude to Downing. He gave a tiny nod and propelled Binchley forward.

They walked out. Downing bowed to Miranda, which caused Binchley to mirror the action to Charlotte, then Downing was leading the stumbling man away.

Miranda claimed Binchley's abandoned spot, hooking her arm with Charlotte's as they walked through the crowd behind the boxes.

Miranda bit her lip. "Did you enjoy dinner?"

Charlotte nodded at the question, unable to part her lips. Why was she anxious *now*? Because the end was imminent? A timetable finally in place? She was no more or less than any of the other girls in society, no matter what her father said. She knew her fate.

But she suddenly couldn't open her mouth.

"Oh dear." Miranda worried her lip, but Charlotte said nothing, still unable. "Your father gave you—"

"I don't wish to speak of him." The words rushed out. A light, feathery breeze brushed her skin. No golden hair in sight, but she could *feel* him somewhere, again, out there on the grounds.

"Very well." Neither said anything for a long moment. "Separate Binchley from his mother, and I think he could be up to snuff," Miranda said tentatively.

Life with Marquess Binchley stretched before her— easy to manage if she could unpin him from his mother's thumb, but drowning in whiskey and gin. And eventual debt, again. The peerage ran under a different set of rules though, which meant they could get into even deeper debt than the rest of society.

"He is an eighth-generation title," Miranda continued in an upbeat voice. "Proper. And he's young. Room to grow."

Far younger than Tewksbury, who was old enough to be her grandfather.

Maybe she *should* run away to the country seat of the Duke of Knowles. Throw herself upon his mercy. A recluse she'd never have to see. Or continue running, straight out of England.

Or straight into the alleys behind an east-side hell.

Her heart sped unnaturally and she missed a step, out of rhythm.

"We were going to take a stroll when two boys walked by saying that you looked like you needed an escape," Miranda said. "I thought it odd but decided to check. I'm glad I did."

"Yes, thank you," Charlotte murmured, paying attention to Miranda's emotional support instead of her words, trying to dam her inner turmoil. She should stay and seek out Tewksbury. Listen to the rumors concerning Knowles. Find her father and put herself forward for the slaughter.

She had never expected a different life. She was bred for this. She was Charlotte Chatsworth.

Yet her feelings continually betrayed that cool pride. The two very different needs pressing against her.

"Do you wish to walk with us? I'll warn you that we will likely find trouble with that lot." Miranda pointed to a group gathered along the side of the main walk.

The smart choice was to stay.

She gripped Miranda's arm in hers and walked from the trapping society crowd and toward the maelstrom instead.

The group, comprised mostly of Downing's relatives and friends of said relatives, called out lively greetings. She always enjoyed standing near them, soaking in their excitement and innocence—even the innocence of the more mischievous ones. Free-spirited and delighted with life. A chance for Charlotte to watch a lovely, vibrant play even through her immovable pane of glass.

Cracking glass. She let loose a breath, trying to free some of her swirling emotions with it. Downing rejoined them, which set the boisterous group in motion. Charlotte walked alongside—not looking for her father or one of her suitors.

Trying not to look for *him*. Though she knew he was there, somewhere. Could feel the charge of charmed danger.

She concentrated on listening to the younger ones gossip and laugh. Admiring the lights and well-trimmed gardenscapes.

Trying to pretend that she was someone else.

That was the beauty of Vauxhall. The ever-present whisper of escape. There was something in the clinging shadows that whispered of freedom—something even the well-lit paths couldn't banish. It would be so easy to slip away.

And many took the opportunity. Though with each passing year, as the collars grew higher and the undergarments grew more restrictive, so too did it seem that society pinched its legs and mouths more firmly together. It had been far easier to slip away without soiling one's reputation in her first year than it was now. She wondered what it would be like in ten. Would simply stepping a foot into the shadows constitute a breach?

But many couples vanished for a few moments here and there. The ones who had an easier road. Or were more reckless.

Or who had an urge that could not be denied. A stirring that needed outlet. A distention that needed ease.

Relief.

She nodded at something Miranda said, and the group walked down the main corridor. Downing's youngest brother whispered something—undoubtedly wicked—and pulled the younger males, groaning, with him toward the lake. Up to no good, that lot.

Downing looked after them with narrowed eyes, but Miranda nudged him hard in the ribs, and, with a grunt, he continued moving forward. There was a set of well-used paths to the right. Crowned in half-light, they led to darker areas, but also looped around to the main road. Perfectly safe to travel in a group. They veered off. Downing's sister and her two friends took the fountain path, chattering about men and bonnets.

That left Charlotte with Miranda and Downing, who were sharing some personal amusement over the split path in front of them. Downing's brows cocked, Miranda blushed. Charlotte felt a thread inside of her tighten and stretch. The shadows whispered giddily around her.

A draft of wind lifted a leaf from the hedgerow and set it swirling into the air, a fluttering voice whispering of other things. Wicked suggestions in the dark.

Light laughter brought her musings back to her surroundings—and her present company. Two wonderful people who had found each other across a barrier she had thought insurmountable.

Charlotte looked at the fork and took a step away from the Downings. She stopped, but the urge pushed at her, some reckless need lifting within her, pushing from the pit.

It was folly to leave the Downings' company. Especially with Trant, her father, and Bethany prowling the grounds. Who knew what she would find—or who would find her—if she ventured off on her own for a few minutes.

She wasn't an idiot. Nor a girl green from the country.

And yet she heard her voice murmuring—"I think I will examine the vines around the corner. Shall we meet at the statue of Venus?"

Miranda gave her a look of complete adoration for giving them a few private moments, then looked back at her husband.

Charlotte didn't wait for a verbal response, or a sensible denial, but stepped around the hedged path, moving into the shadows. She took a few quick strides before she stopped, breathing more heavily than her pace required.

She wished she could lean her head against the coiling bindweed, but it would snag her hair and ruin her coiffure. What was alarming was her urge to do so anyway. She closed her eyes momentarily, curled her fingers around the creased paper she had hidden, and gave a shaky laugh.

She examined the area. It was darker here, of course. She had never trod this path in the night, but she knew it well enough from daytime strolls. It would reconnect with the path the Downings were taking. It would provide seclusion and a way back to her companions.

A giggle rose behind the hedge. It pulled at her wishes and pushed her resolve. She strode forward along the path. If she were discovered here alone, the Downings would cover for her. The proverbial carriage wheel would skip right over them. And her own reputation allowed enough stretch that she could talk her way out of a first infraction as long as she wasn't caught with her skirts over her head. Life would be more difficult afterward, especially with her father, but then too she might not even be caught at all.

Such was the risk of a gamble. Corruption coating perfect thoughts.

She approached a deep alcove and unoccupied bench—the only bench along this path. She touched the stone before sitting, as a wet bum would do her little good. Music penetrated the thick branches with the distant sound of merriment—but didn't drown the sound of the crickets and other night critters, whose chirping increased as she relaxed.

The sounds of foliage brushing and bending suddenly met her ears. Flurries lifted in her stomach. Heavy footsteps crunched along the path.

She tensed. The heaviness of the sounds indicated the approaching person possessed little stealth. And it was one set of footsteps, not two, which ruled out the Downings.

She positioned her body to swing around the bench. To hide behind it in stupid panic. But the footsteps stopped and abruptly changed paths, echoing away. She clenched the stone. What was she doing, *truly* doing, here in the dark?

The path to Venus. It had been written in a quick and scratchy scrawl.

And here she was. Sitting amongst the hedges, *waiting.* *Waiting.* Just like any other boffleheaded chit hoping for a lover. The reckless urge reached up and pushed against everything she knew to be right.

The urge had been pushing hard and fast ever since she'd met him.

"Damn you, Roman Merrick," she muttered, a tad bitterly, too low for anyone to hear, should they be near.

"What did I do now?"

She shot off the bench and whirled around, looking wildly about her, one hand clutched at her throat in terror and shock. Not seeing anyone standing, she wrenched her gaze back to the bench to see an arm propped on the stone, his bottom half hidden behind the bench.

Lying back there the entire time.

She did the only thing that occurred to her in her flurry of wild emotion. She moved forward and kicked him in what she assumed was his backside, cloaked in the shadows as he was. Incongruously, he started to laugh. She lifted her foot to kick him again, but he grasped her ankle. Heated fingers pierced through her stockings, touching her bare flesh through the netting as they wrapped around.

"Don't make me ruin your lovely dress in the grass." Amusement laced his voice as he lifted her leg, pulling her off-balance and causing her to hop on the other. "Or do. It would greatly simplify matters, don't you think?"

"What the bloody hell are you doing back there?"

"My goodness. Such gutter language on a lady so fine." One finger stroked the underside of her calf. Up, up. She tried to pull her limb back, hopping more fiercely, arms whirling around to keep herself upright. "I hope you know other such words because there is simply nothing more divine than the idea of such a classy woman speaking foully as I thrust into her."

Her mouth opened and closed. "What?" she asked, her voice faint. Just like it always was when he uttered such things. Such *promises*. Making her think things that proper ladies didn't.

"I will, you know." His fingers moved farther up, skimming the underside of her knees, reaching around her garters, dipping beneath the straps.

She shivered as he put her foot on the top of the bench, pinning it with his other hand and rising to his knees, running his fingers farther up her leg, over her thigh. My God, he was so close, nothing to stop his fingers from reaching right into her. Her hands slapped down on his, and she could see him smile, his teeth catching the gleam of moonlight.

"But you *do* know, don't you, Charlotte?" He might as well have *slithered* onto the bench, pulling her to him, sliding her over his lap and pressing her down. "You came here—all on your own, *knowing*."

It was the simple truth. She had come, and he had found her.

His hands were around her neck, and their bodies were pressed together *everywhere*. She couldn't remember feeling such a tight-wound thrill—it emanated from the very core of her.

"How did you do it?" she whispered.

"Do what?" He lifted her as if she weighed nothing and worked one leg around to the front of the bench, locking them together fully so that she was *riding* his thigh.

"Get behind me," she breathed.

"Mmmm . . . is that a request?"

She didn't answer, unable to respond as the firm feel of his muscular thigh gripped between hers. But against her neck she felt his lips open into a smile.

"How do you know I wasn't here before you? Waiting?" he asked, moving just the slightest bit so that she slid an inch farther down his thigh, pulling her slowly into place.

"You weren't." Her voice barely emerged.

"So you were daydreaming so intently that I managed to slip behind you? Why not simply slip up your skirts instead? Take you while you were thinking of other things." His lips touched her ear, whispering, "Thinking of me."

"I wasn't thinking of you." She tried not to think of his thigh, which was already up her skirts and burning her below.

She felt his smile again, tracing the curve of her neck, knowing her lie. "I will have to change that then."

"Why do you care? Truly?" she whispered. Some men liked to collect beautiful things, she knew. And his personal space had spoken to a taste for the expensive, but he seemed particular in his acquisitions. Or perhaps she just *wished* such. Dangerous thoughts were ever present around this man.

"Let me ask you this instead, Charlotte—why did you come here? To this spot?"

"I was walking with Mir—"

Her breath caught as his hand trailed up one bent leg, beneath her dress, fingertips kneading the flesh of her thigh above the thin barrier of fabric that remained, so near to where her undergarments parted above him.

"Let's try that question again with a more truthful response, shall we?"

"It is the truth." She gripped his shoulders, staring over his shoulder, eyes unseeing, breath catching, *wanting.* "We were walking."

He drew a pattern up her thigh, long, sloping curves of figure eights that had to brush his thigh as well. "I want you to admit it. Again. Knowing that we are on even ground."

"Why?"

"So that we can begin in earnest. Without all these diversions, entertaining as they are."

"Begin what?"

"Our torrid affair."

She let out a shaky breath. "I'm not having a torrid affair with you."

One finger slipped up, missing the curve of the eight, and brushed the slit in the fabric. She would have jolted had she had anywhere to go. As it was, the action simply pressed her to him and slightly up, and she felt the touch of a bare finger pad against her. Butterfly light and crashingly strong. She exhaled suddenly and lost the ability to inhale.

He, however, did not pause in his exploration. His roving hand continued the pattern of eight, but now with a higher curve, brushing intimately against her on every other curl. Her midsection tightened in waves, undulating as if he were a horse cantering beneath her.

The fingers of his left hand wove into the hair at her nape and tugged—not harshly, but not lightly either. "I assure you," he whispered into her ear, still in full possession of the advantage even in their current position. "It will be *extremely* torrid."

Her fingers dug into his shoulders, her head tilted back to the stars, eyes closed. She wanted to be embraced by the shadows. To do something completely foolhardy and impetuous. Something that allowed her to fly.

"I can't," she whispered. "I can't have an affair."

"I assure you, it is quite simple."

"I'm not married."

"That makes it much easier, don't you think? No witless husband getting in the way."

"It's not possible."

"I assure you, it is quite possible. Or did you think Ganling's daughter impregnated herself out of wedlock last season? And the Usters? Quick marriage there, no?"

She tried to push away, but he held her fast. "You give every reason not to indulge in such foolishness," she said, a little bitterly.

He pulled her back down firmly upon his thigh, stilling her once more at the heated contact. "Foolishness is what gets those into that situation. I think I can safely keep you from that end. There are ways."

His cheek drew along hers, his body dragged against hers, clasped to his as it again was. The fingers of one hand stroked the back of her neck and the other curved around her backside and drew down the side of her thigh. She didn't know what was worse, the way he knew how to get a response from her or the way her traitorous body was rushing ahead to give it to him before he even asked. "Besides, the benefits will outweigh the risks, the gamble, I assure you."

His hand, the lift of his hips, elevated her once again and pulled her fully against him, seated upon him. She felt the entirely male part of him reach toward her, pressing against her, making the feelings spike almost painfully. Awareness, panic, reckless excitement, fear.

"Tell me, Charlotte," he whispered, his lips caressing her cheek, almost brushing hers, his eyes pinning her suddenly, even through the shadows. "Who are you thinking about *now*?"

She breathed heavily, eyes fiercely connected. Firm thoughts about any suitors or marriage plans and plots were nonexistent. Simply hazy mist in the hedges. He was offering her relief.

To sate these new, reckless urges.

Not something simple, though, no matter what his beguiling words promised. She didn't think anything with him could be defined as such.

Who was she thinking about? For the past few weeks there had been only one person continuously on her mind.

"You."

He hummed a little something, his fingers caressing her neck, his eyes not leaving hers. "You admit the most delicious things."

"My lips tend to disobey when you are near," she whispered, giving additional credence to the words.

"Mmmm . . . one of my favorite aspects, I'll admit." His other hand came up to touch her chin, then his thumb ran over her lower lip. "I noticed your lush mouth immediately. Hard not to with such a composed and opinionated opponent. The way your lips come together and part. You shield your eyes, but your emotions still show in the way you expel each succulent breath. And when you press your tongue against the roof of your mouth in anger, trying to keep the emotion from your face, the sides of your throat clench just so, making me wonder how you would look with your tongue wrapped tightly around me."

Stunned and feeling emotionally drunk, she felt his thumb slowly pull across her lower lip, his bare finger running along it fully.

"I notice a lot of things that you probably wish I didn't. But more than anything, I see the cage wrapped around you." He closed the small gap, nose and lips brushing against hers, over and back again. "Why did you come here, Charlotte?" he asked once more.

"I read your note," she whispered.

"And?"

She didn't respond, pride not letting her.

"A man asking to meet you in the gardens, in the dark." His lips brushed her cheek. "Wouldn't that send a proper lady running the other way?"

"I wanted to come." It was nearly yanked from her, like the coating of her pride.

He leaned back with a soothing shush on his lips as he traced hers with his thumb. "I know. I know. Let me set you free, Charlotte."

She had no idea what "setting her free" would mean. But a wild yearning rose from the cavity inside her. A loosening of anxiety. Something that promised relief. Something about this man, about that night in his rooms, had cast a spell. A purely selfish desire to feel again the relaxation and relief that he directly inspired. That she could see *herself* as something more if she allowed him in.

All of which was utter nonsense, of course, the rational part of her mind scoffed. And she would firmly tell him so. After all, if there was a cage, she was the animal and he the hunter. Would she find the exit only to jump witlessly into his snare?

"Yes," her lips whispered, betraying her again.

"Good."

And every thought to the contrary fled as his mouth touched hers.

Consuming.

Something far darker and hotter than she had anticipated. It *burned*. From the inside out. Like a mythical bird erupting, destroying, and beginning anew. She fought against the consumption, pushing back, gripping his shoulders and kissing him back, wanting to force him to feel it too. And he was *pleased*. She didn't have to see him to know it—*couldn't* see him, as her eyes had closed on their own, more stars in the backs of her eyelids than could possibly exist in the sky.

She could *feel* his pleasure.

In the way his fingers alternated between almost gentle caresses and decidedly forceful possession. In the way he brought their bodies even closer together—a feat she hadn't thought possible—rock hardness rubbing through their clothes. In the way he anticipated everywhere that she burned and his hands, his lips, his tongue, his teeth, soothed and inflamed more.

His lips trailed hungrily down her throat, her collarbone, her chest, catching the edge of a partially bared breast—her unconscious arch and their movements baring it farther.

She wanted to complete the need. The need that burned deep within her.

"Behind the bench is a lovely little spot where no one might spot us," he said. She gasped as he unearthed the tip of her breast from beneath the fabric. "And, what is a torrid little affair without some grass stains?"

His low laugh and words, brought her head suddenly back up, and she saw his teeth catch the moonlight in a somewhat feral gesture. "Give the *ton* a right shock. Perfect Charlotte caught with her skirts above her head." He nipped her skin at her jerking reaction to his words, his hand traveling south. "Perfectly delicious."

The words unnerved her, and he knew it. She could read it in his face. He most often said things designed to make her melt, but occasionally, as his previous remarks served, he injected comments designed to put her on edge.

"The thought of simply overwhelming you here"—his fingers somehow worked beneath the layers as if the fabric had ceased to exist—"and giving you what you need"—the hand around the back of her neck forced her to meet his eyes, lips parted, as one finger dipped inside, slowly crooking, with her unable to look away, unable to breathe—"finally taking what I want"—he stroked her and she felt as if the humidity of summer had come early and was everywhere, inside and out—"is consuming."

She felt consumed already. Whatever he was doing to her was making her body respond in sluggish, writhing ways.

He brushed something inside her, and she let out a strangled breath. And she could see everything in his heated ice blue eyes suddenly so close to hers. The satisfaction. The hunger. The possession. "Leave your window open tonight," he whispered against her lips.

And his lips took hers, in an oddly gentle brush, a fleeting touch, before he whipped her around, her dress flying out into a circle. She found herself sitting alone on the bench, the stone warmer than it had been before, but still a shock to her system after being pressed against his heat. The embers still sparked.

She heard the footsteps only a second before Miranda and Downing rounded the corner.

She frantically reached for the bodice of her dress, but everything was in place. And Roman Merrick was nowhere to be seen.

A fiercely wild anger took hold of her as her body tried to gain back its cold equilibrium.

"Charlotte?"

"I am back here," she called, thankful for the dark path and the shadows. Thankful for the cool calmness that she could use as a mask. That she could drape over her shoulders, over her emotions to stop them from consuming her. For the anger seemed to be directed against him for leaving her like this, and the thought terrified her that she might have preferred that he finish what he'd started, even with certain discovery.

"Oh, thank goodness. When you weren't at the statue, I thought perhaps you had decided to leave us. Are you ready to return?"

She couldn't see Miranda's face yet, but she could hear the happiness in her voice, the gratitude that Charlotte had let them have a moment alone, the apology that they had caused her to feel the need to do so. Guilt joined the flurry of emotion within Charlotte, but she was already drowned in the frenzy.

An affair.

A relationship that wasn't under the constant threat of a single night of payment. Nor just the teasing edge of fingers in the brush.

"Yes." The word barely emerged. Return? In what state? But he had taken great care to stroke the hair only at her nape—an area she had pinned with an ornate bauble of paste. She quickly detached and reattached the pin, smoothing up the hair beneath as she did so.

She pressed a hand to her chest, willing it to cool, hoping the skin there didn't appear as inflamed as it felt. "I was thinking maybe we should walk to the lake before we head back. See if the others found trouble," she said.

An affair.

Something more *permanent*. Still taking place in the dark of night, in the shadows, but having a different set of rules and consequences.

She could hear Downing mutter something less than kind about his brother's intelligence. The pair came closer, in range for them to finally see her.

"Excellent idea!" Miranda said.

Charlotte thought so. It would be a good five-minute walk in the night, after all. Plenty of time for her skin to cool before she pitched herself into the depths of the liquid for her stupidity. Or figured out a way to drown her erstwhile companion for starting their actions and leaving her heaving on stone.

An affair.

Something that bound him to her, and her to him, for a period of time. Something heady and euphoric. Something that was both in and out of her control.

She wanted him. *Needed* the feelings he produced. Craved them like a starving woman searching for food.

She pulled her lips into her mouth, running her tongue across them as she stood, the taste of him all over them. Experiencing excitement and terror at the swirling thoughts inside of her. Not wishing to think too much about how she was more like her reckless father than she wished.

Chapter 13

Roman paced outside, the wet grass squishing beneath his boots. All of the windows were dark.

"I hope you know what you're doing," One-eyed Bill muttered.

What *was* he doing?

"Of course I do." He stopped and sent a charming grin the man's way. Bill grimaced but looked mollified. When he had first met Bill, that grin would never have worked, but he had spent a lot of time honing it, and Bill had been properly reformed and enlightened since. Always useful to have people who thought you walked on water.

Andreas liked to knock him into the dark depths often enough.

"You are sure that is her window?"

"Saw her through it earlier before she drew the drapes." But Bill looked shifty.

"One-eye, I swear if you have me entering some nitwit maid's quarters, I'll skin you alive."

"No, it's hers," he said quickly.

Roman watched him silently, making Bill shift nervously, until Roman was satisfied it was the truth. Obviously, someone else had grabbed the man's attention. Probably a maid who liked to pose in open windows, hoping to provide a show.

"Fine. Thank you. Go home and get some sleep for once."

Bill scratched his neck. "Well, you see . . ."

Roman narrowed his eyes, and Bill scratched more vigorously.

"What with all of the dealings . . . it's just that . . . well, and the irons . . . and the fire pits . . . and the trouble . . . and this particular consolidation . . ."

Roman motioned with his hand, trying to encourage him to speak faster. He was fond of the man, but his patience was limited at the moment, as close as he was.

"Well, it's a lot of things, yes?" Bill finished, hope and dread in his expression.

"*Things* that happen every day." She was twenty paces away, waiting to be stripped behind those drapes, and Bill wanted to *talk*.

"Well, not quite at this rate of expectancy." Bill nodded encouragingly, in a way that said he was hoping that if he could get Roman to think rationally, he wouldn't have to keep speaking. "Usually we are more circumspect."

Roman gave him another large, charming smile. Anything to get him to leave. "And these past few weeks we've been quick." He patted the man on the shoulder. "Now go home."

Bill shifted. "Well . . . quick . . . yes. . . ."

"Quick. Yes." When Bill stayed where he was, Roman dropped the smile and narrowed his eyes again. "Things are moving *quickly*. And One-eye, I'm not in the mood for discussion," he warned.

"Right. Well, see . . ." He rubbed his neck again. "Well, see . . . Merrick said. . . ."

Knowledge and rage collided together. Bill suddenly looked quite alarmed, hands held in front of him. "Now, Boss—"

"Andreas told you to watch after me?"

"Now, Boss, it's not like that—"

"Do I look twelve, stupid, and virginal?"

"No, it's not like that, but with Cornelius stirring up trouble—"

"If you don't leave right now," Roman kept his voice low, for once not trying to cover the roughness in the syllables, "I will not be responsible for the *trouble* that happens to either of you."

Bill backed away slowly. "Uh, I'll . . . I'll be at the tavern around the corner." The man beat a hasty retreat before Roman could answer.

Roman kept his eyes narrowed as the shadows sucked in the form of the larger man. He took a deep breath when he was sure Bill was gone, and pushed away the darker emotions that whispered that Roman was not thinking straight, that his actions in the past weeks entitled all of those around him to be wary.

But he'd deal with that later. The twist of fate and press of circumstances demanded his attention now.

He turned back to his inspection of the house, more specifically the one window he was most interested in, letting the thought of her push away thoughts of anything else.

The shadowed drape shuddered as if someone had momentarily touched it.

A slow smile curved, pleasure sliding through him as it always did when he thought of her, and he darted through the shadows of the yard and reached for the first branch of the tree, a tree situated perfectly in line with her sill. Like some fate had deliberately planted the gnarled thing there just for his future use.

He swung himself up easily, ascending each branch in turn until he reached the desired one. He crouched low, eyes already well accustomed to the dark, automatically looking for the easiest way in.

A dark swatch at the bottom started a coil curling within him.

The window was cracked.

Beautiful. She had not only left the window unbolted but cracked as well. God, he was going to enjoy this.

His fingers curled under the wooden pane and lifted, sliding it up slowly enough so that he could feel the notches where the wood might stick. Soundlessly raising it.

He reached forward and drew the drape aside with one hand. A snap sounded. Like the cock of a gun. He tensed, knife sliding easily into his other palm.

Then a pinpoint of light flared, enough for him to see the flint in her hand, the candle on the table. Dressed only in a thin nightgown, her hair plaited down her back.

The knife disappeared back into his sleeve, and he smiled as he slipped easily inside.

"Good evening, Charlotte," he murmured, voice as smooth as he had practiced for all of these years. Never quite ridding himself of the echo of the streets, but that was fine. He watched the slight shiver rake her. There was use in that too.

She looked beautiful, standing in the faint golden light. Not so much from the way her physical features melded perfectly together but in the way she was looking at him, her body positioning—half of her leaning toward him, the other half tight and anxious. Wanting and unsure.

He walked a few quick steps toward her before he slowed and stopped, deliberately gazing around the room. What was wrong with him? It was as if he *were* twelve and virginal. Eager and stupid.

He made a show of coolly inspecting her space, a loose smile on his face, kicking himself.

Her bedroom was . . . neat. Tidy. Unsurprising, really, but something made him pause and look again. There were very few personal objects in the space. For a moment he wondered if this *was* a guest room.

His gaze caught on the dressing table. A white king stood regally next to the cheval glass. A sentinel. He walked over and touched the crown, lifting the piece by its little ivory notches.

"An interesting decoration."

She bolted his way—slipping across the floor on bare feet—and snatched it from him, carefully placing it back on the table, squaring it next to the mirror again. Then as if suddenly realizing what she was doing, she crossed her arms, shoulders hunching up for a moment. The most uncertain reaction he had ever seen her make.

She gave a little shiver that seemed to start in her shoulders and vibrate down to her feet, and his hands automatically reached forward and drew up and down her arms to warm her. She tensed at the contact but relaxed as he continued the gentle, though vigorous, massage.

Small amounts of patience paid big dividends with her. He had felt it in his bones the first time he had spoken to her, and the observation had never failed him. Besides, touching her loosened something within him, a coil that he hadn't even been aware of before she'd entered his existence.

He gradually drew her closer until she was pressed against him, his arms wrapped around her. She sighed softly into his shoulder.

With someone else he would say, "Better?" in a roguish way. But the word stuck to the back of his tongue, and he just kept his arms around her instead. The faint golden shadows embracing them.

"I wasn't sure you would come," she said, her voice barely audible.

"No?" The question came out much more seriously than he'd intended.

"I wasn't sure I hadn't simply dreamed the whole thing."

He raised a brow though she couldn't see it.

"Perhaps I'm dreaming now." She gave a lifeless laugh. "I must be since there is a man in my room, and my mother is naught but a floor above and a room over."

He didn't ask after her father. Roman knew where the man spent most nights. Dividing his hours between the tables and his mistress's bed.

"You opened the window," he couldn't help but point out.

He expected a defensive, sarcastic response such as, "You would just have broken in anyway."

But she said nothing before pulling back a space, eyes meeting his in the faint light. "Yes," she whispered.

"Why?" He internally kicked himself for asking. He didn't need an answer to that question, dammit. She was the one who wanted to know why, why, why. He simply coaxed and *took* what he wanted. And here she was on a candlelit tray. Who cared *why*?

"Because I don't want to feel broken. Because . . ." She pulled her lips in, as if remembering the taste of something unforgettable. "Because you make me feel alive. Because . . . because I want you to burn me from the inside again like you so easily do."

Fine. He cared a lot about why, then. And for someone with such an abundance of pride, she delivered raw statements like flowing water gushing from an undammed creek. Handing him pieces of her soul so easily when it was obvious that with others she normally kept a tight grip.

He was rock hard. God, he wanted to crawl right into her and never leave.

He touched her face, tilting her chin, gently slipping his

mouth over hers. She gave a breathy little sigh, reaching up to touch his cheeks, his chin, her lips opening beneath his, allowing him to deepen the contact. He felt like he was drowning.

He pulled back, unnerved.

"I don't know what I'm doing," she whispered, head tilted back, a half-drunk look in her eyes. Not drunk from liquor, though. Her lower body automatically molded to his as she looked up at him. He could feel the heat of her, burning, pressing against him, making him list five different manners of filthy things he could do to her in the next five seconds flat.

Her eyes pinned him, though, and he swallowed, unsettled.

"Me neither," he whispered back, taking her lips in his. Trying to drown the words, the admission. He stepped her back and laid her on the bed, her golden plait coiling like a tether. He lay down next to her, resting his head on one hand and touching the silk rope with the other. "Sad to keep it chained like this."

She swallowed. "I do it every night. It keeps it tamed."

"Oh?" He pulled the end so that it curled across her chest, examining it in the faint candlelight. "I think we should rectify that, don't you?"

He didn't wait for her response but rose to his knees, crouching next to her, and started to unlace the strands. The back of his hand brushed the tip of her breast, and her stomach clenched beneath the thin gown.

He slowly unwound the strands. Separating each section and letting the loosened silk fall to brush her exposed skin—at her neck, her wrists.

He smiled at the increased rise and fall of her chest and leaned down to run his lips along her throat, up the underside of her chin. Her hands were suddenly on his cheeks and she was pulling him up and into a kiss. Demanding. Hot. And this was why she was going to be *his*.

He disengaged himself reluctantly and chuckled in her ear. "You don't want to go slow, Charlotte?" His hand drew down and circled around her backside, fingers wrapping just a bit farther around, the thin material no barrier at all.

He looked back to see her gazing at him, lips pulling into her mouth again, tasting *him*. And the thought that he might *truly* crawl into her and never leave took him. But there was a thread of uncertainty in the depths of her eyes. That damn tendril of guilt coiled once more.

Here he was planning to rob her of her virginity, after all. Something that some considered a badge of honor on the marriage bed. The loss of which happened far more often than the social elders liked to admit, no matter that they themselves had been young once. Young and foolish, thinking that a warm touch meant love or affection. Or simply wanting the experience, desiring the relief.

He batted away the guilt. He'd make it up to Charlotte. Just like with Andreas, he always did.

He lifted her braid once more and continued uncoiling it, pausing only to pull her to a seated position. He straddled her, keeping most of his weight balanced on his knees, but there was enough pressure there for her to feel him. Her arms were back, supporting her, pressing her, lifting breasts against his chest with every breath.

He pulled his fingers through the freed strands, embracing her as he smoothed them down her back, his rougher cheek brushing her smooth one. He reached down and gripped the bottom of her nightgown, slowly inching it upward, making her arch against him, using her hands to balance and prop herself up, making him rise a little with every pressed arch, like she was a mare, and he the rider adjusting her saddle in motion.

The gown came free, and he pulled it up and over her head, using one hand to hold her as it slipped from her raised arms. She didn't meet his eyes as her hands returned to their previous position, propping her up behind. There was no covering herself with her hands, but pride stiffened her back, straightening her posture as she leaned back on her hands. As if waiting for him to say something and setting herself on edge to hear it.

All sorts of things came to mind. *Lovely, glorious, beautiful*—the way she held herself. She met his eyes, and he felt himself clench. The uncertainty was still present in her eyes, of course, but there was also a demand there, that he fulfill her expectation of him, of his challenge to her.

Nothing could make him harder.

But he knew that commenting on the thoughts running through his mind would make her think he was simply describing her beauty, and it would cause her body to tighten further. So instead he leaned forward, and whispered against her ear, "When I am inside of you, and you are wrapped around me, will you try to burn me too, Charlotte?" He stroked a section of her hair, using it to tilt her head back, eyes as fierce as hers. "I hope so."

He pulled the edges of her hair around her shoulders, over her breasts, her chin dropping back to just above her bare chest, the long strands dripping to her waist, falling to the sides of it in a waterfall of gold. The uncertainty in her eyes was gone; only fierce longing remaining.

He smiled, a slow, absolutely satisfied smile. The cat who was about to devour the cream in one delicious lap.

He set about touching her, stroking her, tasting her. Making the longing turn to fire. He knew how to pull out each reaction. His looks, his charm, had ensured that he had had access to the best teachers. And, thankfully, he had always had enough sense to be choosy.

He wondered if Charlotte knew, really knew, what she was getting into. He didn't want one night. Just as he'd threatened, he planned to suck her dry.

Her head tilted and dug into the pillow, her fists clenched in the bedcovers. Glorious. Doing everything to burn her from the inside as she had requested. He wanted her writhing and screaming, and as the thought trickled, he couldn't help himself and circled her with his tongue, pushing at just the right angle. She arched violently, pressing against him, a cry escaping from her lips.

"Shh, shh . . ." He immediately was at her side, lips on hers, drinking in the reactions as he continued to touch her. He should spirit her away—to somewhere where she didn't have to be caged. Why had he thought to have her here first? He hadn't been *thinking* at all, that was the problem.

He should wait. Should stop.

The thought didn't leave him, even as thirty minutes later she was writhing on the covers, hands clenched around his neck, lips clamped to his, making the most deliciously muffled sounds, and soaking wet below, as he slowly pushed into her.

He shuddered, and she paused, midarch. He stroked her hair, murmuring in her ear. Small, unintelligible noises. She felt like liquid fire around him. And he wanted to slide slowly within her over and over—to make it last forever. Then to take her wildly, savagely—to shake the very foundations of the house with it.

Shit, what *was* he doing? He paused, completely unnerved again.

He hesitated long enough that she pulled back and met his eyes, head pressed to the pillow. Then she smiled, a beautiful smile, and her fingers dug into his nape, and he completed the motion, pushing deep inside, closing his eyes and feeling the wonder of it. Of being inside her.

She clenched around him automatically, pushing her body up for more, the motions innate. Exactly the reactions he had carefully sown. Exactly the promise he had observed in the shopkeeper's back room. Observed even before that, in every memory he had of her.

Wild and wanting. On the edge of losing and taking control.

"It feels . . . I feel . . ." She lifted her hips, allowing him to slide deeper, and another shudder wracked him. "Wonderful."

In his experience, men who caused actual pain for women—mature women, at least, even if it was their first time—had no idea what they were doing. And men who relieved immature women of their virginity didn't survive long in his world. He had a special way of punishing them.

He nipped her throat, pleased beyond measure once more at the things that emerged from her beautiful lips. Ecstatic that he was here, with her, like this. Slightly disbelieving, even with all of his overly grown arrogance, that he was here, with her, like this. "Good."

And with all the confidence and skill that he possessed, hiding the other, more troubling, feelings below, he made sure that the sensations built within her, that she was flying long and high and out of control as he pushed her over the edge, convulsing around him, easily taking him with her as he watched her face, caught her cries.

He buried his face in her neck, shuddering, hiding his face for a moment until he regained control. Then he rolled to the side, taking her with him and watching as she stretched over him, smiling. Her face was soft—softer and gentler than he had witnessed before. A light in her eyes that made his spent body twitch to a semblance of life again.

A look that caused the coil to burn and strange uncertainties to rise.

He stroked her hair without looking away, a gentle embrace in the wild storm that was suddenly raging through him.

Trying to convince himself that he didn't know the meaning of fear. That nothing in the situation suddenly scared the blood out of him.

Chapter 14

"**Y**ou are actually going tonight?"

Roman hummed lightly and put his feet up on the empty faro table that had just been cleaned. Andreas would never be fooled, but there were others in the gaming room, and even if they were cleaning staff or direct reports, appearances had to be maintained. Even if Andreas was angry enough to discuss this outside of their private rooms.

"I can hardly decline, Andreas."

His brother gave him a dark look and snapped an order to one of the boys moving chairs. The boy violently straightened, then rushed from the room to complete the request.

"You are abusing the staff again," Roman said lightly, rolling a pair of dice between his palms. "Besides, you should join me. Give those vultures a right shock."

Andreas narrowed his eyes. He ground a finger into the newsprint. "Did you read the *other* column?"

Roman glanced casually at the paper tossed his way. There were many things in today's paper for them to discuss, but he knew to which Andreas referred. It was the smaller of their problems, in Roman's estimation. A slim reference as opposed to the glaring two-headed vulture on the third page that involved Andreas. "So?"

"I thought you said you had the situation in hand?"

"I do."

Andreas's fingers curled around the back of the chair behind which he was standing. Roman wondered if the wood would hold. They had plenty of other chairs, if not. "Trant is drafting legislation against us."

"It's a rumor."

"It's a *fact*."

Roman laughed unpleasantly. "It's a *threat*. He won't say a word—or do a thing—as long as they marry at the end of the summer. And they undoubtedly will." He rolled the dice in his palm, bones suddenly cracking against bones.

"And you can't *wait* until then?" his brother hissed.

Roman thought of *that* night, in her bedroom, and the three weeks' worth of nights since. Heated liquid gold. "No," he said simply.

"I'm trying to understand."

Roman tipped his head. "There isn't anything to understand." He smiled his charming smile, but his eyes didn't obey. "My actions lack sense."

Andreas hated things that didn't fit into his cold, rational world. Anyone else admitting such things to him would have been derided, banished, or worse. "And what will you do if it becomes more than a *threat*?"

"I have contingencies in place. Trant will prove himself beyond stupid if he doesn't take what is offered. *You know I have taken care of it.* You are acting like a hen."

Andreas's eyes narrowed to slits. "Lately, edge players have been shifting far too rapidly in both arenas for me to feel anything but snappish." He threw the paper away from him. "Not that you would have taken notice."

Roman surveyed his brother. "Especially peevish today, aren't we? I've dispatched cleaners to take care of the edges." He took in Andreas's tightened shoulders, his skin fairly humming with tension. "But you know this too. What has really lodged up your ass?"

"Cornelius doesn't just court the night edges. Whispers point to someone with power backing him. He will move swiftly—"

"And I'll take care of him, when he does," Roman said coldly. He thought of the man who threatened their empire. Who was trying to buy pieces, planting seeds against them—seeds that Roman had helped to water lately with his actions. But Cornelius was just a man—flesh, blood, and bone—who wanted to improve his own slice of the pie. And men could be dealt with.

Andreas pinned him with a dark look. "You go after Cornelius by yourself, and I'll cut off your ballocks with my own knife."

"That hardly sounds pleasant."

"Cornelius doesn't do his own dirty work. And he doesn't hire just one person to complete his tasks."

And neither does anyone of my flesh and blood, was left unsaid. For Andreas would never speak such a thing.

"I've never considered *either* man stupid," Roman said, affecting a light tone and pretending to ignore the tightening of Andreas's shoulders. "I'd like to think I am not either. I know Cornelius as well as you do, so why are you repeating things to me as if I am unaware of the dangers?"

"Because lately you don't seem to acknowledge the danger." And it was as if every emotion in Andreas was pushed into the statement. "You go out willy-nilly, as if you are a forgettable yardsman courting a barmaid. *You aren't.* You don't pay attention to your own safety when she is near. Have you considered what would happen if you were attacked on one of your outings?"

"Yes," Roman replied, watching his brother, trying not

to let his own tension show. Unwilling to admit that he *had* forgotten himself at times in the past few weeks. That if he were killed in the next few weeks, it would assuredly be near her. At her feet, in her bed. Inside of her.

Unfortunately, that last thought just made him think that if he had to choose his final moments, being inside Charlotte would really be the way to go.

"We deal with these issues all the time. For more years than I can count." He motioned to Andreas. "Math is your strong suit."

Andreas rarely appreciated his jokes when he was angry, and the telltale tick in his forehead said that this time was no different. And when that tick appeared, most people ran—smartly—fast and far.

But Roman knew what fueled the anger. Andreas had never handled concern well. And since there were very few people in the world Andreas felt concern for, the emotion always bubbled fiercely when it showed—and Andreas tended to get downright vindictive when faced with the recoil of his own feelings.

One-eye was sure to be permanently assigned to "watching" Roman. Not that the man let him out of his sight for long in any case.

But there was something more to Andreas's reaction— something new—someone had gotten under his skin. Someone besides Roman. Or Andreas's long-disregarded and hated birth family. Roman rubbed his free fingers along his jaw. He *had* been spending too much time away not to know the answer immediately.

Andreas motioned at the paper. "And this other person spreading *rumors*?"

"Probably some frigid, jealous bird. There are plenty."

"Why don't you seek out one of them then," Andreas said darkly.

Roman laughed without amusement and threw the dice onto the table. He saw one of the boys eye them from across the room where he was cleaning the hazard tables. But none of them would dare to breach the space near the brothers without explicit permission. "Because there is a fine web forming. And much profit to be made, besides. Bills in Parliament to thwart, bills to *pass,* lords to form, hands to gild . . ."

Trant to make into a fierce ally. So fierce that he wouldn't pay the least attention to Roman taking his wife after dark.

"You will be recognized if you go tonight. And you won't be able to keep your hands from her," Andreas snarled.

Roman simply smiled. "Someday. Someday, my friend. My brother."

"Never."

Roman arched a brow at Andreas's absolute certainty. Someday his brother would fall hard for a girl and wouldn't have the first notion as to how to deal with his emotions.

He eyed the table. The paper. Slotting something into place as he eyed one of the headlines. Roman removed his feet from the table and picked up the discarded pages. "Mmmm . . . yes, the papers are full of interesting tidbits today, aren't they? That show at the Claremont is sold out. But I know someone with tickets, if you wanted to see it . . . again," he said nonchalantly.

Andreas stiffened abruptly while rising, then turned on his heel and strode furiously from the room.

Roman laughed softly. He'd have a good time with that later—seeing if he could get his stuffy brother to admit anything—but his laughter disappeared as he read the underlying print of his own situation. A tendril of suspicion about Charlotte Chatsworth's purity.

Spiteful speculation fed to the ravenous horde. They

couldn't suspect the truth of the matter. There was no one who knew—about the "fake" night or the real nights since—who would tell. His eyes narrowed. Unless Chatsworth let it slip while in a drunken stupor. But, no, the bet was a secret the man would guard with his life.

Roman dealt with life and death far too often to let things upset him for too long or too deeply. Else he'd turn into Andreas and feel the need to brood endlessly.

Still, there was something about the current situation that he couldn't laugh off. Any show of humor was simply a mask for the darker feelings he drowned, that he didn't want to contemplate. Couldn't.

Some thoughts unavoidably cropped up, though. Actions he undertook with Charlotte would be filled with peril forever. There were certain levels of ruination that neither Trant, or Downing—or the minister or the king or any of the men Roman could influence—would be able to clean up. There was something overwhelmingly enticing about thinking of Charlotte Chatsworth unmarried and completely available, free of society's strictures.

But Charlotte needed society. Even though she might be stressed and anxious in its confines now, society was where she wanted to succeed, dominate, and be happy.

Besides, once she found her place, he could pull her into his lair at will while the rest of society was asleep. And keep her there until she was marked beneath all those layers, and any rings, as his.

Such thoughts were likely what made poor fools marry in the first place. He smiled darkly. Good thing he wasn't the marrying kind.

He looked at the paper again, not wanting to examine the darkness shifting below his thoughts.

Someone was trying to play with his web, and he was going to find out who.

* * *

Charlotte swallowed and looked around the masquerade for what felt like the hundredth time. If he was going to find her tonight as promised, this event would prove irresistible.

It was the gala event of the night, of the week. Some even said of the season. Invitations were always arranged around the Hannings' masked ball. It was an event where things *happened*. Some of the resulting scandals were reported immediately, and some never realized for years.

It was an event where some guests avidly watched and others enthusiastically performed.

She knew Roman meant to find her here. Commoners could secure invitations, especially powerful commoners. The Hannings liked to spice up the guest list in inconceivable ways. Some of their own servants had been known to attend in costume. The uncertainty made the whole atmosphere exciting. And for the *ton,* that made it intoxicating.

She felt the scorch of Bethany's glare. The woman had been attached to her for the past few weeks. As if she could smell the heady scent of Charlotte's doom and needed to discover the place from where it emanated.

And there was a strange feeling surrounding Charlotte. Since the veiled innuendos about her had begun to appear in print, she was on display in a much more dramatic, open way. More men sought her attention—in a far different manner than they had before. One of the more rakish men, John Clark, had been eyeing her from the sidelines, *stalking* her for the past hour. When Roman watched her, thrills coursed through her, whereas Clark's seductive glances made her feel . . . strangely amused and uncomfortable. The more flattery and attention Clark gave, the more he looked like a boy trying on his father's clothes.

Still, the fact that he *was* paying her attention made her nervous. Clark had more social power than the average charmer and could get away with faster behavior. Could catch her somewhere she didn't wish to be caught.

She was sure that Bethany was behind the latest rumors about her fading looks and innocence. Rumors that carried a kernel of truth. Rumors that Bethany hadn't been able to spread before because they lacked believability—the atmosphere all wrong for them. In the past, Bethany would have appeared as a jealous little pest.

But now . . . now it seemed as if Bethany was at the *forefront* of the gossip. Little things added up quickly in the gossip mill. Disappearances. Early departures. Late arrivals. Flushed cheeks. Lingering too long in the retiring room. Whereas in the past, Charlotte had been coldly poised, strictly observing the matron's "rules," now she was skirting them, cutting a corner here, an edge there.

Just enough to allow the tenterhooks of gossip to grab hold.

And she knew she was acting recklessly. But it didn't seem to *matter.* Even as she thought about it logically, she didn't *care.* All rationality had left her. All she wanted was to be with him. To have him inside her. To make him laugh. To experience the joy. Filling the cavity. Making her feel alive.

She felt her flesh heat just thinking about it. God, is this what being in love felt like? It must. Yet she couldn't be in love. She simply *needed* him. As if he had cast a spell on her, chaining her to his dark table for eating a handful of mouthwatering pomegranate seeds. Staring at the remaining seeds and surreptitiously sliding them across the table and into her mouth as well.

Surreptitiously? No, she wouldn't lie to herself. She had boldly and enthusiastically raked them across, then lay beneath, mouth open, to let them fall, juicy and ripe, onto her tongue.

Smeared them across her throat and breasts. There was so much *juice* from such small seeds.

"A dance, my dear?"

She jerked to see Mr. Trant standing before her. She tried to pull herself together as he bowed over her hand. "Mr. Trant." But her voice was entirely too smoky.

She saw heightened awareness in his eyes. He examined her and smiled, but there was tightness to his expression. As if he were both pleased and displeased by the same observed attribute.

"Miss Chatsworth." He inclined his head, and she lifted her chin, pulling the cool mantle to her, letting him lead her to the floor.

Trant was a perfect partner. He danced well and maintained complete control. She remembered her first season, when he had claimed her for a dance. She had thought him charming and smooth, amusing and fun. And since he hadn't been a contender for her hand, their exchanges had been easy and relaxed.

Circumstances on both sides had changed, though, and he had become increasingly political.

"Are you enjoying the night?" he asked, his body perfectly precise as he led them through the steps.

"The Hannings' masquerade is always entertaining."

"Yes. Though one must maintain awareness at such gatherings."

She wondered what Trant thought of the whispered rumors surrounding her, for he still seemed set on his suit.

"One must always keep caution in mind."

Especially when capable hands wanted to smear the crimson juices farther below. Marking her inside as well as out.

Stop thinking of him.

"I invite you to spend the evening near me. I will make sure you are in full view of the assembly."

"That is a very generous offer, Mr. Trant." Her sleeve brushed the sleeve of another woman, Trant turning her just when they might collide. But, of course, he wouldn't make such a mistake. "I will give it serious consideration."

She noticed John Clark watching from the edge of the floor, and again something uneasy slid through her. The rakes had sniffed an opening. They wanted to see if the whispers were true.

She *should* stay near Trant. Or near Mother.

She caught a flash of blond hair curling above a mask, making her breath catch. But the color was too strawlike. Not rich, spun gold.

Her pulse beat uncomfortably fast. Her stomach clenching the muscles below.

Don't show.

She had been looking forward to seeing Roman, but suddenly, everything in her clenched in dread.

"I spoke with your father earlier," Trant said.

His eyes examined her, as if he knew something, or suspected, but couldn't yet be sure.

Don't show.

"I hope you found him well." She tilted her head as they twirled.

"He was more amenable in nature than I usually find him."

She swallowed, keeping the cool smile about her lips. Reading into his statement easily.

Don't show.

Roman could simply crawl through her window later . . . yes, *please*. For here, where two worlds were able to collide, just like at Vauxhall, he was at his most dangerous to her real life.

And with John Clark prowling the edges like a wolf sensing an unguarded chicken in the coop, she needed to secure the gate.

She stuck close to Trant, dealing with his marital insinuations and probing questions, not separating from him until an hour later—the need for breathing room finally overtaking firm caution.

Emotion always led her to trouble. Diabolical feelings had crept beneath her cold mask weeks ago, whispering, and now she seemed unable to rid herself of them.

Whispering of want. Trying to overcome the very real barriers she needed to maintain.

Her mother. She needed her mother—a natural repellant to anything remotely liberated. She walked a clear path to her destination, purpose in her movements, an attempt to dissuade any predators lurking at the edges.

"Merrick hardly cares," a voice hissed, only audible because of a sudden musical pause.

Her feet slowed.

"How much do you owe?"

Three men stood, heads bowed together, a large double pillar behind them with a plant between.

Keep moving! Do not stop!

Her fingers disobeyed, and her fan slipped to the floor. She bent to retrieve it, ducking into the area on the other side of the pillars. Pressing against one, listening.

Foolish girl.

"Forty."

One of the men whistled.

"A thousand at the races, a thousand at faro, a thousand to my tailor. All spread here and there. You have the same liabilities." The man's voice was harsh, pride stung.

"I don't owe one man forty thousand pounds."

"He consolidated my damn debts. *Every single one.*"

"Well, old boy, I have to say, you left yourself open for it."

"I did no such thing."

"Shouldn't have dabbled there. I told you so that night."

Smack.

She jerked as the wooden pillar she was standing behind—a pure decoration along with the dozen others in the room—shook at the smack of the man's hand.

"*She had it coming.*"

"And now *you* do."

"I need you to help me, not treat me like a child."

"I don't have twenty, no less forty, mate. Besides, bad business to get involved."

"Do you know what they *do* to people who don't pay?"

"Ask your brother to help."

"He'd rather serve me up to them himself."

"Beg then. Only way around it. He can put the matter before Parliament. Heard whispers from others. Wanting to do something about them. Wanting to see them ruined. Or . . . have something else happen to them."

"Shut your trap," the third voice hissed. "Do you have a death wish? You don't know who might be listening."

There was some grumbling, and some nervous stuttering, and the men moved away.

She swallowed. How she had avoided hearing all about the Merricks before, she didn't know, as the least mention was a shout to her ears now.

She wondered what the men had meant about Parliament and ruin. About *something else* happening to the Merricks.

The air at her side stirred, drifting across her bare shoulder. She stiffened.

"Hear anything interesting lately?" A staccato-edged melody.

Thoughts of newly interested rakes or political gossip or something decidedly more deadly retreated under the onslaught of twining emotions. No one in the *ton* possessed such a voice. That street accent lurking in the syllables beneath.

With her back still pressed to the pillar, she turned her head to see Death—or surely the visage of such—leaning against the pillar next to hers, only a few feet away, separated only by the fans of a fern. His head tilted back, just enough so she could see perfect lips smirking beneath a full-hooded cloak.

"No."

His mouth curved, though his eyes were lost to shadow. She had a feeling he had been standing there for far longer than she wanted to admit. She had become much more observant since he had entered her life, and she always seemed aware of him, but perhaps only when he *wanted* her to be.

"You look beautiful clothed in white, golden hair knotted and curling over your shoulder. Some kind of Greek goddess?"

"Some kind." She looked him over, tension and dread slipping beneath the pleasure that always rose up to override everything else when he was near. Happiness that he *had* shown and was next to her. "So, Death? Aren't you missing a few accessories?"

"They took my weapon at the door. Said they didn't want any 'accidents.'" He easily closed the gap between them. Touching the small knife at her waist. "How did you manage to keep yours? Dainty, yet strong enough that you could unman someone if you stuck it just so." He made a motion to an unmistakable spot on a man. "No one thinks you a threat?"

"Their mistake." She tossed her head and smiled. Easy banter that she had been unable to let loose with anyone other than her sister and Miranda, until this man had stormed into her life.

"And you? Come collecting?" she asked lightly, as he leaned down and into her. Their banter nearly as intoxicating to her as their physical actions. She loved flirting with this man.

"On a mission for souls." His lips brushed her ear, his hood brushed her hair. "Don't worry, Charlotte, I will take gentle care of yours."

They were out of view of the traffic lanes. And for a long moment she wished everyone else beyond the pillars would disappear, cease to exist.

"I wasn't sure you'd come," she said, her voice so low as to be a whisper. Conflicting desires battled each other—fear that he had arrived, pure bliss that he stood in front of her.

"I have an invitation." He languidly tapped his chest and stepped back, leaning against the pillar next to her, a proper distance in the event that anyone came upon them. "Do I need to check you for yours?" His mouth jerked wickedly beneath the hood. "Search you for it?"

She rubbed her bared arms, wary thoughts overriding the others for a moment. "Actually, the night has an ill feel to it." Danger and unease. She watched him for a reaction but couldn't see anything but his lips beneath the dark hood. "Perhaps, perhaps we can meet later. I . . . I'll come to you?"

"Will you?" There was something strange about the way he said it. Something she couldn't discern.

Her mouth opened without her consent. "I can't see your eyes." She reached up to push his hood back, and her thumbs brushed his cheeks. He stilled, and she froze as well. Sometimes she said and did the most absurd things when near him.

Especially because if anyone stepped around the closed-off space, they'd be able to see him. But *she* needed to see him, had to know what he was thinking.

She pushed the hood fully back.

A dark mask circled his temples. Black ovals rimming clear, light blue. Golden hair curling about his crown, falling to brush the mask. Straight nose and full lips beneath. Not a haughty, patrician face. Not the hawkish or mousy features of many of the men in her sphere. But straight, hard lines dipping into sensual curves, over and over again around his face and body.

"Better?" His voice sounded amused, but there was something shuttered in his eyes, as if he didn't quite know how to respond—wasn't sure what she wanted from him.

She pulled his hood up so that it covered his hair although she could still see his expression, his eyes.

A waltz started up, heavy and pulling.

He smiled flirtatiously, as if trying to dispel the haze. "Is this where I ask you to dance then?"

She blinked. "You can't dance with me."

"I assure you, I know the steps." He looked amused, but again it was as if he was using the emotion to push at a barrier.

"No, I mean, people will notice us."

There was something dark and completely visible in his eyes before it cleared, and only amusement remained. "You think someone will peer under my hood? See if there is a face beneath?"

She wanted the banter. She wanted *him*. But the wariness that had been creeping upon her had sunk in its claws. Rational thought, which had been far too long missing, pushed through. "No, but even if it takes weeks, it is a game for the *ton* to identify those beneath the disguises. Rarely does anyone remain anonymous for long." She threw a hand to his costume. "All it takes is for someone to bribe the butler who read your invitation."

He smiled lazily and fished a paper from the dark cloak. "Would it do your reputation ill to be seen dancing with"—his eyes dropped to the vellum—"Mr. Reginald Barton then?"

Her lips parted, then pressed together. "You stole his invitation."

"*Borrowed. Borrowed,* Charlotte." The lazy smile was still about his lips, but there was something tight in his eyes. "I have my own invitation, but I knew you wouldn't want to be seen with me."

"That's . . . that's not it." Pride stiffened her spine. She wasn't a snob.

"I can dance with a maid and one or two of the courtesans as well, if you'd like. People who we can be assured will keep their silence if any of them figures out who I am. Women of my kind." He flashed a smile. She couldn't smile back though.

"Come Charlotte, you're not *frightened,* are you?"

Her stiff pride told her to respond in the negative. "A little, yes."

He bowed low over her hand, his hood swinging back down to cover him completely from her view as his lips lingered on her clothed knuckles. "Don't be. I will take care of things."

And she wanted to believe him. *Did* believe him. That was the problem. That was always the problem.

"Come, my Charlotte." Death tugged her from the

shadows and into the moving bodies. "I can play nice."

And, indeed, he did seem to know all of the proper steps for the waltz, smoothly leading. Though there was something a little too *earthy,* a little too sensual to his movements. It made her heart beat faster. Leading her in a three-beat rhythm that far too closely mimicked *thrust, pause, release.*

"I told you I can play nice," he whispered far too close to her ear, his body automatically pulling hers toward his, closer than was deemed acceptable.

"I hardly think your mauling is *nice.*" She felt hot, out of control, not nice.

He smiled, but he did increase the space between them. It simply made her body strain toward his, like magnets too near to each other.

"How is that, oh prudish one?"

Fantastic. Wonderful. Never let me go.

"Adequate. Where did you learn to dance?" she asked.

"Ratcliff Highway."

"Very amusing."

"You'd be amazed at what you can pick up in the rookery," he said casually, his voice picking up a stronger cadence for a second, chopping and slurring the last words.

She watched him steadily through her mask. He looked every bit as relaxed as he usually did, but there was a slight tightening of the dancing turns, no pause in evidence for a few steps. *Thrust, break, pull.*

And then he was twirling her about again as if nothing had happened, the intimate dance regained. *Thrust, pause, release.*

"I never realized Death was so fleet of foot."

"The fleetest. Always dancing in the shadows."

"Always waiting for his next partner?"

"Dancing through a long list until he finds the perfect one." His voice was like the drink he always kept stocked—hot and strong, invigorating and calming at the same time.

She wanted to see his eyes. So badly in that moment that she literally yearned for it.

He twirled her. "You spent quite a long time with Trant. I wasn't sure you'd ever separate."

She dipped her head to hide her pleased expression at his tone and looked at him again with a calm gaze.

"One would think you jealous, *Mister Barton*."

His teeth flashed, and the hand gripping hers stretched, thumb curving along the inside of her wrist and stroking there. "Terribly jealous. Beastly."

"You have no reason to be." Her voice hitched.

A finger stroked a long, deep line. They were in the middle of the floor, dear God, and he was touching her familiarly. "That is good to know. I didn't realize you had accepted the inevitable."

She couldn't help asking the question, her body demanding things her mind was screaming no to. "What is the inevitable?"

He leaned down, pulling out the pause of the rhythm half a beat too long, the rhythm pulling back against them. "That you are mine."

She had no idea if there were other people near them, if her sleeve was brushing someone else's, if they were narrowly avoiding collision after collision, if he had swept her off the floor completely, and they were someplace else. Because her entire focus was on him. She couldn't see anything past him. Anything to the left or the right.

Dangerous. Deadly. Literally. Figuratively. In every way.

"As much as it tickles me to be out here, dancing with their princess underneath their noses, I'd rather have that princess naked and writhing beneath me."

Her traitorous body continued to respond, giving an affirmative reply to his words.

His hand tightened upon her back. "In fact, there is a perfect little room beyond the retiring rooms, around the corner, three back on the left. A perfect place to despoil a goddess."

Her body leaned across the space separating them, then pulled back sharply, to keep the distance between them, even as the words curled and made her body respond.

She had to remember where the *devil* she was.

She looked into his shadowed hood. Perhaps not so much Death in front of her as something far darker.

"No."

"No?" A wicked smile crossed his face, visible beneath the edge of his hood. The music came to a close, and she wondered if he would release her. Or if he would continue to hold her on the floor and never let her go. He bowed over her hand. "I have a feeling that you will find the way."

He disappeared into the crowd.

"Who was that, my dear?"

Charlotte started as Trant moved into her view. When she was near Roman, everything else became a blur. Here, where he could mingle with others, he was deadly to her. Death waiting to snuff her reputation. Her position. Emily's future.

"I believe that was quite possibly the Hannings' main footman. Though he'd have me believe he is the King." She moved to the edge of the floor in measured strides.

"Perhaps I should speak with him?"

Charlotte shrugged. "If you'd like. He is probably over yonder." She waved negligently toward the crush of people near the terrace doors.

Trant watched her, weighing her words against her cool expression. She watched him calmly, blood racing inside.

"Perhaps you'd care to dance again, Miss Chatsworth?"

She *wanted* to be around the corner from the retiring room, three doors back on the left.

"Of course."

Trant danced more closely to her this time. Though he strained away too—the edge of his movements showing two different desires.

All the while, her body leaned toward a back room.

As they turned, she saw her mother, Marquess Binchley, John Clark, Bethany Case, and any number of anonymous young women in pink or white. Women in red and gold.

Married women standing entirely too close to men who were not their husbands. Married men dancing attendance on women of the same. The way of her world. Political and social matches with little emotion involved. Entirely acceptable for her in a few years' time, as long as she was discreet.

Then she thought of Miranda and Downing . . . the perfect pair, never needing to play that game, always having each other. A real marriage.

She pushed the thoughts roughly aside. Not for her. Never for her. Her father had made sure of that. She could only grasp the hope of the *future*.

As long as she was discreet . . .

As long as she didn't get caught red-handed. For even she, as an unmarried woman, knew the identities and pairings of many of the married women and men who had relationships on the sly. Open secrets. Acceptable as long as one was circumspect.

Though . . . though it might never be acceptable with Roman. Not in this arena. She would still need to keep a relationship with him secret.

Would still have to end things with him upon marriage, hoping that in a few years . . .

She swallowed, responding automatically to Trant's queries and comments, while keeping the space between them set and firm.

As soon as she was able, she slipped away, not able to stand it another minute. Knowing what awaited her in the back.

Pleasure and doom.

There were women coming out of the retiring room, so she coolly smiled and entered, then waited a moment and walked out, anticipating that she might have to repeat the actions if guests were in the hall. But the hall was blessedly empty. A strike of fortune. She quickly walked forward and turned the curve.

There was a small alcove ahead, but this hall was far more likely to be empty, and anyone who would be in the alcove would have had to have been waiting. Only Bethany—or Trant—would have such foresight, and Charlotte had just seen both in the ballroom.

She looked over her shoulder. The hall was still clear. She touched the handle to the third door on the left, fingers shaking slightly, as they always did when she slipped away. Waiting for someone to jump out. Waiting for the inevitable to happen.

The handle turned, and she pushed the door ajar, walking inside. The door closed behind her, and a lock slid into place.

A warm body pressed her against the wall, warm hands pulling her head and mouth to his. Eyes unadjusted to the dark, all she could do was feel him.

"A small detour with Trant?" he whispered against her lips.

She wondered how long Roman had waited in the ballroom and where he had been standing.

"He asked me to dance again. He wanted to know who you were."

"The death of him." Roman's hand lifted her dress, his fingers slowly touched her. She could make out the curve of his lips, obviously pleased at what he discovered. "I wonder what he would do were I to muss you beyond all recall? Sending you back out with red cheeks, crimson lips, flushed chest. Gloriously debauched."

"He would likely expire." Her breath hitched as he touched her perfectly, repeatedly, exactly as he had mastered weeks ago. "One moment before I did."

"Then I could sweep you away," he whispered in her ear. "Never let you go."

She said nothing, letting the thought of it wash over her, burning her, making her arch against him, his hand moving deliciously. The picture they would make if anyone would walk in, a cloaked man with his hand thrust up her white skirt and she arching back against the wall, likely ruining her coiffure, screwing the strands free.

"Do you know what I'm going to do to you, Charlotte?"

"Yes."

How could she not know? She had been living in this fantasyland for weeks now. Weeks since he had come through her window. Nights drenched in revelation and wonder. Relief and tension.

"Do you?" His lips attached to her neck, just for a moment. Her heart beat furiously. She trusted him not to make a mark. *Trusted him far too much.*

"I'm going to press you against this wall. And you aren't going to be able to walk for a week."

She pressed against him as he lifted her, her voice coming out in pants. "Oh?" Her covered breasts slid across his covered chest. He was still fully clothed, but she knew from experience that stopped nothing. Her head hit the wall as he slid into her, suddenly, firmly, roughly, fully.

Yes. Every week. Every night.

"And you are going to know exactly who put that hitch in your step." Pinned to the wall, his hands around her backside, lifting her onto him, beyond strong, using her back and shoulders against the wall as if he would split her in two. A lovely, lovely death.

Why couldn't she have this? Him?

"Me." He pulled out almost entirely and thrust in again—*and, God, she felt like she might die from it*—as he touched something deep inside. Overwhelming heat stole over her entire body.

"Yes." Her hands curled around his neck, and she arched her back a little more, digging her shoulders in, letting him have anything he wanted.

She arched partially out of her gown. The tip of one breast scraped the roughness of his chin. He sucked it between his lips, and she writhed back, pushing down on him, hindering his movement for a second below as she pushed back hard, grinding against him.

"Mine." His eyes were fierce, and he wasn't a restrained man, but there was a core that was protective and almost gentle, beneath it all. Never frightening her with anything but her own feelings for him. He lifted and pulled her down against him again, claiming her, and she felt the lift, the stamping inside her. Not long. The wave raced toward her.

Why couldn't she have him?

"Always." She realized she said it out loud, whispered it. But there was nothing that she could do about the admission as his eyes sharpened. It was infinitesimal, but he paused before his withdrawal, the wave still racing toward her. He didn't say a word, but he pressed slowly into her so deeply that she saw stars and forgot how to breathe. He did it again—a deep, penetrating, slow movement that cracked her world.

And she was breaking apart as he slid along the inside of her, almost gently—if there was such a thing as fiercely gentle—over and over, his hands in her hair, his mouth drinking in her cries.

He held her to him, his forehead pressed against hers. Then he kissed her again, long and lingering. "I should have stolen you later this evening when there would be no need to return you."

"You want to keep me all night?"

"And maybe even into the next." He was still within her, and she couldn't help the clench. His fingers gripped her shoulders.

She looked at him from under lazy lids as they disentangled themselves and righted their clothes. "I think people might notice my absence. I don't think the 'tell Mother I'm going with the Downings' and 'tell the Downings I'm going with Mother' gambit would work tonight."

He smiled as he smoothed down her dress. "I love that maneuver though."

"I know you do," she said wryly, removing a pin from her crown, smoothing her hair, then pinning it back in place.

He took the next one from her, and she let him. He always knew how to put her back together again. "Classic switch. Simple, useful. And easily believed. The two parties hardly exchange greetings, and you've already put the assumption in people's minds that if you aren't with one, you are with the other."

"But dangerous to use too often. I am sure Miranda knows."

"Of course she does," he whispered into her hair. "And that just means that you have her approval."

Dangerous words, winding down to her core.

He tweaked her knife as he straightened the rest of her.

"Jealous?" she asked lightly.

"Of your ability to unman someone who flirts with you? Immensely."

She smiled and pressed a hand against her chest, willing the color down.

"Do you wish me to open a window?" he asked.

"No. I'll just let you amuse me for a moment more."

He backed up to lean against the back of the settee, and she had to withhold the elated smile, the knowledge, that he did so in order to resist his impulses. That he *would* touch her otherwise—like a call he couldn't resist.

"Like a court jester?"

"Like the one in Sam's naughty picture on the wall."

The edge of his mouth lifted. "Why, Charlotte, I'm shocked."

"Are you? Does that mean you won't consider attempting the movements within?" she asked innocently, pleasure running through her at the heat flaring again in his eyes.

"If I had known you wanted to enact that scene, I would have used the bloody desk over there in the manner it should be employed." He pushed back to a standing position. "In fact . . ."

"You think I'll make it easy?" She smiled at him, knowing that her color had receded enough to return to the gathering. She walked backward, disengaged the lock behind her back, and wrapped her hand around the door handle. "The jester pushing up the queen's skirts? You'll have to catch me first."

She turned the handle, peeked into the hall, then ducked out, pulling the handle down as she closed the door.

A small, secret smile curved her lips. He could have caught her if he had wanted. But that he hadn't just made it more exciting for next time. Another experience to look forward to.

She touched the back of her hair, her smile growing. He always knew how to pin it—as if he'd memorized everything about her. She tried to keep her grin from going silly, knowing she'd have to check it in the retiring room, just to make sure. But she always felt she could take on the world after she saw him like this. The euphoria beating through her. Nothing able to touch her.

"Well, well, well," an unwelcome voice said. "Miss Chatsworth . . . using the back rooms."

Chapter 15

Charlotte froze. She hadn't even thought of safety a moment ago, too busy wanting to play. Roman usually scouted exits in advance. But she'd been careless. Caught in the euphoria.

Affairs were hard work. No wonder people were so frequently discovered.

She was about to be ruined. Emily's chances dashed. She had always known the consequences of her actions, yet her emotions had simply bypassed any and all sense.

"So the rumors have it true." John Clark *rolled* around the corner alcove and leaned against the shadowed wall, smiling. "I can't believe my luck."

Charlotte turned to face Clark, left hand still frozen, fingers curling tightly around the metal handle. *Stupid.* Her mind so caught up in Roman that she hadn't *thought*.

She could detect him pressing against the other side of the door, listening. A click away from emerging. Confirming that indeed she had been meeting with someone. Perhaps even going so far as to show Clark exactly who inhabited the other side of Death's mask.

"I don't know of what you speak, Mr. Clark," she said with far more calm then she felt, unwilling to cede anything. "I mistakenly thought this was the retiring room and searched for light before realizing my error." Her hand was still wrapped around the door handle, gripping it like it was the only thing holding her to the cliff.

Clark clucked. "I wouldn't have batted an eyelash to believe that at the beginning of the season. But now . . ." His head tilted. "No. There is something different about you. Not so cold anymore, are you? Someone finally thaw out your skirts?"

The handle moved beneath her hand, bending from the other side, and only force of will kept her gripping it, forcing it back into resting position, tugging the door against its frame.

"I think you have imbibed too many spirits, Mr. Clark. You are making highly inappropriate suggestions."

She could twirl on her heel and return to the ballroom or the retiring room. Roman was more than capable of disappearing should Clark look inside. Or of taking care of himself.

It was the latter that kept her hand wrapped around metal. Trapped, and with her hand upon the proverbial latch, as it were.

"Am I?" Clark's smile grew. "I think we should speak more of my suggestions, Miss Chatsworth." He tilted his head and looked at the door, then dismissed it and whoever might be behind it. "Unless you enjoy the spread of ugly rumors?"

"Blackmail?" She twisted her lips, hand firmly gripping the metal, working more fiercely to keep it in place, with physical strength she hadn't realized she possessed. Of course, perhaps Roman realized that if he used more force to open the door, he would rip her shoulder from the socket. Hopefully he realized that. "How bourgeois."

"Actually, blackmail hearkens back to the best of kings." He walked to within a foot of her.

Her eyes narrowed. And she wondered why she felt all

sorts of distasteful feelings at Clark's threat yet had felt none of them when Roman had initiated his pursuit.

Because she had returned his desire, and Roman had known *it.*

"You won't blackmail me," she said flatly.

He smiled, a very confident look in his eyes, as he reached toward her. "No?"

She wasted no time or thought and with her free hand stuck her small knife directly forward, into the tender space between his thigh and crotch, just as Roman had unknowingly demonstrated earlier. A flick away. Clark froze, smile dropping, not anticipating the action in the least.

"Not if you want to be able to use *it* again," she hissed.

His hands rose slowly in surrender, eyes narrowing. "You will regret this."

"I don't believe I will. And if you spread any rumors, I will make sure that this little scene is repeated to its conclusion."

He backed slowly from the knife, and she felt confident enough, knowing Roman was on the other side of the door, not to panic at the realization that now that surprise was not on her side, Clark could physically overpower her. She had been raised to be a lady, a hostess, with sharp words on her side but with little sense of physical self-preservation.

In Roman's world, she would be little more than a slab of meat on the chopping block.

And in her naïveté and wrapped in her cold persona, she had never been exposed to this type of danger before since she had never posed a challenge to the rakes. They had seen her as a cold fish, a statue on display.

Only recently had she begun to think of *herself* outside those terms. Wild emotion surged at the revelation, but she pressed it back down. She had to remain focused.

"This isn't over," Clark said, dark promises in his eyes

before he walked around her, giving her a wide berth, continuing down the hall, cloak swishing along the floor.

She swallowed, then stumbled forward as the door opened and Roman pulled her inside. He tilted her chin, touched her shoulders and hands, looking her over, as if for injury, as she pressed against the back of the closed door. Again.

Her eyes adjusted more quickly this time, and there was something far darker than Clark could ever claim in the depths of Roman's eyes. A darkness that made her feel safer. She closed her eyes. Breath coming quickly. Heady success mixed with lingering fear.

She'd fought off Clark. Taken care of him herself.

But she'd been *caught*.

Not in some shady tale of her arriving late, but observed with her fingers wrapped around the door of a back room.

The only thing that could have been worse was if Bethany had seen her. Hell, Bethany could have turned the corner at any point and seen her with *Clark*.

"Come."

She opened her eyes to see Roman reaching toward her, eyes still raking her. She automatically put a hand in his, pausing only to wonder why she so often did as he willed without question. His fingers curled around hers, clasping her clammy, though covered, hand in his warmer one.

He pulled her toward a very large portrait of a snowy, austere man that hung in the middle of the wall, and ran a finger down the side, lightly tapping.

"What are you doing?"

"Clark will return any moment with someone he trusts in order to catch you here with a witness."

Fear overtook the dissipating feelings of heady success. "We have to leave."

"Either that or kill Clark."

She opened her mouth. "We . . . we have to leave."

"I thought that would be your choice." He ran a finger along the frame, his voice almost *disappointed.*

"What are you doing?" she said, pulling at him to move toward the door, the window, anything.

He pulled her firmly against his body, his other hand moving along the gold scrolls. Finally, he smiled and pushed.

The entire frame rotated, opening up to a dark space behind. A corridor.

She stared at it in disbelief, then looked at his faint smile.

He raised a brow, obviously amused. "Did you think I would ask you to meet in a room lacking escape?"

"How did you . . . ?"

He lit a nearby candle. "Drunken tongues turn spare and loose when on a winning streak. And people frequently forget that I am far from the person I pretend to be when playing." Her stomach tightened at the words. He stepped over the low wall and lifted her into the corridor, shutting the painting behind, sealing them inside. "And the middle Hanning likes to joke far too often about his uncle Bernard overseeing his liaisons and keeping him from trouble."

Roman's candlelit smile looked almost demonic as he peered down the narrow, dark corridor for a second, holding the light up.

She concentrated on the passageway rather than her ragged nerves. "You, er, you know how to exit this hall, correct?" Being trapped inside a wall and having to pound against the wood to be freed seemed a conspicuous end to a secret liaison.

"I do not." He said it a trifle too cheerfully. "I didn't want to spoil the joy and surprise of figuring it out under pressure. I think it comes out near, or in, the library, though."

She shut her eyes, damning his penchant for risk and her foolishness for always jumping after him with both feet. "Why don't we just wait for Clark and his cronies to enter and exit the room, then go back through?"

"Because they might wait outside the room, and you need to return to the ballroom quickly. Besides, where is your sense of adventure?"

"I left it in the hall when I stuck a knife into John Clark's crotch."

"I think I am jealous."

"I can remedy that," she said darkly.

"Promises, promises." He raised the candle again, looking down the hall. "I'll go first. There are a few cobwebs that will not look best attached to your head."

She pressed her forehead between his shoulder blades and felt him chuckle as they began to move.

The trek was short, but it gave her time for recrimination. She could barely work up relief when he figured out the locking mechanism to the library and cautiously opened it.

He stood silently, listening for a few long moments. "Wait here," he whispered, then slipped out. Moments later, he opened the passage door fully and lifted her into the darkened room.

"*Voilà*, the library."

She leaned against a set of bookcases as he closed the secret panel—a column of leather books that gave a peculiar metallic click as the wood pushed flush.

"I believe the passage continues to the conservatory as well." His fingers ran over the spines at the edge of the case. "We could make Clark and his cronies chase us all over the house, if needed."

She gripped and released a fold of her dress. "I know that for you these meetings are a grand lark," she whispered, the words accompanied only by the sound of his fingers slipping over the leather spines. "But when I am thinking correctly, I feel them as the deepest danger."

His fingers paused, silence permeating the room for a moment before he resumed whatever it was he was doing. "On the contrary, this is one of the most dangerous situations I've ever found myself in."

The placement of the lamp on the table in front of her left her features open for view and his hidden, as always.

She gave a short laugh. "I saw you at the Hunsdens' shop, remember?"

"How could I forget; it was the highlight of my day."

She closed her eyes. Seeing him was always the highlight of her days. *Stupid girl.* "I—I don't think I can do this anymore," she whispered.

She heard a click and opened her eyes to see the bookcase opening again. Dratted man had been discovering how to open the passage from this side. Lovely. Roman gave the wooden panel a firm push, and it clicked flush again with the surrounding panels.

"I beg to differ." He reached over and stroked her cheek, eyes shadowed, but a faint smile about his lips. "You have been doing so, and *well,* might I add, for weeks now."

"We will be caught. I was *just* caught."

"And you dealt with it quite well." The faint candlelight highlighted his lazy mischievousness. He tilted her chin and pressed a roaming kiss to her throat. "Though being near me does put you in danger." Darkness entered his tone.

"That's not it."

"Have you bored of the chase?" he said against her skin.

The light-headed feeling from both the threat of discovery and his presence indicated she was anything but bored, but she didn't trust herself to respond.

He leaned away, backing up a pace. "Do you wish to leave, Charlotte? You came here of your own accord." He indicated the door, then smiled, though it didn't reach his eyes. "Well, it was another door you entered. But the question remains."

The question really was more *why* did she come? Night after night, he called to her—from the gardens, from underneath her window, in her dreams—and she repeatedly flung herself to, and at, him.

Who was this new Charlotte who had taken over completely?

"I hardly know you," she said to herself, whispering.

"No?" He said it lightly, suddenly roaming over to a cabinet in the corner, taking the light with him. "I didn't think you really wanted to."

She blinked at his back. "What?"

With his back to her and the light at his side, she couldn't see his face. "I thought you were perfectly happy in this exchange," he said, fiddling with one of the doors of the tall cabinet. "Exactly as is."

"What exactly is this exchange?" She folded her arms, uncertainty running through her, as it always did when they danced around this subject, trying to define whatever it was they had. For when she wasn't losing herself in carnal bliss, she had to accept that she had a life outside of that bliss. That it was only temporary freedom she found in his arms.

"It is what you want it to be, of course. As it always has been."

Something shifted uncomfortably. For Roman Merrick *took*. Freely and unabashedly admitting to it. It was something she counted on actually. That she simply couldn't resist him and didn't need to. That she didn't need to think on the choice. She could just be . . . Charlotte.

"I was under the impression that it was what *you* wanted it to be," she said stiffly. "You are the one who collects after all."

"Am I?" One of the inlaid glass doors of the cabinet opened beneath his hand, and he tapped the pane with a finger, producing a hollow sound in the silent room. "Do you plan to allow me to collect forever?"

"No, of course not." It was surprisingly hard to say. "And don't make a mockery of me by trying to imply that you would stay well pleased with me for any length of time." Her voice was tight, the admission pulled from her.

The tapping of the glass echoed inside her, the only sound in the room for long moments.

"You are quite the conundrum, Charlotte Chatsworth," he said at last.

She tightened her arms, hugging them uncomfortably to her. She looked to the dark windows of the room. Soulless eyes peering in from the night. "I am hardly a mystery when compared with you."

"But I am quite simple, in fact." He cocked his head toward her, back still turned. "My wants and desires easy to discern."

She stared into the shadows of his profile, waiting for him to laugh at the joke.

"You, on the other hand, don't know what you desire, do you, Charlotte?" He closed the door and turned to lean back against the wooden case. "Do you want the freedom or the cage?"

"I desire freedom, of course." But she also desired it for others. For Emily. Whom she had to protect. Who was affected by her rogue actions. A pawn someone like John Clark could use.

Roman extended his hand and made a casual twisting motion toward his chest. "Freedom comes in many guises, though. And sometimes, that which is within is the hardest to release."

"What . . . ?" She swallowed, unwilling to finish the question. Unwilling to face whatever he might say. Whatever was inside.

"But we—you—have tarried here far too long." He motioned to her, then to the door. "I can't seem to help myself from tarrying with you. Why do you think that might be?"

As usual, something underlying his words pulled her to him. So much so that she had to stop the movement of her body. For his first words were correct. She needed to return to the floor posthaste to make a respectable exit. She should have been out there already to mitigate whatever venom John Clark chose to spread.

Her continued presence in the room, with him, was almost frightening. What was she doing?

"You . . ." She chewed the inside of her cheek, trying to stop the words. "You could find me later, perhaps?"

Damn weakness.

He hummed a little something. He was studying her, she knew it from his positioning, from the feel of his stare, but his eyes were hidden in shadow.

Charlotte waited a moment too long, uncertainty and apprehension running through her. He remained motionless, watching, as if trying to solve the *conundrum,* leaning against the cabinet, pulling deeper shadows to him. She turned when the moment grew to discomfort and walked to the door, peering out, waiting for a threesome of girls to pass before slipping into the hall after them. Not looking back.

He didn't stop her. And she should be happy about that.

She needed to understand this *compulsion* for him and do something to remedy it, to even out her emotions.

The library was a few doors from the retiring room. She bit her lip. Roman always knew what he was doing. Still, Charlotte slipped inside, half-anticipating her appearance to be wild and disorderly now. But she looked perfectly put together. No traces of being pressed and frenzied, of being caught and forced to sneak through a dusty secret passage laced with spiderwebs.

She gathered her courage and exited with a group of women returning to the ballroom; then headed toward her mother as sedately as she could, hiding her emotions behind her strict carriage and mask. She didn't feel any whispers or secretive looks cast her way to indicate John Clark had carried out any of his implied threats.

She also didn't feel the relief of knowing she wasn't ruined yet. And such odd feelings required intense examination, for she had felt such converse emotion ever since she had spent that first night with him. She found her mother quickly and stayed at her side for the remainder of the night. Her mother kept sending suspicious, cool glances her way, but said nothing.

From the lack of immediate whispers, it appeared that Clark intended to find a different way to extort revenge. She had seen him staring at her across the room soon after she had reentered, a glittering look in his eye. Then he had suddenly disappeared, as if the devil had yanked him back to hell.

Off plotting, no doubt. For he didn't have a solid hold on which to pin the rumor. It would be his word against hers, and, at the moment, hers held more weight.

Though that would change in the blink of an eye should she be caught again—especially by a second person. She was going to have to pay even more care in the future.

The future. She found it difficult to breathe as she watched the masked dancers twirl—anonymous friends and lovers finding each other. Silly. But she couldn't bear to think of a future that didn't contain clandestine meetings with him. She tried to stop the threat of tears. One way or another, their affair would come to an abrupt end. *How*, was the only question.

Clark had been easily taken care of. The man hadn't presented even a remote challenge. Boring task really, but for the emotions evoked by what Clark had planned to do to Charlotte. That had made the task . . . less boring.

The night had long since blended into the morning when the chair on the other side of the table scraped against the floor. Roman continued to roll the dice at his two-person table, stretched back with his arm over the back of his chair, watching the pips turn. He hardly needed a card printed with a spade to tell him who currently occupied the other seat.

"Lord Downing."

"A trifle conspicuous in your nightly maneuvers for once, Merrick."

"I hardly feel the need to hide from you, my lord. Or your wife." He spun the dice over to him. "It would be stupid to think you unaware of . . . affairs. As for others, who would hazard the correct guess?"

Downing's expression matched his black attire. "You dance in a deadly game."

"Do I?"

"On a number of fronts, I believe."

"Ah, yes. But it is not those other fronts that concern you."

The viscount studied him. "Your brother will be called to account soon."

Roman kept his muscles from stiffening and shrugged nonchalantly. "Andreas will do as Andreas wills."

"There are those who would make deals for your brother if you were willing to negotiate other things."

"Ah. But I am not willing. I have my pieces already in place, and Andreas well understands my goal." He tipped his head. "Is that all, Lord Downing?"

"I could call in your marker."

A single shovel with which to bury him. Downing had said nothing the night Roman had won Charlotte. But he had known. Had helped Roman cover the cheat in the tense minutes after the hands were revealed. And even now, Roman wondered about Downing's motives.

"Could you now?" Roman smiled. "But then, I don't think you will. I don't think your wife will allow it yet. You will be made to see how things play out, just like everyone else."

"You take unnecessary risks."

He'd go brood with Andreas if he wanted to be chastised. He waved a dismissive hand. "No one knew it was me tonight. For you, it was hardly a deduction to make when you saw an unknown man dancing with her. But who else would even think to link my name with hers?"

"Trant."

"Ah, Trant." Roman smiled. "Interesting thing about Mr. Trant is his ambition. Rules everything in his life."

Downing's expression didn't soften. "You are maneuvering for Trant. Why? It does not seem to be in your best interests."

"When you find what rules a man, you control that man."

"Binchley is easily controlled by drink and his terror of his mother."

"Ah, but intelligence and ambition are difficult to

bestow, whereas offered power is not. Controlling men in power—" He waved his hand. "Is easy. It is simply a matter of finding the right key."

"And what do you think will happen when it becomes obvious to others as to what rules you, Merrick? What your key is?"

Long practice at the tables prevented him from going rigid. "We shall see *if* it occurs, shall we?"

Downing tossed the dice back across the table. "We shall. And perhaps you should reconsider the scope of your actions while waiting for the inevitable. I wouldn't want to join the voices clamoring for your removal. Nor to sign these." He tossed a sheaf of papers—a petition—on the table. "Good evening, Merrick."

Chapter 16

"**H**eadache?" Her mother peered at her dispassionately across the carriage space. "You've been plagued by headaches this season. Interesting, as I don't recall you complaining of the malady in years before."

"Perhaps I have caught your ailment, Mother."

"Mmmm." Viola watched her coolly. "That would be a shame."

Charlotte tried to decipher her mother's expression, for she was suddenly quite sure Viola wasn't speaking of headaches.

"You hardly danced at all," her mother said. "Though there was a very interesting interlude between your dances with Mr. Trant. Who were you dancing with, Charlotte?"

Charlotte wondered how many people had noticed their dance and commented. She pressed two fingers to the bridge of her nose.

"I don't know that I recall, Mother. A footman perhaps. I'm sure someone will suss it out."

She hoped that statement would not prove true.

"Your father will be quite displeased, Charlotte. You may want to rethink your . . . strategy?"

"Yes, Mother."

"Marquess Binchley will be an easily led husband."

Charlotte nodded.

"A woman could do worse than a witless man." The emotions in her mother's caustic voice were pronounced. And there was something almost desperate in her eyes. Strange.

"Yes, Mother." A witless man who would have them as beggared in the future as they were now. One thing about Mr. Trant. Titles be damned, he would never allow himself or his family to be beggared or ruined. His pride and ambition were far too marked.

That didn't mean she wanted to be pledged to him either. At the moment, she wished simply to disappear into the night. Free.

Every time she thought of anything marriage-related, light eyes dark with promise pushed into her thoughts instead. She'd been unable to perform on the marital stage since Vauxhall.

Since Roman, really.

Viola retired quickly after they arrived home, irritation coating her night salutations, leaving Charlotte alone in their front hall.

Charlotte's fingers brushed a bright swath of fabric hidden in the rack of outer garments. Uncovered just for a moment. A smile formed, straight from her heart, washing away her malaise.

She pulled her fingers along the fabric, then walked steadily upstairs, trying to hide her smile. Thinking about what she could do to the intruder while Anna was helping Viola undress.

Charlotte didn't pause on the landing—feeling confident that she wouldn't be attacked on the stairs—but she kept her eyes moving as she walked down the hall to her room.

She opened the door, checking for shadows beneath the bottom edge. She pushed the door back quickly, but it didn't squish a body; nor was anyone waiting in the shadows.

Under the bed was the next best bet. Though she could hardly check in her current state of dress. Still, she'd keep her ankles away. It had taken a fortnight for the throbbing in her throat to ease the last time. She'd never shrieked so hard.

She eyed the wardrobe. It was a tight fit. She would make the gnat regret it if any of her clothes were damaged.

She touched the knob. It gave way too easily. She jumped to the side when a flurry launched from the interior. The gangly body flew through the air, then landed lopsided against the end of the bed with an "ooomph."

Charlotte snickered before lighting a lamp. She turned to see two large, disgruntled, brown eyes.

"It appears that someone has breached my domain." Charlotte groaned, hand to her forehead. "Where, oh where, is my shining knight to save me?"

"You knew I was here. It was supposed to be a surprise!" Her sister's light brown hair stuck up every which way as it was wont to do in the mornings—or when she shoved herself into, say, a wardrobe.

Charlotte held out a hand to help her up. "The whole house brightens when you enter. I can hardly be unaware."

Emily smiled happily, giving her a hug before dusting herself off. "Oh, well that is fine then. I missed you too. And good show, by the way. I thought I had you for sure. How was your night?"

Charlotte pushed down the excitement that spontaneously appeared with any thoughts of *him,* and the anxiety that always lingered, and smiled at the girl she had all but raised while their mother had been in and out of her constant depression. "Fine. But I didn't expect you home until next week."

Had thought she had more time to pretend.

"Tree fell through the south wing. Mrs. Stanwick had to close things down for a few days to get it patched up and decided to extend break for those who wanted to leave early."

Charlotte's chin dropped, temporarily suspending all thoughts of the dripping sands of the hourglass. "A tree fell through the wing?"

"Yes." Emily's lower lip drew between her teeth. "Not sure how that could have occurred."

Charlotte raised a brow but didn't ask. Emily would come clean eventually. "How are things at our fair house of higher learning otherwise? Help me undress while you tell?"

Mrs. Stanwick was the best governess in their county. So highly regarded for her strict propriety that she had been able to take on multiple girls, with parents vying to get their daughters enrolled in her classes.

All the better, for Viola Chatsworth had wanted little to do with her daughters, or anyone else, for that matter.

"School is . . . school is fine." Emily picked at the coverlet, then pulled up a brisk smile as she helped Charlotte. "I bested Margaret Smith in all subjects."

A sliver of tension returned, far too easily. "Has she been bothering you again?"

"No."

Everything in that single word shouted the opposite. Charlotte felt the guilt like a sharpened blade. The Smiths were country neighbors and Bethany Case nee Smith's animosity toward Charlotte had been passed down the family line.

Margaret, the more physically blessed of the two sisters, hadn't needed the extra edge to make Emily's life miserable.

Charlotte pushed the heel of her palm to her forehead.

"Are you pained?" Emily asked, somewhat anxiously. "Why didn't you say something sooner? Anna said you were sick earlier, but I didn't believe it. You are never sick. Not unless you have cause to avoid something or someone."

Charlotte pushed against her sudden headache. "If you tell anyone that, you'll ruin all of my mad designs," she said as lightly as she could.

"Like I'd tell," her sister scoffed, looking relieved. "Now, I want to hear all about your night. About the Hannings' masquerade—I simply cannot bear the thought of another two years before I'm able to attend. And don't omit any details about your suitors." She wagged a finger. "You have been incredibly tight-lipped in your notes."

She thought of how it would look on the page. *Dear Emily, I think you will be most interested in the knowledge of my torrid affair with a man from London's underworld . . .*

"The masquerade was quite tame this year." The back rooms on the other hand . . . "And my suitors are the same ones you already know of, goose. Quite a lack of interest there. For *your* interest, though, there are a few men who have returned from recent travels who are quite handsome and witty. Who dance like dreams and speak like angels."

Emily put her chin on her hand, sighing. "That sounds lovely. I can't wait until I can accompany you."

"I wish that as well." Charlotte swallowed. "You will brighten the halls."

"What I want to know is why you don't find one of these dreamy angels instead? One should *not* be bored by a suitor."

Charlotte snorted.

"Who do you truly fancy?" Emily wheedled. "You've

not written anything tangible in *weeks*. I'm liable to start believing Margaret Smith's tales."

"Oh? And what does Margaret Smith have to say?" She tried not to tense too noticeably. Sometimes the truth to rumors was far easier to sift through from the information that passed between towns.

The knowledge of where and with whom she had been spending time would destroy Emily's future chances in one swift stroke.

She *knew* that. But had been drowning in her own desires instead. Wanting this *one* thing . . .

Emily waved a hand. "Nonsense. As usual. But hurry and let me undo your hair so you won't be a slugabed in the morning. Mother said I can accompany you on your appointments tomorrow." Emily looked as excited as a sixteen-year-old could when told she'd get a taste of society.

"Did she? I don't know . . ." And though Charlotte said it teasingly, she honestly didn't. What if . . .

"Oh, hush, you wretched thing." Emily hurriedly helped her, then all but stuffed her under the covers. "Can't be late tomorrow."

"Emily, we won't be late."

"Ha," she muttered, capping the light. "I will have my day." She waved her fist.

"Yes, Captain." Charlotte rolled her eyes, waiting for her sister to leave.

The edge of the bed dipped, the covers lifting.

"What are you doing?"

Emily stuffed herself next to her, giving her an incredulous look in the adjusting shadows as she made herself comfortable. "What does it look like I'm doing?"

"But . . . don't you want to sleep in your own room?" Roman . . .

Emily stared at her. "No," she said baldly, flipping over

to her side. "We always do this first night back. Honestly, Charlotte, I'll start to think you truly perplexed."

It took Emily twenty minutes to stop chatting and start softly snoring. Emily, who had her boxed in against the wall. Charlotte closed her eyes, hand to her brow. Wonderful. Trapped. Just where she needed to be if a slippery and deadly visitor made an appearance at her window. Her unlatched window—as it had remained for weeks.

Again, what the hell was she *doing*? What was she *thinking*?

A scrape at the window caused her to go stiff as a board, but it was only a branch in the wind. A creak in the floor made her whimper. A whisper of sound outside made her pray that he ignored her request to find her later.

The shadows passed from quarter hour to half hour to full hour, then over again.

The remembered sound of a light laugh and feel of fingers gently stroking her cheek finally pulled her deep to sleep.

It felt like twenty minutes later when Emily pulled at her arm. "Up, up."

Charlotte allowed herself to be dragged up. She touched two fingers to her forehead. The headache hadn't ceased. Anxiety, plans, revelations, fear, and the grip of a charmed smile not letting her free. The decisions she made here and now would have an impact on more than just *her* future. She *knew* this. Had breathed the knowledge of it for years.

Had put all her past plans in jeopardy because of him. Because of her *own* needs.

She had half expected to wake to his smile, to Emily's yelp. Wondering and waiting. Fearing and dreaming. Not sleeping.

She didn't think she could look any better than she felt.

Emily stopped her tugging and surveyed her. "Actually, you don't look all that well. Are you truly sick?"

"Thank you for that lovely examination of my sterling appearance." Charlotte pushed her hand away. "I'm perfectly well."

She peered into the mirror, though, just to see the ghastly image. She paused, fingers at the corners of her eyes. Was John Clark right? Did she look different now?

"Are those wrinkles?"

Everything in Charlotte froze at the teasing, and her vision seemed to magnify the edges of her eyes, gaze frantically searching for the lines. She tore her gaze away, determined not to give in to the folly. *Stupid, silly fears.* She didn't want the pictured image to change, as it used to, into the cold, decrepit reflection she had invariably seen staring back. The image had changed recently into something very nearly approaching vibrant. She closed her eyes and ran fingers along her cheek, the tips of her nails lightly scraping as they came to rest at her chin.

Her eyes opened to pin her sister. "Very amusing." Charlotte tried to keep her voice light. "Help me dress? What should I wear?"

"Pink."

Charlotte shook her head, looking through her decidedly pink-free wardrobe.

"What is this?" Emily asked. Charlotte looked over to see her sister sitting on the edge of the bed holding a note. "It says, 'Everything taken care of. Apologies for last night, my snoring beauty.'"

Charlotte plucked the note from her sister's grasp, clutching it in her shaking fist. Damn man had come in through her window after all and left it on her pillow. *After* she had fallen asleep. *Next* to her sister.

Emily's brows creased as she examined her. Hysteria rose within Charlotte.

Charlotte waved her shaking hand. "A note for Miranda that she shared with me last night. Snored something dreadful the other night, I guess. The note must have slipped into my cloak or dress."

How long had he stayed? What if Emily had awoken when he was there?

Emily regarded her seriously. "Charlotte, you aren't having an affair with Downing, are you? Miranda will be seriously displeased."

The hysteria bubbled over.

Emily twiddled a pin between her fingers an hour later as Charlotte put the finishing touches on them both.

"My new correspondent is far more attentive than you have been. I'll have you replaced in a thrice, dear sister, if you don't increase your efforts."

"A new correspondent, hmmm?" Charlotte pulled a brush through her sister's hair.

"Yes, Lady Downing linked us together. He is incredibly prompt. Unlike some, hmph." Emily gave her a look.

Charlotte stared at her sister's image in the mirror for a long moment, uncertainty flowing through her. Only confidence in her friend stemmed troubling thoughts. "You started writing a man? Who?"

Emily shrugged. "Don't know. The measured sort who is probably shy in person, but on paper he is quite the wittiest man I've come across. Probably some vicar's son chafing at his binds."

Charlotte felt the corner of her mouth tug. "A vicar's son?"

"Held hostage somewhere, only my letters getting

through to him. I've decided I will rescue and marry him."

"Indeed." The other corner joined the first.

"Don't ruin my imaginings, Charlotte. You are far too sensible."

"Someone needs to be," she teased back, picking up a pink ribbon for her sister's hair.

Emily said nothing for a long moment, and Charlotte looked in the mirror to see her sister staring at her with a doleful expression.

"What?"

"Nothing. Where are we off to first?" The bounce returned to her sister's movements as Charlotte finished tying the ribbon. "Somewhere brilliant, I hope."

"Lady Hodge's parlor."

Emily's face fell. "Lady Hodge is eighty, if a day. There won't be an amusement to be had."

Charlotte shrugged and didn't try to hide her smile. She'd need it for the coming morning. "Did you not want to come?"

"Fine, fine."

"I was dreadful," her sister uttered darkly after their fourth such visit a few hours later.

"You were wonderful. No one noticed," Charlotte assured her, as they eased into the well-trod shopping lanes, unabated tension thrumming through her.

No one had given Charlotte any odd or satisfied looks. And one person had even gossiped that John Clark had suddenly decided that very morning to visit the Continent.

Charlotte prayed his accommodations didn't include a wooden box.

"My cup hit my saucer so loudly it was as if I'd tossed her prized plates through the display glass."

"No one noticed." *Everyone had noticed.*

"*Everyone* noticed. I might as well have thrown the plates. I'm doomed."

"You aren't doomed." She wouldn't let her be.

"I'll never secure a husband."

"Because your cup hit your saucer a tad forcefully? It was of no consequence," she said as lightly as she could.

Emily gave her a disbelieving look. "Don't try and convince me that you weren't noticing such things about the other girls."

"You will hardly find such harsh scrutiny elsewhere. It is in the dance of the older women where such a thing is required. And you are young. You did well."

"I couldn't answer a single question without babbling. And you were nice enough not to incline your head when I'd already put my foot in it. Damn tongue might as well be a straight toboggan on a sharply curved path for all of the grace it possesses."

"Language. And you did a fine job."

"I probably ruined *your* bloody chances too. You should put me out. To pasture."

"If you don't watch your language, I'll consider it."

"Father will be so angry."

"At your language?" Charlotte looked down her nose. "Undoubtedly."

"No, at my lack of skill."

Charlotte's eyes narrowed. "You have plenty of skill. And Father will say nothing."

"He will. He's always going on about how . . . well, he just will," she finished lamely. The words whispered between them anyway.

He's always going on about how I have no beauty or grace to claim. How I will have to rely on you to make a good match. Or for someone to take pity upon me.

Charlotte stopped suddenly, Emily coming to rest next

to her as the crowd moved around them. The tension *pulsed*. She put a forceful hand on her sister's shoulder. "If the fools can't notice what is in front of them, then you don't need them," she said, somewhat savagely.

Emily blinked in shock.

"You are the prettiest girl in England." Bright eyes and cherried cheeks, so full of life. "And better than that, the *smartest*."

Emily raised a brow, the lingering hurt retreating back. "I think you have gone blind."

"And I think it's those other fools who are." Charlotte squeezed her shoulder and urged her back into motion, tension still throbbing. "Pay them no attention. We will change them. Force them to *our* will."

"We will?"

"Yes."

Her sister didn't respond for a long moment.

"What happened?" Emily asked quietly as they crossed the street.

Charlotte tried to pretend ignorance. "They don't know true beauty when they see it."

"No. That isn't what I was asking, and you know it. Don't . . . don't leave me out. You've been so happy in your letters—though infrequent and *vague*, don't think I didn't notice—but I assumed it meant this season was *good*. Yet, today, at the stops, you seemed . . . angered."

Charlotte tried to smile. "I told you that I would make up for any uptight nonverbal reminders I might give."

"No, not those. I appreciate those, as idiotic as it all is. I mean, who *cares* if you take a sip of your tea? Maybe someone is *thirsty*."

"Emily—"

"No, don't distract me. I'm not sure what to make of it. You *don't* seem to enjoy socializing or the *ton*. I remember the bubbling excitement when you were set to debut. The notes and thrilled words. And I thought you had recaptured that . . . but you haven't, have you?"

No. She had been ignoring the pit. Filling it with *Roman, Roman, Roman.* But the cavity still remained, deadly, patiently waiting. Waiting for her return like an old friend.

She didn't wish to lie to Emily. But she also wanted her sister to look forward to her first season, unhindered. Full of anxiety about her success, undoubtedly—there was little to calm those types of nerves—but with all of her optimistic illusions still in place. She could walk through the ballrooms and feel the lively air and dance the night away without a care. What the young were supposed to feel. What many of the young women enjoyed.

If Charlotte made a grand match, she could ensure that Emily wouldn't be a puppet on their father's string. She could have all the time she needed, could revel in the parties and fun. Emily wouldn't even have to marry should she choose not to. Charlotte had always planned to work it out with her future husband. On the side, away from their father.

That was what she had always planned—where she had concentrated her efforts. But now other possibilities bloomed, disjointed and new. Tenuous and dangerous.

. . . as long as Emily was happy . . . as long as Charlotte could *make* it so.

"Just a rough night, is all, nothing to worry over."

Emily said nothing, but Charlotte knew her sister didn't believe her.

"You said you wanted to go to Grubbins'." Charlotte pointed at the milliner's ahead, and Emily's eyes lit up. "And we are here."

"Oh! Margaret Smith will be over-the-moon jealous."

Emily tore from her side the last few steps through the crowd and slipped inside.

Charlotte clutched her reticule.

Perfection. It was what she had clung to all her life.

If she could marry perfectly. If she could *be* perfect. Surely, she could make everything well for Emily.

For herself.

She hadn't believed in fairy tales and white and black knights come to save her. *She* was their white knight. Emily's white knight.

She had drifted so far from the path of perfection, though. And into an unknown, exciting, frightening place. One full of all of her fears—ones which keenly whispered that one day she would look into icy eyes and see nothing there but disinterest. Murmuring wary commands to her to control that disinterest by conquering or rejecting it before it appeared.

So much easier and safer surely to be a perfect portrait, unblemished and still. Coldly calculating. Rebellious thoughts crushed to marble.

Warmer, softer thoughts plunged into the hollow under her fear.

Perfect.

Someone bumped her elbow and her grip involuntarily opened, popping the bag from her hand. A thief's tactic. She hurriedly bent down to retrieve it and her fingers met strong golden ones already clasped around the fabric.

She suddenly couldn't remember how to breathe.

She stared at the long, strong fingers. Ones that could handle a knife or the delicate ivory of an expensive queen.

The fingers brushed hers, and shivers spread through her limbs. Out and about during the day so rarely, but somehow always running into her whenever her thoughts strayed . . .

Her eyes rose slowly, halting at his lips, staring at them, pulling her own between her teeth. Knowing how they *felt*. On hers, against her neck, pulling perfectly across her skin.

"Well, this is an unexpected surprise," those lips murmured.

The way his mouth curved she knew it wasn't a surprise in the least. She couldn't pull her eyes away.

"If you keep looking at me like that," he whispered, his lips moving slowly over the words, savoring them, "I may give in to my urge to do something very *undisciplined*."

That snapped her eyes straight up, along with her body. He seemed to anticipate the movement and gracefully rose with her, the bag still clutched between them.

She stared into eyes the perfect shade of frost over a clear blue lake. Frost that was violently melting under the searing look he was giving her.

"Let me go," she whispered, words unable to separate from her breath. The hard edge of propriety that she always crowned herself with in public disappeared like so much fog under the blazing sun.

"I don't think I can." His words held the edge of her whisper. "Unless you wish it."

She needed to spare a look to the passing crowd, to see if anyone was watching, but she couldn't look away. The faceless crowd sifted around him, bodies, both male and female, drawing toward her companion, then subtly shifting away. Something about him still both pulling people to him and pushing them away, on edge. A deadly predator wrapped in an entrancing hide.

The thought that she was just as susceptible to his lure as anyone else on the street made her uneasy. Any feigned perfection disappearing like mist. He always made her feel *raw*.

And with that rawness, stripping away all the artifice she had carefully cloaked about her over the years, was the fear that there would be *nothing* left on which to cling.

"Are you well, Miss?" he asked loudly, his previously intimate look and question replaced with a stranger's propriety. "Let me help you to the side." He slipped his warm palm beneath her elbow, steering her out of the path of the people passing by and into the vacant area in front of the shop. His dangerous aura pocketed them from stray limbs.

She set her chin. Trying to push away the sly, undermining thoughts that she could give away her control.

"It's the middle of the day. You aren't supposed to exist," she murmured, then, for the benefit of anyone listening, said loudly, "Thank you, sir."

"Of course, Miss." He handed her the bag, bending toward her as he did. "Afraid that I will take over your waking hours as well?" Slippery graveled words full of promise.

She had no illusions that she would control all of her fate, but she could forge a large part of it behind the scenes once settled. Subtly manipulating, coldly crafting, hiding her warmer feelings under a carefully wrought veneer only broached by a chosen few. The clear path toward a ruling matron written like a recipe on a page.

She had long sought that recipe, had worked hard to divine the perfect ingredients. She knew exactly what needed to be done.

And that was the danger of predators at the top of the chain. They tended to destroy the best of plans.

That deep voice promised things she couldn't even comprehend, even after weeks of knowledge. Whispering over her skin. Shuddering through her veins. "I may just do so."

Splayed on bedsheets or across a garden bench or in a back room. Forgetting where and who she was.

Emily burst from the door. "Charlotte!" She waved something pink.

Charlotte scrambled in front of him, pushing him behind her in some crazy, idiotic gesture of secrecy.

Someday, *God, someday,* she had to believe she could have something wild and free. Unrestrained. Something warm and alive. Something dangerous and out of control. Something like the man behind her.

That she could have *him.*

But not today . . . in the bright light of the sun, with Emily waving and her thoughts going in too many directions . . .

She had to hold it together *today.* The perfect statue, cracking irrevocably, pieces falling even as she scrambled to glue them back in place. Or to tear them off herself.

"Charlotte," Emily breathed as she skirted the crowd between them. "What is taking you so long? Look at this." She held up a pink bonnet—the light color the very hue of innocence.

Get back in the store!

"That will look divine on you, Emily." She thrust her bag toward her. "Why don't you purchase it."

Get back in the store!

Her sister cocked her head to the side, eyes drifting past Charlotte. "I say. Are you a friend of Charlotte?" There was something odd and penetrating in her gaze.

"Miss Emily, is it?" he asked from behind.

Charlotte stiffened so abruptly that it had to be excruciatingly noticeable.

Roman appeared at her side and smiled charmingly at her sister, the deadly aura retreating a space and making him seem almost safe. But it lingered about him, as if unable to dissipate completely. "That bonnet will look quite striking with your hair, Miss Emily."

"Really? Do you think so?" Emily's rosy cheeks grew redder. Attention caught sufficiently that she didn't seem to realize they had not actually been introduced.

"Definitely. A rose in spring."

Charlotte stepped between them again. "Emily, go buy the thing." She shoved a few notes to her sister and forced her to back up a pace.

Charlotte didn't spare more than a glance at her sister's eyebrows, which were now nearly touching her hairline before turning to him.

"Thank you for your help, sir. Good day." She nodded at him tightly, pointedly.

"Perhaps in return you might help me find a bonnet for my aunt?" He smiled, a much-less-*polite* smile than he had given Emily, the danger all but cloaking him again.

"I don't think so."

"She has been sick. I am hoping this will lift her spirits."

She'd eat Emily's new bonnet if he had an ill aunt. "I'm sure you will make a splendid purchase."

"But I would love to have your gifted opinion. Perhaps Miss Emily's too."

"No. Go away," she whispered harshly. "You are making a scene."

"Am I?" The edges of his mouth curved. "And here I thought it was you making it."

Two women stood a few paces away, bent heads together, whispering.

Panic rushed through her, all coolness completely gone. Her breath caught. If someone identified him, there would be talk of her connected to Roman Merrick, which would lead to other things. Last night had proven that. The maelstrom surged. She tried to draw breath, but it became difficult for a moment.

His eyes narrowed and wandered over her face. At the moment, she couldn't even pull forth the calm veneer she usually hid behind in public. He tipped his head to her. "Actually, I just remembered an urgent appointment. Thank you, Miss."

"No." She reached out a hand before she could stop herself. "I . . . I'm sorry. I can help you with your purchase if you still wish it."

He examined her for a long moment. Why couldn't he be a man of the *ton*? Someone she could have a yearning flirtation with. Able to freely express that lift of a butterfly's wings in her stomach. Able to marry him and live in stunned wonder, chained to her bed, the rest of her life.

His lazy smile suddenly appeared. "Perhaps I might take you up on that offer in the future then. Good day, Miss."

He turned, and she watched as he slipped into the crowd and disappeared. She stared after him for long moments, trying to corral her chaotic thoughts.

Beyond his unsuitability to her world, and hers to his, Roman Merrick was *not* the marrying kind. Even if he suddenly became a *prince,* he'd probably thumb his nose at them all.

Charlotte turned to see Emily examining her and pulled up a forced smile.

"Who was that man?" Emily asked.

"I have no idea." Charlotte gestured toward the shop. "Shall we purchase your bonnet?"

Emily held up a bag. "I already did." A sly smile appeared. "While you were staring off into space. Bit distracted, Charlotte?"

"No. Gunter's?" She briskly started walking in that direction.

"Charlotte, you can't fool me with an ice." Emily called behind her, obviously hurrying to catch up. "Well, I suppose you can," she huffed, pulling alongside her. "And I'll have you know that I want one now, but you knew him."

"Fine. He is an acquaintance of Father's. No one of import."

"I think he might be the nicest-looking man I've ever seen." Emily cocked her head. "Downing has serious competition. I think I will develop mad tendres for them both now."

Charlotte stopped abruptly. "You will not."

Emily raised a brow. "Really? Gotten under your skin that far, has he? Sounds like a bloody fine bloke to me. What's his name?"

"Language! And stop speaking of him."

"Strange name, Language. What is his first name? Handsome?" Emily cocked her head. "No, wait, that is probably his second name. First name, Incredibly, then?"

"Emily."

"Really? I don't think Emily does him justice."

The yearning, the want, the defeat, all mangled together and knotted violently. "Emily," she said, her voice cold and clipped, "I'm going to kill you in a matter of seconds." She pinned her sister with an ice-covered look. "Out of the love I once felt for you, I will give you a choice as to what method I will employ. Carriage wheel or strangulation?"

Emily raised her hands in surrender. "Fine. Buy me an ice then."

Charlotte started moving again.

"But," her sister's voice called from behind, "I think you should know that Incredibly Handsome looks at you as if you are the only person in the world too."

Charlotte pushed away the elation, the terror, and wondered if she could strangle her sister *and* throw her under a carriage at the same time.

As he leaned against the bricks of the alley, Roman watched them pass: the younger one nipping at the elder's heels. Charlotte turned and said something deadly to her sister, who threw up her hands.

But the mischievous grin on the younger girl's face as she called out, then chased after her sister, who was once again striding forward, spoke to their relationship.

Charlotte's pleasure in the younger girl was obvious.

He wondered what Charlotte would do if she ever discovered that her father had tried to exchange one sister for the other. To have the younger one, barely out of leading strings, take her place in his bed. A sacrifice to keep his trophy from scandal.

He reached in his pocket and turned the clip between his fingers, leaning his shoulders farther into the edged bricks. That warm protectiveness was going to cost her.

He'd exploit it himself, if needed. He found that lately he was feeling the urge to use everything at his disposal.

He laughed without amusement at the thought. At the weakness that wound insidiously through him, slithering, squeezing, debilitating, at the thought of her.

Pictured the panic, the internal lesions, showing on her face before he had turned to go. *Before she had called him back.*

He could have overpowered her before that. Could have made her come to him even there in the middle of the crowd with her panicking over the talk they were sure to cause. He had seen the way she hovered there on the brink, sensuality and reserve threatening to break.

And he hadn't been able to bring himself to do it.

There was an audible snap triggered between his fingers. Shit. He pulled the pieces out of his pocket, examining them. Broken.

Shit.

He tried to push them back together, even knowing that the piece was irreparably damaged. Shit. He curled his fingers around the broken edges and stuffed them back in his pocket.

Out of control. When she'd grabbed him, telling him she would help him anyway, willing to take him into the store where she'd be observed by any number of people . . . his mind had stopped properly functioning.

He had gone to her room last night to demand answers, to force her to make choices. But had changed his plan after seeing the other body occupying her bed. Had decided to approach her in the middle of the day.

He had the sneaking suspicion that even though Charlotte had been dead to the world when he'd been in her room, *Emily* had seen him crawling back through the window and sliding it shut. Which made things . . . quite interesting indeed. Messy and uncontrollable, just as he usually liked it. So why he was feeling distinctly uneasy was the question.

The chaos was pushing at his plans, longing for some stability. Slightly terrifying, the idea of order and future plans. Especially when the edges of all the choices were torn and muddied.

Weakness.

He pushed away from the bricks, striding down the alley, turning onto the pavement, making people veer from his path.

He could win everything he wanted or lose it all in the same roll.

All he had to do was pick the right dice. Start the last

game. He had an appointment in half an hour. One that would put every pip in its place—simply waiting for her hand to roll as she willed.

He could see the end. Could feel fate gripping him by the ballocks. Twisting them and telling him that she was fickle with her chances. And that if he didn't move *now* . . .

He narrowed his eyes and pressed farther into the lane, seeing the edges of the shadows following him. Had they seen him with Charlotte? Bloody stupid, not paying attention as he should. So hard to when she was near.

He slipped into another alley, enticing the shadows to follow, feeling the broken pieces of the clip in his pocket. He needed to pick up another from his stash. And he needed to take care of the men behind him—find out if any of his enemies knew about Charlotte—then be on his way to the appointment.

After all, the future Lord Trant awaited.

Chapter 17

"I'll accompany you home for the evening, Mother. Then I want to peek in on the Pevenshalls' gathering before it ends."

Charlotte had found Roman's note in her reticule—anytime the man touched something, she now assumed a note was left behind—telling her to work a blind that evening.

Her mother's eyes narrowed before she nodded sharply and held her arm out for Charlotte. They found her father gaming in one of the large side rooms, foxed and losing, trying to escape from his debts and mortality. But he retained enough judgment to nod stiffly and remain mute about their departure.

As their carriage jolted forward and picked up speed—the driver seeming to have forgotten how to properly use the ribbons—her mother's glacial stare pierced her.

"I will deal with Father's displeasure," Charlotte said, anticipating her mother's words.

"To *attend* the Pevenshalls'?" Her mother's jaded eyes switched to the window. "You think yourself so *clever* lately? Trying not to rely solely on that pretty face your father keeps on display?"

Charlotte swallowed, alarmed, heart lurching along with the carriage as it took too sharp a turn. "What—"

"Save your explanation. I truly don't care to hear it." She didn't look at Charlotte as she grabbed the leather cord near the window, keeping herself steady and wooden, as always.

Charlotte kept the pleasant, stretched smile upon her face as she tried to balance herself against the violent pitching. "Very well. You looked quite lovely tonight. I heard a number of people mention it."

Who cared about Clark finding her in a deserted hallway when her mother *knew*? *For how long?*

"You can save your misplaced pity as well."

The carriage rocked violently again.

"Very well." The smile hurt. It always hurt. "Would you like me to fix you a cup of tea before bed?"

Emily was spending a long evening at an event for younger ladies and wouldn't return for hours.

"No. Leave me to the house alone. Go meet your lover. Be like your father." Her mother gripped the strap as they pulled in front of the house, the traffic quick, especially with the furious way Henry had driven.

"He did the unthinkable." Her mother's voice was whisper tight. Charlotte had wondered how Bennett would succeed in hiding the bet from Viola. It seemed he hadn't. "I cannot fault you for your actions."

Viola paused for a moment, her hand hovering above the door handle, body tight with . . . Charlotte's hope lifted . . . regret?

"And I . . . I care not," Viola said quickly, face turned away as she pushed the handle down.

"Ver—very well." It was hard to speak over the choking block in her throat, to utter the expected response. Charlotte found it even more difficult to move as her mother hurriedly dismounted and firmly shut the door behind her.

Fingers clenched into the seat, then released. Clenching, releasing. Scraping. Breaking.

Tears pricked as a card at the bottom of the stacked house wavered. It would so easily pull all of the rest down when it fell. She hadn't realized that so many people could flick the cards holding the supports.

The carriage jolted forward. She jolted with it and immediately rapped on the trap. Forgotten inside, for she hadn't given Henry new directions. The carriage would return to the stableyard or to the house of her father's mistress—even worse.

She rapped again, as hard as she could manage, to no avail. She wondered without amusement if she should just sit back and let the carriage take her where it willed. Then ask Henry to take her to Blackfriars, so she could toss herself over the edge.

The carriage stopped abruptly, flinging her forward.

The door opened and a dark figure swung into the interior of the carriage. Shadowed fingers reached forward to grab her, with cloth to bind her.

Chapter 18

The door slammed shut, the carriage immediately jolting forward once more.

Strong fingers caught her shoulders, steadying her, then ran softly along her jaw. Golden hair caught the slivered light. The length of cloth was a dark cloak. For her.

Her lips remembered how to move. Her lungs, to breathe. Henry was a good man, but he could easily be bought for a few pounds of gossip. Charlotte knew Bethany wasn't above such a tactic. "The driver—"

"Oh, we switched him out after you climbed inside at the last stop. One of the boys paid 'to drive a handsome carriage' for a few hours. Your driver is off drinking somewhere warm no doubt."

The vehicle took a breakneck turn.

Roman steadied her again, then gave three hard raps to the trap. The coach immediately slowed. "I think I might have a talk with Johnny about his aspirations, though. When he professed himself 'energetic' to be a coach driver, I didn't realize he tilted so far to the literal."

She couldn't muster proper outrage over the uninformed switch of her driver as an onslaught of dark want took her—his finger smoothly stroked her chin, promising relief, promising to make her forget.

"My . . . my mother knows."

He tilted her chin, eyes examining her. "Does she? What does she know?"

"That you exist."

He didn't seem surprised. *Why* didn't he seem surprised? "And what will she do with the knowledge?"

"I don't know," she whispered. "Nothing. Everything. We don't get on well." Actually, that wasn't true. They got along perfectly well as long as Viola wasn't doing something she didn't wish to do. "My mother is solitary."

And cold, so cold sometimes. Charlotte clung to the regret that she had seen though—she knew she saw it in her mother's eyes occasionally, before they turned cool and empty once more.

Charlotte *clung* to the emotion—the thought of it at least. Pride falling to the *need* for it.

She looked at Roman. Her need for *him* strengthened each time they were together. Which scared the devil out of her.

Miranda, Emily—relationships that were lovely and enduring, for she was needed while needing in return. Like Miranda and Downing—partners, needing each other. Wonderful, not weak. Reciprocated, not one-sided.

But there were other relationships in her life where she was the flat-out loser in the dynamic. And events were promising in so many small and large ways, ways that she didn't want to think about, that the top of the hourglass was nearly empty for this one. That she would be abruptly cut off from him. That it was already written in fate's hand. All while *needing* him . . .

He tilted her chin again, looking into her eyes, reading her. "Don't be sad, Charlotte. Everything will be well."

She tugged him closer. Needing the proximity. Fighting against the weakness of it even as she embraced the comfort. "Will it? How can you so calmly say so?"

"Does it change how you feel, Charlotte?" His lips brushed the hair above her ear. "About this? About me?"

His fingers stroked. Promising that she could be terrified over her mother's words and knowledge later. Over the weakness in wanting him so keenly. That she could pretend that the conversation with her mother hadn't happened. That Emily hadn't *met* him. That Charlotte could think about consequences tomorrow. In the morning. Another day.

"No. None of it changes how I feel."

So little time left to pretend. She kissed him, wanting it to last forever. Pushing the thoughts from her mind forcefully and deliberately.

He responded immediately, then flashed a grin, whatever had ailed him earlier, and last night, gone. Or buried too. "A gentleman would hardly take advantage of a lady in distress."

"Good." She kissed him again, curling her fingers in his hair as she did so. "I am with the right man then."

"Oh?" He smiled against her lips, leaning into her.

Kissing, kissing, kissing her as if she could be consumed by it and made whole. Or if he could.

"This is folly," she whispered against his lips, as the carriage continued rolling farther away from her home, taking her somewhere far from where she should be. Though everything in her said she should be right with the man whose forehead was pressed to hers.

"The best things usually are." Each breath drummed in concert with the feeling of his fingers stroking her. The drugged feel of heated eyes connected to hers. "But I couldn't let you escape for the night with so much time left in it."

So little, so little. Already running through the last grains of sand.

She pulled back a few inches so she could raise a brow. So she could stop being *weak*. She would *own* this in the here and now. Her *choice*.

"Escape? Where would I escape to?"

"The land of sunshine and fluffy rabbits? Hardly a place I can enter."

"Rabbits?"

"Rabbits scare the devil out of me. Unassuming creatures, waiting to rip out your throat when you least expect it." He caressed her chin, eyes dropping to her lips. "You invite them in, pet them, love them, and they piss all over your boots and rake their back claws across your skin on their way out. Leaving you unshod and with permanent scars."

She laughed, feeling the ease trickle through her that he always brought. "I'll make sure to save you from feral rabbits, shall I?"

His eyes met hers again, and for a moment her laughter caught at the piercing look there before his mouth pulled into a charming grin, and her laughter spilled forth, tightness giving way to relief. She swallowed back the strange block in her throat, unwilling to let stray thoughts mar the moment as they separated.

She watched him settle back on the seat. "No mask tonight, dear Death?"

"Against better judgment," he said lightly.

She leaned back into the cushions as well, pulling the edge of his cloak through her fingers, drinking in his expressions. "Where are you taking me, leader of my follies?"

He put his boot heel on the edge of his seat. A move that would cause a society matron an attack. "Family card game."

She blinked. "Pardon me?"

He spread his arms wide. "You said you didn't know me last night."

Something thrilling and downright terrifying ran through her. Even if she had meant that statement in reference to herself at the time, here he was offering up part of himself.

She opened her mouth, but nothing emerged. Her entire being shut down by the ecstasy and terror pulling at each other.

"There is no fear for your reputation as none of the players will utter a word about you. And I thought you might like to get to know Andreas better. Would be good for him too, liking someone in society." He looked amused at some private joke, the heel of his boot grinding into the edge of the seat, back and forth.

She didn't respond, as doing so would just produce stuttering.

"He doesn't bite too hard, I promise," Roman assured her, and for the first time she had met him, he sounded *earnest.* Her world flipped again.

"I . . . I don't play cards."

"Not at all?"

She swallowed. She rarely admitted it. For many ladies played cards just as hard, or harder, than some of their male counterparts. And solid contacts existed in the game parlors.

But when asked to play, she always demurred.

"I hate them." She looked away, clenching her fingers in the fabric of his cloak. Why had she divulged that? She met his eyes, determined to revive their banter, but stopped. It was *unnerving,* his complete lack of surprise.

"Of course you hate them. But you've never really played, have you?"

"My father tried to teach me to play whist long ago."

She had stubbornly refused to show any aptitude for it. She knew it was childish, but it had been something in her control, and she'd needed the outlet.

"Yes, and your desire to abstain in no way stems from your irresponsible father's decisions. I am happy you do not let his idiocy rule your choices."

She sighed. "Will you not let me have my immaturity?"

"Not in this." His smile was dangerously cheerful once more.

Maybe . . . "You play for money."

"Nothing to worry about." He waved a hand. "And you'll do wonderfully. I'll help."

She grimaced, but nodded to satiate him. Once play began, and he was immersed like her father, she could retreat to watch and keep at least one of her comforting, old standards of control in place.

She pulled up the hood of the cloak when the carriage rolled to a stop. Roman said something to the driver after he helped her dismount, then led her through the back door, where they were immediately beset. Five boys stood there, three *hopping* and nearly bursting at the seams.

"Sir, sir, there is a run on table four," a small boy said.

"And that bastard Treverly is cheating again, but Jimmy can't catch how he's doing it," a larger one eagerly spoke up.

"—Gimling's up. Charity has the rue. Tyson can't be found."

"—Bernie's drunk."

"—Captain Stabley punched Johnny Tinsdale. In the *groin*."

"—We ran out of Popler's."

Roman let go of her hand and clapped his hard. "Boys." There was immediate silence.

"What night is it?" His voice was deceptively even.

Eyes widened, and nervous looks ensued. A few curious gazes finally turned her way, trying to pierce through the shadows of her hood.

"Sir?" The largest boy seemed to accept the task of voicing the single question.

"Shut down four, tell Jimmy to watch the side, have Gimling deal with Charity, Tyson will be here at three, ring Bernie's bell—hard." He barked the last. "Take the pitch off Tinsdale, send to the highway for more, and for the love of cheating St. Nick, *go to Donald with these*."

They hopped to, the smallest one, with a jagged scar the breadth of his forehead, even sent a cheeky salute as his tiny frame disappeared through the door to the hell proper. Loud voices and the clink of chips rose, then muted as the door swung shut.

Roman shook his head in annoyance, though there had been something oddly pleased in his eyes for a moment at the smallest boy's cheek. He took her hand and led her up the stairs. She said nothing, nerves grabbing hold of her again. Pushing down thoughts and desires.

They walked through the hall, opening that same door he had unlocked so many weeks ago. She could hear voices as he pushed it open and ushered her inside.

All talk stopped as three heads turned their way. The click of the door engaging sounded like a gunshot in the silence. Only long practice stopped Charlotte from shifting. She concentrated on the darkest gaze. Andreas Merrick looked coldly furious.

"Good evening," Roman said, drawing next to and slightly ahead of her, enough so that she could see him in her peripheral vision, a wide smile on his face.

She couldn't move, though. Couldn't understand how Roman didn't feel at least a little intimidated by the stare the darker man leveled upon him.

"Indigestion again, Andreas? Shall I have one of the boys make a remedy? The lot of them would be overeager at best." Roman tossed his keys to a side table and blithely moved forward, grabbing a side chair by its wooden top.

The scraaaaaape of the chair echoed long and uncomfortably as he pulled it excruciatingly across the floor. It took what felt like an eternity to drag it into place. He blithely nudged Bill's chair leg with his foot, and the one-eyed man snapped to sudden attention, scooting his chair over to make room.

Roman gave him a blinding smile, then sprawled in the added chair.

Silence reigned. The three men stared at him, then the two men—not including Andreas—shot surreptitious looks to her. She couldn't see what Andreas's facial expression was, but she was pretty sure it was unpleasant. Roman smiled at him cheerfully.

The silence was obvious. Roman was one over from the chair he had occupied that first night—and the other nights they had spent together here. Reserving *his* chair for her.

She swallowed. What was he doing? What was *she* doing? But Roman gave her that slow smile, the one that always did funny things to her insides—that intimated she was the only woman alive to him—and somehow her feet moved her forward, her hands shaking as they pushed back her hood, fingers lingering for a moment before dropping.

"Charlotte, this is Milton Fox, who manages things for us." Roman indicated the auburn-haired, beefy man, who was gawking at her though trying to be surreptitious about it.

She stopped beside Roman and felt warm, familiar hands reach up to help her out of the cloak, folding it behind her, but she could barely acknowledge the actions as she woodenly sat.

"And you've met Andreas and One-eye." Roman seemed more than a little amused as he waved a now-free hand at the others, hiding any smile as he bent his head to gather chips at the side.

"Good evening, milady." Bill nodded his head to her. "Nice to see you again. You look quite fetching. Like a golden statue."

"No," Roman said, face hidden as he picked up chips. "More like one of those golden, snowy birds, don't you think, One-eye? The ones that sing so prettily when you let them free?"

Bill blinked. "Of course. That too, milady."

She swallowed around the block in her throat, looking at Roman's bent head.

"It is nice to see you as well . . . Bill." She had no idea what the man's last name was, but she sure as December wasn't calling him One-eye. "And thank you for the compliment. Please, call me Charlotte. I'm not a lady."

Well, that had not come out quite as she'd intended. Luckily, the other two men—she couldn't bear to look at Andreas—were too kind to say anything, but Roman chuckled and slipped a glass of the calming drink in front of her, then started stacking chips in front of them both.

Bill's eyebrow rose at the drink, so blithely placed, then at the piles, and he shuffled his hands together in glee. "Good pots tonight." Milton also smirked.

Charlotte had no idea what the chips meant, but whatever they were, the amount was more than she had. Which made her refusal easy. She curled her hand around the short glass. "Oh, I'm simply watching."

"You are doing no such thing. You will play with these." Roman indicated the stacks he had formed.

She looked uneasily at the chips, then at the faces surrounding her. Bill nodded encouragingly, eye drifting happily to the stacks in front of her. Milton nodded as well. Andreas militantly stacked his chips in small piles with one hand, his other arm hanging over the chair back. It was an oddly informal posture on the dark-haired man. His dark eyes suddenly lifted and caught hers. Fathomless pools of black menace. Threatening her with something dire.

She jumped a bit at the look. She turned to Roman to tell him that she couldn't play with money she didn't have, and was surprised to see his eyes narrowed dangerously at the man across the table. She swallowed and looked back to see Andreas casually stacking his chips in larger piles, looking nonchalant, as if nothing notable had occurred.

"Now, who is dealing first?" Roman asked.

Her mouth opened again to tell him that she wasn't going to play, and his hand clamped around her thigh, his eyes piercing hers. Her lips stayed parted, and she could see in her periphery that Bill quickly took up the cards. Dealing five piles.

And still she couldn't pull her eyes from Roman's. Couldn't pull her thoughts away from his hand. Undoubtedly, each of the other three people at the table could see his hand or otherwise *knew* where it was placed. She was so used to any physical gesture simply being between the two of them—she was so used to having almost *no* physical contact with anyone in public, period—that her mind froze.

Her eyes broke free, and her hands automatically raked in the cards piled in front of her. His warm hand squeezed her thigh in approval, then lifted.

Well, when she lost all of his money in the next five minutes, *he* would realize his folly. It had been idiocy staking her a small fortune, judging by the looks of the piles.

Still, her pride made her think of the money as her own. So when he peeked over her shoulder, then leaned forward and threw in a few more of her chips, she balked. "What are you doing?" she hissed, raking them back. She didn't know what they were playing, or what she had, but that wasn't important. "Are you playing, or am I?"

His brows rose, and she heard Bill snicker.

And such was how the games went, though she reluctantly accepted Roman's advice more times than not. She ended up doing much better when she did, unsurprisingly— her piles dwindling due to her inexperience, especially surrounded by sharps, but filling out when she followed his pointed suggestions. He patiently explained each new game, usually tweaking the others as he did so.

"Bill can hardly play Loo without reminiscing about his uncle. The memories get him nice and drunk, and you can then pluck whatever you need from his dwindling chips."

"Andreas thinks Speculation involves deciding which frown to use. I think his *'dire things will happen to you for making that comment'* frown is especially nice, don't you?"

"Milton still maintains a prostitute gave him Vingt-et-un. We keep trying to tell him it was his sister, but he won't listen. See?"

"Commerce is a bore, but Andreas doesn't know how to have fun, so we pity him and play it. Milton will never admit it, but he hates the game with a passion. Andreas will never admit it, but he encourages us to play so Milton's trousers get in a twist. Bill will never admit that he finds their bickering amusing and cheats shamelessly when they do it. And *I* will never admit that I instigate half of it."

Even with Andreas being barely civil, playing was surprisingly fun, though frighteningly fierce, at times. For people who called it a "family game," they played like they would eat the others alive if given the opportunity. Even Bill, who had been more willing to bet kindly against her at the beginning, once she started following Roman's advice, he eagerly joined the bloodbath, including her in the letting.

Her mind had stopped working properly when she realized the first pot had been three hundred pounds and that it was considered "measly." She had decided that the better part of retaining her sanity lay in playing as if it were all an illusion of chips and paper.

Though that was likely how her father got into trouble, and she then had to banish that thought as well.

In the course of events, her coiffure had lost its shape, and one of the short locks around her face kept slipping into her eyes. She finally gave in and brushed it away, trying to tuck it behind her ear. Without looking away from his cards, Roman reached into his pocket and handed her a fresh clip. It was one of hers, likely forgotten at some point in the past. He always had one handy.

She smiled and took it from him. "Thank you."

She opened the pin in her teeth and pushed her hair into place, her eyes automatically looking up as she withdrew the pin from her lips to secure it. She froze as every eye but Roman's was on her. She swallowed and clasped the pin in place, breath coming too fast as she blindly gathered her cards.

"Interesting little bauble to have in your pocket, Roman," Andreas said.

"Hmmm?" He was examining his cards, which she had quickly figured out meant he wanted the others to think it was a good hand—whether it was or not. It was a frustrating tactic to a beginner like she, because he just as often did nothing when he had a good or bad hand, and she had wrongly assumed otherwise at first, thinking she had him figured out. "Charlotte always forgets one when she needs it most."

"It is very fetching on you, milady." Bill looked over the top of his cards nervously—looking from Andreas to Charlotte, then back again.

She swallowed, but Roman seemed as if he wasn't paying attention to the undertones. "Thank you, Bill," she said.

"I didn't realize you were such a connoisseur of women's accessories, Bill," Andreas said unpleasantly.

She narrowed her eyes at Roman's brother, but Bill didn't seem to take offense. "Spiffing lady needs a few shinies. Though some don't need nothing to make them pretty. Like milady here. Good stock."

Charlotte blinked.

Bill addressed himself conspiratorially to Milton over his cards. "Mother is quite a shiner."

Charlotte's hand jolted.

Roman pinched the bridge of his nose and pushed his fingers out and over his closed lids. "So that was it. I swear, if I had ended up there instead, you'd be called One-arm."

Bill looked at his cards, affronted. "Got it right, didn't I?" he muttered. "Didn't see you complaining after."

Charlotte looked from one to the other. "What—?"

Roman waved her question away and smiled charmingly. "Nothing."

She looked back at her cards, willing to let it slide for now, too caught up in the fact that Bill might fancy her mother—her mother, who knew about—*no don't think of her in anything but the abstract. No one* fancied Viola, she was far too cold. Like . . . like Charlotte.

Andreas snorted, and the uncharacteristic noise made her look at him. There was malice in his gaze as he looked at his brother. "Works on her too, does it? For now." His dark gaze swung to her, almost dismissively. "They are speaking of watching your house to determine the location of your bedroom." His voice was snide. "Roman can't be arsed to solve such things himself."

She looked at her cards for a second, deciding how to play the verbal hand; how to deal with the thick tension in the room. She looked at Bill, and said lightly, "You watched my house?"

"No, obviously One-eye watched your *mother*," Roman said lightly, as if unaffected by Andreas's words, but the edges of his cards curled.

Bill leaned toward her over the cards bent to his chest. "What kinds of flowers does your mum like?"

Charlotte stared at him, uncomprehending for a moment. "You want to know what type of flowers my mother likes?"

He wanted to know what sort of flowers *frigid Viola Chatsworth* liked?

Bill looked abashed at whatever he read in her face, and leaned back, shuffling his cards. "Awk. No, never mind me. Mouth has a mind of its own sometimes."

From the corners of her eyes, she saw Andreas open his mouth, and Roman as well—probably to counter whatever his brother was about to say.

"Blood roses," Charlotte blurted. "She adores them."

It was one of the few pleasures her mother seemed to have in life.

Bill perked up. "Really? Got a thing for bloody red myself."

"I'm in hell," Andreas muttered, throwing his card play on the table.

"Now, Merrick. First thing you should know about a lady—she likes to be appreciated. That you've taken the time to discover her likes and dislikes. Especially if you are serious in the courting."

Charlotte stared at Bill.

"My mistake," the dark man across from them said viciously. "I'm somewhere far worse than hell."

"Now, Merrick. Second thing you should know about a lady—she requires tender handling. Especially the most prickly variety. Sweet cores underneath, but easily damaged. Sensitivity goes a long way. And the full bloom is well worth the scars from the thorns."

"Yes, Andreas," Roman said cheerfully. "You should pay close attention. No finer courtier than One-eye."

Bill nodded solemnly. "Boss knows, though he can't follow my instructions. Too impetuous. Good thing milady here likes his tactics. You, however—"

Andreas leveled a look of utter death at him.

Bill scratched his neck quickly. "—right. Whose hand?"

Milton looked as if *he* was dying, his face purple. "Your turn. Three up." He coughed into his sleeve, then coughed again, something suspiciously like a snicker in the hack.

"Er, so, Merrick," Bill said. "How's Na—"

"Fine."

"Oh." He blinked at the quick answer. "Good. And how did—"

"Fine."

"But weren't you tracking—"

"Fine."

Roman wasn't even trying to hide his grin at their exchange. There was something diabolical in his eyes as he watched his brother.

"Yes, Andreas," Roman said. "How is your *tracking* going?"

"Roman." There was a clear warning there.

Roman smirked.

Bill scratched his head. "I thought—"

"*Fine*." Andreas all but snarled the word.

Roman simply grinned. But the depth of anger in Andreas's final answer shut Bill up for a few hands. However, not even Andreas Merrick and his deadly one-word answers seemed to keep the man's spirits down.

"Oh, heard something today," Bill said. "Eight's on the out and McGregor's in."

Milton's brows rose as he looked at the cards played on the table before he threw his own. "That means the whole clan is. Good fortune there. Though it won't stop a move should they play the wheel."

"Awk, Milt, no wheel ever worked with Boss around. Too good at pulling that trick himself. Corns would never know what hit him."

They might as well have been speaking Norwegian for all Charlotte understood. She examined her cards, if she played the queen . . .

"Cornelius has a few players who aren't to be underestimated, One-eye," Milton said, throwing a look over his cards. "You know that. Roman might be the best at confidence games, but it is easy to be overpowered by a large force running multiple good cons. If Cornelius sways enough good people . . . best to be cautious, is all I'm saying."

Charlotte pretended to keep looking at her cards, but she focused on Roman from the corner of her eye—could *see* the tightness he couldn't hide.

"Best to be cautious," Roman said, nodding. Idly. Too idly.

Bill and Milton immediately returned their gazes to their cards, shoulders tight. But Andreas's eyes held a black gleam.

"I couldn't agree more. In fact, I think we should

discuss such caution at length. I'm sure that Miss Chatsworth would be enthralled by such a discussion. Perhaps we should even speak of the games in more detail. The ones currently running. I think she'd be decidedly *interested*."

Andreas's smile was dark. But Roman's gaze promised dire consequences should he continue speaking.

Charlotte watched, unwillingly transfixed, exceedingly anxious with the conversation—both stated and unstated. She concentrated on Andreas as his eyes turned to hers, dark and deadly. Cruel. He was going to say something that would tip her world on end. She *knew* it. And all she could do was stare.

Roman's brother *was* the kind of man a person wanted to examine because there was something intriguing and enticing about him. A predator luring his prey closer. Sending the same prey skidding from him, overpowering them with the sinister waves he exuded.

Unlike Roman, who would idly or hotly gut a person, then be on his way, Andreas looked as if he'd stay to coldly enjoy the fear and pain.

There was a rap on the door. "Enter," Roman said. Relief that they were being interrupted was evident in his voice.

Charlotte shifted, and Roman's attention turned to her at the unusual gesture.

A boy peered around the corner. "Boss? We need—"

All of the men were in sudden motion, even Andreas. Flicking some sort of symbol, signal, whatever, with their fingers.

Roman looked surprised for a second, any lingering anger temporarily overpowered.

"—someone to come down. Donald even said so," the boy at the door finished.

One-eye cackled evilly. "Been a long time since you lost, Boss. Never seen you move so slow."

Charlotte had no idea what he meant, Roman had moved so fast that she'd barely been able to see the motion. It had only been a hair later than the others, his attention on her.

"Well, bound to happen sometime," he said lightly, pushing back his chair. "I'll return in a few minutes," he said to Charlotte. Then he sent a look full of dark meaning to Andreas, who tightened his lips.

One-eye cheerfully explained the meaning of the motions as Roman disappeared from the room. "You have to wait for the request to be uttered. Not fair otherwise. On card night, whoever is slowest has to deal with the problem." He shrugged, smiling, obviously happy to have a change of subject as well. "Been a long while since it was Boss. Right surprising."

Andreas looked even more unpleasant than usual. "Is it?"

One-eye shifted. "Aw, Merrick. He barely even showed it."

The darker man gathered the cards. "All it takes is one moment of inattention."

Silence descended. Milton started whistling—loudly in the suddenly quiet room. Andreas raked the rest of the cards in tight, controlled motions.

Then the edge of his mouth curled viciously. "What do you say, Miss Chatsworth? Wouldn't you like to know the implications of what we were speaking about before Roman left?"

Andreas's smile was . . . unpleasant. Bill shifted, obviously wanting to interject something.

"There seems to be a split in opinion as to whether I should," she answered calmly. She could feel all of their eyes touch upon her. "And I admit myself curious, but I don't see any dire need for me to know about it at this time if it makes Roman uncomfortable."

That didn't mean she couldn't ask Roman later. Seduce him into explaining if she had to. But what it came down to was that she trusted Roman, and she didn't trust Andreas. At all. Wouldn't allow Andreas to plant dark seeds. Not when there were plenty of seeds of destruction already sowing.

"You will sacrifice your safety for Roman's comfort?"

"I didn't realize that my safety was at the center of the matter."

Andreas leaned forward, shuffling the cards in his hands. "No? You have no idea what you are playing with, do you, little society girl?"

"I suppose I do not, Mr. Merrick."

"Merrick . . ."

Andreas gave Bill a black look, turning his head to do so. She could see a badge of scars at his neck, diving down the back of his shirt. She knew intimately that Roman had similar markings. Wounds littering his frame. Speaking of fights and death and survival.

It should have been humbling that she thought so much of her social survival, when pure survival was a far greater fear. Overcoming a lifetime of thought that if one didn't have society, then one might as well end it all, was a humorless thing.

"We've been hearing of your help with Sam," Bill suddenly said, trying to break the tension. "Right swell of you."

She focused on Bill in relief. "He has good ideas."

"Well, as that may be, it's nice to have you with us tonight, milady."

"Thank you, Bill. Though you must tire of entertaining Roman's guests," Charlotte said lightly.

"Oh, no, milady." He looked uncomfortable.

She smiled. "It's fine, Bill."

"No," Andreas said coldly, shuffling the cards again. "He means Roman's never invited anyone else."

She swallowed, thrill and fear again snapping together at the revelation. Pushing at the knot within.

"You don't like me," she said calmly, deciding to state the obvious and get it out of the way. And to avoid the other aspect of his words. She was used to being disliked though it stung a little more deeply that Roman's brother seemed to hate her.

Bill patted her hand. "Merrick don't like anyone, milady. Don't take it personal."

"I don't like careless fools," Andreas said, coldness underlining each clipped word. "And I especially *dislike* people without regard."

Charlotte kept her face impassive and tried to concentrate on the details of the man across from her. Such as how Andreas had such a crisp, patrician accent. Any street accent an overlay, unlike Roman, who held the exact opposite.

"I don't mean your brother any harm."

"No?" Andreas laughed without humor. "Wonderful." He threw a card with a flick of his fingers to the place in front of Roman's empty chair. "She doesn't mean harm." He flicked another card, but this time to Bill.

"Now, Merrick—"

But the look Andreas leveled on Bill made Bill's mouth clamp tight. Disapproval shone from his eye, but he looked down, ceding to the other man.

Charlotte narrowed her eyes on Roman's brother. "There's no reason to be foul to your friends just because you dislike me, Mr. Merrick." She could be just as clipped and crisp.

Andreas's eyes darkened. Anger and confrontational excitement in their depths.

Bill tried to intercede. "Don't worry about me, milady, Merrick's always . . ."

But his words trailed off as Charlotte and Andreas exchanged gazes that could strip paint.

"I can be as foul as I wish." He flicked a card from a line in the middle of his fingers as if it were a dagger. She wondered how it didn't stab straight into the wood of the table in front of her, but it slid underneath the ones already piled. "And I have to say that I more than dislike you at present, Miss Chatsworth."

"I can't say that I find you remarkably charming or favorable either, Mr. Merrick. It's a wonder anyone tolerates you at all."

He stopped dealing, his fingers tightening around the cards.

She'd never admit it aloud, but he scared the devil out of her. Whereas Roman was probably equally as dangerous, he didn't show it in quite the sinister way Andreas did. Roman had heat, a depth of feeling for other people. Andreas felt like black marble. Lacking feeling and warmth.

He smiled, a very cold smile that made her feel as if she'd never truly felt the emotion at all. "Most people don't."

She didn't know how to respond to that admission, so she didn't. Bill and Milton were paying very close attention to their cards, not waiting for them to be fully dealt before lifting and studying each one as if it held a secret they had long been searching for.

Andreas leaned forward, just a slight movement, and she resisted the urge to pull back in her chair. "I repeat— you have no idea what or who you are *playing* with."

It wasn't a question. "I didn't realize I had to run my actions by you."

Andreas gave a cold laugh. "I know why he likes you. It is beyond obvious. But I will hold your life *forfeit* if something happens to him."

His tone was anything but idle.

Everything in her stilled. Not in the heated way that it did when Roman touched her. Or in coolness as when her father threatened her. This was pure animal, survival instinct.

Cold, social skills were the only thing she could call upon, like old friends. "Pardon me?"

"No." Clipped. Final. A duke could do no better. No one in her vast acquaintance could.

She thinned her lips into a smile. "It is not every day that I receive threats to my life. I want to make sure I have the wording correct. And how is Roman's life in danger?"

Bill opened his mouth, but a slicing hand gesture from Andreas had Bill studying his cards again, beyond agitated. It seemed that no one save for Roman ever spoke back to Andreas.

"You'll go your way. I'm sure that you *will* accept Trant's proposal in a few weeks as well. Be a fine *lady* and leave the room as messy or clean as you entered it." He started flicking cards again.

"I think you grossly overestimate my impact."

"For your sake, let's hope so."

The door opened, and she knew Roman entered, but her eyes were still frozen on Andreas.

"I'm promoting Peter. That's all there is to it," Roman said, and she could hear the door close.

Andreas's eyes held death and destruction, then he looked down at his fingers, *blinked,* and only boredom remained in his expression as he finished dealing.

"What did I miss?" Roman plopped into his chair, hands pulling his cards toward him, quick eyes taking in everyone at the table, narrowing in turn. "Everyone's getting along well, I see." Pinning Bill, whose eye slid from his. Charlotte wondered if the man would spill the conversation later, or if Andreas would get to him first.

She wasn't sure she wanted Roman to know.

The hand played quickly. No one spoke much, as everyone seemed quite eager to avoid Roman's eyes.

Surprisingly, she easily won, her cards clear winners.

"Milady wins this hand. Good game," Bill said more cheerfully.

"Did you think she would be the one to lose?" Andreas asked, as if it were an insignificant question, only the darkness in his eyes stating otherwise.

Silence met the pronouncement and stretched uncomfortably. Roman's quick, narrowed eyes took in the players, trying to piece together what had occurred.

"Another game of Commerce?" he asked, almost casually, concentrating on Bill.

"Think it's time to turn in, Boss," Bill said, chuckling uncomfortably, not meeting his gaze. "Milt? See if the boys have things in hand downstairs? I'll even come with ye on the rounds."

Milton shrugged into his jacket, scraping his chips into a cap he pulled from the sleeve. "Can't turn that down. There was some trouble at the highway last night. Gent murdered. Be good to have three eyes there for a few minutes tonight."

They said their farewells, adding more gentlemanly ones for Charlotte, then slipped from the room more quickly than she imagined they normally would.

Andreas tapped his tricks on the table, then threw them into the center. He made a dark noise and rose, grabbing his jacket in one smooth motion. He turned and walked to the door.

"I'll speak with you later," Roman said evenly at his departing back.

Andreas didn't halt, just signaled something over his shoulder. Something that she guessed wasn't exactly a kind gesture. The door slammed behind him.

Silence stretched over Charlotte as Roman's eyes remained narrowed on the wood.

"What an ass," he finally said.

She cleared her throat. "Your brother doesn't approve."

He made a little hand gesture. "He doesn't approve of anyone."

"No." She laughed without humor. "You shouldn't have brought me here. It will just cause you trouble."

"What did he say?" The question was casually asked, a thread of coaxing beneath.

She pressed her lips together.

Roman sighed and pushed his chair back, obviously confident that he would find out later. "Don't pay whatever it was any mind. It's just his nature. He's overbearing. Especially with recent events."

She stared at him, disbelieving, as he rose, stretching. "Overbearing?"

Roman stretched farther, his shirt lifting a bit to show a peek of skin beneath. "My God, I was just up, and still, how do people sit in those knobby, wooden chairs for so long?"

"You are spoiled."

"I know." He grinned widely, his eyes lighting with that rare boyish charm that was so odd on such a sinful face. "It's brilliant, no?"

She shook her head but couldn't stop an answering smile, trying to fully push away the lingering unease Andreas's words had caused. "You are a menace."

"Also brilliant." He swept forward and suddenly lifted her up and over his shoulder.

She let out a surprised squeak. "What are you doing?"

"Being a menace." He strode forward, kicked the door to his bedroom fully open, and plopped her down on the bed.

"This is hardly proper," she said breathlessly, anticipating his next movements already.

"There is nothing proper I want to do to you anyway." A finger stroked down her throat.

"I can't stay all night," she whispered.

He smiled and leaned forward. "We'll see."

Chapter 19

Loose hair fell across her eye, and she had the strangest urge to blow it from her view. Emily did that, but Charlotte had never dared.

She touched his collarbone, tracing it down to his sternum. There were old and plentiful wounds there. She circled one at the top, then moved to the next.

"Cataloging my imperfections?"

"From where did you get them?"

"Here and there."

She circled a third that undoubtedly had been made by a knife, then pinched him in response to his nonanswer. He caught her hand and flipped her. Her hair spread in all directions, leaving her free to observe him. He pinned her hands above her head with one hand, and her breathing sped back up. One bent leg pressed her hips to the bed.

"I'd rather examine you." His free fingers traced down her collarbone and followed the same path she had taken but veered off when he reached her left breast, tracing the perimeter, watching it with a lazy smile as her chest rose more rapidly, pushing it higher toward him.

He leaned down, his roughened cheek resting on the edge of one breast, his lips breaths away from the other. "You realize"—every puff of warmed air hit her—"I could do anything to you right now. Anything I want."

She squirmed, strangely aroused by the thought. Then again, she had given complete trust to him in this arena weeks ago. "You do realize you already did things to me?"

One finger traveled up the inside of her thigh, and the tip curled slowly into her. She arched against him, still pinned beneath. He withdrew the touch and began making lazy patterns on her thigh. Her breath came quickly now, for at any moment he would repeat the motion. She knew it. Could feel him smiling against her chest. His amused breath against her exposed nipple.

"There is your *perfect* thigh."

She tensed at the word.

His finger slipped over her thigh, then just as easily slipped into her, her body once again ready, curving in a little more, brushing against the shockingly potent place that he'd already overcome her with.

"And your *perfect* smoothness."

She clenched around the digit, body trying to lift up. His palm cupped her, and his thumb rubbed between. She panted out a breath, then another, all calmness and coolness erased.

"And your *perfect* reaction."

"I hate that word." She breathed the response.

"I know you do," he whispered against her ear.

"Who are you?" And unlike earlier, this time she purely meant it as a question to him.

He pulled back and met her eyes steadily. "Simply a man."

"I know so little about you," she whispered. "Sometimes I'm not even sure you are real. While you know everything about me."

"What flowers you like, what time you rise in the morning, how you take your tea? Hardly things that others don't know or can't learn."

"No." She kept her eyes locked with his. "Not those things."

"How you like to be touched?" He pulled a finger over her thigh, the sensitive inner flesh that always made her shiver. "How your body responds best? What makes you moan?"

"Not just those either." She shook her head slowly, tilting it back on the pillow, something choking and fearful and overwhelming taking hold of her.

"What you hope for? What you need?" He leaned forward and whispered in her ear. "What you fear?"

Everything she feared. Things she didn't want to admit to herself. Foolish, vain things. And things she both wanted, and needed, him to know. That terrified her far worse than anything else ever had. For this man to have her secrets—what would that mean? She couldn't have anything lasting with him. She would be married. This would come to an end. And even if she went the way of the *ton*—affairs and liaisons after the production of heirs— he would undoubtedly lose interest. Men always did once they put the trophy away.

And yet, it whispered between them. That he knew her secrets. That he held them close. That he might *always* do so.

"Yes." The word barely emerged, and in fact she thought she might not have spoken it at all, except that she could see the reflection of it in his satisfied expression as he leaned back again.

"And you?" she whispered. "What do you fear, Roman? You, who seem fearless."

His satisfied expression immediately turned blank. He released her, his leg retreating, only his tapping fingers on her hipbone remaining.

She didn't think he would respond, but she kept silent, not

wanting to fill the silence. Hoping he would start speaking.

For how long had she let him give her what she wanted and needed yet not asked after him in return? Something of their conversation from earlier, before they'd come here to play cards, echoed between them, unspoken. Unresolved.

And he could so easily say nothing.

"A cage. No exit," he said.

Her throat clenched. "A confirmed bachelor?" she said lightly.

"Mmmm."

His tapping fingers began drawing lazy patterns again. "A raven, a dove or rabbit . . . life extinguished."

Her heart beat faster. She wanted to ask—

"No choices." He sucked suddenly at her throat, at the beating pulse there. "Choices taken away."

Her eyes closed. When they reopened, he was drawing patterns once more—across her chest and down her stomach.

"There are so many things to fear, aren't there, Charlotte? Silly things." He touched a lock of her hair, pulling it over her shoulder. "Real things." He touched her hand, fingers circling her fourth finger from the right. "Dangerous things, and things that make no sense." He smoothed his hand down her stomach and over her hip. "Better to live now than fear what is to come."

His eyes met hers, and her breath caught. As if he were asking her to rid herself of all her fears. Fingers touched her cheek.

"Are you playing other games with me, Roman?" she whispered. "Are you playing with me for sport?"

Was any of this real?

One finger drew down her cheek. "Yes. No. Yes."

She hadn't asked three questions aloud though. Which corresponded to which?

"Charlotte, who asks for everything. Charlotte, who asks for nothing in return for herself."

She opened her mouth to speak, to deny, but he gently pushed his fingers to her lips.

"My parents died when I was ten," he said absently, as if speaking of the weather. "Half of London seemed to perish that winter."

She swallowed as his fingers moved down her throat. She knew of what he spoke. She'd been too young to remember it herself, but they had not visited the city for an entire year.

"There was no one else. No money left once the creditors came through. We didn't have much to begin with. And I was too stupid to understand that I should have taken what little money was lying around and fled." He laughed, an old laugh. "Like the debt-ridden aristocrats fleeing to France."

He traced the curve of her breast.

"Took to the streets instead—nowhere else to go. The orphanages were far too crowded—then the sickness swept through them faster than in the rookeries. I found Andreas a few months in. Patched him up. Made him tolerate me."

"His parents also perished in the sickness?"

"Mmmm . . ." He drew a pattern underneath her breast, then circled the tip, not coming too close, but teasingly coming just close enough to make her body tense.

"Tried to work as chimney sweeps for a while. Stupid, terrible job. And Andreas wasn't cut out for it."

She blinked at that.

"Boys can be . . . unkind . . . on the streets, unless you already are someone, or are protected by someone. And sometimes not even that helps. The newest sweeps get tortured and beaten. And, well, let's just say that Andreas didn't take well to anyone laying a hand on him. Or, after I'd forced him to accept me, on me."

"Runaway," she murmured. Abused child. From a wealthy house too, perchance, with the way he spoke.

Roman laughed without warmth. "No, but that is his story to tell."

His fingers pulled along her collarbone, making her shiver.

"Our second week on the job, and I thought I'd never scrape the soot from my lungs. Andreas was up the bricks, cleaning, when one of the boys lit the straw beneath, telling him he was going too slowly and had better hurry."

She closed her eyes, his hands moving over her like burning rushes.

"I knocked it away and got thrown into the bricks for the trouble. Bastards charged us for that later, when we couldn't get the blood out of the mortar."

His lips coasted over her throat, and she thought of the faintly raised scar behind his ear that she could feel sometimes when her fingers ran through his hair.

"Andreas went silent. That should have been their first hint. But the idiot then shoved a poker up the chimney, trying to do damage. He lit another rushlight when that failed."

"What happened?"

"Suffice to say, Andreas dropped to one knee amidst the flames and shot out swinging."

"And the boys?"

"One ran like the coward he was. One never quite learned to work his jaw correctly again. And the one who had been in charge still wears his patch today." The last was said a bit fondly.

Her head jerked up. "But . . ."

Roman merely shrugged. "People change. I trust him

with my life now. Another tale, and one that happened years later. As Bill says, fate can be a pox-ridden whore. And I've always had a tendency to collect strays." His finger worked beneath her chin, then down her throat.

"With one swift stroke though, we were mostly left alone. Became crossing sweepers the next day with the notoriety in our empty pockets, seeing as we were already a set, and that is when everything changed."

He didn't say anything for a moment, simply stared at his fingers ghosting over her skin. She took his hand and turned to her side, propping the side of her chin on her hand, fingers playing over his.

"We started running errands for Nicholas Merrick, a small-time thug who managed a gaming hell and ran a few *businesses* on the side.

"We started working more and more at the hell. Took the notice of the owner. Sent me to *school*. To gain some polish." He flashed a smile, letting his full accent through. "To make contacts."

"And your brother?"

"Andreas hardly needed *school*." Again the accent. "Instead, he got the quick and dirty education in keeping—and cooking—the books."

"Took over the business a few years later when Old Merrick kicked it. Then bought out the owner. Earned enough to buy some land. That turned into two plats, then three."

Landholding was key. She knew better than anyone. The Chatsworths should have sold their country estate long ago, but her father needed the status. Landholders had far more rights.

"We quickly made people take notice. Between the two of us, with such different and complementary skills, it was easy."

Roman the face of the business, its charisma and mercurial danger, and Andreas the hardened, ruthless spine.

"More land, more businesses. Started buying debts when we earned just enough prestige to make it work. If there is one thing people hate, it's creditors, after all. You have to carry enough weight to create a pause. A big enough stick to get things done. And a twist to how you do things, for we usually don't take the debts ourselves, we just make them available. Which helps some people and ruins others."

She pinned him with a look. "Depending on if you like them."

He feigned a look of outrage. "You make me sound like an ogre. Next thing I know, you'll be calling me Andreas."

Charlotte wanted desperately to know if he held all of her father's debts. If that is what had her father drinking more heavily, acting more desperate.

His eyes held hers, watching, *waiting* for her to ask.

"No, I think I'll continue to call you Roman."

His fingers worked into her nape, pulling her head back slightly, exposing her neck. "That is good. I am fond of my brother, even when he is being an ass, and would hate to have to hurt him."

His lips grazed her skin. "There, now you know all about me," he said lightly.

There was something entirely *too* light about the statement. She touched his cheek, making him look at her. There was no emotion so easily defined as *fear* in his light eyes. Nor of concern or trepidation. Yet . . .

"While that tells me a very abbreviated version of your past," she said softly—and some seed that had long been there, fed small chugs of water, growing slowly without her notice—suddenly pushed out its leaves. It made her breath quicken, stirrings of panic pushing at a strange river of calm. "I know much about *you* already, do I not?"

He raised a brow, but there was something dark in his eyes, quickly covered. Something that made her heart increase. *So very close.*

"Oh?"

"And all of those boys downstairs, running around, clean and clothed. From the streets? Chimney sweeps and crossing sweeps and orphans?" Her voice nearly stuttered at the end, reacting to his expression—he was going to *deny* it. And yet, she knew. She *knew.* That little one with the scar? The pride and satisfaction on Roman's face?

The *something* swelled within her. Terrifying. Exhilarating. She couldn't control her breathing. She needed to look away from him, but couldn't.

"Don't be fooled." His eyes narrowed, and she wondered what he read on her face in that moment. "We hire them for our own benefit. Who takes notice of a child, after all?" He said it offhandedly, with a dismissive wave of his hand.

With worship in their eyes, and thin layers of fat filling out their frames? She simply stared at him, the seed sprouting shoots in multiple directions. The feelings intensified. She cut a shoot before it grew too large, but it was simply replaced by a dozen others.

Normally she might wonder why she was panicking so fully at such a small series of internal revelations. But while the revelations themselves might be small, the consequences were anything but. For one revelation just pushed at a dozen thoughts and feelings that were already present, pushing them all together into a maelstrom within her. Pushing into one giant whole.

"You actually gave Trant's money to a fund for orphans, didn't you?" The words emerged a little hysterically.

"Only to irritate him."

"And—"

Her words were cut off as his mouth covered hers. His hands wrapped around the edges of her waist and pressed her into the bed. "No more talking," he said against her mouth, lips trailing over her cheek to her ear. "You have no idea what I've done in this life. It would curdle your blood. Make you shrink from me in horror. Giving a few boys a place doesn't make a dent in my sins."

"There are few of us without sin."

"And there are a few of us with too much to ever be overcome," he said in a low tone.

"You don't think you deserve love?" she asked softly, rubbing her cheek so that she was speaking into *his* ear. Something inside of her rotating her panic and her need. Rotating all focus to him.

He froze.

She gently pushed him to the side, to his back, rolling over to straddle him. She pushed her hair back, leaning down over him.

"Why not, Roman? Do you see it as a cage? Or do you see yourself as the animal that the cage keeps out? The cat from attacking the canary?"

"Charlotte—"

"You want something. You think you might find it in *me*," she said hurriedly, terrified, elated, uncertain, assured. "And yet you are terrified too, aren't you? I'm not alone in this."

He was going to say no.

She pinned his shoulders, leaning over him, hair a curtain around them. "Tell me I'm alone in this feeling." She slipped down so they were touching. He was already hard against her.

"Tell me." She curled her fingers into his shoulders, lining them together. "Tell me if you can."

"No." He looked pained. His eyes closing as she brushed him, slipping along him.

"Why?"

"Always bloody why." He pulled her hips so that she was over him, a thrust away from being completely inside of her. She shifted before he could do it, smiling at the frustrated expression on his face. But there was something vulnerable there too, not wanting to answer her question, and that was what she pressed against.

"Yes. For I want to know." She pulled her hands over his chest. "All of you."

"You won't. I won't let you."

"That will likely be true," she stated, feeling strangely *calm* all of a sudden. Calm and in control. "So I'll tell you instead, Roman Merrick, that regardless of what happens after tonight, with whatever games you are playing outside of this—" She leaned down, touching her lips to his ear. "I will thank my lucky stars that you won me that night. That I've had all of these nights with you."

"Don't thank me," he said hoarsely. "*Don't* thank me."

"Thank you," she whispered, kissing his ear, the side of his throat. "Thank you." Up under his chin. "Thank you."

"I cheated. There was nothing lucky about it," he said harshly, though his body strained into hers. "I cheated in that hand."

She pulled her head back so she could see his eyes, their bodies still straining together, not caring about the words they exchanged. "You cheated to win me?"

"To beat Trant." His teeth gritted together.

She searched his eyes. The heady excitement rushing through her at seeing everything she wanted to see. The debilitating terror rushing through her *at seeing every-thing she wanted to see*. "Mmmm." She smiled at him, controlling the excitement, the terror, channeling them into her want of him, to the moment. "Well, then I will thank *your* lucky stars that you didn't get caught. And that you needed to beat him so badly on that *specific* hand."

He closed his eyes as she slipped down his frame, kissing each scar she came across, and there were many. "Charlotte—"

"I want you to know what you have given me, Roman."

"Given you? Taking your virginity? Making you sneak around to see me? Ruining your future?"

She continued kissing him. "No. For other things. Things that I will never be able to repay."

"Repay?" he asked harshly.

"Yes. For you have given me . . . me." Movement in her reflection once more. The drive to be something more *now,* not later. Still uncertain, still a little broken. But helping to replace bitter strength with something more self-assured and far stronger.

She kissed her way back up. She could see him arguing with himself, eyes tightly shut. "Charlotte—"

She slipped over him. That perfect feeling of being joined together. Like the first time, like the last time.

Of finding someone she could love. Someone in the least likely or appropriate place.

His voice cut off, his hands automatically going to her hips, pulling her more fully on him, clasping her to him.

"You know my fears," she whispered. "The silly and the real."

Silly things like beauty and growing old and her worth wrapped up in everything superficial and fleeting. Real things like Emily and her parents and losing herself.

"And you make me want to be better than those fears."

Even if she never saw Roman again after tonight, and the thought physically hurt that she might not, she was determined to *keep* that movement.

To keep the emotions the man below her inspired. A man who she both *knew* and knew not at all. For he *was* playing her in some way still. A game within.

"Charlotte—"

She rose and lowered herself again, pressing against him, and he closed his eyes, pulling her hips down to capture the deep curl of feeling underneath. God, it felt so wonderful. She had never realized that her body could feel this way. Could produce such spectacular feelings. And if that were only it, then she could dismiss it all as physical pleasure.

The problem was that she felt a similar euphoria whenever he was near. When he smiled, when he tweaked her, when the danger danced along his skin, sparking her. *He* was where the feeling emanated from. Becoming a hundred times as potent when he was inside of her.

Her body moved with the thoughts, wanting to please him, wanting to please herself, *them* together.

He groaned, drawing her more firmly down each time, moving her hips, pulling her that extra measure so they were so fully joined she didn't know if they'd be able to separate. Then moving with her body to do it again. Never one to passively accept anything. Always demanding the same from her. "Charlotte, I—"

Vulnerability. Pupils swallowing the blue with desire. Need. Alarm.

She leaned over, rubbing her thumbs along his cheeks. "Shhh . . . all will be well, Roman. You have nothing to regret." She watched his eyes, rims of sky around dark tunnels of black. "For no matter what . . ." She leaned down to his ear. "I won't regret having and loving you."

The certainty of the statement—the terror and euphoria collided. She felt the balloon fill . . . not a distention of despair but filling with a mist of warmth and determination.

Squeezing her, as she squeezed him. And she was riding the wave of it as he went rigid beneath her, as he pulled her mouth to his, consuming her, plunging up into her again and again, driving her to the brink.

One finger grasping sanity's edge as the rest of her fell over into the abyss.

He smiled cockily at her an hour later. "I should return you just like that." He kissed the side of her neck as she continued to dress, everything about her appearance thoroughly debauched.

She sent him a raised brow. "Are you feeling the sudden urge to make a visit to the parson tomorrow?"

His shirt was half-done up, sleeves rolled, golden hair half-curling and falling in disarray around his face. He looked just like the decadent, fallen angel she had first thought him.

He touched her cheek, crooked smile still in place. "Mmmm, do you know any?" He leaned forward and touched his lips to hers. It was so perfect, she heard what had to be a choir of angels.

Though if she was being honest, it sounded more like the stamping of hell's minions. Cacophony growing closer from every direction. Still, she decided not to be picky. Angels were obviously a rowdy bunch.

She closed her eyes and leaned in to him, one hand gripping his half-open shirt, fingers of the other wrapping around the band of his arm.

The muscles beneath her fingers tightened suddenly, immeasurably, and the next thing she knew her nose was pressed against his back.

And the whistle of something whirred past her ear.

Chapter 20

She didn't know how he moved so quickly, moving both of them together in one sharp, seamless movement. She had no idea how he had spun her behind him like that, nor how they moved from the bed to the wall so swiftly, but she found herself flattened against the smooth surface, his back pressed against her, his body completely blocking her. Long and wicked-looking knives glinted in his hands.

She had just watched him put that shirt on. How had he hidden knives in his sleeves without her noticing?

And Hell's minions, indeed. It sounded like the entire neighborhood was outside, trying to break down the walls.

Roman's entire body stiffened, and she had the feeling he would be doing something far different if she weren't pressed behind him. It was as if he were expecting, almost resigned, to being shot or—

A second whistle ended in a ping, shattering a decanter near her head. A spray of glass erupted to the floor, thankfully away from them.

Thankfully? She saw the flat knife that had fallen amidst the glass. Dear God, someone had thrown a knife at them. Suddenly, the whirring sound that had accompanied their movement to the wall connected with the evidence before her. A *second* knife.

But Roman still didn't move. And the noise of the crowd far below grew louder.

"Merrick." A voice called, and she could see black boots step forward out of the door's shadows. She couldn't see anything else, blocked as she was. "Merely a warning, as you've obviously guessed since we aren't currently trading blood." Something hit the ground, near their feet—a black card with a picture of a man hanging upon it. "I was hired. I have *missed*. Our debt is satisfied."

"Who?" Roman's voice was deadly flat.

"A surprise, to be sure. I hadn't realized the ass was so *well* connected." The voice was equally flat, almost bored, with just the slightest hint of irritation. "And if it'd been *he* as my target . . ."

It didn't seem possible, but Roman's body stiffened further.

"Ah, family betrayal. A lovely thing. Though I don't believe anyone else has pieced it together," the voice said, musing. A sudden increase in the rage of the crowd below nearly drowned his words. "But fair warning. The stirrings are enough to cause comment—everyone waits to see what will happen."

Something fairly *vibrated* about Roman's body. He wanted to be somewhere else *now*. But he tilted his head, waiting, and a second later the dark boots disappeared soundlessly into the shadows.

As soon as the man disappeared, Roman was in motion. "Andreas." There was something of anguish to it.

Wait, what? Andreas had attacked them? Or had them attacked? And was the entire building under siege?

Roman's hand whipped, and the knife in his right hand disappeared. He knelt and in two smooth motions pulled a pistol from under a pile of clothing and pulled a cord under the bed with his other hand. He cocked the pistol, pressing it into her hands, eyes locked with hers. "Shoot anything that moves. Reinforcements will be here in one minute."

Then he was darting through the partially opened door.

Charlotte frantically looked around, but there was no evidence of whoever had been throwing knives at them. And she had the very certain notion that Roman wouldn't have left if he had thought otherwise.

She held the pistol gingerly in her numb fingers before curling her fingers tightly around the handle, jerkily aiming it at everything in the room that caught her attention. She might have never held one before, but that didn't mean that with the choice between pulling the trigger and having one pulled on her, she wasn't going to choose the first option.

She listened to the roar below and clenched tight fingers around metal. She couldn't even comprehend what was happening.

Andreas had betrayed Roman? Had hired someone to kill him? And what . . . people were rioting below to make sure no one escaped alive?

But . . . but Roman had gone after Andreas. What would *Andreas* do to Roman? Especially with Roman in emotional pain over his betrayal? Andreas could *kill* him.

Her mouth opened, her throat worked, but no sound emerged. Killed while she stood here stupidly waiting— while a crowd tried to break down the building at its foundations and destroy everything within.

Her feet moved through the bedroom door and toward the outer door without mental consent. She attempted to open the outer door, but it was locked tight. It took a precious thirty seconds to unlock the *three* locks. How . . . ? She shook her head at the unimportance of the question. The hall was empty, but the only other door in the hall was ajar—Andreas's room, sharing the other half of the building's upper floor with Roman.

Her breath came in pants, but she crept to Andreas's door, pistol waving all over the hallway toward any noise.

Then everything went suddenly silent. So silent. Nary a shout from the streets below.

She slowly peered around the edge of Andreas's door.

Her first impression consisted solely of bodies and blood. Then her gaze snapped to Roman, who was crouched, hovering, over someone half-propped against the wall. She took a step forward. Roman spun around and for a split second she saw her life end. His knife hit the wall half a pace from her, as, at the last moment, he threw off his aim. The blade vibrated outside of the tip of its sheath.

"Shit. God. Charlotte." He closed his eyes tight, then they shot open. "Stanley," he shouted. "One-eye, Milton, Bertrand, Lefty! Upstairs, now!"

She wasn't sure her body would regain movement, the pistol frozen in her fingers for all eternity. She heard feet furiously stamp up the stairs and down the hall.

"Sorry, Boss, but someone started a riot and—" The young voice abruptly ended as a boy appeared at her side, stopping dead just inside the frame of the door. She could feel at least one other body at her side, but her head stubbornly stayed forward, unable to move or look to see.

"Johnny, whiskey, needle, and thread. Peter, the special knife, two candles." There was nothing soft about Roman's voice, and his accent was so thick she could barely discern the words.

The scene finally snapped into sharp focus as someone next to her pried the pistol from her frozen fingers. Roman was crouched over *Andreas*, who looked as if he'd participated in a war, one leg bent at an odd angle. And there were five other bodies and a flood of spilled blood on the floor.

"Dammit, don't touch that." Andreas, fortunately, or *unfortunately,* still alive, tried to swat Roman's hand away from a bloodied gash in his chest.

"Stop being a fucking lightskirt." But Roman's voice was steady—too even. "Charlotte, can you sew him up?" Roman didn't meet her eyes for a moment, but when he did, they were carefully blanked of expression.

"No. No *bloody* way," Andreas said.

Roman looked relieved to look away from her and back to his brother. "She's a lady. They have to know how to sew a perfect stitch. It's a requirement."

Charlotte knew quite a few ladies who were abysmal at it, actually, but she thought it best not to add her thoughts. They kept slipping to the dead bodies splayed on the floor anyway. The blood soaking the floor was like too much wine spilled at a Bacchanalia. She was pretty sure the man nearest her had not died *pleasantly.* And another one . . . she didn't know you could actually stick a blade through bone like that.

She snapped her eyes away, focusing instead on a lock of hair that was falling into Roman's eye as he argued with his brother.

"It's the best option."

His hair was always quite fetching.

"She's not *touching* me."

"She'll do you up right."

A much nicer color than hers.

"No."

And his eyes. They were fetching as well. Very fetching all around. She felt fetching too when she was around him. "Fetching," what a strange word. Like fletching, but without the "L" that made one's tongue do extra work.

"Why are you whining? She will—*shit!*"

Huh. The ceiling wasn't gold here, but the wood was quite dark.

"See?" a voice hissed. "Bloody useless."

She wondered if they planned it that way—to echo themselves in their décor.

Roman's face appeared in her view. How'd he get up there? "Charlotte? Charlotte, are you hurt? Did Slade hit you without me realizing it?"

He sounded panicked, and she felt his hands moving over her. She tried to reassure him. He would always be so pretty, unlike her. Her mouth opened, but before she could say anything, his eyes went wide, and she found herself twisted to the side.

A good thing really, as she proceeded to retch all over the floor and what looked like a bloody stump. But that didn't make sense. There were no bodies over on this side of her. She retched again, only Roman's soothing hands keeping her from falling into the swirling mess.

"She *fainted*." The voice sounded farther away than the wall. "Ladies *faint* at the sight of blood. And then *vomit*. Except they call it 'casting up their accounts' because they are too *ladylike* to use the real word. *Bloody useless*."

Roman uttered a string of words—quick and angry—but she couldn't catch them with his thickened accent and through her fuzzed thoughts.

"I will *not*," Andreas sounded furious—not that that was different from usual.

Fifteen minutes later, and with a cold compress pressed to her forehead, she watched from a chair as they bickered over how to stitch up the wound.

"Now, Boss, you know you ain't no good with a needle." Bill rubbed a hand along the back of his neck. "And the only good blood-and-bones can't be found. Damn riot. Smart bastards to start it. Kept everyone busy downstairs. Lucky we didn't lose anyone."

She had been studiously avoiding watching the boys clean up the bodies. It had taken six trips. She closed her eyes and pressed the pad harder against her forehead, trying not to think about why five bodies necessitated six trips.

"Anyway," Bill continued. "Merrick is the best one with a needle. A rotten ass of a doctor, but he gets the job done."

"Exactly." Andreas held out his hand imperiously. "Now bring me a damn mirror and give me the damn needle, so I can sew it up my damn self."

"You'll end up stabbing yourself," Roman said flatly. "Your hands are shaking. You've lost too much blood."

"My hands are not shaking." Andreas's voice was deadly.

Charlotte threw the cloth down on the table. "Just give *me* the damn thing."

"*No.*"

She stood up and strode around the—*wine*—on the floor. "Give it here." She held out her hand, and Roman gamely handed the needle to her.

The wound had been cleansed, so she could see the blade line.

"Have you ever even seen this done?" Andreas snarled.

"No," she said bluntly. "But you are sorrier-looking than my first embroidery attempt, so shut your gob."

Surprisingly, he did. She thought it might be because he was too tired to do anything else, though. He glared but closed his eyes, leaning his head back against the wall. He had other injuries too, but the chest wound was by far the worst. Somehow his leg looked completely normal again. Obviously a trick of her mind before she'd fainted.

She threaded the needle. A simple series of straight stitches. She had been able to sew a perfect line since she was eight. That's all she needed to do. She put her finger on top of the needle and placed the tip against his skin. Of course, sewing through cloth and sewing through skin were hardly equal tasks. She hesitated, point pressed.

"Just push it through," he said viciously, eyes still closed. "What difference does it make at this point? You'll probably faint halfway through the first stitch anyway, then I can just do it myself."

She set her jaw and pricked the skin, pushing through to the other side of the gash. "You know exactly how to motivate me, Mr. Merrick. Congratulations."

She finished the half stitch, pulling the thread through as carefully as she could. She peered up to see his eyes still closed but with something looser in his expression.

"Are *you* going to faint, Mr. Merrick?"

He peeked one eye open to look at her, death promised in his glare.

She looked down, satisfied, and started the next stitch, settling the scene into a rhythm as she worked.

Andreas took a swig from the bottle in his hand a few minutes later, far calmer. "I don't know whether to be insulted or pleased that they sent five men after me and Slade after you," he said to Roman.

But now that things were being taken care of, Roman was unresponsive, rolling a pair of dice under his palm, across the table, over and over, staring at them as if doing otherwise would produce dire results. Charlotte spared him a quick look as she threaded the needle with a new line. She was nearly done stitching. Apprehension slid through her, but she couldn't identify why.

Bill looked pensive. "Maybe luck of the draw. Slade's expensive. So they sent one pot one way and the other"—

he shrugged—"to the other. But they didn't make the proper inquiries, or else they would have sent Slade after you instead, Merrick. There's only one person in this world who Slade would show himself to, and they submitted his name to the fold." Bill shook his head and shot a glance at Roman. Charlotte's apprehension grew at the concerned look in Bill's eye as he too watched the steady crackle of dice.

Andreas smiled, eyes closed once more. "Does my heart good to think that the bastard's reputation took a hit tonight."

"He'll probably hold it against *you*," Bill pointed out.

Andreas smiled thinly. "I hope so. It will give me opportunity when they send round two."

"Only thing in our favor is that they might think Slade can't do the job properly and not hire him again. How did people without an arseload of inquiry figure out how to contact him anyhow? S'not easy. It has to be multiple factions working together, Boss, you were right. Bad communication is to our advantage."

"Who's Slade?" Charlotte asked, pricking Andreas's skin again with a far steadier hand than she had any reason to claim.

She could see Andreas study her from beneath cracked lids. "He's an assassin," he said finally.

"I put that together, actually," she said calmly, pulling the thread through. "But *who* is he, and why didn't he kill us?"

"What difference does it make *who* he is?" But Andreas moved his fingers slightly around the neck of the bottle, belying his words. "Wouldn't have killed you anyway unless you saw his face, or he was paid to put you in a grave. Roman was the target."

"Slade's the best," Bill piped in, then held out his

hands. "No offense, Merrick." Bill addressed Charlotte again quickly. "Boss saved his arse years ago when Slade was still wet behind the ears." His brow furrowed, and he turned to Roman. "You know, Slade might have chosen his target. Taken you instead, Boss. To protect you like."

Roman shrugged. He looked bored. "Perhaps. Though why now?" And now his voice sounded anything but bored. Vicious, angry, savage. "This happens all the time after all." He swept the dice, flinging them harshly against the wall. He threw back his chair and went to the sideboard.

Andreas's eyes narrowed on him. Charlotte's unease turned into a raging tumult.

"What's crawled up your breeches?" Andreas demanded.

Roman fished through glass containers, ignoring him, clinking bottles together.

"Stop abusing my liquor."

"Walk over here and stop me." Roman's voice retained the vicious thread as he grabbed a bottle, nearly breaking it along with another as he yanked the glass container from its pocket.

"Roman." The voice held warning. A warning laced with some unidentifiable emotion. And like before, her body instinctively reacted to the threat underlying every aspect of Andreas, and her shoulders rose and tightened.

Glass shattered somewhere behind her.

Andreas thumped his own bottle down roughly, and she found the needle plucked from her hand. She blinked at her empty fingers. Shock overpowering everything else.

"Out! All of you. Now," Andreas barked, holding the needle, threaded and still attached to him.

And it was as if everyone had a pressing urge to use the commode, as they all stumbled over each other trying to get to the door. She stared at the madness.

"You, out too," Andreas hissed at her.

She bristled and opened her mouth to respond, but something in Andreas's eyes stopped her. Something neither cold nor cruel. Something almost approaching fear. And it stopped her.

She looked from one of his dark eyes to the other, and in other circumstances she might have been surprised to notice that his eyes weren't inky black—they were a very dark blue. And as if the realization that Andreas wasn't a fathomless pit, and instead was just very, very dark, made a difference to her worldview, she rose and stiffly walked to the door.

Roman stood rigidly by the sideboard, gripping a bottle, aggression vibrating underneath his skin. His mouth tightened as his eyes slid past her, still not fully meeting her gaze. Saying nothing.

But as she touched the handle of the door, the words came, dark and harsh, as if torn from him.

"Do not leave this floor."

She gripped the handle, turned it, and walked stiffly into the hall, where a gaggle of men and boys shifted uneasily. She shut the door behind her just as the shouting started.

Charlotte curled into Roman's plush seat and idly moved pieces on the chessboard. The yelling—and a few conspicuous thumps and sounds of breaking glass—had ceased half an hour ago. There hadn't been a peep since, though neither Andreas nor Roman had emerged. They had either killed each other or worked through the argument, as stupid men did.

Bill, who had been the only one to remain with her—having sent the others to various defensive stations or tasks—had looked relieved, so she was inclined to the latter view. Some of the words had penetrated the wood, though most of the time it had been obvious that they were too aware that there were others near.

Still, it had become evident that Roman felt he had endangered her life. That he would always do so. Andreas had not been kind, saying she had been in as much danger the day before, and yet he hadn't cared then.

That hadn't gone over well.

She had finally given up waiting outside and numbly walked to Roman's room, which had already been thoroughly searched for intruders and cleared, and closed the door behind her.

She had then leaned against it for long moments, with her eyes closed and a delayed whimper on her lips. Finally, after gathering herself, she had moved to the table—not a desk, for there were no *desks* in his personal rooms—and sat in his cozy, well-loved chair.

Roman was going to push her away. That much was clear because that's what stupid people did.

Stupid people like she, too scared to grab the *good* that she could have.

Smart people like she, with enough regard for others to understand that her actions didn't impact just her alone.

She moved the white queen, dragging her rigid hem along the squares.

She should let him push her away. Make it easy.

Make *life* easier. Make life safer. Make life so less vibrant and bright and warm.

She heard a door shut down the hall, then Roman's door opened. Andreas strode inside, dark and deadly, though the sinister air that usually surrounded him was conspicuously absent, and there was a slight hitch to his stride. Probably more to do with the loss of blood than anything else.

He regarded her for a long moment, taking her measure. She took his right back. She figured that she had poked a needle through his flesh, she might as well tell him to go to hell too.

"If you are here to tell me to stay away from Roman, you can—"

He gave a humorless laugh, eyes dark. Dark *blue*. "I'm not." It was hard to hold his piercing stare, truly, but she did so, determined. He lifted his chin, regarding her as if she were a mangled insect that somehow still managed to stay alive. "If you make him happy, then I will *tolerate* you."

Only the stubborn urge not to allow him to flummox her moved her tongue. "That is very sporting of you." At least, that's what she figured she should say. "Thank you."

She couldn't read his expression for a moment. "But just because I know why he likes you," he said, "doesn't mean *I* have to like you."

"Of course." She smiled without humor. "I'd hardly think you a man to be swayed by cool manners or a pretty face."

His finger nearly vibrated as he jammed it in her direction. "If you think he likes you because you are beautiful or finely mannered, then you are as stupid and useless as I once thought you."

She blinked.

He turned and was almost to the door before he stopped and angled his head slightly back toward her. "Oh, and thank you for stitching me up."

And then he was gone.

Roman had tried to grab Andreas before he entered the room, but even injured, his brother was a slippery bastard.

Andreas exited again, an unreadable expression on his

face. Roman moved to walk past him, but Andreas's hand shot out, gripping his forearm.

"Don't be an idiot." Then he strode off, likely heading somewhere to get soused.

An idiot? That was what he had been to think that everything would be fine. That he could control the chaos when he wanted to. That nothing could touch him.

He hadn't much cared that anything could touch him before. He still didn't. But that it could touch *Charlotte* . . .

He could feel the lingering coil of absolute fear. Fucking unpleasant emotion. His hand shook. An inch to the left, and *he* would have killed her.

From his post just outside Roman's door, Bill tilted his head in question. Roman wanted to shake his head and walk right by his room. Even with the door wide open and her able to see him do it. Better than seeing that overlay of her face lifeless and frozen. Shit, he had just admitted no more than a few hours past that one of his fears was—

She appeared in the door, her features very much alive. "Are you not going to come in, Roman?" Her voice was soft. Almost as if she *understood* what was going through his mind.

But then again, maybe she did.

His feet took him toward her, unwillingly, and he entered the room, pulling the door shut behind him. But he couldn't meet her eyes. All of his cute games. His plans and traps. His excitement that maybe . . . just maybe . . .

"You did not endanger me." Soft, so soft, her voice as it attempted to absolve him of damnation.

He gave a brittle little laugh. Andreas had already rung him up one side and down the other, and that hadn't helped. He opened his mouth to say so.

She touched his cheek, making him meet her eyes. Bright blue rimmed with gold. "Everything is well. See?"

And she gently pulled his head down, her lips gliding over his forehead, over his eyelids.

One hour earlier, and he would have had something easily witty to say to that.

"Everything is not well, Charlotte."

She took his hand and pulled it to her throat, to the heavy beat in her neck, then down her chest and around her waist.

He shuddered, then slowly withdrew his hand. "I'll have One-eye and three of the others escort you home."

"Why?"

"You will be safe with them."

She gripped the open edges of his shirt, giving him a shake. "I will be safe with *you*."

"*I know*." He grabbed her wrists against her chest, spinning and pinning her to the wall. "Because I would skin anyone alive who dared to touch you."

He could feel her heart beating nearly through her chest. A black, ruptured emotion slithered through him. She was *afraid* of him.

She pulled his mouth to hers, almost savagely, and he shuddered under the onslaught of need that rushed through him. To possess her. To keep her. To protect her. To never let her stop pulling and kissing him as hard as she was able.

Every dark desire that he had first felt for her remained true, but with the certainty that she would push back to dominate him too. Equally.

What he *wanted* from her. *Needed* from her.

But what was best for *Charlotte*?

He pulled away, breath harsh. "Go home, Charlotte."

"You are being foolish." She stepped toward him again.

He pivoted and walked around the table, picking up the decanter of One-eye's specialty—for he needed all of his wits about him—putting furniture between them, not letting the desire to chain Charlotte to his bed overtake him.

After all, she had been threatened there. The thought spilled a cool river of ice down his spine. "Don't tell me of foolishness." He gripped the glass cylinder. "I *cheated* to win you that night, Charlotte. After the way the Delaneys spoke of you, after seeing you in the market, trapped, then digging into your charity works, seeing you again in the Hunsdens' shop? Wanting to meet you the normal way, but knowing then that would never be possible?"

She reached a hand toward him, eyes wide and full of emotion at the serial confessions, but he pushed backward, even with the furniture already lodged between them.

"I *cheated*. Do you know what could have occurred if Trant had proven that? And now? That I have been poaching a highborn woman considered incomparable? They wouldn't need to pass legislation against us. And do you know the games I've played with you? And with everyone around you?" He gave a humorless laugh. "Do you?"

"Don't tell me of your regrets," she hissed, anger replacing all of the softer emotions in her face. "Not now when you are obviously beyond sense. *I regret nothing.*" She slashed her hand through the air.

His personal motto. And at the same time, regret slithered over every thought he now possessed.

What was best for Charlotte? The answer was obvious. And for once he needed to overcome his selfish desires.

"Go home, Charlotte."

"So that's it?" She straightened, her lovely pride stiffening her frame. "You are finished with me? Finally?"

He discarded the glass and moved so quickly across the room, around the furniture, that he saw the surprise that she couldn't hide.

"No." He touched her chin, made her meet his eyes.

Charlotte needed society and the life she had been born to, and he would put her back on that path, but he wouldn't let her believe herself a passing fancy in order to do so. "I would never be finished with you, Charlotte."

Something far more contorted than simple confusion graced her face. "Roman." And her voice was soft, questioning. "Do you think you might come to love me? If you weren't . . . giving . . . me back? Someday? Just a little?"

He was frozen. Absolutely frozen. He couldn't speak a word. She lifted her chin a notch and pressed a soft kiss to his lips at his nonresponse. And still he remained frozen. He saw her walk to the door and grab Bill's arm. Heard their footsteps filing down the hall. Leaving.

Leaving. Never hearing his whisper that he already did.

Chapter 21

She hadn't seen him in a week. Always looking to the shadows, desperately *hoping* he would be there. Fearing what his absence meant. Both to what lay broken between them and to his own safety.

But she only saw the men shadowing her. Bill usually, and sometimes "Lefty," a man she had seen so often that she had forced him to introduce himself. Milton had appeared a few times. She'd even seen Andreas once, waiting outside of an event in the shadows, arms crossed, eyes dark and grumpy.

But no Roman.

She had taken the warnings Bill had given her to heart and not sought Roman out. She would not put Roman in more danger by going to the hell just yet. Bill said "soon."

The only problem was she didn't know what would happen if and when "soon" finally came. She wondered if a single word had ever caused such anxiety.

"Charlotte, I say, what the devil is wrong with you? You have been as grouchy as a troll and as jumpy as a three-legged foal."

She pinned Emily with a look, but her sister smiled in response.

"Come on, Charlotte," Emily coaxed, pulling ahead of

her, walking backward. "Race you home. The morning was a dead bore. Please? For me?"

Charlotte bit her lip, feeling the memory of hot eyes upon her, releasing and holding her, spurring her forth. She started running, uncharacteristically giving in to her sister's demand.

Emily whooped as they raced.

They arrived home flushed and slightly breathless a few minutes later.

"Brilliant," Emily exclaimed, tugging off her outer garment as soon as they were inside. Charlotte smiled at her, blood pumping, feeling better than she had in days.

"Mr. Chatsworth is closeted with Mr. Trant," her mother said from the parlor, without looking up from her stitching.

Charlotte stilled, her fingers on the edges of her pelisse.

Making an offer.

She didn't respond, and her mother's eyes suddenly met hers, brows raised. Asking the silent dark question of whether she cared—of whether her *lover* would care.

Charlotte removed her pelisse slowly, handing it to their butler along with her reticule. "Is he?" she responded calmly. "For how long has Mr. Trant been here?"

"An hour now."

Hammering out details.

It wasn't the first time someone had closeted himself with her father with an offer. But she was reaching the apogee—drawing ever closer to the last.

Emily looked confused. And strangely concerned as she followed Charlotte farther into the room.

"One would think Mr. Trant was buying into the rumors," her mother said, stitching, eyes on her piece. Charlotte hadn't stitched in a week. Hadn't been able to without thinking about that night. "That he wishes to secure your obedience quickly."

Charlotte sat stiffly in a chair. There was a tea service on the table. "A cup of tea, Emily?"

Emily hopped forward and poured as if she'd always been a dab hand at it, offering a cup to Charlotte, then balancing her own perfectly on her lap. She gave Charlotte a fierce, supportive smile.

Their mother's eyes didn't lift, her response apathetic. "Adequate, Emily. Perhaps in two years, you will not be a complete disappointment to your father."

Charlotte's smile froze in its response to Emily's. "Better than adequate, Mother," she said smoothly. "And Emily is far from a disappointment. In fact, she handled that as if she had never been anything other than perfec—" Charlotte looked at her sister. "She handled that just like the magnificent woman she is."

Emily's smile resumed its brilliance.

"You coddle her." Stitch, stitch, unending stitch. "How did she do on your rounds today?" Viola's tone said that she had already come to her own assumption about Emily's performance.

Charlotte kept the stiff smile about her lips. "Emily did extremely well. I remember a time when I was far less certain of where to place my cup or how to enter conversation."

Viola's mouth pinched. "As if you have ever tipped a cup." She jabbed her needle through the cloth.

"And besides that," Charlotte pressed on, "Emily's presence fairly lights a room on fire. She will start her own fashions, mark my words."

Viola made a little noise as she worked another endless stitch.

Emily's face drooped for a second before she grasped onto Charlotte's words again. Charlotte could see the thoughts tumbling there on her face. That she believed in *Charlotte's* words. That she would make her own happiness.

Charlotte *wanted* to make sure she had that chance. It had been her most desperate desire for so long. Her own happiness easily pushed to the side, for *Emily* had always been her happiness.

And now . . . Yes, now. That was the question.

Charlotte looked at their mother. Had *Viola* ever been happy? Charlotte thought of the miniature portrait she had once found in the attic—one her grandparents had commissioned upon her mother's debut. The girl within had been sparkling. Vivacious.

The woman across from her though looked like a dimmed reflection of chipped paint. And yet reflections could hold their own shine. They simply needed polishing.

The malaise seemed to feed on itself, insidious. Her mother begging off appointments and leaving Charlotte to attend on her own or with one of their neighbors. She wondered why no one had ever broken her mother of the spell.

Why hadn't *she*? Because . . . because Viola was her mother. Untouchable in the same way her father had once been.

And Charlotte could see how the malaise might have taken hold. How the anger had turned to bitterness, then resignation. The darker emotions never truly leaving, merely hiding behind the melancholy.

How Charlotte could go down that path herself if she wasn't careful. How she might have contributed to her mother's descent if only in that she had done nothing to stop it.

Charlotte narrowed her eyes. When was the last time her mother had been to the park? To an event outside of the *ton*?

Charlotte pushed forward in her chair. "Let us go to the park and the fair this afternoon."

Emily pushed forward too, more than eager for an outing that would prove entertaining.

"Mother?" Charlotte asked.

Viola waved a hand, well used to simply polite inquiries. "I'm sure you will find it amusing."

"All of us will find it amusing. You are coming with us." Charlotte said it calmly but injected just the right amount of steel.

Her mother looked up, and her eyes narrowed before the malaise took hold once more. "I don't feel up to it. You two go."

"No," Charlotte said in the same calm, steely tone. Her sister's eyes widened, and Emily shifted in her seat. "We wish you to accompany us."

She could feel Emily saying "We do?" in her thoughts, but wisely her sister held her tongue.

"I have the headache, Charlotte," Viola said with more asperity, unused to her daughter arguing with her. Charlotte found it easier to do things without her parents, so she always took the easy excuses tossed her way, finding accompaniment with others—mainly Miranda for this past season.

Selfish and easy, yes, and perhaps unwise.

"Fresh air will do your head good."

"Aunt Edith needs looking after," her mother said with a wave.

"Anna can look after her just fine." Aunt Edith was a convenient excuse they used to explain her mother's frequent absences and general state of fatigue. The elderly woman lived next door, rarely emerging, content to do . . . whatever it was she did. Emily liked to say she was a spy, but Charlotte thought maybe she was simply a hermit sitting on her husband's fortune. Bennett, her nephew, was always trying to figure out a way to get his hands on it since he was her closest family member.

Regardless, Aunt Edith made the perfect excuse. That Viola Chatsworth was so *devoted* to family was something that the matrons admired. It kept tongues subdued. It also hinted, wrongly—but no one outside of the family *knew* that—that the Chatsworths would one day be out of debt, inheriting Edith's money.

"Aunt Edith doesn't like Anna."

Charlotte wasn't sure Edith liked *Viola* either. But then, she seemed to tolerate the deception as long as Bennett kept his paws away from her paintings.

"Aunt Edith will be fine. You don't need to attend her today."

Her mother's eyes narrowed, pinning her, stitching forgotten. "Then perhaps I merely don't wish to go with *you*."

No one ever made her mother attend an event that she didn't wish. She could shred a person to ribbons if she chose. Bennett dealt with her as little as possible.

"You will feel better," Charlotte said, gently. "I want you to feel better."

"I don't wish to go," her mother hissed in reaction. "With an incompetent"—she pointed her needle toward Emily, then Charlotte—"and *perfection*."

Charlotte held her mother's wild eyes, determined not to allow the words to hurt. Or to look at Emily's assuredly devastated face and give in to the rage.

In part because . . . because Viola had never said a word about Charlotte's *activities*. Not since the night in the carriage. Her mother had been tight-lipped and surprisingly nonjudgmental, when she could have decimated her with a few well-chosen barbs.

She thought of Roman's slipped words that at the be-

ginning of their relationship he had needed to overrun
Andreas's prickly exterior to get to the real man beneath.

She took a deep breath. "Then you can go with your
daughters."

Heavy silence fell and stretched.

Charlotte disregarded her pride. "We wish you to come
with us. Please."

"I will make the outing hell for you." Viola's voice was
almost pleasant as she jabbed her needle into the piece.

Charlotte nodded. "I know. I still wish you to accompany us."

There was a strangled sound, and her mother threw
down her stitching and swept from her chair and through
the door.

Emily stared after her, wide-eyed and unsure. "Charlotte, what are you doing? It . . . it is more fun without her."

Charlotte tipped her head, not wanting to utter anything
that could be construed as agreement in case Viola was
standing on the other side of the wall, listening. "Let's
give her a chance, Emily. Do you not wish she would come
with us, happily?"

Emily didn't look convinced. "I suppose."

"If she comes back, give her a chance. Otherwise, we
will go ourselves. Yes?"

Emily slowly nodded.

Charlotte half expected her mother not to return, but
ten minutes later she did. Charlotte swallowed, trying to
restrain the tendril of optimism.

Her mother gave her a dark glance. "Very well. The
sooner we get this farce over, the better."

It was more spirit than her mother had shown in years.
And the rope of guilt that she had let her mother linger
in her own cage knotted about her neck. She had always
accepted that cages were necessary—that it was just the

way things were. Charlotte swallowed uncomfortably.

"Excellent," she said softly. "Thank you, Mother."

Viola nodded sharply. Charlotte looked more closely at her, at her expression, at her tight lips. *At the deep fear underlining her irritation. Along with something else, something she couldn't identify.*

Scared of her daughters? No, that wasn't quite it.

Oh. Charlotte felt the revelation—the *revelations*—so keenly it almost choked her. She pushed aside the one tied to Roman and concentrated on her mother. Viola had ever been a vicious woman when it came to their father. And she had encompassed her daughters in that vitriol—then hadn't known how to stop.

Behind the fear in her mother's eyes, behind the irritation, there was *hope*. Choking hope.

"Yes," Charlotte said firmly. "It will be wonderful, just the three of us. We can change dresses and—"

A door opened. Footsteps and voices.

Trant emerged in the doorway to the room, her father a step behind him. Her father shot her a look full of dark meaning. Deal with Trant—or else.

"Mrs. Chatsworth, Miss Chatsworth, Miss Emily." Trant nodded to each of them, his eyes quickly focusing back on Charlotte. "If I could speak with Miss Chatsworth privately?"

Viola's expression gave away nothing, but she eyed Charlotte for a long moment. "Of course, Mr. Trant." Her mother ushered a wide-eyed Emily from the room.

Trant motioned to another chair in the room. Charlotte woodenly rose and accepted the offered seat. An ornate chair her parents hadn't yet been able to part with. Uncomfortable, but beautiful. Trant drew the door shut and approached her again, hands behind his back.

"I've spoken with your father."

"Yes." She called upon her manners—and they held her stiff. They never abandoned her except when Roman Merrick called them to his control.

"And he still proves . . . stubborn. Unwilling to believe my assurances."

"My father often does not follow where others want to lead." He never followed where she did.

"He does not realize the extent of the mistake he makes, allowing me to speak with you instead. You know what I desire." His eyes took her in. Admiring her posture and carriage. Her teeth like a good horse showed.

"Yes."

"We could make a good team, Charlotte."

She looked at him steadily, at the use of her Christian name. "Of course we could, Mr. Trant."

"The things we could accomplish together . . . Things beyond your father's narrow view."

Rule the *ton*. Climb the social vines. Create their place at the top.

Trant needed her, or someone like her. And the farther he climbed, the higher she would ascend. Unlike Downing, who cared not, and Marquess Binchley, who lacked vision, Trant's ambition would push him high.

"Yes, I am not unaware."

She wasn't a duke's daughter, or an heiress, but she was exactly what he needed and could have. Poised, impeccable, the perfect hostess, with the grit to rule. And her father had made her attainable. Had limited his own ambitions with one simple round of cards.

Had both freed and chained her with the same.

"I know you aren't. It is one of your many fine attributes. Your father plays a game still. Holding me off until the end of the season, though little does he seem to realize that it is far too late. But it is not your father whom I have to sway at this point. You are the one who holds the power."

She kept her face cool. The twisted smile down. "My father holds my strings still. I hardly think it would be within your plans to elope."

He roamed around her chair, a finger brushing her shoulders. She stiffened automatically, muscles tightening. "No, no it would not."

Trant desired power and prestige. Standing, and an unsullied reputation.

The whispers about her were making him livid. She could see it there behind his eyes. He was a meticulous planner, and factors kept slipping from his grasp.

"But you are the one who will make or break a contract. I don't remember you pushing or lamenting Downing's offer or lack thereof." She could feel him leaning closer. Her skin prickled uncomfortably, but she held herself immobile as he continued speaking. "You could have pushed it through. There was a moment when Downing was still thinking clearly . . ."

She thought Downing had never been thinking more clearly than when he was outwardly showing his love for his wife. But it was true that there might have been a moment there, a moment he would have regretted forever, and that Charlotte hadn't pushed. Hadn't been able to after she had spoken with Miranda in the dark of the opera. Stolen away in the cavern of a box to watch them together. To see the adoration. To hear her future husband's mistress speak of him.

Trant suddenly was before her. "You are the one who handled your father's bet and decided things in Merrick's hall that night."

"It is not in my nature to have a mark upon our honor."

"And that does you credit," he all but purred. "But might

there have been . . . something else? You have been . . . sloppier lately," he said. "Not up to your usual standards."

"You are correct." Her directness made him start, his eyes narrow. For he was not one to admire directness when it was pointed at him. "I believe you would deem my emotion and actions as 'rebellious.' "

His face was cool, but there was appreciation as well. "It is a relief to know you can be objective, dear. That you understand and can correct the behavior."

She looked at the wall. There used to be a painting there. A beautiful landscape showing girls in a meadow. Girls with unbound hair and movement in their limbs. It had been one of the first things her father had sold. "I am able to correct the behavior."

"I know. Or else we wouldn't be having this discussion."

"Perhaps you are rethinking your plans, Mr. Trant."

"I am. But things are not too far gone to correct. Jealousy is an easy excuse with which to dismiss the rumors. And marriage will quash the rest," he said.

"I see."

"Do you? I will tell you something that no one else yet knows. The King is drawing up Letters right now. He knows which way the wind blows. He sees the future. And by this time next year, I will be an earl." One finger ran along her shoulder as he turned. "And you, my dear, you will be a countess. And not just any countess, but the wife of the future minister as well."

She wasn't surprised by his ambition. Or by the information that he was to be titled. And least surprising was the crisp coolness that coiled within her, waiting. Winning cards lay before her. Chance blossoming and offering her a perfect hand.

"That sounds like a very fortuitous state of affairs." She tried to keep her voice calm. And she found that it wasn't difficult to do so. A few months ago, she likely would have felt some heady relief. Something that said she didn't have to continue along her rocky path, her father's path.

But that path had disappeared over the cliff, and the one now before her was shrouded in a different kind of darkness.

"I see you are happy to have your sister back," he said, eyes narrowing when she didn't gush over his offer, expression also satisfied that she could still act so coolly.

"Yes."

"Such a carefree, happy spirit."

Charlotte said nothing, not remotely surprised that Trant knew her weakness. Only that it had taken him so long to use it.

"Your sister will want for nothing. I have many connections."

Coldness spread. For here it *really* was before her. Actual bargains to be made, deals to be sealed, opportunities to be seized.

Her father thought his pawn was in here placating Trant. Securing his compliance to wait until the end of the season.

She thought back to what Roman had said. That the power rested in her lap. The problem was that internalizing that revelation also meant decisions could no longer be pushed aside.

"I simply wish for Emily to choose her own path." Everything in her voice said that there was nothing simple in the statement. That this is where negotiating began.

"Then that is what she will have," he whispered in her ear, excitement in his tone that they had reached the crux. "When I am minister, she might choose to become a patron of the arts. A courtier to a queen. Married to a simple man with children in the country. Anything she wants."

The whispered promise of *out of your father's hands* lingered. Not having to worry about threats of Lord Kinley or his ilk.

She lifted her chin in interest, not willing to give away her position yet.

He paced around her chair again. "I'm a greedy man. But I could also offer . . . some freedom for you. Eventually." There was a hint of warning behind the words. He knew. Her heart beat in her, vibrating up her throat coldly. She should have felt no surprise at the certainty of the revelation. "Even with your current . . . *rebelliousness,* there is still barely a hint of talk. And with a ring on your finger, that all gets wiped clean." His fingers trailed across her chin as he came back into sight. "Perfection," he whispered.

She remained motionless. An expressionless bust.

Not only did he know, but he was willing to let her have some sort of relationship with Roman afterward.

Why would he agree to that? She didn't have *that* much power. And while Trant was the type of man who could coldly work arrangements out at a later date, that he would use that incentive *now* . . . Something tugged at her thoughts, demanding attention.

"Still." His fingers left her skin. "You play your part, and I will play mine."

Give him heirs. Be the perfect wife in the social and political spheres. Have a secret life on the side.

The questions continued digging at her—*why? And why now?*

She could have everything. Why then did her stomach clench so painfully? She could have everything she'd thought she'd wanted if she simply, patiently *waited* for it.

"You offer much," she said.

"I want much in return." His eyes examined her. "But nothing that you are unable to give."

She lifted her chin. He didn't require warmth or personal feeling. Obviously didn't expect anything remotely smacking of it.

And though Trant's motives were clear, pieces of him were hidden and twining beneath his calculating eyes. Less able to manage than another husband but also ambitious enough to claw them to the top.

She suddenly wondered when she reached the peak, how difficult it would be to stand upon the high, cold precipice, shivering, balancing, finding it hard to draw breath.

No, that was a coward's way of thinking.

She worked with the cards she was dealt. She always had. A curl of cool air blew from somewhere. *This was what she had been bred for.*

These cards were better, no, more *perfect,* than any she'd been dealt before.

She smiled tightly at the man in front of her, and something inside of her, something that had been hanging by a fingernail for so long, finally broke.

The fair was lively. Emily was as enthusiastic as always, even if she kept sending Charlotte concerned glances when she thought she wasn't looking. Viola was silent, and Charlotte would have normally pinpointed her expression as brooding, but on second glance it was almost contemplative.

Charlotte had a feeling that the three of them planned to exchange quick, pensive glances all day when they thought the others weren't looking. She wondered what Emily and Viola were thinking—or brooding—about. She wanted to ask, but then she'd have to explain her own thoughts. Her future and her plans. Set the words and patterns to reality.

They swirled around her, tendrils of air that needed something firm to attach to. For she'd forced their carriage to stop at the Downings' on the way to the fair. Had run inside to speak to Miranda. A tumult of words and feelings, and admissions, all bursting free.

Knowing that everything might blast back. Turn on end, leave her dying.

And still she had done it. Pushing past the fear, pushing past the responsibility.

Roman . . . what would he—

She froze, seeing Bill walking toward them. It wasn't an unusual sight to see him these days, but to see him looking so solemn, his hands behind his back, approaching as if he meant to speak with them was. Her heart clenched. Had something happened?

She anxiously looked past Bill, hoping to see golden hair, but the crowd churned, the fairgoers laughing and talking, their voices too loud and piercing.

Bill finally came to a stop, standing before Viola, who looked at him as if he was a bug in her porridge.

"Milady, I couldn't help but notice that your beauty shines brighter than the bloodiest of veins."

Charlotte wasn't sure whether to give into hysterical relief that nothing was wrong with Roman or to stupefaction at Bill's words. Emily appeared firmly set on the latter.

"Pardon me?" Viola said coldly. But Viola didn't push up her nose. Nor did she move away.

"The crimson blush of a violent sunset. Slaughtering my poor heart."

Bill's hair was neatly combed, and he was dressed in a dark but dapper outfit, eye patch rakishly angled.

Charlotte's eyes automatically raked the crowd for blond hair again. Slaughtering *her* poor heart.

"*Pardon* me?" Viola had never worn such an expression in Charlotte's sight before.

"Only the light touch of your hand to my brow can stave the carmine mist."

Carmine mist? Charlotte's brows furrowed, looking back at the man whom she had very much come to like, suddenly wondering at his sanity. But he was staring straight at Viola.

"*Pardon me?*"

Bill solemnly took his hands from behind his back and offered a bouquet of flawless roses to Viola. "For you, milady."

Viola stared at the man, her fingers automatically taking the flowers. She looked at the bouquet in her hands. "Blood roses are my favorite," she said, and Charlotte couldn't read her tone.

"A beautiful choice, for a beautiful woman." Bill bowed. "Good day, milady."

Viola lifted her eyes from the flowers to Bill's retreating back.

"I . . . what the devil just happened?" Emily whispered, staring at their mother, then looking into the crowd to see Bill's figure disappear.

"Language," Charlotte said, almost absently, her eyes locked on the crowd that had swallowed him in.

"Yes!" Emily said, voice perkier. "There he is."

Charlotte froze. "Pardon me?"

"Incredibly Handsome Language. I've taken to calling him simply Handsome though, in secret," Emily chirpingly confided, then waved a hand at someone over Charlotte's shoulder.

And now that she knew he was within the crowd, she

couldn't look. "Emily, what are you doing?" Charlotte hissed. Even Viola had recovered from her stupor and noticed, looking to where Emily waved.

She waited until she could wait no longer, then turned and bumped into a warm body, a warm hand touching her waist to steady her.

"Pardon me," she said, shivering beneath his hand, not looking up. All the thoughts and emotions in the last few hours, in the last week without Roman . . . all swirling around.

"You have nothing to apologize for." Gravel under honey. "While I, on the other hand, have many such things. And yet I can't stop touching you, even when it is better that I stay away," he whispered, too low for the others to hear. "Everything will be better. Soon. After this. Tonight."

He stilled suddenly. Almost a complete absence of movement, his hand still touching her. She startled and looked up to see him gazing at something over her shoulder. Deadly ice, those eyes.

"Pardon me, ladies." There was something venomous in his voice. Lethal and promising. He fluidly stepped around her, fingers drawing along the waist of her gown. Leaving a piece of paper tucked up in the ribbon under her breasts.

She turned, flustered, gripping a hand over the tucked paper as if it had the answer to every question she had ever asked, and saw him stalk toward a man who stood across the street. A man with a feral look to him. The man scowled upon seeing Roman, turned, and scurried into the crowd—not seeing Andreas standing nearby, a hellish smile about his mouth as he smoothly pivoted and followed.

Roman's pace increased as he moved after them, crowd parting around him. Expensive clothing moving with the stretch of his muscles. Savagery with the edge of polish. He disappeared from view a moment later.

"I say, Charlotte." Emily just kept blinking. "Each time I see him, I'm rendered stupid. Can I keep him? Or set him on Margaret Smith?"

Viola's eyes were narrowed, and she looked at Charlotte for a long moment before she looked to Emily. "Do you know that man, Emily?"

"I have only partially met him. Charlotte was rather abrupt with him last time." Emily gave her a teasing grin. "I look forward to meeting him at a ball though. I bet he knows well how to dance."

Viola's eyes were piercing. "Who is he, Charlotte?"

Emily blinked, brows furrowed as she looked from her mother to her sister. Obviously thinking with the way he was dressed and the fact that he had known Charlotte, it meant he was of the *ton*.

Charlotte looked at her mother evenly. "An acquaintance of Father's."

And she saw everything in her mother's eyes connecting the threads. *Knowing*.

Viola looked at the flowers in her fist. "And the other man?"

"A friend of his. Acting completely on his own." She added the last instinctively.

Viola said nothing for long moments, then she lifted her chin, looking at Charlotte, expression unreadable. "Very well." She turned and began walking slowly, flowers in the crook of her arm. "Shall we see whether the sweets here are any good?" she called over her shoulder. "Quality sweets, even in such an unrefined guise, should never be sacrificed."

Emily looked as if she'd been goosed, but a wild and thrilling emotion ran through Charlotte. Hope.

Charlotte quickly caught up to her mother, with Emily a beat behind. "I didn't realize you were interested in sweets, Mother."

"Perhaps that has been my trouble all along. Not choosing to change circumstances to my advantage." Viola brought her chin up farther. "If one isn't offered a sweet, it is up to that person to take one or make her own."

"But—" Charlotte looked at the hem of her expensive dress as it floated above her equally costly slippers. "Sometimes you can't simply take one. It upsets the whole balance."

"Of course it does. And makes it incumbent on others to find their own paths." Viola waved a hand at Emily. "Take your sister. You don't think that she would lose her way in this world if something happened to the rest of us, do you? Bah. She's always been the quickest of our lot."

Emily blinked, but Charlotte smiled, tension and giddiness mixing, pressing her lips together.

"She'd probably take over France, or destroy it, if someone let her in on the strategy meetings. Your father is an idiot not to see it." There was a lot of relish in the statement, their mother's voice flowing like a dam finally broken. Free. "He lost his way long ago, thinking there was only one way to skin a rabbit. And I lost my way brooding over his choices."

"But there is clearly a best way to skin one." Charlotte gripped her skirt, lingering tension still thrumming through her over her choice. "And sometimes pieces must be sacrificed."

"No, we aren't playing chess," Emily said softly, breaking in to the conversation, putting her hand upon Charlotte's arm. "And it is not necessarily that there is a best way, only one that is *easiest*."

As their mother had pointed out, Emily was far from

stupid, and she had obviously put things together quickly.

"I—I plan to make my own mistakes, Charlotte. My own choices. Would you take that away from me?"

Charlotte looked at her, shocked and confused. "Of course not, Emily. That is the point. You will be able to make any choice that you wish."

"At your expense? Do you think I could live with that knowledge?"

Charlotte took her shoulders in her hands. "There is nothing for you to feel guilty about. *Nothing*. It is my choice."

"And so too do I want to make my own. But not on the back of yours." She tipped her chin up. "I will make Father proud. Or I will make him rue his estimation of me. Either way, I want to do it on my own. And I want you to be *happy*. I—" She sent a quick look their mother's way, who was pretending interest in a stall at their right though obviously still listening. "I can't believe I didn't piece it together sooner that he was not of the *ton*. But I saw you one night. Maybe, er, more than one night. Together. And didn't think on that aspect."

Panic took Charlotte.

Emily gripped her hand. "Charlotte, I've never seen you so happy and relaxed. And I know that even though you are arguing with me now, you have thought of alternatives. You simply need to be confident as you walk down *your* path." She shrugged, a smile loosening her lips, her shoulders letting loose a tiny bit. "Besides, you'd never leave me. If I wanted to join you, you'd make sure I had a place to stay. Maybe I could get a dangerous Handsome to call my own."

Their mother gave Emily a look but was waved over by a matron a few paces away before she could respond.

"His name . . . his name is Roman," Charlotte said, unable to move anything but her lips.

"Is it?" Emily looked at Charlotte slyly from beneath her lids as their mother drew past hearing range. "Nice to know. Almost as nice as the deal you made with Miranda to sponsor me should things go badly."

Charlotte reacted as if *she'd* been goosed. "How do you—?"

Emily hummed. "Best to keep my secrets to myself." She hummed a little more, walking away. "Like how it has been quite drafty in the house lately. I should speak to Anna about leaving windows open."

Charlotte looked after her sister, stunned. Then she narrowed her eyes and decided maybe the carriage wheel was still the way for her to go.

Emily laughed, seeming to understand the thought, and raced away. Charlotte raced after her, and *part* of the burden she had shouldered for so long slipped away.

Chapter 22

The address was highly respectable. A little *too* respectable. Charlotte had *walked* from her family's house, a mere five-minute jaunt. And into an even nicer section of town. Only hiding her identity from the dozen or more people she had encountered—and knew socially—because she had worn Roman's large cloak and kept her head lowered.

She stood on the stoop, knowing that if she turned around, there would be at least one person looking her way. For there was always someone looking for a bit of gossip to be had. Always a Bethany to be found.

Though not for much longer.

Charlotte swallowed. Everything she had believed would make her *content* was awaiting her at home. Freedom from her father, freedom for Emily, an assured place in society. If it wasn't pure happiness, that was a dream she had parted from long ago.

A dream that had once more crawled through her window and slipped beneath her covers nearly two months past. A dream that had carried her here to this stoop.

She rapped the door with the gleaming knocker.

The door opened immediately. And there he was, golden and gorgeous, leaning languidly against the jamb, the light filtering around him, stroking him. He smiled slowly, only the underlining thread of tension strumming beneath his muscled skin giving him away.

Sleeves rolled up, golden forearms tracked with old scars, clothes assuredly hiding a plethora of weapons that would shine under the lights. Scars and risk.

Eyes hooded and uncertain.

She smiled and walked past him into the foyer. Chancing the disillusionment that might one day grace his face. The shattering of confidence and dreams. The force constantly pushing and pulling within her between external bravery and internal vulnerability.

But there was a little of that in everyone. Even in the man standing behind her.

He closed the door, and it was a loud sound in the empty entryway. She gazed around her, pushing back her hood, but it didn't seem as if anyone lived in the house. "Yours?"

He tilted his head. "Let us say I'm borrowing it for the night." He motioned toward the stairs. "The parlor has a few pieces left, though the new owner will have to furnish this place soon, don't you think?"

She blinked, not really caring about whoever owned the place. Someone wealthy—the address and size of the house guaranteed it. And undoubtedly someone with clout since the neighbors on this particular block were quite powerful and able to dictate and influence who could purchase property.

The parlor was roomy, and thankfully there were a few pieces for them to sit upon and use. In fact, there was a bookcase full of games and books and a small liquor rack that looked very similar to Roman's.

"No servants or service. Hope you don't mind." He kicked back on the settee, putting his feet up on a low table. But his voice sounded strange, almost as if he were hesitant.

She perched next to him, wanting to blurt out all manner

of things, trying to find something inane of which to speak instead in order to hide her nerves. "I don't mind serving myself, but perhaps you should remove your feet?"

A full smile drew across his lips, banishing some of the hesitancy. "I'll ask permission later. Or forgiveness."

That sounded more like him.

She touched his cheek. "You are well?" She gave up on engaging in a battle of words—too relieved to see him whole and unharmed.

He froze beneath her hand, then ever so slightly leaned into the touch, eyes closing for a moment. "Of course. Fixed any threats to your safety, didn't we?"

She examined his serious expression. There was nothing amused about it at the moment. "I . . . I don't know?"

The edges of his eyes pinched, and he withdrew her hand from his cheek, holding it in his. "I'd never have met with you otherwise. I would have had One-eye tell you to come another day."

That was something she would address in a moment. But first . . . "Does that mean you are safe?"

The skin around his eyes stayed taut. "I will never be safe." His entire body vibrated as he leaned toward her. "You have no idea how many times this past week I planned never to see you again."

She swallowed at the sudden cold his words produced but said nothing as he continued.

"To let you live your life without a trace of me in it. And yet, selfish bastard that I am, here I am." He tipped her chin up, his gaze switching from one of her eyes to the other and back again, trying to read her. "But I will never be safe. Do you understand that, Charlotte?"

He—and Andreas—had made it blindingly obvious, so the answer, if not the emotion that accompanied it, was easy.

"Yes," she whispered, having thought things through all week, even with immediately knowing what her answer would be. "And if I have to sew *you* up, if I have to wait up every night, then I will."

He stared at her, fingers frozen on her chin.

She took his hand in hers, a reflection of his previous motions, and pulled it to her lap. "So, yes, Roman," she said calmly. "I know."

His eyes shut for a moment, and he shook his head minutely before opening them again. "There is no wonder in me, no question, as to why I am here. Only that it is not the right choice for you."

She grabbed *his* chin. "And yet you *are* here. And I am *glad*."

A sliver of a smile curved his lips, the light she so loved there in the back of his eyes.

"Now—" She primly crossed her hands in her lap. "Tell me what has happened in this week that you've been absent from my window."

He reached out and tugged one of her curls, coiling it in his fingers. "We took care of all threats to you. But there are outside forces that must be dealt with." His eyes tightened again.

"Outside forces?"

He smiled grimly. "A . . . rival. And Andreas's *family* must be dealt with."

She blinked.

"But I will always keep *you* safe." His eyes went fierce and dangerous, just as they had in the Hunsdens' shop so long ago. "No one will dare try something like what happened the other night again, not with you anywhere in the vicinity. I made sure the repercussions of such actions would be seen as . . . decidedly unpleasant."

"What did you do?"

The tight smile didn't fade. And neither did a word cross his lips.

"Roman."

He laced their fingers together. "I just had to lay some groundwork—make the consequences known. That if someone hurt you, even unintentionally during an attack on one of us, that they had better make sure to eliminate me as well as half the city of London. I have dozens lined up to do my last bidding—which would be to get revenge for you. Bloodily."

She opened her mouth, but nothing emerged.

He watched her carefully. Waiting, she realized, for her to bolt in terror.

"Why?" she whispered.

Stabbing pools of piercing blue pinned her. "I would destroy the city if something happened to you. I can't even bear the thought of it," he whispered.

She couldn't speak for a moment, emotion clogging her throat. Love and fear, pain and desire plugging the channel.

And then she couldn't stop the words, she simply blurted them out.

"Trant proposed."

Roman's entire body stiffened, then he turned fluid, playing with her fingers. "Did he?" There was a loose smile about his lips as he leaned back into the cushions.

What are you doing? Get yourself together! Stop rushing!

"And did your father accept?" he asked.

She opened her mouth to respond, but the words all clogged together, tumbling around with her emotions. She had practiced three times in front of a mirror, and even on the third try she had tripped and stumbled.

She withdrew her hand—with difficulty, for she wanted to stay exactly where she was, for eternity. Surprisingly, he let her go. She couldn't look at his face, though, to see the expression there, or else it would all just tumble out with no sense of order. And there was still that thread of lingering fear in her—that she could be wrong.

She rose and walked to the liquor stand, lifting a replica of his favorite decanter—half-full—with shaky fingers. She grabbed two glasses, guessing that it was One-eye's easy brew, and she need not worry about any hint of inebriation coloring her words. She poured more steadily than she had any right to claim. "I will tell you of the conversation. But first, what else did you wish to speak to me of tonight?"

"Getting more slippery, are we, Charlotte?" He rose as well, pressing his shoulder against the case that held all manner of games and puzzles and accepted the glass from her. His eyes were unreadable, but intensely focused. His body almost vibrating against the wood. "But I find I can't concentrate on other matters at the moment. Are congratulations in order?"

Congratulations. It depended on how one thought of the word. For she could secure all of her old goals by wedding Trant. And such a conclusion would necessitate congratulations.

She could marry Trant, become a countess—perhaps even more one day—and still have Roman. And when Roman grew tired of her, she could bandage her heart and look to other shores. Emily would be taken care of. Would have freedom to choose. Would have powerful relatives sheltering her.

The right choice. The safe choice. The smart choice.

A choice given to congratulations.

And she knew that Roman would understand such a choice. He prized determination and survival. She would be showing good use of both by accepting Trant's proposal.

He expected her to accept.

She could even see it in his eyes now, that he assumed all of the above. That he had long expected this particular order of operations to occur.

Only his remembered words from that first night said otherwise and pointed to other desires. *Will you possess me right back?*

What will you do, Charlotte? Hmmm? The answer to that, the desire to know that answer—that is my motive.

"You don't wish to speak of your decision, Charlotte? But I find myself curious about what was said." He smiled winningly, but even as he could read her, she found that she could read him too. The way his eyes moved and the position of his body. His words so at odds with his expressions.

"I am quite sure that is true." She looked straight into his eyes. "After all, you created this situation in order for a decision to be spurred."

His eyes immediately dropped to his drink, hiding his gaze for a long moment before he looked back up. He motioned his glass toward her. "Why would you say that?"

"It took me far too long to suss it out, I'm sorry to say. But it became more obvious as Trant was speaking. As I connected a thousand small things together with your words the other night. You. You engineered it so Trant would receive a title *soon*. And that he would be willing to negotiate with me extensively in order to secure it quickly. Probably even backing up such negotiations with a bodily threat or two," she said lightly, not feeling the emotion at all. "Knowing exactly what to say. Giving me far greater power than I had before."

He looked neither resigned nor apologetic about any of her statements. He simply tipped his glass, watching her.

"What is interesting," she continued, "is if you could so easily move Trant's title forward, why wouldn't you secure one for yourself?"

And now everything about him screamed tension. "I have no desire to be titled. I *never* will hold that desire." The warning in his words was quite clear.

She watched him, the coil within her growing tighter, readying. The script she had practiced in front of the mirror was long tossed away, the right words suddenly finding their way to her tongue. She hummed a bit. "It would make life simpler, easier."

He set his glass down, eyes carefully blank. "I don't like simple. Or easy. Those choices are for people with no imagination. Or drive."

"And what happens when your game ends? Does another immediately begin? Or do you wait a few months before starting a new quest?"

His eyes narrowed, trying to read her. But she held her lips still, her chin immobile, determined not to make it easy. "It depends on the type of game, of course. And what I have at stake."

Yes. It was one of the aspects about him that her internal fear could see past. He played games with people—many, many people—but when he collected someone, they were *his,* seemingly forever. The evidence of that was all over the establishment he called home.

And . . . and *she* was part of his collection. That was blatantly obvious from his words to her, from his threat to the populace of London's underground. The question was . . . would such a collection *be* permanent?

"Are you truly set against marriage?"

His eyes shuttered. He didn't respond.

She tried again. "Are you—"

"I would never ask it of you," he said harshly.

Wild thrill overlaid the coil, thrumming against it, at his tone and his wording. "No? Not Roman Merrick, who takes as he pleases?"

He stepped forward and fingered a lock of her hair. He didn't respond for a long moment. "I have recently been cursed to find that what I please depends on what pleases you."

"Oh? What would you say then if I told you I have no wish to marry Trant?"

She could *feel* his body loosen.

"No?"

"No."

"I will take care of things with him, if you'd like me to." He tilted her chin. "Break the betrothal for you. You can take your time and marry someone you like better."

"That won't be necessary," she said simply. "The breaking part, that is. I didn't accept."

He stilled. "Pardon me?"

"I didn't accept Trant's proposal. In fact, right now he is likely plotting my downfall."

"You didn't accept. Even—"

"Yes."

"Charlotte—"

"No, it will be well, Roman," she tried to reassure him because he had the strangest look on his face. "I understand that you aren't interested in marriage. And I find myself quite intrigued at the possibility of simply being free. Between Emily, Miranda, and me, and strangely enough, I believe Mother too, we will figure out how to keep Father from doing anything drastic to Emily. The bride has to accept a marriage these days, more's the pity for Father. And I think it will do many wallflowers good to see me as an unrepentant spinster, if I can keep Trant from talking. In fact—"

"Charlotte, stop speaking."

She blinked at him.

"Charlotte, I'm . . . I'm a selfish man." His fingers slipped over the curl he was holding, smoothing it down, his eyes tracking his hand's movements as if entranced—or uncertain. "It was the truth when I first met you and remains the truth now. I played with you unrepentantly." His eyes met hers and they were serious and shuttered. "I set you up. I—"

"I know."

" . . . what?"

"I know. You were actually quite honest with me about it. I just didn't think far enough around the edges to understand at the time as to *how* you were setting me up. Or perhaps part of me *did* understand. Perhaps that would explain many of my own emotions these past weeks. That I did understand on some level."

She peered up at him. "You may have played a game with me, but you never did anything that was debilitating to me. In fact, you made events more favorable for me, in a sense. Trant would never have offered so much otherwise. Never given me the assurances that he did."

"Charlotte—"

"No, please. I need to finish. I don't understand totally. Not really. For all that you say you are selfish—and believe it—you would let me marry Trant if I should wish it, wouldn't you? And yet, I feel as if . . ." She had to swallow deeply, for it was a wrenching thing, putting herself forward, even with her confidence riding high. "I feel as if you do care deeply for me. Just as I do you."

He stared at her for a long moment without responding—so long that she felt her confidence falter, her heart breaking a little. She couldn't control her involuntary step backward, the rise of her shoulders.

He quickly reached toward her, touching her hand, stilling her.

"Do you remember what I promised? So long ago?" His tone was unreadable, his voice gravelly.

She swallowed, heart pounding, nerves ragged once more. "That you were going to possess me."

"And?"

"You asked if I would possess you back."

He smiled, that slow, gorgeous smile, and stepped, *stalked*, the single pace to her. "You realize, Charlotte, that I would have carried on an affair with you for years." His fingers wrapped into the back of her hair, tipping her head back, voice whispering. "But you possessing me back? You will be mine for eternity."

"My looks will fade," she blurted, heart beating from her chest, emotions pushing against the clog in her throat. "I'll grow weathered. Old."

"So will I." He traced her jaw. "I might even age *ungracefully*."

"Roman, I'm being serious."

He touched her cheek, then looked into her eyes. "So am I. I don't love you because you are beautiful. Oh, it makes me aroused beyond measure to see your lovely cheeks flush and your perfect breasts heave in passion. To have you tightly clamp around me, your body made for mine, every *perfect* curve and smooth, flawless expanse of skin. But it's not why I love you."

"You love me?" she whispered.

He pulled her fully to him, fingers drawing along her cheeks, over her lips. "It's not why I wrap my fingers in your hair, why I clutch your body to mine, why I absorb every passionate whisper from your lips."

His mouth traveled over her neck, whispering in her ear. "It is because you are a stubborn, proud woman who I don't wish to live without. And even if you grow old and weathered, and do so *ungracefully*, I'm counting on you being too stubborn to admit it. To browbeating me into seeing you as the goddess I always will."

She pulled his mouth back to hers, their lips hovering just a breath apart. "You will never grow tired of me. I won't permit it." She backed him up until he was against the back of the settee.

"Good. But we need to address a few things first. And at the moment, I feel furnishings are at the top. The back of this couch, for example, is amazingly awful," he said, lifting her against him. "We will have to purchase something to replace it."

"Oh?" She tilted her mouth up to his. "Are you planning to ruin it, then?" She found herself not altogether unaffected at the images of how that might occur.

"I think we can ruin it six ways to Sunday." His fingers gripped her hips, pressing her to him.

She laughed against his lips. "I will have to make sure to be in the park to watch you carry out the pieces."

"Showing the broken and battered planks from where you rode me dead, and the eruptions of cushion stuffing from where your fingernails tore through. The image is quite appealing. Give the neighbors a right shock. Maybe steal a few replacement pieces from them while they're still gawking."

He cocked his head, a cunning smile stretching.

"I can have the minister invite us to his social next week. Might as well start bleeding from my wrists now. Together, we can carefully scout his pieces for our collection here."

She stared at his lips, at the curve of them and the way they formed the words. They always looked quite stunning.

His hands lifted her chin so she was looking into his eyes. "Charlotte"—he sounded concerned—"I'm jesting about stealing their furniture. Though Liverpool's wife has quite a good eye for comfortable pieces. Are you going to faint?"

"That isn't fair," she breathed, certain she had heard his other words incorrectly. "You holding that over me. That was the first time I have ever fainted."

His eyes pinched. "I . . . do you . . . do you truly understand what you are entering into by choosing me?"

She smoothed his brow. "Shhh. Yes. We will figure everything out together, yes?"

He smiled. A beautiful smile that settled any lingering fears. It was true. What's more—she *believed* it.

"Of course we will." His fingers worked at the buttons near her neck.

"And I will be able to come and go as I please?" she asked as he worked, her mind trying to fill the blank spot his words had provoked a moment before.

His brows pinched. "Of course you would. Why wouldn't you?"

"Well, I don't want any of your boys barring me from your rooms."

"Well, that's fortunate, as I don't plan to have them around here much, except for the ones who want to be footmen and the like."

"I . . ." She stopped his fingers. "Did that mean I heard you correctly when you intimated that this is . . . *our* . . . house?"

The corners of his mouth lifted, and his eyes were delighted. "Without price, that expression on your face."

She narrowed her eyes, but all she could feel was *hope,* glorious hope. "I'm going to become a spinster."

"Mmmhmmm." He finished the buttons and tugged a string. "But I hear that St. George's is lovely this time of year," he said casually. "And you look so *perfect* in white." And before she could respond, he pulled her, gasping, over the edge of the couch, madly laughing all the way.

Chapter 23

He used the front door.

It was entirely too normal. Disconcerting even.

"There are a few things we should discuss, Chatsworth." Gravel and honey poured over her, even two rooms over, making her think of the previous night. Of all the nights in her future. She could hear the door lock shut in the foyer. "Merely tiny details, Chatsworth, I assure you."

Slippery, scheming man.

He came into view, and the warmth and happiness lit, then spread. She could smile gently as a well-bred lady should. She could be restrained and embody the kind and soft woman she had once wished desperately to be.

Instead, she let the feelings push and her grin spread. Her heart grew.

Roman winked and made a naughty gesture at her as he sauntered past the sitting room, leading her father. She supposed both the wink and the gesture were meant to reassure her.

They did.

Thankfully, Viola was looking elsewhere at that moment, a small, secretive smile about her lips, though Emily erupted in giggles.

"I really, really like him, Charlotte."

"Yes, Emily." She smiled as her father started shouting. "I really, really like him too."

Emily would be socially provided for. Viola would be financially provided for. Charlotte would be emotionally provided for.

And Charlotte would make quite sure Roman would never lack for anything either.

"Oh!" Emily sat up straight. "Why didn't you tell me that Bethany Case was throwing the ball to announce your engagement? Margaret was absolutely *formal* when she extended her felicitations. It was *wonderful*."

Charlotte wasn't sure Emily needed to know that Bethany had been *persuaded* to do so by her husband, who was a frequent *client* of the Merrick hells and had the bills to prove it. It had been unnecessary to ask Roman how he had made that particular choice. He had obliquely said that they could have the prime minister do it instead, should Charlotte prefer.

Charlotte did *not* prefer. Not in this instance. Bethany would host *the* event of the season—for *everyone* would be talking about it. And she would be forced to smile happily at Charlotte and Roman the *entire night*.

Roman really did know too much about her for her own good. She was looking forward to turning the tables on him. Frequently.

St. George's? She'd simply settle for waking up next to him every day. Who wanted one night when she could have them all?

She smiled. And as he exited her father's study, with another wink in her direction, she found herself unable to feel anything but hope and joy.

***Don't miss Andreas
Merrick's story, coming from
Avon Books in Fall 2011!***